SURVIVING THE COLLAPSE

JAMES HUNT

1

CHAPTER 1

Dozens of knobs, buttons and lights lined the roof of the Boeing 737 cockpit just inches above Captain Kate Hillman's head. The view beyond the windshield was gloomy. The aircraft rumbled through the grey skies spitting patches of sleet, snow, and heavy winds.

"New York has a funny way of welcoming you home." First Officer Dan Martin shook his head, keeping his hand steady on the flight stick. "My brother said it's going to get down to ten degrees tonight."

The headphones that both pilots wore crackled with air traffic control's voice. "Bravo one-eight-five-six, this is tower, we've got a roadblock down here because of the weather."

"Timeline for the delay?" Kate asked.

"Twenty minutes. Redirect heading to one-one-nine."

"Copy that, tower," Dan relayed. "Redirecting heading to one-one-nine." The navigation screen tilted toward the new coordinates, the big bird turning slow and steady. Once adjusted, Dan looked over to Kate and raised his eyebrows. "Did you hear me? Less than—"

"Ten degrees," Kate said, reaching for the flight plan that she had been given prior to takeoff. She flipped through the pages quickly, scanning the data. "We should have been ahead of this weather." Kate flipped the "fasten your seatbelt" sign and then picked up the phone to address the passengers. "Ladies and gentlemen, please remain in your seats. The weather has caused a slight delay, but we'll land as soon as possible. Thank you."

The inside of the cockpit rumbled, and the muscles along Dan's forearms tensed. Kate hung up and noted Dan's white knuckles. "First storm?"

"Yeah," Dan answered.

"Easy on the stick. She'll do most of the work. Just keep it steady. Radar has the storm passing in a few minutes."

Another burst of icy sleet smacked the windshield, and the jet rumbled in discontent. Kate shook her head, clicking on her radio. "Tower, this is Bravo one-eight-five-six, requesting an ascent. We're getting tossed around pretty bad up here."

"Copy that, Bravo. Request granted. Ascend to thirty-five thousand feet."

"Ascending to thirty-five thousand feet," Dan replied, pulling back on the stick.

The jet climbed higher, the nose pointed up as it broke through the worst of the clouds. Kate watched the altimeter. "Twenty-five thousand." It ticked upward. "Thirty thousand."

The plane jolted and tossed both Kate and Dan in their seats. The notebook in Kate's lap crashed to the floor, and the altimeter's gauge dropped one hundred feet in the blink of an eye. The straps over Kate's shoulders dug deep and tight into her flesh. When the inertia of the fall ended, the warning beacon on the port engine blinked.

Kate shook off the disorientation and checked the engine status. "One is rolling back."

Dan looked at her sharply then at the display screen.

"Two is holding." Kate flipped channels to the control tower. "Mayday, mayday, mayday, this is Bravo one-eight-five-six. We have lost thrust on our port engine, requesting immediate emergency landing."

"Copy that, Bravo one-eight-five-six."

Kate took control of her stick. "My aircraft."

"Your aircraft," Dan said, letting go of the controls.

"Get out the QRA," Kate said, the stick stiff in her hands.

"Bravo one-eight-five-six," tower said. "Redirect toward LaGuardia, heading two-two-zero. Runway one is clear."

"Heading two-two-zero. Copy on runway one." Kate placed her right hand on the ignition key. "Restarting engine." A twist. Nothing.

The big 737 groaned as Kate steered through the clouds, the jet struggling to maintain altitude with only one engine.

Dan scanned the Quick Response Action checklist. "Master on or off?"

Kate glanced toward the display. "Off." She tilted the stick to the left, adjusting the aircraft to the new heading toward LaGuardia. "Gears down."

"Gears down." Dan reached for the lever and pulled it down. The mechanical drone of the wheels descending from the plane's belly ended with a clank.

Kate checked the heading, altimeter, and speed. The weather provided poor visibility on approach. But she trusted the instruments to do their job, along with the coordination from air traffic control.

"Bravo one-eight-five-six, you are on course," tower said. "Watch your speed."

"Give me flaps," Kate said.

"Flaps extended," Dan echoed.

The gears in the wings ground as Dan adjusted for the landing, helping to steady the big bird on its approach.

The 737 broke through the clouds and the worst of the storm, and Kate finally had a glimpse of runway lights, and the sprawling airport and surrounding borough of Queens.

The computer's automated alert system kicked into gear once they cleared fifteen hundred feet, lights flashing in coordination with beeps and its robotic voice. "Warning, pull up. Obstruction. Warning, pull up."

"Two hundred feet," Dan said, his voice shaking from the steady rumble of the aircraft.

The big jet tilted left, then right, then back to left as Kate struggled to keep it steady. She knew the storm had slicked the runway with ice and rain, so she'd have to keep the plane as level as possible to avoid a spin. She measured all the inputs, all the variables, letting the instruments help guide her path.

"Fifty feet." Dan extended his arm to brace for landing.

The computer's warnings blared again, and after twenty feet, it recited the elevation countdown. Kate tilted the nose up slightly just before impact, and the hulking jet's wheels squealed and screeched onto the runway. The plane started to spin, but Kate pulled back on the thrusters, and the aircraft slowed to a crawl.

Dan exhaled, leaning back into his chair. "Nice job, Captain."

Kate's muscles slowly relaxed as she leaned back into her seat. Beyond the cockpit's door, the muffled excitement and relief of applause broke the cabin's silence.

"Bravo one-eight-five-six, please taxi toward gate twenty-one. We will have emergency operations on standby."

"Copy that, tower."

Once docked at the gate, Kate and Dan stepped out of the cockpit and triggered another round of applause. Dan immediately pointed to Kate, and she smiled curtly but waved off the adoration. As the passengers were escorted from the plane, one by one, they offered their thanks and gratitude.

With the plane empty of passengers and crew, Kate grabbed her overnight bag, jacket, and flight cap and followed Dan through the gate.

"So what happens now?" Dan asked.

"We'll be interviewed separately by the NTSB," Kate answered, her pace brisk as she removed her phone and powered it on. "Then an investigation will review the cause of the engine failure. So long as there wasn't any negligence on our part, we'll be back in the air."

Dan hurried ahead of her and then blocked her path. His cheeks were suddenly white. "There wasn't any negligence, right? I-I mean, I followed protocols to the T."

"We'll be fine, Dan. We did everything right. So far as I could tell from the cockpit." Kate stepped around him, and when they exited the tunnel, members of the NTSB were already there to greet them, along with a union rep and airport security.

The interview was quick, mechanical, and efficient. Kate answered the questions honestly and candidly. She offered no fault to her first officer, crew, or herself. The board members thanked her for her time, and once they were gone, the union rep pulled her aside.

"The review shouldn't take longer than a few weeks, but until you're cleared, you're grounded," he said. "I'll contact you when we know more."

Kate nodded and then sat in the quiet of the conference room. Alone, the moments replayed in her head. It had happened so fast, it almost felt like a dream. She'd only been through one engine failure scenario before, five years prior. It was a malfunction in the master computer caused by inclement weather. She assumed this was a similar error.

Still alone, Kate took a few slow breaths. She lifted her hand, keeping it level in midair. Despite the rush of adrenaline, it didn't shake, steady as a rock. Repeated vibrations drummed against her thigh in her pocket, notifications of the texts and calls she missed while she was in the air.

The most recent call was from Mark, but the other ten were from her lawyer, who had also sent her a text marked urgent that simply read, "Call me."

Kate's stomach tightened, but she forced herself to dial. It rang twice before he answered.

"Kate, where the hell have you been? I've been trying to get ahold of you all morning."

"I had a flight," Kate answered. "What happened?"

Dave paused and then exhaled as though he were holding in his breath. "The parole hearing was moved up today. Can you make it?"

Kate hunched forward and rubbed her forehead in exasperation. "Shit. I don't know. They still have my statement on file. Do I really have to be there?"

"It always makes a more formidable show of resolve when you're there personally," Dave said. "It sends a message to the parole board that he shouldn't be let out. You—"

"All right," Kate said. "I'll find a way to make it up there."

"Good. Meeting is scheduled for five. See you then."

The call ended, and Kate collapsed backward in her chair, slouching. She glanced down at the wings still pinned on her uniform. She'd been flying for more than twenty years. She'd just managed to land a Boeing 737 with a port engine failure safely through a storm of sleet, snow, and wind. But when Kate lifted her hand again and brought it to eye level, she couldn't keep it steady.

She grabbed her bag and left.

Terminal D was packed with tourists heading toward gates with flights to all over the world. Los Angeles, London, Miami, Toronto, Tokyo, Hawaii, Paris, Madrid, Moscow. To Kate, airports were the ultimate melting pots. Millions of people, all from different backgrounds and geographical locations, passed through them on a daily basis. And while her main route was from New York to Chicago, she'd done her fair share of travel to different parts of the world.

She missed those far-off places sometimes, but she had requested the new route personally. The fact that her family had moved eight times in the past seven years had taken its toll. An ultimatum was given, and Kate didn't hesitate to choose her family over work. With her tenure at the airline and her excellence as a pilot, her bosses didn't hesitate in their approval.

Just before the airport's exit, Kate spotted the customer

service desk. She weaved through the masses funneling outside and noticed the weather had cleared up. She flagged down one of the employees. A young girl came over, and when she noticed the wings on Kate's shirt, her face lit up brightly.

"Captain! What can I do for you?"

"I normally fly into JFK, and I need to know the quickest way to get into Manhattan from here. My apartment is on the south end of Central Park."

"Taxi will be the most comfortable, but with the weather and traffic, it'll take you hours to get into the city." She leaned over the counter and pointed past the doors and down the street. "So long as you don't mind the cold, there's a train station two blocks south. The N will get you to Grand Central. From there you can hop on an uptown train."

Kate nodded her thanks, but before she got away, the girl called out to her.

"I'm in flight school," she said proudly. "Got any tips?"

Kate kept walking but turned back toward the girl. "I'll tell you what my flight instructor told me." The electric doors opened, and cold blasted Kate's body. "Don't crash." The girl laughed and flashed a thumbs-up. Kate waved back, and the electric doors closed.

Outside, Queens greeted Kate with a cold, dirty whoosh of city air. She skipped the line for taxis and zipped her coat up to her collar.

Tiny puddles of frigid water filled divots and potholes along the sidewalk and roads. Everywhere Kate looked, there were people. People walking, people driving, people running, people talking, people, people, people.

Horns blared in sporadic patterns and acted in coordination with the steady buzz of voices as the official New York City soundtrack. Up until six months ago, she never would have pictured herself living here permanently. But while the city was congested and dirty and overpopulated, there was always something to see and do.

Crates of fruit and vegetables sat out in front of a grocery, a few customers browsing the goods with skeptical eyes. Kate stopped in front of the fruit and wondered if they needed anything at home. She examined an apple and reached for her phone.

Kate scrolled through to Mark's name when she suddenly remembered the voicemail he'd left her. She quickly pressed play.

"Hey, you're probably still in the air, but I wanted to let you know that Holly came down with a fever this morning. Mrs. Dunny is going to keep an eye on her until you get home, but you might want to get her some cold medicine on the way. Love you and can't wait to see you tonight."

Kate immediately turned from the fruit, dropping the apple into the crate as she dialed her daughter. It rang five times and then went to voicemail. She redialed. Five more rings. Voicemail. She left a message.

"Hey, Holly, it's Mom. I'm on my way home. Dad told me you were sick, and I just wanted to see if there was anything you wanted from the store. Text or call me. Love you."

She hung up and pocketed the phone, confident that her daughter wouldn't call her back. Over the past year, their interaction together had dropped significantly. She might as well have been invisible. Mark had chalked it up to preteen angst, but Holly didn't act the same way with him.

And while the ultimatum for stability had come from her husband, Kate had really done it for her daughter. The constant moves, the days at a time away from home, had created a barrier between Kate and her little girl. A resentment had built up. And after six months of stability and the repeated promise that they would no longer have to move, Kate hadn't made much progress. Mark reassured her that it would just take time, but as the days continued to roll past with their relationship unchanged, the resolve of that statement began to crack.

At the corner of the sidewalk, Kate broke away from the

steady flow of pedestrians and climbed the stairs to one of the N train's elevated platforms. She reached for her metro card and swiped it, making her way topside, shoulders brushing against the huddling masses trying to stay warm. She leaned against one of the posts and checked her phone again. Still no response.

She pocketed the device and flipped the collar of her jacket to guard herself against the stiff wind. Her stomach rumbled, reminding her of the skipped breakfast.

The thump of the train against the tracks triggered the eager eyes of passengers desperate to get warm. As the train slowed, everyone huddled near the platform's edge, hands rubbing together vigorously and toes tapping impatiently.

The doors swooshed open, and a mash of people collided into one another, fighting for the warmth of the train car, as if this were the last train in existence into the city.

Once the bulk of the people had boarded, Kate wedged herself into a small space in the back corner of the train car between an old woman in a bright-pink sweater and a man in a black trench coat.

The doors whooshed shut, cutting out the cold air, and Kate's cheeks warmed from the heat pumping in through the vents. Bodies swayed back and forth as the train jolted forward.

Kate closed her eyes and leaned against the corner wall, her right hand still wrapped around the pole to keep her steady and her left clutching the phone. She wasn't sure how Mark would take the news of the parole hearing being moved up to today. He hated her going almost as much as she did.

The phone buzzed, and Kate smiled as she read the text.

Hey, mom, sorry I didn't answer. Throat hurts bad. Could you get me some popsicles on the way home?

Kate typed a reply, but before she hit send, the train jerked to a stop and flung her into a cluster of bystanders. The wheels screeched loudly, the grinding metal matched only by the screams and gasps of fear, confusion, and pain as bodies were slammed into walls, the floor, and each other.

Kate let go of the phone and thrust her arms out to brace for the fall. Her palms struck the floor hard, and a sharp pain flashed in her elbows and shoulders. The same momentum hurled her luggage forward and slammed it against her back. Finally, the screeching of wheels ended, and the metro stopped.

Groans, heavy breaths, and screams pierced the air in random jabs. Kate lifted her head and saw that she lay on top of the legs of the man in the black trench coat she had stood next to, who quickly stood, heeling Kate in the chin. She gritted her teeth through the pain and rubbed it vigorously.

Dozens of other bodies slowly lifted their heads, looking up in confusion.

"What's going on?" A voice filtered through the air. "Why did we stop?"

Another chimed in. "Did the power go out?"

Panic escaped worried lips, and once it caught the surrounding ears it spread like wildfire.

"What happened?"

"Is someone coming?"

"I have to get home!"

"I have to get to work!"

"Please… help."

The last plea was nothing more than a whisper, and Kate turned around, still rubbing the red mark on her chin. The elderly woman in the pink sweater sat on the floor, her back flush against the wall and blood dripping down her forehead.

Kate rushed to the woman's side, and the old woman lifted a shaky hand and grabbed Kate's arm. Her grip was weak, her hand cold as ice. "I-I can't get myself up."

"It's all right," Kate said, trying to find the source of the gash beneath thick curls of grey and white. "You have a cut on your head. Does anything else hurt?"

"No," the old woman answered, her voice shaking.

"Can you remember your name?" Kate removed her jacket and placed it around the old woman.

"Grace." She closed her eyes and swallowed. "Grace Nettles."

"Okay, Grace, I'm gonna try and sit you up. Is that all right?"

Grace nodded, and Kate turned and smacked the calf of the man who'd kicked her. "Hey, help me get her into the seat."

Trench Coat spun around, his hair disheveled with tiny wisps of what looked like a toupee sprouting wildly into the air. He blinked in annoyance at Kate and Grace and reluctantly dropped a knee and grabbed Grace's left arm.

"On three," Kate said. "One, two, three!" The pair lifted Grace in coordination, and she clung to Kate's shoulder as they guided her to an open seat. She collapsed into the chair, her frail hand immediately searching for the tender spot on her head, then grimaced when she found it.

Grace retracted her finger quickly and examined the blood on it. "Oh, my."

"It's okay," Kate said, trying to see if the woman's eyes were dilated. "We're going to get you some help." She grabbed Trench Coat's attention. "Hey, look after her while I find the metro worker on board and see what's going on."

Trench Coat jerked his arm from Kate's hold and stepped back. "Listen, lady, she's not my responsibility. I've got my own problems." He took one step before Kate pulled him back.

"There isn't anywhere you can go right now." Kate squeezed his arm tighter. "Stay with her. Make sure she doesn't pass out, fall, and hurt herself again. Got it?"

The man lowered his eyes to the wings on Kate's pilot uniform. When he lifted them, the tension in his body relaxed, but he still jerked his arm away in defiance. "Yeah, all right."

When Kate turned to face the car, the majority of the crowd was already focused on her, watching what she'd done with the old woman. She glanced down at her appearance, wondering if she had blood on herself, but then slowly realized she was the only person on board with a uniform. She was a pilot, and despite the times, that still garnered respect.

Kate cleared her throat. "Do we have a nurse or doctor on board?"

A black hand rose above the heads in the very back, and it was followed by a high-pitched voice. "I'm a nurse."

Kate waved her forward. "All right, everyone, let her through."

With the old woman in better hands, Kate trudged toward the front of the train but then stopped after she instinctively reached for her phone, finding it missing out of her pocket. She spun on her heel, searching the ground for where she'd dropped it, and spotted it under one of the subway seats. She bent down to get it and pressed the home button, but the screen remained black.

Kate frowned in confusion and pressed it repeatedly, but nothing happened. The crowd around her began examining their own phones in the same frustration. All their devices showed the same black screen.

The back door to the train car was forced open, and a metro worker stepped through. His girth made him open the manual doors as wide as they could go, and even then he had to sidestep to get inside. "Ladies and gentlemen, please remain calm!" He huffed a labored breath. "Is anyone in need of immediate medical attention?"

"We have a woman with a concussion." The nurse stood, a bloodied napkin in her hand. "She needs to be taken to the hospital."

"I'm fine, really," Grace said.

The metro worker eyed the blood, and a thick gleam of sweat broke out on his forehead. "God. Um, okay. Is there anyone on the train that's a nurse or a doctor?"

"She is," Kate said, pointing to the nurse in scrubs who had just addressed him. "Do you have any communication with the other trains?"

"Um." The metro worker licked his lips, the beads of sweat

on his face worsening, and then looked back to the eager crowd. "No."

The crowd erupted in a series of gasps, groans, and curses. Hands were tossed in the air, and cheeks reddened from anger and the growing cold. The metro worker's double chin wiggled as he struggled to find his voice among the angered crowd.

"HEY!" Kate shouted at the top of her lungs. "HEY! LISTEN UP!" The fervor died down, and Kate pushed her way next to the nearest chair where she lifted herself above the crowd. "There isn't any reason to panic. They have procedures for things like this." At least she hoped so.

"My phone isn't working." A young man lifted his device high above the heads of the crowd. "Like, it's not even turning on, and it was working fine before the train stopped."

A series of grunted agreements echoed back, and Kate raised her hands to quiet the growing panic. "Mine isn't working either. I don't know why, but—"

The train car rattled violently, and a bright burst of fire and light plumed into the northern sky. Gasps erupted in simultaneous spurts as heads turned toward the explosion. The blast rumbled in Kate's chest worse than the turbulence in the jet. Kate knew the blast's origin. It was around LaGuardia.

2

The elevated tracks rumbled from the explosion. Every face on the train stared at the rising plume of smoke that blended into the grey clouds that had again begun to spit snow. Once the rumble from the blast subsided, the growing dissent of panic took its place.

Trench Coat was the first to step through the crowd. He shouldered people aside, his eyes fixated on the metro worker. "Let me off this train, now!" He thrust his gloved finger at the ground, his mouth tightening into a straight line.

The crowd on the train latched onto the man's dissent, waving their broken phones in the air, demanding the same action. The hulking mob circled the metro worker and shoved Kate aside, squeezing her up against the walls with the old woman and the nurse who'd stepped up to help.

Kate pushed back against the hysteria. "Enough!" The attention turned from the metro worker and back toward her, and she noticed the puffs of icy air from her labored breaths. With the power off, the heat on the train had stopped as well. The cold was already biting through her coat and gloves. "He's doing everything he can, and he knows just as much as we do."

"So what?" Trench Coat flapped his arms at his sides in exasperation. "We're just supposed to sit and wait for someone to come and get us off this thing?" He pointed toward the explosion. "That was at LaGuardia, which means it was a terrorist attack."

The car drew in a simultaneous breath at the word.

"The power, our phones?" Trench Coat stepped toward Kate, the crowd parting in his path. "It's all a part of the attack. They're taking out transportation hubs." He spread his arms and gestured around them. "What do you think they're going to hit next?"

Affirmations of the man's words rang on the train like bell peals, the tides of consciousness shifting toward madness. Fear brought people toward the edge, inching their toes off the side. It wouldn't take anything more than a stiff wind to knock them over.

"You might be right," Kate said, keeping her voice calm but her volume loud. "But panicking and bickering with each other isn't going to get us off this train any quicker."

Trench Coat stepped backward, and the crowd deflated. Kate pointed toward the window, the faces in the crowd following her finger. "There's a platform with a railing. It looks wide enough to walk on, and we can follow it down to the station." She looked to the metro worker for confirmation.

The big man nodded quickly. "Yeah." He wiped the snot leaking onto his upper lip and gestured toward the narrow path. "We use it for maintenance. It should be safe."

A woman peeled her face off the window, and she tapped the glass, stealing everyone's attention. "All the cars are stopped. Nothing's moving down there!"

The outburst triggered another series of teeth-chattering discord, but Kate clapped her hands together. "Hey! Let's focus on what happens next, all right? And that's getting off the metro."

Kate stepped from the seat, and the crowd parted as she walked to the metro worker. She pulled him to the side and kept her voice low and the worker close. "Can we open the doors without the power on?"

"Yeah." He nodded aggressively. "There are override latches on all the exits. And the electricity in the rails won't be live since we're not moving, so we shouldn't have to worry about anyone getting hurt if they fall."

"Except for a broken leg," Kate muttered to herself and then turned back toward the crowd, their attention split between the scene outside and the back of Kate's head. "All right, listen up, folks! There are emergency latches on the doors that—" She turned to the metro worker. "What's your name?"

"Bud."

Kate refaced the crowd. "That Bud is going to show us how to open. The rails won't be live with electricity, but I still want everyone to act like they are. Anyone who's sick or hurt is going out first." She eyed Trench Coat, who had hidden himself back in the crowd. "And anyone healthy enough to assist those people should."

Trench Coat rolled his eyes.

For the moment, the tension thawed. Bud started at the front of the train, letting people off, and then worked his way back. Once Bud had left, the Grace tugged at Kate's hand.

"Good job, Captain."

Kate smiled. "Thanks. How are you feeling?"

Grace sighed. "Wishing that I hadn't lost my license."

The pair laughed, and the nurse stepped close. "Can I talk to you for a minute?"

"Yeah, sure."

The nurse made sure to tuck them into a corner and kept her voice low as they huddled close. "We've got a problem."

"What is it?" Kate asked.

"If the roads are blocked, that means emergency services are going to have a hell of a time trying to get anywhere, and that means anyone on board that's hurt beyond minor cuts and scratches might be in real danger."

Kate looked to Grace, who had rested her head back on the glass, gently holding the rag up to her head where she'd been hit. She bit her lip and then looked down to the streets below, which were clogged with stalled traffic. "All right. So what do we do?"

"If this is a terrorist attack, and from what it looks like, it's a big one, then that means the National Guard and the Red Cross will be called to help assist. I volunteered for the Red Cross when I first got out of nursing school. Their protocol is to coordinate with emergency services to figure out where they're needed most. If we can get any of the sick or injured to a police station, we'll be able to track them down."

"There's a police station on 21st and 35th Ave." A young man, earbuds still in even though the phone in his hand no longer produced any music, leaned into their conversation and then stepped back when Kate and the nurse glared at him. "Sorry." He lifted his hands passively. "Didn't mean to pry."

"No, it's fine," Kate said, taking a step toward him. "How far of a walk is the station from here?"

The kid couldn't have been older than twenty, but he had dark, puffy blotches beneath his eyes. It reminded Kate of scratches on a new car. "Less than a mile."

"All right." Kate turned to the nurse. "We need a count of everyone that needs hospital attention. We'll make sure those folks have priority off the train and get them to the police station quickly."

"Yeah, okay."

"I can help." The kid finally removed his earbuds and pocketed the phone in his jacket. "Just tell me what you need."

"You run up and tell Bud to send anyone down with high-priority injuries or illnesses. Then collect any able-bodied people that can help. Tell them where we're going. And try to get big guys. We might need the muscle to carry people."

"Got it." The young man darted off through the open car doors and wove his way through the crowded aisles. Kate smiled as he parted. The kid had a good heart. He reminded her of Luke.

The sudden thought of her son made her worry. Were the attacks isolated to just New York? Then she thought of Holly in the city, stuck in their apartment, alone with Mrs. Dunny. She needed to get home. She needed to make sure her family was safe.

"Captain!" The kid called her from the second car, slightly out of breath as he jogged to the door. "We've got a pregnant woman up front who thinks she might be going into labor and one diabetic that'll need his insulin shot in about an hour. He doesn't have any on him, but he has some at home."

"Where does he live?"

The kid sighed. "New Jersey."

Kate turned to the nurse. "Will the police station have any medical supplies like insulin?"

The nurse grimaced. "Maybe, but probably not. The Red Cross will."

Kate returned to the kid. "Get the diabetic down here, and the pregnant lady if she can move." She turned back to the nurse. "You go with the kid and see if she's actually going into labor. If she is, we'll need to find a wheelchair if the contractions worsen."

"Can you watch her?" The nurse said, handing Kate the bandage she was using for Grace.

"Sure." Kate sat next to the woman, who was concentrating very hard on the floor between her feet. She placed a hand on the old woman's shoulder. "How are you?"

Grace closed her eyes. "A little dizzy is all." She swallowed and then slowly leaned back. "Feels like I just went on a merry-go-round." She chuckled. "Haven't been on one of those since nineteen fifty-six." She turned to Kate, still smiling. "You're not from around here, are you?"

"I'm not from anywhere really."

"I imagine you travel a lot," Grace said, gesturing toward the pilot wings.

"I do." It was one of the reasons Kate had become a pilot in the first place. As a young girl, she had dreamed of traveling around the world. Meeting new people, experiencing different cultures, living a life with nothing to her name but a backpack full of clothes and a map. But reality didn't match up with those dreams.

The parole meeting suddenly penetrated her thoughts, and Kate shuddered. She pictured Dennis, sitting in that chair in the middle of the room, looking at her. He was always chained by the wrists and ankles, but that never stopped her skin from crawling. Youth had a way of making you pay dearly for your mistakes, and Kate had paid in spades.

"Dear, are you all right?" Grace asked.

"Huh?" Kate looked over, slack-jawed, then tried to hide it with a smile. "I'm fine."

Grace took hold of Kate's hand and gave it a reassuring squeeze. "Thinking of your family? Well, don't worry. By the time you get back to them, this will all be over."

Bud returned from the other train, raising his hands to address the crowd. "We've already got people moving. The platform is two blocks to our south. Everyone keep in a single-file line, and move slowly and carefully. No pushing, no running, and make sure you give enough space for the person in front of you." He walked to Kate and Grace, extending his hand to the elderly woman. "Okay, ma'am. Let's get you some help."

The nurse and the kid returned with the diabetic and the pregnant woman, who cradled her stomach as she waddled through the doors.

A foot of space separated the metro from the emergency railing, and when Kate brought Grace to the precipice, she wavered. "Sorry. Another dizzy spell."

"I'll go over first." The kid jumped the gap with ease and held out his arm to help Grace cross. Kate handled her gently, but the kid practically lifted Grace on his own and landed her safely on the emergency walkway.

"Keep her steady," Kate said then turned to the pregnant woman. "You're next."

The woman waddled forward, belly exposed, and her hand gripped Kate's arm like a vise. She breathed in quick, short bursts, and despite the frigid air a sheen of sweat covered her face and neck. "God, it's getting worse."

"Just breathe," Kate said, wincing from the grip on her arm. "Kid, a hand?"

The boy made sure Grace was safe on the railing before he reached out his arm. "Okay. Got her."

"On three," Kate said. "One, two, three!" Kate pushed and the kid pulled, and the pregnant woman landed breathlessly on the other side and winced from another contraction.

The diabetic got over without much help, and with the three of their sick and wounded across, Kate went next along with the nurse. Kate turned back and saw the line of people already on the railing from the other cars. They had all waited just as the metro worker had told them to. And Kate noticed that all of them were looking to her.

"Everybody keep a slow and steady pace." Kate stole a glance to the long fall to the road below, and she quickly grabbed the railing for support. "No need to rush it."

Kate shuffled forward, while the kid helped Grace and the nurse guided the pregnant lady right behind them.

The commotion below continued to pull Kate's attention away from the emergency walkway. People had walked out of stores, and car doors stood open and abandoned. There were shouts of panic and fear. Most of the heads were turned north toward the pillar of smoke. Kate's eyes were pulled toward it, and when she watched the column twist and then meld into the grey skies, another explosion erupted and rattled the train tracks.

Instinctively, everyone ducked. Kate turned to the east,

toward the sound of the explosion. A few seconds of silence passed before another column of smoke rose into the sky, and the mood on the ground below transformed from mild anxiety to full-blown panic.

The same reaction spread to the crowd on the rails, and Kate watched the man in the black trench coat shove people aside and sprint up the railway, his feet teetering close to the edge. "Out of my way!" He waved his arms angrily and left a trail of dazed and confused bystanders in his wake.

"Stop!" Kate thrust her arms out, but the man continued his bulldoze down the platform. He swayed right a little, and the people he passed followed suit as the orderly line was wrinkled by chaos. "Stop!" But it was too late.

Kate yanked Grace and the kid forward, pulling them away from the stampede. When the old woman couldn't keep pace the kid scooped her up in his arms. Kate kept an eye on the nurse, who pushed the pregnant woman forward as fast as the woman's legs could waddle, but she couldn't see the diabetic man.

A shriek pierced the air, and Kate turned in just enough time to watch a woman fall from the safety of the emergency walk. She screamed all the way down, her voice ripping into the air. A thump sounded, the scream ended, and Kate looked away, tears forming in her eyes.

Kate reached the platform first, and she spun around and pulled the old woman and the kid toward the wall, away from the structure's edge. The nurse did the same for the pregnant woman, but the diabetic man led the charge down the steps and onto the street with the rest of the train passengers.

When the platform cleared, Kate hunched over and placed her hands on her knees, with her backside up against the wall on a poster for some band playing at a local bar. She stared at the tips of her shoes, and after a moment, and with a shaking hand, she wiped the snot from her upper lip and straightened herself out.

At first glance, everyone was still in one piece, though the pregnant woman looked one contraction away from spilling the baby right onto the dirty platform.

"How bad are the contractions?" Kate asked.

"Fucking bad! GAHHH!" The woman's cheeks reddened, and her whole body spasmed as she shut her eyes tight and waited for the pain to pass.

"She has maybe another hour before the baby comes," the nurse said. "But it's hard to tell."

"Another hour?" The woman slapped her hand onto the wall for support. "Mary, mother of Christ."

Kate turned to the kid. "All right, hero. You lead the way to the police station. I'll take care of your lovely lady." She took Grace's hand and followed the kid down the subway steps, past the turnstiles, and to the street level.

People sprinted and screamed in terror, unsure of where to run or what to do. The kid brought them out of the street and away from the worst of the maddening crowd. They clustered at the corner of a coffee shop, and the kid gestured down the street. "Two blocks that way."

Kate followed, her eyes surveying the blank traffic signals overhead. A dog sprinted past her, causing both Grace and Kate to jump. The animal barked randomly on its run, then disappeared down an alleyway. They passed an apartment building, and Kate saw the pillar of smoke that belonged to the LaGuardia explosion still drifting up toward the sky.

A cold blast of wind knocked a stack of newspapers over the sidewalk in front of them like an accordion. One of them flattened against Kate's shin, and she ripped it off.

"It's just around here," the kid said, separating himself from the group. "It's right—" The kid turned the corner and stopped in his tracks.

Kate followed, her hand still gripped tightly in Grace's, but when she saw the police station, she let go. "Oh my god."

Hundreds of people poured off the front steps of the precinct, the sidewalk jammed with more pedestrians than it could hold. They clambered over one another, fighting to get inside, fighting for answers, fighting because they had no idea of what to do next.

A few people stood on the outskirts, blood dripping down their faces. One man lay on the concrete off to the side. He was motionless.

The nurse bumped into Kate with the pregnant woman, and all five of them stood in shock on the street corner. "What the hell is going on?"

Kate spun around, gripping the nurse by the shoulders. "Is there another hospital nearby? Another place where the Red Cross might show up?"

The nurse gawked at the hordes in front of the station. "I… I…" She shook her head, her eyes reddening. "I don't know." She let go of the pregnant woman's hands and backed away. "I have to get out of here. I have to go home."

Kate shook her head, following the nurse step for step as the pregnant woman leaned against the building for support. "No, we need you." She pointed back to the woman. "She's going into labor."

"I can't help her." The nurse backed up more quickly now. "I'm sorry." She spun around and sprinted away.

"Wait!" Kate took a handful of quick steps but ended the pursuit as the nurse vanished into the panicked masses. She held the sides of her head, the atmosphere too overwhelming. There were no sirens in the distance signaling help. She saw no police on the street, no signs of authority anywhere.

"Hey." The touch of a hand on her shoulder accompanied the voice, and Kate spun around to find the kid standing there. His eyes were wide, his nose red from the cold. He gestured back to what was left of their group. "What do we do?"

The pregnant woman shut her eyes, both hands over her stomach, grimacing in pain between short, quick breaths. Grace was next to her, her weathered hand brushing the sweaty strands of hair off the pregnant woman's forehead.

"Hospital," Kate said. "I don't know if anything will be working there when we show up, but it's the best shot we have." She looked to the kid. "Do you know one that's close?"

"Ah, maybe?" He shut his eyes to think. "There might be a small one off 30th Ave." He opened his eyes, nodding. "Yeah. That's the closest one."

"We need to hurry." Kate relayed the plans to their two other companions and departed the chaotic scene of the police station. And just as they turned back down the street away from the precinct, gunshots fired.

3

Broken-down ambulances and police cars dotted the roads leading to the hospital. Behind one of the emergency vehicles were two paramedics lifting a man out on a gurney. He was bloodied, the cold already causing the claret to crust and grow brittle. The paramedics wore the same bloody stains over the chest of their uniforms.

The hospital's entrance wasn't as hectic as the police station, but there were still dozens of people that passed in and out of the ER's now permanently open sliding glass doors.

Inside, the cold stench of bleach and antiseptic blasted Kate's senses, but it was a small price to pay for the relief from the cold. A faint glow of warmth still lingered, either from the number of bodies or from the heat still trapped inside from before the power failure.

Hospital staff scurried back and forth. Cries of pain and pleas for help echoed down the darkened halls. Two nurses sat behind the ER station, their bodies shaking with adrenaline as they searched for files in darkness. One of them held a lighter, examining a sheet with medication doses.

"Room twenty needs their antibiotics bag, and eighteen needs their pills." The nurse, husky with short-cropped hair and a tattoo that crawled up the side of her neck and out of the collar of her scrubs, slapped the folder into the chest of another nurse.

"But all of the equipment is on the second floor, and the elevators aren't working." The second nurse was a mouse compared to the husky woman. "I can't even see what I'm doing up there!"

The husky nurse opened the mousy woman's hand, shoved the lighter into it, then closed her fist. "There. Now go." The bark was accompanied by a shooing hand, and Ms. Mouse scurried away.

Kate rushed to the station, grabbing the husky woman's shoulder just before she was out of arm's reach. "Excuse me, I have a woman—"

"Little busy, sweetheart." Husky Nurse easily removed Kate's hand and flung it away, moving quickly toward the double doors that had a sign with the letters "ICU" etched over the top.

"Hey!" Kate sprinted after her, sliding in front of the woman and blocking her path. She thrust a finger into the nurse's face, and the woman wrinkled her nose in annoyance. "I've got a pregnant woman in labor and an elderly woman with a possible concussion. They both need help." She gestured to the kid, who had one arm out for each of their patients to grab onto.

Husky Nurse turned to look and then pinched her fingers in her mouth and whistled, high and loud. "I need a wheelchair and a doctor, now!"

An orderly brought the wheelchair and slid it under the pregnant woman's backside then looked to the nurse for direction.

"Get her down to room seven. I'll meet you there." She clapped the orderly on the back, and the woman was whisked away, panting heavily.

Just before the pregnant woman passed through the double doors, she looked back at Kate, the kid, and Grace and smiled, her cheeks a bright cherry red and covered in sweat. "Thank you!"

"You're welcome!" Kate waved back, but the woman had already disappeared.

"Your mother can take a seat here, and we'll get to her when we can," the husky nurse said.

"Oh no, she's not—" But the nurse was gone. Kate returned to the kid and took Grace's hand. "She said someone will come out in a second." But as Kate examined the ER's lobby, she wasn't sure how long that would take.

While they waited, more and more people poured inside. Some were bloodied, some were scared, most were both. Another twenty minutes of this steady influx, and it would be the police station all over again. "We should leave."

"What? Why?" The kid asked. "This is probably the safest place to be right now."

"No generators," Kate said, talking to herself. She looked to the emergency exit signs. They should have been glowing, alerting people to their presence, but none of them worked. "Hospitals have generators as backups in case of power outages to keep the equipment running." She shook her head. "None of them are working here."

The kid let go of the old woman's hand. "S-so what are you saying? Everyone here is going to die?" He shouted the last words, and Kate hushed him.

"I don't know." Kate pressed the back of her hand to her forehead. "I need to get home."

"Go." Grace's voice was soft and weak. She shifted in the plastic chair, and folded both hands in her lap. "You've done enough."

Kate joined her in the empty seat to her left. "Listen, it's only going to get worse. You can't—"

"I'm seventy-nine years old." Grace smiled and gently patted Kate's hand. The gesture was similar to the one that Kate's grandmother had done whenever she had a story to tell. It was reassuring. It was safe. "I'll be fine. It might look bad now, but things will turn around." She leaned in close. "But we'll need people like you out there." Then she pointed to herself. "To help more people like me." She looked to the kid. "They'll need people like both of you." She placed her weathered hand against Kate's cheek. "Go. Be with your family. It won't be long before I'll be with mine."

What was surely meant to be comforting instead filled Kate with a sadness that swelled in her chest. It was the way the old woman spoke and the double meaning of her words. But Grace was right. She needed to go home. She needed to be with her daughter and husband. And she needed to get in contact with her son. "All right. But if someone doesn't come by to check on you in five minutes, then I want you to raise hell."

Grace laughed. "Oh, I will." She turned to the kid and extended her hand, which he took gently. "You know, I have a granddaughter about your age. She's very pretty." She leaned in close and raised her eyebrows with a coy smile. "I'll put in a good word for you. She's crazy about me."

"Thanks." The kid smiled, blushed, and then let the old woman's hand go.

Grace returned Kate's jacket, and then Kate and the kid walked toward the exit, and both turned back one last time once they reached the door. They each raised a hand to Grace, sitting in that plastic chair, bundled up in her pink sweater, and a kind smile over her face.

Grace waved back. They never saw her again.

4

Around every corner, down every street, in every neighborhood they passed, the scene was all the same. People scurrying around, afraid, confused, panicked. Anything that sat on the sidewalk in front of stores was either broken or looted.

Kate shook her head, numb with disbelief. "I can't believe people sometimes." She looked to the columns of smoke that had faded somewhat against the greying sky. The clouds had darkened. It wouldn't be long before they started spitting snow again.

"People do weird stuff when they're scared," the kid said, his eyes always looking, always scanning. "My uncle was an alcoholic, and he used to beat up my cousin when he was good and drunk. It went on like that for a long time. He's a little older than me, and he still can't be around drunk people. You try and get him close to a bar and he freezes up. Can't speak, can't move. He goes catatonic." He stopped and gestured down a street. "If we turn here, we can make it to the Lincoln Tunnel to get back into the city."

"Tunnel?" Kate raised her eyebrows. "No. We haven't seen any traffic moving for the past six blocks. Everything's dead in the water, including the tunnel. I'm not going into a concrete tube buried under the river with all of this happening." She gestured ahead. "Let's take the bridge."

"The closest bridge to us right now is Williamsburg." The kid glanced back down the street. "That'll take me longer to get home." He looked back to Kate. "My mom's sick." He tapped the side of his head. "Kind of a mental thing. Has a hard time keeping track of stuff. The longer it takes me to get home, the more she's at risk of wandering out into all of this and getting herself hurt."

Kate studied the worried lines on the kid's face and was suddenly reminded of how young he was and that she didn't even know his name. "Hey, listen—What's your name?"

"Doug."

"Doug, take it from a mother who has a son about your age. The only thing your mom would be concerned about is you getting home safe in one piece. The bridge is safer, and we'll have better line of sight into the city. And trust me, when you're heading into a storm, line of sight can save your life."

Doug nodded but offered a final longing glance toward the direction of the tunnel. When he faced Kate again, that steady assurance had returned. "Yeah, that makes sense." He pointed down the road they'd been traveling on. "But I need to hurry."

Kate did her best to keep up with Doug's jog. While she would have preferred to keep a steady speed walk, she didn't want to hold the kid up any longer than she had to. And she didn't want to lose him. Not because she didn't think he couldn't take care of himself or that she couldn't find her own way into the city but because of something inexplicably simple. She didn't want to be alone.

In the maddening storm that swirled around them, they were each other's lifeboats, and they needed one another to stay afloat, lest someone else come along and try to drag them down into the dark abyss of the cold waters.

Intermittent screams and the crash of glass had replaced the city's bustling motorists and honking horns. Destruction had replaced production, and Kate still hadn't seen a single authority figure since they'd left the police station. Had they all gone home? Had they all been absorbed into the mob?

After fifteen minutes on the run Kate winced and clutched her side, slowing to a walk. "Doug!" She stretched out her hand and then leaned up against a storefront, the sign on its door flipped to "closed." "It's just a cramp. Give me a minute."

Hesitantly, Doug slowed and then jogged back toward her. Kate lifted her arms into the air, doing her best to draw in long, deep breaths. The knives digging into her sides had lessened, and she paced in a tight circle. "Don't get much cardio anymore." She smiled, but Doug wasn't paying attention. She was slowing him down.

"You sure you're all right to keep going?" Doug asked.

"Yeah," Kate answered, the tip of the knives still prodding her ribs. "I'm fine." She turned away from Doug to hide the pain, and when she did she noticed the name of the storefront where she'd stopped. It was a pharmacy. She pressed her face against the dark glass, unable to see anything inside.

"What are you doing?" Doug asked.

"My daughter's sick." Kate peeled her face away from the cold glass. "And you said your mother needs medication, right? We should look inside. See what they have."

Doug snickered. "I doubt they're open."

A bell at the top of the door chimed when Kate pushed it open. Inside, like the rest of the city, the power was out, and the only light provided was what shone through the tinted windows at the storefront. The back of the store and half the aisles were covered in darkness.

The pump of the shotgun froze both of them in their tracks.

"Who's there?" The voice shouted from the darkness.

Kate lifted her hands, squinting into the darkness. "We need medicine."

The man with the gun remained hidden in the shadows. "You some junkies looking for a high?"

"We're not junkies," Kate said, hands still raised and her eyes focused on the barrel of the shotgun. "My daughter's sick." She tried to swallow but couldn't. "I just need some things for her. I can pay."

The man grunted. "Pay? With what? Credit Card? Debit? There aren't any machines working. No electricity." He finally emerged from the shadows. Sunlight revealed a weathered face, cheeks wrinkling and sagging. Liver spots dotted his bald head, but his blue eyes were still vibrant as they stared down the shotgun's sight. "Go."

Doug tugged at Kate's shoulder. "C'mon. It's not worth it."

But Kate stood her ground. "I'm not leaving until I have medicine for my little girl."

The old man didn't waver, didn't move, didn't flinch. "What's she sick with?"

"Sore throat, fever," Kate said. "I think she has the flu."

The old man lowered the shotgun, and Kate and Doug exhaled. He walked past them toward the front door and flipped the lock. "Won't be long before they start breaking glass to get in here. Damn animals. C'mon. Let's get your little girl some medicine."

A few candles glowed behind the counter of the pharmacy, where most of the prescription drugs were stored. "I'll give you a few general antibiotics in case that flu turns out to be something bacterial." He snagged a few bags off the aisle and then shoved them into Kate's arms. "You can grab some over-the-counter pills on your way out. Aisle three."

"Thank you," Kate said, stuffing the pills inside her jacket. "Thank you so much."

"Do you have any SSRI medications?" Doug asked, eyeing the rows of medicine.

The old man grunted. "Probably gonna be a lot of people

down on their luck after all of this." He stepped backward farther down the aisle. "A particular brand you're looking for?"

"Celexa, if you have it," Doug answered.

"Here." The old man tossed a bag at Doug. "Now get out."

They retreated down the aisles, and Kate stole a variety of cold medicines and throat lozenges and added them to her stash of antibiotics.

Once outside, Doug took a few steps then stopped. He stared at the medicine clutched in his hand. His expression glowered contempt, and the corner of his eye twitched. It could have been the cold, but his eyes reddened in the anticipation of tears.

"What's SSRI stand for?" Kate asked.

"Selective serotonin reuptake inhibitors," Doug answered. "It's for depression." He looked at her, almost as if he were waiting for her to make a joke at his mother's expense. "That's what's wrong with my mom."

"I'm sorry." Kate gave a soft touch to his shoulder. "I can imagine that's hard."

"Harder when you're alone with her." The tears fell, and Doug turned his head away, wiping at the corner of his eyes quickly. "I'm fine." He stuffed the medicine into his jacket pocket. "We need to get moving." Without looking at her, he broke into another jog.

Kate's body groaned, but she caught up to him easily enough. The knives returned to her side for a moment but didn't linger as long.

The pair cut through neighborhoods, staying off the main streets where most of the looting and chaos was taking place. But the houses and apartments they passed were calmer, more stable. Kate assumed home had that effect on people. Though there were a few exceptions.

"Danny!" A young woman stepped from a small house, cradling a crying baby in her arms. "Danny!" She had been screaming that name since they'd turned down her street, her voice shrill and panicked. "Danny, come back!"

"Shut it, lady! Danny ain't here!" The angered voice was thrown from a window in one of the apartment buildings. Kate looked to see where it came from, but the coward had already ducked back inside.

"Oh, god," the woman said, and the baby let out a high-pitched shriek. She gave her a soothing bounce and kissed the top of her head. "It's all right, Liddy. Everything is going to be okay."

Kate locked eyes with the mother briefly as she continued her search for Danny's whereabouts. Kate assumed it was her husband or boyfriend. She was a young woman, not much older than Doug.

A few hours ago, if the woman had wanted to talk to Danny, all she would have had to do was call his cell phone. It was so easy to talk to people now, and it could be done at any time, from anywhere in the world.

The sight of the woman made Kate grab her phone, but the blank screen was a reminder of just how easily all of that could be taken away. In the blink of an eye Kate, and the rest of the people in the city, had been cast into the stone age. No cars. No phones. No power. And then Kate stopped, a terrible thought freezing her in place.

"What is it?" Doug asked. Then, noticing the phone in Kate's hand, he lunged forward excitedly. "Did you get it working?"

"If the power went off, how does that affect our phones? They have batteries in them." Kate lifted her head and saw that the woman with the baby who was screaming for Danny had gone back inside. "And the cars. They've all stopped working too." She frowned. "How is that even possible?"

"I don't know. Some type of wireless computer virus maybe?" Doug shrugged, shaking his head from the lack of conviction in his own answer. "Everything has computers in it now, right? Or at least some component."

"Yeah," Kate answered. "Maybe." She tucked the phone back in her pocket and then zipped her jacket all the way to her chin.

The first few flecks of snow fell and dotted the sidewalk. "Bridge isn't much farther, right?"

"No," Doug answered. "One more street, and then it's down on the right. We're almost there."

Kate took the lead the rest of the way. On her run, the mother's cries of 'Danny' replayed in her mind. How many other people were screaming for their loved ones? How many people didn't know the condition of their friends and family? She looked up to the grey clouds that blanketed the sky. The snow thickened, and she squinted to avoid the snowflakes stinging her eyes. She never wanted to be that woman on the street. She never wanted to have that fear of the unknown.

But the closer they got to the bridge and the more people Kate saw on the street, funneling out of the city and into the boroughs of Brooklyn and Queens, she also had another thought. How many of these people were leaving friends and family behind? How many of them gave in to the fear and instinct of survival? She'd seen enough of it on the train to guess that those numbers were higher than they should be. The mob mentality had taken control. And despite Grace's plea that there needed to be more people like her and Doug, Kate had her doubts about how many of those "good people" were still hanging around the city.

5

Thousands of people crammed onto the small sidewalk of the Williamsburg bridge, funneling themselves off the island and onto the mainland, desperately trying to get out of the city. Every face carried an expression of hastened panic, and hands clawed forward, people shoving one another aside.

"Looks like we're the only ones trying to get back in," Doug said then shook his head. "Power must be out in the city too." He spun around, unsure of what he was even looking for. "God, how far does this thing go?"

Kate eyed the pedestrian walkways that lined either side of the bridge. Not an inch of space remained. She looked to the road and saw that many people had chosen to climb over the stalled cars that clogged the bridge. "We'll have to go over the cars."

"Yeah," Doug replied, nodding nervously.

Two women passed, clutching one another, muttering to themselves loud enough for the whole neighborhood to hear. "God, who were those people? Why would they do that?"

Kate reached for the woman's shoulder. "What people?"

The woman spun around, snarling like a rabid dog. "Don't

touch me!" She lunged as she barked, and Kate stepped back with her hands in the air.

The second woman calmed her friend. "We saw one of the attacks."

"Attacks?" Doug and Kate asked simultaneously.

"You're talking about the blasts?" Doug asked.

"No. The people with the guns. They came out of nowhere. We were near Times Square when it happened." She cast her gaze to the ground, and her lips quivered.

"Terrorists," the other woman blurted out, her expression still rabid. "They're animals!"

"C'mon, Mary." The friend pulled the woman forward, but Kate still heard her screaming as they disappeared into the crowds.

"Animals! Rabid animals!"

Kate followed the back of the woman's head until she couldn't see her anymore.

"Looks like we can get on the road there." Doug pointed between a black truck and a red Mercedes sedan. "It'll be hard crossing all the way over though. Especially with so many people leaving."

"We'll just watch our footing." And just as Kate spoke, she watched a woman fall from the hood of a car, twisting her ankle as a friend tried to help her up before she was smashed to a pulp by the stampede of people behind her. The sight triggered the image of the woman who had fallen off the walkway of the elevated train tracks and the resounding splat that ended her screams.

"Kate," Doug said, snapping her out of the daze. "You coming?"

"Yeah." Kate followed, the pair pushing through the hordes streaming off the bridge. Most looked like they didn't even know where they were going. They were simply lost and aimlessly following the masses.

The crowd and its madness thickened the closer Doug and Kate got to the road on the bridge. The pair squeezed through, Kate's shoulders knocking into arms and chests and stomachs as they pushed closer.

Doug glanced behind him twice to make sure Kate was close, but she had latched onto the back of his jacket without him even knowing. That same impulse from before flooded through Kate's veins. She didn't want to lose him, a kid she had met less than an hour ago. A kid that she never would have even spoken to had the train not stopped. A kid that was the only person who stepped forward to help when things got bad. A kid who stayed when everyone else ran.

They reached a truck, and Doug climbed into the bed. He turned and offered his hand, which Kate grabbed hold of. Elevated by the truck bed, Kate had a better view of the carnage clogging the bridge and the steady stream of people still trying to escape.

"Holy shit," Doug said.

Every car on the bridge was wrecked. Piles of metal and tires formed like anthills. And through the wreckage, she saw the lifeless bodies of those still inside, unnoticed by the people that passed over their metal tombs.

"Look at this," Doug said, sweeping his hand over the chaos. "No cops. No authority anywhere. How the hell are people supposed to get any help?"

"They're not." Kate thought about what the pair of women had said about the terrorists with the guns. An old rhyme entered her mind. Like shooting fish in a barrel. "C'mon."

Hoods and roofs buckled underneath their feet, and more than once Kate was forced to crawl then slide down over the fresh snow that melted against her pants and jacket. After the first dozen cars, her joints ached.

"Holding up okay?" Doug shouted back to her, pausing on the hood of a Chrysler as a fresh wave of New Yorkers passed them on their way to Brooklyn.

"Yeah." Kate hopped off the front bumper of a jeep and landed on the first open patch of concrete she had seen on the bridge since they had started walking. "Just need a break for a second." She squatted, letting her muscles stretch, and then stood.

The cold and the exertion chipped away at Kate's stamina. The skipped breakfast didn't help either. And despite the cold, she began to sweat. "Do you have any water?"

"Yeah, I think I have some left." Doug swung his pack around and opened the largest compartment. He rummaged through while Kate glanced to the south.

The Brooklyn Bridge sat on the horizon, the suspension bridge larger than the one Kate currently found herself on. She had taken Holly there the first week they moved. She remembered all the bike locks that people attached on some of the support cables of the walkway. One of them was hanging out all the way over the center of the road, which meant the daredevil who had put it there dangled twenty feet in the air over traffic.

Kate wasn't sure of the tradition's origin, but it was one of those small things that made big cities feel like home. And she'd been to enough of them to know New York was unique.

An explosion plumed over the Brooklyn Bridge, tearing apart Kate's memory as the blast echoed over the river. Kate jerked away from the sound, turning her face as if the blast was close enough to hurt her. Another explosion rumbled in the distance, and this one pulled her attention back to the bridge.

A second plume of smoke rose on the opposite end of the bridge, and Kate watched brick and concrete collapse into the East River, dragging cars and people with it.

The crowd on the Williamsburg Bridge froze at the sight of the horror unfolding to the south. And then, slowly at first and then all at once, screams and the stampede of footsteps replaced shock.

In the explosion of panic, Kate watched three people disappear beneath churning legs and feet. Heavy footfalls stomped over the vehicles like a tidal wave.

People slipped on the slick surfaces fresh with snow and landed hard, shattering windows and denting metal. Everyone clawed and scrambled forward, fleeing toward safety.

"Kate, run!"

Doug's voice snapped Kate out of the stupor, but she lost him in the crowd. She rocketed herself into the growing projectile of human bodies that fled toward safety. Another explosion rocked the Manhattan Bridge toward the north, two more blasts jettisoned debris into the air, and the bridge joined the Brooklyn in its collapse into the East River.

Kate's heart hammered wildly. Adrenaline washed over the pain radiating from her knees and hips, and she grew numb against the bodies that rushed past her.

The end of the bridge drew closer, and it was clogged with people sprinting from the city. They came from everywhere, bottlenecking at the bridge. Another blast rumbled, and this one shook the ground beneath her feet. Kate lost her balanced and tumbled forward over the hood of a truck.

Screams replaced the monotonous whine of the blast. Two pairs of feet scurried past Kate's line of sight, and she pushed herself up, her chest still vibrating in a low hum from the blast. She wobbled once she was upright and sloppily placed one foot in front of the other as she restarted her escape.

Others joined in Kate's retreat, and then another blast thundered on the bridge, this one closer than before. A wave of heat warmed Kate's backside, but she didn't turn around.

The ground suddenly buckled, and the foundation of the bridge gave way. Kate kept her pace, the muscles along her legs wobbling like jelly, and she didn't stop until she tripped and skidded to the pavement, her gloves tearing on the concrete.

Kate heaved for breath and fought the urge to vomit. She turned behind her and saw nothing but grey dust where the bridge once stood. It was like a smog of destruction, and every once in a while, someone ran into the fog, and then someone ran out.

"Doug!" Kate's voice cracked. It was dry and tired. "Doug!"

Figures darted around Kate as the fog spread, swallowing her up with everything else. Visibility dropped to less than a few feet in front of her face. She clawed at the dust, searching for Doug, but she couldn't see him. A million thoughts raced through her mind. Had he been trampled? Was he caught in the explosion? Did he fall into the river?

Gunfire broke Kate's stream of consciousness and jump-started her pulse. The gunshots fired in the same hastened rhythm as her heart. Blanketed by grey haze, they seemed to come from every direction. The gunfire chased screams as the slow, huddled masses of people escaping the bridge suddenly returned to their frenzied pace.

Kate finally jumped into the rat race and kept her head low. Gunfire blared to her left. She shuddered and ducked lower. She veered from the road, choosing to head for the cover of buildings, and as she did, she saw them. They were nothing but silhouettes, their arms lengthened by the rifles in their hands. She wasn't sure if they could see her, but she darted to the corner of a store to escape execution.

Fear clawed the back of her neck, traveling down her spine and invading every cell of her body. The gunfire, the smoke, the screams—it all funneled that primal emotion of survival through her veins. The ability of higher thought ended, and everything was replaced with a single message: run.

Dust trailed off her as she sprinted. Like an extended blur, it followed her until her legs tired and her lungs exploded in her chest. The snowfall lightened, but it had already covered her tracks with fresh powder.

The farther she ran, the more she noticed the faces in the windows of the stores she passed. In turn, they watched her through the glass, clutching their broken and useless phones like some kind of life support.

Kate caught her reflection in the glass, and at first glance, she didn't recognize herself. The dust-covered monster couldn't have been her. What she saw now was a frightened animal.

Adrenaline propelled her forward, and the more ground her boots chewed up, the faster those sounds of gunshots and the sight of the ruins of the Williamsburg bridge faded. She made it ten blocks before she stopped. She hunched over, wheezing, then hacked and coughed, spitting snot and saliva onto the pavement.

With her motion ended, pain returned. Feet, hips, knees, everything ached. After the stop, she could only limp. And she traveled the next thirty blocks to the street where her apartment building was, fighting the urge to collapse.

Like Queens, Manhattan was in chaos. Screams bellowed from subway entrances. More gunshots thundered to the west. Glass shattered to her east. And while most people had sought shelter, thousands still roamed the streets.

The more she separated herself from the bridge and the fighting, the stranger the expressions became on the people she passed. She had been touched by the madness that had descended on the city, and people recoiled from her. They hadn't seen the horror yet. They hadn't experienced the real fear. But once they did, they'd change. It was inevitable.

A city of nine million people would fight. And if this was happening elsewhere in the country, which Kate was beginning to have the sinking suspicion that it was, that meant they could go a long time without receiving any aid.

And as those realizations washed over her and she saw more confused people with their red, cold noses pressed up against the windows of shops and apartments and houses that she passed, Kate knew she had to get off the island. She had to get her family away from the teeming masses that would do anything to survive.

It was like Grace had said: there weren't enough good people in the city, and even if Kate was able to round up all of them, they'd still be outnumbered one thousand to one. Those were odds that she wasn't willing to put her family against.

6

Thirty stories up, New York looked different. The roads that pumped life and movement into the city had suddenly clotted without warning. Rodney Klatt examined the streets below in a sort of stunned silence from his apartment window.

Vibrations from the explosions around the city had ended, but from his location, they were barely more than a rumble of thunder. He had gone to the roof to see where they'd hit, and his mouth dropped as he watched bridge after bridge collapse into the river.

Manhattan was isolated now, cut off from the mainland. There were the tunnels, of course, but that was only if the people doing this hadn't flooded them, and Rodney's souring gut was telling him that they had.

He moved to his couch, sitting down slowly. He eyed the bags he'd pulled from the closet that were already prepared for a quick escape. Food, water, medical supplies, clothes, knives. He had a gun. It was a .38 revolver. He owned it illegally, of course, and its only purpose was for reassurance. Never did he expect to ever use it.

But the gunfire on the streets had prompted him to remove it from its case. And here he sat, in the dark of his apartment, his supplies bagged and sitting by the door, with his .38 clutched tightly in his hand. He wanted to get used to holding it before he went out. At least that was what he was telling himself.

He'd prepared for stuff like this, but up until now, it had only been practice in preparation for a worst-case scenario. And now shit had hit the fan, and it was time for the rubber to meet the road. But for some reason he couldn't pull the trigger.

A part of it was the people he heard in the hall. His neighbors, some of them friends. People had knocked on his door, yelling his name to see if he was home, but Rodney had kept quiet. He was scared to confront them, scared to pass them in the hallway with his backpacks and his gun.

In all his planning and drills, he'd always done things alone. He thought it'd be better that way. No one to hold him back, no one to slow him down. And it would lessen the amount of supplies he'd need to bring. But in all of his planning, Rodney Klatt forgot the one element in a true crisis situation: fear.

Violence had erupted on the streets. People had gone crazy, and the only thing they could focus on was their own survival. They were all scrambling, searching for what Rodney had in those packs and what he possessed in the cabin up north. It was arrogant to do everything alone, to keep his thoughts and his fears to himself.

There was safety in numbers. It was one of the reasons he'd lived in New York for so long. Here he was nothing more than a tree lost in the massive forest. In a city of nine million people, no one even noticed him.

Three more knocks pounded on his door. "Hey, Rodney! Are you home, man? We think that there might have been an attack. Everyone is meeting on the twentieth floor to talk about it. Starts in ten minutes."

The knocking ended, and Rodney turned away from the door and back toward the window. He pressed his palm against the glass. It was cold and frozen, like the world below. His hand left a greasy print as he removed it and then returned to the couch.

The cushions smooshed beneath his weight, the support of the couch nonexistent. He'd been saving up for a new couch for the past four months. One more paycheck and he would have had enough money for the La-Z-Boy he wanted.

But there wouldn't be any more paychecks. His job at the utility company no longer existed. Nothing was going to be the same. Everything had changed in the blink of an eye, the flick of a switch.

Rodney released the revolver and set it down on the cushion next to him. He ran his palms up and down his thighs. His jeans were cold like the window. The weather was already seeping into the building. It wouldn't be much longer until it was just as cold inside as it was outside. Night would be worse.

He knew the bulk of people would stay in their homes, telling themselves the power would come back on. But Rodney knew better. The combination of the power, his phone not working, and the broken cars below all told the same story. An EMP had gone off. Everything with a computer processor in it was fried. No more utilities. No more transportation. No more food and water coming into a city that depended on it every day.

Nine million people. The number was too staggering, too unreal. It would take another couple of days before people started to become really violent, maybe even less considering the frozen tundra that New York was about to transform into. He had to get out. And he had to get out now.

Rodney sprang from the couch and donned the backpacks at the door. He rechecked his inventory in the bags. It was enough for the journey north and then some. He swung the straps of the pack over his shoulders and then reached for the revolver. He lingered a moment, looking at it before he placed it in its holster. He placed his hand on the doorknob of his front door but then froze.

The meeting. All those people I know, friends I've made since moving here, they have no idea what's happening. They have no idea what's going on, and that's not going to change anytime soon. It's not like the six o'clock news will be airing tonight, and they can't get online to research.

But was that his problem? Was it his fault they'd chosen not to be prepared, informed? No, it wasn't. So why couldn't he leave?

Rodney let go of the doorknob and leaned up against the wall. His stomach twisted into knots. That nauseating feeling he associated with bad Thai food and roller coasters spread through his body. He shut his eyes, shaking his head. "Shit. Shit-shit-shit-shit!"

Quickly, and before he changed his mind, Rodney opened the door and stepped out into the hallway, beelining it toward the stairwell. His feet fell quietly against the steps, the floor numbers descending numerically on his way down.

The bannister was cold against the palm of his hand, the metal smooth as he glided down. He passed the twenty-eighth floor, then the twenty-seventh. The twenty-sixth, twenty-fifth... by the time he reached the twenty-fourth, he found himself slowing a little. He passed a woman he didn't know in the stairs on the twenty-third, who was frantically running upward. He frowned at her as they passed, though she didn't pay him any attention. She was covered in dust and snow, her eyes wide and focused on nothing but the steps in front of her.

Rodney knew she was one of millions following the same instinct. Get home, get to family, find my friends. What he had observed from his window on the thirtieth floor wasn't chaos at all, simply a reorganizing of value within the city. And right now, that value was people. People who knew things, people who understood what would happen next. People like him.

Rodney stopped on the twentieth floor and stared at the exit door. He glanced toward the stairs leading downward. And then, just as quickly as he'd left his apartment, he exited onto the twentieth floor. He couldn't save everyone. But he might be able to save a few.

* * *

BY THE TIME Kate reached the thirty-fifth floor of the apartment building, the muscles in her legs were jelly. Gasping for breath, she shouldered open the exit door from the stairwell and clawed at the wall to pull herself toward their apartment.

The weather had frozen her stiff, and every step forward was jerky and spastic, akin to the walking dead. Some of the apartment doors she passed were open, the residents inside peeking out to watch her pass. If they spoke to her, she didn't hear them. Only two thoughts consumed her mind. Get to her family. Get them out of the city.

Kate found their apartment door open, and when she stepped inside, the fatigue in her muscles and the pain in her joints vanished. "Holly!" She sprinted into the apartment and found her daughter on the couch with Mrs. Dunny on the chair across from her. Kate exhaled. "Thank god."

"Mom?" Holly pinched her eyebrows together, sitting up from her position on the couch, the blanket falling from her chest.

"Mrs. Hillman!" Mrs. Dunny jumped from her chair as quickly as her old bones would allow, her jaw slack as she gawked at Kate. "My god, what happened?"

Kate cried, squeezing Holly tight. "I'm so glad you're okay."

"Kate?"

She spun around and saw Mark exiting the bedroom, his tie undone, hanging loosely around his neck. After a moment's pause, Kate flung herself into his arms.

"Jesus." Mark squeezed back, his hands gently prodding her body, trying to make sure that she wasn't injured. "Where did you come from?"

Kate finally pulled back, wiping away tears that smudged the snow and dirt against her cheek. "I was on the train when everything shut down. And I saw the explosions." She cleared her throat. "I got your message that Holly was sick before my phone died, and I just... I just... had to get home."

Mark cupped his hands on her cheeks. "You were out there?" His expression retained worry but showed signs of relief as he pulled her close. "Thank god you're all right."

"Mrs. Hillman, what is going on out there?" Mrs. Dunny asked. "What were those explosions?" Her eyes grew large and fearful, and she clasped her hands together in front of her sagging bosom as if she were praying.

Kate stepped back from Mark and took a seat on the couch with her daughter. Her body groaned in thanks for the rest, and she leaned into the soft cushions. Heat still lingered in the apartment, and her face thawed. "Nothing is working. Cars, phones, no power anywhere in the city."

"Yeah, it was like that on my way home from work." Mark took a seat on the armrest. "Once everything shut down at the office, I came straight home. They wanted me to stay, but with Holly sick and me not being able to get ahold of you, I couldn't stay."

Kate placed a hand on his knee, and Mark rested his hand on top of hers. She smiled. "I'm glad you came home." She looked at Holly and suddenly remembered the medicine in her jacket. "I stopped at a pharmacy on the way here."

"They were open?" Mark asked.

"Not exactly." Kate unzipped her jacket, and out spilled the medicine and antibiotics. She handed Holly the cough syrup and then gathered up the rest and placed them on the coffee table. "The bridges are gone, at least the ones across the East River."

Mark ran his fingers through his hair and stood, pacing back and forth in tight circles. "If the bridges are down, then that means they'll have to use the ferries to bring help over."

"I didn't see any boats working on the river either," Kate said, removing her jacket and flinging dust and snow to the side.

"There isn't any way off the island except for the tunnels, which I didn't want to chance coming through on the way here. Not with those people—"

"What people?" Mark asked.

"You didn't see them?" Kate asked.

"No. As soon as the power went off, I came here. I told you that."

Kate recoiled from the bite in Mark's answer. She frowned, and he flapped his arms at his sides, sighing.

"I'm sorry." He returned to his seat on the armrest. "It was hard being in the dark. I didn't know where you were, Holly was here alone, and—" He slouched and rubbed his face. When he peeled his hands from his cheeks, they were a bright red. "I thought I'd lost you."

Kate grabbed his hand. "Me too." She turned to Holly and held her hand, which was warm with fever. A sick child in a world with no hospitals and no doctors.

"Listen, we need to get out of the city," Kate said. Strength returned and steadied her voice. "It's bad out there right now, but it's only going to get worse."

"What about the Hudson River bridges?" Mrs. Dunny asked. "Are they still up?"

"I don't know," Kate answered. "But after what we saw out there, I doubt it."

"We saw?" Mark asked.

"Huh?" Kate replied, turning to him.

"You said 'we saw.'"

"Oh. There was this kid on the train. He helped me with an older woman and got her some help." Kate's voice grew distant. "We stuck together until we got to the Williamsburg Bridge. We were on it when it collapsed. I don't know if he made it. There was so much gunfire."

Mark shot out of his seat. "Christ, this is like 9/11 on crack!" His cheeks reddened further, and the vein along the side of his neck throbbed. "You're right, we need to get out of the city." He spun around, facing Kate. "Did you see what they looked like? Where were you when they started shooting? Did they follow you here?" He arched his eyebrows on that last question.

Kate stood. "I don't know who they are, what they want, or where they are right now." She pulled Mark out of earshot of Holly and Mrs. Dunny. "We shouldn't be talking about this in front of Holly. It's not anything she needs to hear."

"So what do we do?" Mark asked. "We try and go to the tunnels? How are we supposed to move her when she's sick? What if she gets worse? What if we have to stop? What if we run into those people on the streets?"

"One problem at a time," Kate answered.

"We should go to the meeting on the twentieth," Mrs. Dunny said.

"What meeting?" Kate asked.

"I heard some of the neighbors talking about it." Mrs. Dunny opened her purse and rummaged inside until she removed a stick of gum. "Management wanted to get everyone together, see what people knew." She popped the gum into her mouth, her attitude rather nonchalant about the whole idea. "Personally, I think it's just to keep people from going crazy."

Kate nodded. "We should go." She turned to Mark. "Can you stay here with Holly?"

"Me?" Mark gestured to Kate's appearance. "You show up like that and people will think the world is ending."

"Isn't it?" Kate asked.

"I'll stay with Holly," Mrs. Dunny said. "I don't need to hear a bunch of people hooting and hollering about stuff they don't know anything about. It's all just speculation. This thing will blow over. It always does."

The old woman spoke in a frame of mind that Kate found most of the elderly did during times of crisis, and she had noticed that in New York, the habit was twice as bad.

Kate knelt by Holly's side. "We'll only be gone a minute, but we'll be right back, okay?"

Holly immediately looked past Kate and to her father. "Dad, do you have to go?"

Kate's heart fractured at the words, and she let go of her daughter's hand as Holly reached for her father.

"We'll only be gone a little bit." Mark kissed her forehead, and Kate forced a smile. "Promise."

Kate turned toward the door, but Mark grabbed her wrist. She spun around. "What?"

He looked her up and down and then grimaced. "Might want to change."

Kate examined herself. "I'll make it quick." A trail of dust and snow followed her into the bedroom, and she wiped her face as best she could with what water remained in the pipes, which was ice cold and burned her skin.

A few smears of dust and frost lingered on her neck and ears, but she looked more like herself again and less like the ghost woman she had seen in the reflection of the shop windows she'd passed. She closed her eyes and gripped the granite of the sink's counter, fighting against the trembling and fatigue of her muscles.

All right, Kate. You've got to go into this thing with both eyes open and figure out how to get your family off the island. That is the priority. After that, it's finding a safe place for Holly and Mark to stay until whatever is happening is over. Then it's off to get Luke.

Kate opened her eyes, and nodded at her plan of action. And then, as if to test herself, she slowly lifted her hand and held it out flat, concentrating on keeping it steady. But it wouldn't stop shaking, no matter how long she stared at it.

7

When Rodney opened the door to the common area, he slammed the edge into a man standing nearby. The commotion triggered every head in the room to turn.

"Sorry," Rodney said, squeezing through, his backpack smacking into a woman's shoulder as he closed the door behind him. It clicked shut, and he sidestepped toward the back behind the crowds.

The manager shook off the disturbance, clearing his throat. "As I was saying, the power is out in the entire building."

"Cell phones aren't working either!" a voice shouted among the crowd.

"Nothing's working!" another added, and so began the low rumble of dissent.

Rodney kept quiet, wanting to see, wanting to hear how they'd react. While he hadn't left yet, that didn't mean he wanted to die here, and there still might be someone useful he could take along. He had what everyone wanted: a way out.

"Everyone, please!" the manager shouted, arms extended high and over people's heads. "I understand everyone's frustration, but the purpose of this meeting is to unearth the facts of what we know and don't know."

The door opened again, and this time Rodney's was one of the heads turning to see who entered. It was a woman and man, presumably husband and wife. The man was fairly put together, but the woman had flecks of dirt and snow littered in her hair. He thought about the explosions and then furrowed his brow. Had she seen what happened?

"If anyone has any information about what is going on, please, now is the time to let your voice be heard."

Rodney watched the woman and the man whisper to one another. Then the man nudged the woman forward, and she slowly raised her hand.

"I was out there," she said, shouting above the murmur of the crowd. Again, heads turned, and the room went silent.

The manager up front motioned her toward him. "Let her through, let her come up here."

The crowd stepped aside, and the woman moved past. Her steps were slow but deliberate, as if she was biding her time and thinking of what to say. She looked nervous, due either to the crowd or to what she'd seen outside.

By the time she reached the front of the room, the murmur had started up again, but it shushed itself when she stepped up on the chair, hovering above the crowd. She kept her fists balled at her sides, and she cleared her throat.

"My name is Kate Hillman. I live on the thirty-fifth floor with my husband and daughter." She swallowed, scanning the crowd, and she finally relaxed her hands. "I'm a pilot with Nova Airlines, and I landed at LaGuardia this morning before the attack."

Rodney squinted at her but remained silent as everyone else whispered.

"I don't know much, but I can tell you what I've seen!" She raised her voice, taking command of the room. "Transportation is down. Cars, metro, buses, planes, trains, boats, all out of commission. Whoever is doing this has also blown up every bridge over the East River."

"What!" The comment triggered a general outrage that flooded through the crowd like a virus. "All the bridges are out!" "How are we supposed to leave?" "How are we supposed to get help?"

Half of the people bickered among themselves while the other half barked at Kate.

"Everyone, please, calm down!" She waited for the crowd's roar to quiet then drew in a breath. "The bridges over the East River are gone. And while I didn't witness it firsthand, it's probably safe to say the bridges over the Hudson have been destroyed as well. The people responsible for all of this are still in the streets. I don't have any proof that all of this relates to the phones, cars, and power not working, but I think it might."

Rodney looked to his left and to his right. The mood in the room shifted. Everyone was calmer. And it was because of her.

"Police, emergency services, anyone that you think can help you already has their hands full," Kate said. "And I think if there is a way to get off the island, then we need to do it and go quickly."

"But how?" a woman shrieked. "The bridges are down, and you said the boats aren't working."

"Power boats aren't working," Kate replied.

Rodney smirked. She was smart. He looked to Kate's husband. He'd have to come, most likely, and the daughter too. No way she'd leave them behind. But if she'd already seen what they were up against, he'd have a better chance of making it out the other side.

"So what?" a man asked, flapping his arms at his sides in exasperation. "We're supposed to swim across? That water is freezing!"

"I don't know how we cross." Kate shut her eyes, and her forehead creased. "Rowboats, paddleboards maybe, anything that can float and we can move by hand. But if we go, we should go together, and we should go soon. Trust me."

Kate looked to the manager and then stepped down. The crowd parted again as she walked back to her husband, but this time she was stopped and questioned along the way. Rodney couldn't hear what they were asking her, but everyone was ignoring whatever the manager was saying. He was old news. He hadn't seen the shit. She had. And Rodney wanted to take her with him.

* * *

It all happened so quickly that when Kate tried to recall what she'd said and what people were asking, it was nothing but a haze. But despite her words, no one offered any suggestions. No one had a solution. People started to trickle out, and Kate grabbed Mark's hand. "C'mon. Let's go."

A few heads turned to watch her leave, and Kate made a beeline for the stairwell the moment she was in the hallway. She reached for the door handle but paused as she stretched out her hand.

A slight tremor rattled her hand back and forth. Kate pulled her hand toward her, examining the vibration. She slowly turned her hand palm up, watching all the muscles twitching simultaneously. She was exhausted, stretched beyond her means.

"You okay?" Mark asked, gently coming up behind her.

"Yeah." Kate balled her hand into a fist and then turned toward him. She slouched, exhausted. "I don't know how we're going to get out of here."

"I might be able to help with that."

Kate and Mark turned toward the voice. It belonged to a young man. He was about Mark's height and maybe only a couple years older than her own son. He was bundled in a jacket with a hiking backpack strapped securely to his body.

The man kept his distance and a casual stance. "Getting out

of the city is only going to become harder the longer people stay. You're right in wanting to get out now."

Kate squinted at him. He spoke like a person who had a secret key that could unlock everything. It made him come off as arrogant. She didn't like that. "Do you know what's going on?"

"I have a few theories."

"Care to share?" Mark asked.

"What you did in there was impressive," he said, ignoring their questions. "People looked up to you. That's valuable now."

"I don't have time for this." Kate turned to leave, and Mark followed.

"I can get you and your family off the island," he said.

Kate stopped. She turned. "How?"

"I have a boat," he answered. "A sailboat. It's docked on the west side of the city."

"How far?"

"The George Washington Bridge." He shrugged. "If that's even still there anymore."

Kate paced in a circle, biting a lip that had already started to blister from the cold and dehydration. She stopped, then arched an eyebrow. "Why didn't you say anything in the meeting?"

"You saw what happened in there." The man inched forward, keeping his voice low, and then checked behind him to make sure they were still alone in the hall. "People are scared. And fear makes people irrational. You really want to risk going out there with people that don't have their shit together?"

"And do you really want the death of the people you leave behind on your conscience?" Kate asked.

The man stepped back, grimacing. "Listen, I came out here with an offer, and if you—"

"You didn't come out here with an offer," Kate said. "You came out here with an ultimatum." She looked him up and down, taking in the cargo pants, boots, gloves, and backpack. He was prepared, and she was betting that he had even more supplies waiting for him on the boat. "You want to go, but you don't want to go alone. Is that it? Afraid of what might happen when you're stuck out there on your own?"

"This was a mistake." The man shuffled past her toward the hallway door.

Kate turned and followed him inside the stairwell, upset by the fact that he was leaving, upset over the fact that she may have missed her one chance to get her family to safety. "So you can live with that? Letting these people die?"

"It's not my fault they're not ready," he said, descending the staircase.

"Then help them!" Kate curled her body forward, and the heightened scream stopped him in his tracks. He turned to look up at her, and she frantically ran her fingers through her hair. "I don't… I don't know what to do. My daughter is sick. I don't know if I should move her. I don't know where to go." As badly as they wanted to come, she denied the tears their fall. "If you know what's going on, then tell people. If you have a way to save people, then save them." She gripped the railing for support, fatigue suddenly catching up with her again. "A world where you're by yourself isn't much of a world to live in, is it?"

The man looked at his feet and shut his eyes. After a minute, the tension in his body relaxed, and he looked back up at her, his expression softened. "I guess not." He stepped to the stair just below her so they met at eye level. "But you should know that the more people we take, the longer it will take us to get to the boat." He pointed toward the hall. "And if everyone decides to come, I won't be able to fit them on the boat in one trip. Time is an ally that we don't have right now."

"We give people the option," Kate said. "If they want to come, we explain what'll happen. If they don't, well…"

"If they don't, they'll be wishing that they did."

Kate nodded. "You're probably right."

"I'm Rodney." He extended his hand, and Kate shook it.

"Nice to meet you."

The pair lingered, and before they ascended the staircase,

Rodney cleared his throat. "If we're all about being up front, then there's something else I should tell you." He wouldn't look at her as he spoke. "After we get across the river, there still won't be any help on the other side. What's happened here is more than likely happening all over the country."

"How is that even possible?" Mark asked. "Was it a bomb or something?"

"Kind of," Rodney answered. "It's a piece of a bomb, a nuclear bomb actually."

Kate raised her eyebrows. "We were nuked?"

"It was an EMP," Rodney answered. "It's a device that fries and renders anything with a circuit board useless, and in today's world, that pretty much means everything. Cars, phones, computers, utility companies, they all run off computer circuits. The terrorist group responsible knew what they were doing."

"How long?" Kate asked.

Rodney shook his head in confusion. "How long what?"

"How long until things get up and running again?"

Rodney chuckled to himself, and then the smile melted, and in its place was a hollowness that Kate had never seen in someone before. "Every decision that you make right now, that anyone makes now, will have ripple effects that extend for years."

Kate reached for her wedding band. The metal was cold, almost freezing to the touch. "Then I guess we better make some good decisions."

8

The emotions in the room rolled up and down like turbulence on a bad flight. Kate let Rodney take the lead, and she jumped in to help corral the masses when he couldn't reel them in. He told them exactly what he had told her and stressed the importance of leaving.

Kate watched the varied expressions of the people in the crowd. They ranged from fear to skepticism, from uncertainty to disbelief.

"So you're saying that the power is never coming back on?" a woman asked.

"I'm saying it's going to be a long time before we're back to anything normal," Rodney answered.

"But those terrorists in the streets," a man said. "They're just killing people. How are we supposed to fight that? They have guns."

A general murmur of agreement flooded through the room, and Kate noticed that Rodney was getting frustrated. She stepped in before he made a tense situation worse.

"Listen, everyone," Kate said, and the room hushed. "You know everything we do. We're not holding any details back. Leaving is a risk, but staying might be a bigger one. We don't know what's across the river and what we'll face, but we know what's here, and it's only going to become more dangerous." She looked to Rodney then back to the crowd. "My family is going with him, and he's leaving within the hour. If you want to come, then raise your hand. But we need to know now."

The room shifted and swayed. Hands fidgeted, lips were bitten, and tongues whispered in ears. At first, no one moved. Groupthink had taken over in the form of hesitation. And then, finally, a hand rose in the back, which Kate was quick to point out.

"That's one. Anybody else?"

More glances between people, more whispers, and then another hand shot up on the left. Two more on the right. Three in the middle. Then one in the front. Kate waited until the division in the room grew uncomfortable.

"All right then," Rodney said. "Everyone who raised their hands, please come up front."

The door opened in the back, and a slow leak drained the room of everyone that was staying at the complex. Kate watched them go, pairs talking to one another. She saw mouthed expressions of "they're crazy to go out in that" and "it can't really get much worse" and "they'll get shot the moment they step out of the building."

With so many people staying and so few coming with them, Kate questioned her decision. Wasn't the best course of action in a survival situation to stay put and wait for rescue? Everything she was doing now was against her flight training in a crash-land situation.

But there was no black box for this, no hidden beacon switch that she could flip to notify the Coast Guard. This was all instinct, and despite the walkout, after everyone had gone and she saw the eight people that had stayed, she felt calmed.

"Don't bring anything perishable, not unless you're going to eat it today," Rodney said. "Water bottles, blankets, any medicines that you have should come with. But you don't want to overpack. Remember that everything you bring you must carry. Overpacking can slow you down and hurt you in the long haul. And we can probably forage for food along the way."

"Forage? What are we, Yogi Bear looking for a picnic basket?" the middle-aged man with a receding hair line scoffed. He turned to the rest of the group, the gold necklace dangling from his black turtleneck swaying with his movements. He had thick eyebrows and a pronounced brow, most likely from Eastern European ancestry.

"What he means is stealing." A young woman spoke up. Short blond hair styled in a pixie cut framed a pretty face. She had blue eyes, and even with the gloomy winter weather that had plagued the city for the past month, she still had the remnants of a tan.

Rodney held up his hands. "That's not—"

"Of course that's what you're suggesting." The Eastern European man crossed his arms. "If we are going out there, it's best to use plain English. We're not going to have time for subtext or feelings when shit hits the fan."

Kate stepped in, but Rodney stopped her, nodding. "He's right." He addressed the crowd, and everyone stiffened. "We're all going to have to get used to doing things we don't want to do. Things that before the EMP went off may have been considered illegal." He looked at the man who'd made the comment. "But when it comes down between us staying alive and someone else, we need to understand that it's us."

"But not at all costs," Kate said, uncrossing her arms. "We lose ourselves, and we're no different than the people tearing apart the city." She leveled Rodney with a mother's gaze. "We help who we can."

"And what if someone decides to help themselves to her?" Rodney pointed at the young woman with the pixie cut, and she jumped. "You want her blood on your hands? I know I don't." He dropped his hand and addressed the small crowd. "I want to make one thing very clear: My main goal is to survive. I could have left, and I almost did, but I stayed to find people to join me. I recognize that there is strength in numbers, but other people will have that strength too. And when push comes to shove, I will act to protect my interests and the interests of the people around me." He turned back to Kate. "Anyone who has a problem with that should stay behind."

Kate opened her mouth, but she felt Mark's familiar hand on her wrist, and she turned back to him. He gently shook his head. And as he did, she pulled away from him, crossing her arms, but remained silent.

"All right then." Rodney finished addressing the crowd and instructed them to head toward their apartments, gather the supplies he had spoken about, and meet back here in thirty minutes.

"How do we know how long thirty minutes is?" the girl with the pixie cut asked, holding up her dead phone. "Nothing's working, remember?"

"Good point," Rodney said, exhaling, tapping his foot. "Um, I don't know, just—"

"Give us your apartment numbers," Kate said. "We'll swing by to get everyone on our way down. Just make sure you pack everything quickly. And that way we can have Rodney scan your apartment to see if there was anything he might think would be useful that we missed."

"Yeah," Rodney said. "Good idea."

Kate used a scrap sheet of paper and pen from a desk drawer in the corner. A business center was tucked away in the rec room's corner, which basically boiled down to nothing more than a computer and a printer, not that either of them had worked before the EMP.

EMP, Kate thought. It felt ridiculous to say, but from Rodney's description, it was anything but funny. Some invisible blast wave had brought the whole country to its knees. It really was like flipping a switch. Only the switch flipped one way.

The crowd dispersed, mumbling, after Kate collected the

apartment numbers, but she noticed the air of hopefulness in their words. She even saw a smile crack over the blond girl's face at something the old man had said.

"I need to go back to my apartment," Rodney said. "I'm willing to bet not everyone will have a suitable pack to carry their supplies. I know I've got at least one spare I can loan out."

"We're apartment 3563," Kate said. "Come up when you're done, and we'll start working our way down. We'll try and pack quickly."

"Yeah. Okay."

And with that, Rodney left, leaving Kate and Mark alone in the rec room. Mark kept his gaze on the tips of his shoes, shuffling his feet like a kid in trouble. "Don't be mad."

"Be mad about what?" Kate asked, shrugging exaggeratedly. "Over the fact that you don't seem to mind going to whatever lengths are necessary?"

"To keep us alive," Mark answered, finally tilting his face up toward hers. He pointed toward her clothes and her face and her hair. "Look at you! Look at what happened on your way here! People just left you to die!" He spun in a half circle and paced away, shaking his head. "If it comes down to picking between strangers or my family, then I pick family every time."

"And you think I wouldn't?" Kate asked. "Mark, I would do anything for you and Holly and Luke. But if we walk out there thinking that everyone we see is out to get us, then we're not going to make it down the block!" Her voice thundered in the room, and Mark flinched. "How long until we turn on each other? How long until we sacrifice somebody we know to save ourselves? I saw people do that on the way here, and I know you think you can use that as an excuse to do that in return, but that doesn't make it right." The tension in her body slackened, and she leaned back against the table that had been set up in the front of the room. The manager had set out bottled water for people to drink. Not a single person had taken a bottle when they left. She grabbed one and gave it a squeeze. "They really don't know how bad it's going to get."

"What?" Mark asked. "Honey, I can't hear you."

Kate walked to her husband and ran her hands through his hair. "I wouldn't have made it here without help, and we need to remember that. I don't want us to get lost out there. Right now there are too many people that are."

Mark kissed her lips. When he pulled back, he rested his forehead against hers, both their eyes still closed. "We won't. I promise."

IT TOOK Rodney five seconds to find the extra pack that he kept in his closet, but he found himself returning to the window where he'd watched the city descend into chaos. The snow hadn't let up, and the weather blocked his view of the ground below. He remembered the last weather forecast he had heard before the power went out. He checked it every morning for both the city and upstate New York.

A blizzard was on its way down from the northwest. It'd arrive in two days, and it brought with it a projected snowfall of ten to twelve feet. It would make roads impassable and bury anything that was caught in it. He had to get to the cabin before that happened. But with the number of people now hitched to his wagon, it would slow him down.

Kate's words lingered in his mind. In a perfect world, he knew that she was right, but what had descended on them was anything but a perfect world. It was cold, and vicious, and it would take without asking from them, so why should they grant any leniency in return?

Rodney kicked the leg of his sofa and grunted. He should have just left when he had the chance. For him, the meeting had been nothing but a showing of weakness. And he wasn't sure if it was worth it. The woman was clever, sure, and he could always use the added muscle of manpower. Except for the old man, there were now four added men in their group, all of whom looked healthy.

There was still a chance for him to leave. He could dart down the staircase before anyone was the wiser. After all, they were waiting on him. And it wasn't like he couldn't get the boat together by himself. He'd already run through this drill a hundred times.

But every time he got close to leaving, every time he was on the verge of forsaking the people in their moment of need, he stopped. A well-worn line had formed in the carpet as he paced nervously.

The spare backpack slouched lazily by the front door. Rodney stared at it then looked back out the window. Nothing but a sheet of white and grey outside now. The buildings next door were barely visible. If he was going to lead these people through the city, then that meant he was responsible for their well-being. That weighed on him more than anything else. If they died, then their blood was on his hands.

And could he wash it off after it had been spilled? Could he handle that heavy a burden? Doubt crept into his mind. It nagged at him, pulling him toward the door. *Leave,* it whispered. *You don't need these people. They're only going to slow you down. And you need to move fast.*

"But they'll die if they don't get out of the city," Rodney said, not even noticing he was speaking aloud.

And what about the supplies at the cabin? You have enough to last years, but only by yourself. The more people show up, the more they'll consume. If everyone survives the journey, you won't last a year. And do you really think that all of this is going to get sorted out in a year?

"No." Rodney rubbed his eyes, a hot swell of panic rising inside him. The conflict pulled him harshly in both directions. The whispers grew louder, more violent, more panicked.

Just go! Run! Leave them! You want to live? Then go, go, go!

"AHH!" Rodney slammed his fist against the wall, which

rattled and knocked a picture frame to the hardwood, face down. A harsh crack sounded as it made contact, and Rodney muttered a curse as he shook his hand in fatigue.

When he turned the picture over, bits of glass lingered on the floor. Rodney carefully brushed away the glass and then removed the picture from inside.

It was the only photo in the entire apartment, and looking at it now, he felt guilty that he hadn't even considered bringing it with him.

The picture consisted of an eight-year-old Rodney and his father. Both were decked out in fishing gear, covered in matching rubber suspenders used for fly fishing, compliments of his mother.

The little boy in the picture smiled from ear to ear, struggling to hold the trout with both hands. It was his first fish, and his father gave a big thumbs up, laughing. Whenever he thought of his dad, he could never picture him not laughing. He was a big man with a big heart.

But sometimes it was too big.

His father had owned a construction company, and while he did good work, he was too lenient with his accounts receivable. People brought their sob stories to him, and he would cut them slack every time. That pattern had bankrupted his company and nearly put his family on the streets.

At the time, Rodney was too little to really understand what was happening. His mother told him the details years later but said never to mention it to his father. He was ashamed of what had happened, well, more embarrassed than ashamed.

A few years ago, Rodney had finally racked up the courage to ask. He and his father were on one of their fishing trips, and they'd returned to the cabin with a string of trout. It was a quiet evening, and the sunset had painted the sky a magnificent array of blues and oranges. Mountains and treetops greeted the sky on the horizon, and a cool breeze offered enough chill in the air to make it cold.

"You never told me we were almost homeless." Rodney had blurted it out, just like that, and his father froze in mid-scaling of one of his trout.

"It's not something I like to talk about, son." He kept his head down, concentrating on his fish, finished it, then picked up another one.

"You're always telling me that there are ways to learn from failure," Rodney said, doing his best not to try and sound like he was mocking his father. He noticed the muscle around his father's jaw twitching from annoyance. "So what happened?"

His father laughed, flicking off a spray of scales that speckled the front porch. "What happened was people didn't do what they said they were going to do." He worked the fish more vigorously. "People will say anything to get off the hook. The parasites will suck you dry if you let them." He turned, pointing the knife toward his son. "You hear me?" His voice thundered, and Rodney flinched, recoiling into his seat.

"Yeah, Dad," Rodney answered.

His father's anger was something Rodney had seen only a handful of times over the course of his life. Most of them were reserved for when Rodney had done something bad. But after a minute, his father's expression softened, and he dropped the knife and the fish back into the bucket. He leaned back in his chair, shaking his head.

"The older you get, the less you can see the world in black and white." His father looked out toward the forest as he spoke. "For a long time, I thought that doing the right thing meant doing the right thing for everybody. But if you do that, it'll drain you, and you'll have nothing left for the stuff that really matters." He turned to Rodney. "Like family."

"You're a good dad," Rodney said. "Best one I've ever had." He grinned, and his father belted out one of his boisterous chuckles.

The smile lingered, though his voice didn't match his expression. "There's nothing wrong with helping people, Rodney. In fact, it can be one of the best feelings in the world. But you should get to a point where you can recognize the difference between someone who really needs help and someone who's using you." The smile was gone now. "It was something I never learned how to do."

They were words Rodney had remembered well, and it was a lesson he took to heart. But after a long pause, his father added more.

"You have to take care of yourself first. Because if you can't do that, then you sure as hell can't take care of anyone else. And once you have a family, you take care of them next, and then you widen that circle to friends, and then strangers." He rubbed together hands that had grown knobby with arthritis, though at the time there was another invisible enemy attacking his father from the inside. "But don't be cynical. I lost a lot of money, but most of the people that I helped really did need it, and one of them even helped me find a job after it was over. Keep the faith, Rodney. Don't lose hope."

A tear splattered on the trout in the picture, and Rodney wiped at his eyes before another fell. He collapsed back onto his couch and sobbed silently. Six weeks later, his father had been gone. Cancer. It had gotten into his blood marrow and spread like wildfire. It was quick enough that he didn't feel much pain at the end but not so quick that he escaped all of it.

His father had always been a big man, but by the time he passed, he'd lost nearly one hundred pounds. Nothing but bones and skin and sullen, sunken eyes. Six months later, his mom passed. Heart failure. Both of them wanted to be cremated, and Rodney spread their ashes at the cabin.

With no siblings and no other real family to speak of (Rodney's dad had a brother who had some children over in Colorado, but he'd met them only twice), Rodney was left on his own. He'd sold his parents' house but kept the cabin and then used the money that they'd left him to live comfortably on his own in New York. But now people needed help. He was prepared with more than he needed.

Rodney folded the photo and shoved it into his pocket, where he felt the cool of a metal. He tugged a chain, the silver retreating from his pocket in a thin line until it removed a pocket watch. It had belonged to his father.

The front of the watch had an engraving. *Be better.*

It was his father's creed. He used it to challenge himself, to challenge the people around him, and to challenge his son. Rodney pocketed the watch, and then checked his face in the mirror and waited until his eyes were no longer red then grabbed the spare backpack as he shut the door on his way out.

* * *

MARK WAS busy helping Holly pack while Kate sifted through the cupboards. They didn't have much in the way of canned goods, but she found some trail mix and protein bars that she added to their food pile. Hopefully it was enough to keep them fed until they got to... well, wherever the hell they were going.

Kate had thought about that a lot since the meeting. They had a way to cross the river, but after that, then what? If this was as widespread as Rodney believed it was, then how was she supposed to get in contact with Luke?

"All right," Mark said, stepping out of Holly's bedroom. "I think I've packed up everything she needs, so I'm going to put a bag together for us. You think we should try and take the rolling luggage?"

Kate picked up one of the protein bars and then dropped it. "I don't know." She leaned against the counter, staring at the food. "What are we going to do when we cross?" She looked up. "What if it really is the whole country?"

"I think Rodney is just exaggerating," Mark answered. "There's no way these people could have done this to everyone, right?" He walked toward her and kissed her. "Let's not jump to conclusions."

"Yeah," Kate replied, exhaling. "You're right."

"And I'm sure that Luke is fine." Mark rubbed her arms. "I know that you're worried about him. But he's a smart kid."

"Yeah." Kate pulled back, biting her lower lip. "First thing we do when we cross the river is find a working phone."

A knock at the door made them both jump, and Mark answered it. Rodney stepped inside, his pack already strapped to his back and the extra bag in his hand.

"You guys ready?" he asked. "The weather's getting worse by the minute, and it's going to be hard getting the boat across in this."

"Just finishing up." Mark disappeared into the room, and Kate rummaged through the rest of the cabinets.

"Everything I found I put on the counter," Kate said, her back to Rodney as she pushed aside a bag of rice. "Anything you'd recommend bringing?" He didn't answer, and she turned around, finding him at the counter, staring at her. She frowned. "What's wrong?"

"There's something I need to tell you," Rodney answered. "Something that I held back when I was talking to the group."

Kate crossed her arms. "What is it?"

"After we cross the river, I'm not staying anywhere near the city." Rodney spoke slowly. "I have a cabin in upstate New York. I've outfitted it with enough supplies to last me years on my own. I have access to fresh water and good hunting and fishing. I also have medical supplies and enough space to fit six others."

Kate shook her head slightly in disbelief. "What are you saying? You're going up there to hide?"

"I'm going up there to survive. And anyone who is interested in doing that is more than welcome."

"You're acting like the world is ending."

"That's because it is," Rodney said. "It could take years for the country to rebuild."

"Why are you assuming the worst?"

"Why are you not?" Rodney stepped around the counter. "You saw what's out there. You've seen what people are like when they panic, and the panic isn't over. Highly populated areas are going to be the worst. Look, we don't have to stay at the cabin forever, but for at least a month until things settle down. Then we poke our heads out and see what's happening."

Kate's stomach soured, and she felt a warm sensation crawl up her throat. "This can't be happening." Before, it had all been just talk, but now somehow it felt more real, more violent, deadlier. "You really think it will be that bad?"

"Not *will be,* Kate," Rodney said. "*Is.*"

The young man had seemed to age a decade in the time that had passed since their last conversation. Mark reappeared from their room with his rolling luggage, and when Kate looked at him, he let go of the handle.

"What's wrong?" Mark asked.

Rodney looked down to the roller in his hands and tossed him the spare pack. "Use that instead." He paused. "You'll want to have your hands free."

9

Kate kept close to Mark and Holly on their descent. Every few floors, they stopped and collected the rest of their group. Rodney checked their supplies, scanned their rooms, and they moved on. It was quick, efficient, calculated.

One personal item, that was all anyone was able to take. Whatever held the most value and could be stashed away in their pack. The rest was food, water, and medicine. The advice was met with groans, eye rolls, and pleading, but in the end, everyone listened. Partly because Kate had backed him up.

Kate's experience on the street, combined with her career as a pilot, had given her clout with the group. Leadership had been thrust upon Rodney and Kate equally, and nothing passed without their approval. Whenever Rodney suggested something, everyone looked to Kate to confirm and vice versa.

Once the group was collected and all the gear and supplies were sorted out, they descended to the first floor. Beyond the walls of the building, the winter winds howled with a ferocity that sent a shiver down everyone's back.

A ball of anxiety grew in Kate's belly. It rumbled and protested with every step down, but she pushed past it.

Rodney stopped at the door at the bottom of the stairwell and then turned to the huffing and puffing crowd behind him. "All right. You keep your eyes on me." He reached into his pack and handed out the rope that they'd all be tied to. It was a method that mountain climbers used to keep each other safe and accounted for. "And you keep at my pace. You move where I move. You run when I run. And you stop when I stop. You're my shadows, got it?"

Everyone nodded, the group scattered in a broken line. Glen, the old man with liver spots on his head, and Laura, the girl with the blond pixie haircut, were directly behind Rodney, followed by Barry, the Eastern Europe man. Then it was an older couple from the tenth floor, Stephen and Jen, followed by a young married couple from the nineteenth, Kit and Sarah. And then Holly, Mark, and Kate brought up the caboose.

"I have a few alternate routes in case we run into trouble," Rodney continued. "It'll take us longer, but it'll keep us safe." He held up the rope once everyone was secure. "I cannot stress this enough: do not deviate from the group. You try and pull us one way when I'm going another, and we fall. And if we fall out there, we might not get back up."

Holly sneezed and then coughed, and Kate instinctively reached up and pressed the back of her hand to her daughter's forehead. The girl was burning up.

"Everyone ready?" Rodney asked.

Nervous nods responded in answer.

"All right then," Rodney said, turning toward the stairwell door. "Let's go."

The door opened, and they passed through the lobby in a blur. A crowd was huddled inside to weather the storm, all of them people who didn't live in their building but were seeking a place to hide. Kate didn't see their faces as she passed, but she felt their stares as they left.

Outside, the air froze Kate's lungs, and she'd forgotten how bitterly cold it was. The chill ran through everyone, even stiffening the rope.

A blanket of white cascaded from the sky, and Rodney was forced to slow his pace to a crawl as wind whipped from the left, forcing Kate to shield her eyes from the heavy flurries with her arm.

Visibility dropped to less than a few feet, but Kate recognized some of the street signs they passed. There were even people still in their cars, waiting out the weather. Kate locked eyes with a woman in a passenger seat, holding a little boy. A man, presumably her husband, sat in the driver's seat. She only got a glimpse of the woman's face as they passed before the snow blocked them from view, but she saw envy in the woman's eyes. Envy of her movement, envy of the sight of action, envy because they looked like a group who knew where to go in the middle of a city that had no idea how to react.

Except for Rodney, most of the group kept their heads down on their march uptown. Rodney had warned them that it would take a few hours, but none of them, Kate included, had really understood just how far and how strenuous that trek would be in the cold. It took less than twenty minutes before they were forced to stop.

"I'm sorry!" Glen yelled above the howl of the wind as he leaned against the side of a building. Snot had frozen to his upper lip, and he kept coughing. "It's my lungs. Used to be a smoker." The parts of his cheeks that weren't covered with frost were cherry red.

"It's important not to overdo it," Rodney said, shouting at the group over another whistling howl. "Once you stretch yourself beyond the point of fatigue, you're doing more harm than good." He glanced around and then turned back to the group. "But if we have to stop every twenty minutes like this, it's going to take until nightfall to reach the docks, and we'll freeze to death by then."

Glen nodded, taking the hint, and pushed himself off the side of the building. "All right. I think I'm better now."

And so they trudged on against the winter storm. Kate kept checking on Holly, though she couldn't see her daughter's face beneath the cover of the ski goggles and the scarf.

"You all right, sweetie?" Kate asked, no longer able to feel her nose anymore.

"Yeah," Holly answered, her voice muffled through the scarf. She kept hold of her father's hand, and she looked up at him. "Dad, if I get tired, will you carry me?"

"Of course, baby."

A vicious crack thundered through the air, more metallic than the natural howl of the wind, and they stopped.

"What was that?" Mark asked.

Kate shook her head, her eyes never leaving the back of Rodney's head. "I don't know! It sounded like—"

Gunfire exploded to her left, and a harsh tug at Kate's waist yanked her feet from beneath her. She smacked hard onto the concrete, the contact made worse by the harsh cold.

Shock rippled through Kate's body, a sharp pain radiating from her left hip where she'd landed. She gasped breathlessly, her view from the ground nothing but white sheets of snow. Before she had time to think or check on Mark and Holly, another vicious tug from the rope pulled her backward, and Kate flailed her arms against the concrete to try and gain any traction.

The scream came from up front, and Kate saw nothing but the flailing arms and limbs of their poor conga line, her eyes glued to the back of Mark's head.

Kate crawled toward her family, but a gust of wind blasted snow on her right side and knocked her off balance. Her heart pounded wildly, and she blinked away the snowflakes collecting in her lashes, which melted and stung her eyes. She wiped her cheeks and scrambled to her hands and knees. The tips of her boots and her gloved hands slipped wildly over the sidewalk as she reached for Mark and Holly, who squirmed on the ground.

Kate screamed and clutched Holly's arm as Mark floundered on his back. A million scenarios raced through her mind. Mark was shot. Holly was shot. They were bleeding, they'd broken something, they were dying.

"Holly! Holly, are you all right?" Kate cupped her daughter's face, still unable to hear her own words. She pulled down the scarf that covered her daughter's mouth and saw that she was screaming something, but her lips were moving too fast. "What?"

A hand jerked Kate's shoulder. She jumped and saw Mark propping himself up on his side. She looked ahead to their group that looked like nothing more than huddled clumps of white struggling to get up. But she saw one person remain on the ground.

A woman hovered over the body. She shook it violently, but the individual didn't respond. More people gathered around them. One of them was Rodney. He was pointing somewhere, trying to pull the woman away from the person on the ground. *The body on the ground,* Kate thought.

Muted thuds echoed in the distance, and everyone shuddered. But Kate couldn't take her eyes off the man on the ground and, more importantly, the woman who wouldn't leave his side. Rodney was suddenly by Kate's side, shaking her shoulders. She looked up at him, the howl of the wind creeping back into her ears along with his mute screaming.

"Kate, we have to go!" He pulled her up and cut her rope.

As they passed, Kate heard the woman's hysterical screaming. Heads turned to look down at the scene, and Kate noticed the patches of crimson mixed with the snow.

It was Kit and Sarah. A red slush had formed around Kit's head, which was slowly being covered by new snowfall. Sarah howled, her shrieks matching the high-pitched ferocity of the wind. Kate kept her head turned behind her as Rodney and

Mark led her away from the scene, and she watched Sarah lay her head on her husband's stomach until their figures disappeared amongst the sheets of white.

But long after they had separated themselves from the scene, and long after in the years of recovery, Kate would still hear that woman's screams whenever there was a harsh wind. It was a warning, a bleeding memory that left a scar she'd always carry.

10

Rodney pressed forward, pulling what remained of his team of survivors through the storm. It had been several blocks since he'd heard gunfire, and while some of the group might have kept their eyes behind them, Rodney kept his eyes forward. He had to. If he didn't, then they'd all die.

The shooters were everywhere. Rodney chalked up the man's death to a freak accident, a stray bullet. It wasn't his fault. And he'd warned them it would be dangerous. He hadn't forced any of them to come. No, it wasn't his fault. It wasn't—

"Rodney, stop!" Kate grabbed hold of his shoulder and spun him around. The others were behind her, huffing and puffing breaths of icy air. "I've been calling you for the past block."

Rodney noted the haggard looks on everyone's faces. He could see them better now. The snowfall had stopped, but the residual frost on everyone's face told the story of the powerful storm.

"We need a break," Kate said, gesturing toward the group. "Just a few minutes to thaw."

"The storm's over," Rodney said. "Now's the time to gain some ground."

"And we'll gain more ground if people can move without

wanting to collapse every five seconds," Kate said. "Don't push past the point of fatigue, remember?"

Rodney looked back to the group. They swayed back and forth like trees ready to be felled. It would only take another chop of an axe to knock them down. Rest wasn't a bad idea.

"All right," Rodney said. "But only for a few minutes. I don't want us to get caught in that bad weather again." He glanced down the streets, noting the lack of people outside. "Of either variety." He wasn't sure if the rest of the group grasped what he meant, but Kate understood.

A Thai restaurant was the first door that opened, and inside they found three Asian women huddled in the back. Rodney lifted his hand in an attempt at a friendly wave, and after a moment's hesitation, they reciprocated.

The shortest girl approached as they all took seats at the tables near the window. Even though the power was off, it was noticeably warmer than outside.

"Nothing's working, but..." The girl twisted her hands together nervously. She couldn't have been older than twenty. "We have water and drinks. Cold drinks, obviously."

"Water would be great," Rodney said. "Thank you." They held eye contact for just a half second longer than normal, and then she smiled and spun around quickly. And for a moment he tried to catch his reflection in the mirror to see what he looked like.

"Rodney." Kate nudged him again and then pulled him a few steps away from the rest of the group, who'd already collapsed in their chairs. She lowered her voice to a whisper. "How much farther to the docks?"

Rodney wiped his face, flicking off bits of snow and frost. "If we keep at the pace we were and the weather continues to agree with us, it shouldn't take longer than forty minutes."

Kate nodded, but her lips twitched.

"What?" Rodney asked.

"Now might be a good time to talk about the cabin and a plan for what happens after we cross the river," Kate answered.

"Especially after what happened with..." She trailed off, shutting her eyes. "Oh my god, I don't even remember their names."

"Kit," Rodney said. "And Sarah."

"Right." Kate sighed and dropped her shoulders.

The young Asian woman returned with bottled water and handed them out to the group. She smiled at Rodney again as she passed, and this time Rodney watched her leave.

"Hey," Kate said, smacking his chest. "You can get her number another time."

"That's not likely," Rodney muttered under his breath.

"C'mon." Kate pulled them back over to the group, and she rejoined her family.

Rodney noticed that Kate's daughter was shivering. She sipped water and wheezed between gulps. Her father handed her a pill, and she swallowed it reluctantly. Her lips were blistered with fever.

"Listen up," Rodney said.

Heads rose halfheartedly.

"We need to talk about our next steps," Rodney said. "After we get to the dock—"

"We just left them," Laura said, her lip quivering as she quickly covered her mouth to muffle the light gasp.

Glen reached over and patted her shoulder. "It's all right, young lady."

Laura shrugged off his hand and threw her arms down by her sides in defiance. "No, it's not all right!" She stood, trembling as she stared Rodney down. "You said it was better to leave. You said it was safer."

"I also told you there would be risks," Rodney said, a harsher bite to his tone than he had intended, then turned to what remained of their group. "I didn't force anyone to come with me. In fact, I had planned on going alone." He snarled and clenched his fists. "I thought I was helping people. I thought I was doing the right thing. I thought... I thought..." His anger deflated, and he collapsed into the nearest chair. "If you want to blame me for what happened, then go ahead."

"No one is blaming you," Kate said, rising to his defense. "We all made the decision to leave."

Laura lowered her head and sheepishly retreated to her chair. She pulled a napkin from the dispenser on her table. She wiped her nose and then crinkled the napkin into her fist. "I'm sorry. I didn't mean—"

"It's fine," Rodney said, an air of petulance in his voice that he tried to mask with a smile that looked more annoyed than friendly. "Really." He thumbed his nose and then leaned forward at the table. "What I'm about to tell you I already told Kate at the apartments before we left."

Eyes widened and heads nodded aimlessly as Rodney told them everything. The cabin, the supplies, and how long he thought it would take before the rest of the country managed to pull themselves up by the bootstraps.

"Help isn't going to come," Rodney said. "Once we cross the river, we head north. It's going to be a little cramped, but I can promise you it's going to be better than staying anywhere close to the city."

"We should go," Kate said, backing Rodney up again. "After everything we've seen and everything that's happened, it's a good idea."

Glen nodded. "I agree. And who is to say that the effects of this..." He turned to Rodney to make sure he was saying it correctly. "EMP? Didn't manage to travel that far north." He smiled. "We might be on our way to the Garden of Eden."

"Yeah," Rodney said. "If the Garden of Eden got to three below at night." He stood. "We have two days to get to the cabin before a bad northwestern storm dumps twelve feet of snow, because once it does it'll make finding the cabin like looking for a needle in haystack."

Everyone nodded, finished their waters, and chomped down on a quick snack of protein bars. As his group did that—he stopped to think about that for a moment. His group. It was even wilder than he could have imagined. He walked to the back of the restaurant, where he found the waitress who had served them.

"You guys are leaving?" she asked.

"Yeah. Thank you for the water though." And for some reason, Rodney gently took the girl's hands in his own. "If you can, you need to get out of the city. It's only going to get worse." He gestured to his group. "The bridges are gone, but you can come with us. I have a boat that can get across the river."

She looked at Rodney confused, and pulled her hands back. "I-I can't. My mother, she's at home. I can't leave her."

Rodney nodded. "The power isn't coming back on, if that's what you guys were waiting for." He backed away. "I don't know if it'll ever come back on." He spoke the words more to himself as he distanced himself from her. "The tunnels might be open, but it'll be risky to use them. Be careful."

"Wait." The waitress followed a few steps as Rodney reached the door. "Where are you going? Why don't you think the power is coming back on? Who are you?"

Rodney stopped at the door, feeling the frigid blast of the weather outside. A tiny bell jingled. He looked back at the girl, and for the first time in his life since he had moved to the city, he found himself desperately wishing to remember a face in a sea of the faceless.

Six months from now, he wanted to find this little Thai shop and get a table and have her be his waitress. She'd laugh, he'd laugh, they'd get dinner and they'd date, and they'd be happy.

"Gather as much nonperishable food and water as you can," Rodney said, and then he was out the door, gathering his group together for the last portion of their trek to the boats.

The sun was trying to peek out from behind the grey clouds above, and for a moment the whole city was peaceful, blanketed under a sheet of white as though it had been put to bed and tucked in for the night.

But it wouldn't be peaceful for much longer. Violence would come like the storm lingering in the northwest with an unforgiving force that would do everything in its power to crush them into dust.

Rodney thought of the girl and her smile, and suddenly that only made the foreboding worse.

* * *

KATE KEPT her head on a swivel for the rest of the journey. Every once in a while, a high-pitched whine filled her ears, and she'd wince in pain. Residual noise from the gunshots that she hoped wasn't permanent.

Walking around the city that had just been blanketed with snow made it less intimidating. All of the cracks and dirt and trash that normally littered the ground were covered with a cleansing whiteness. But every once in a while, there would be a scream or a shatter of glass or a gunshot, and that façade of safety would crumble.

It was all some type of joke, a sick, cruel joke with a punch line that only the terrorists who did this understood. The type of joke whispered at secret meetings. It was the type of joke that was told by no one with a sense of humor and left people joyless.

"Unbelievable," Kate muttered to herself. She stared down at her boots as she shuffled through the slush. Every step disrupted the fresh white powder and churned up the black dirt underneath. Their group left lines of grey and black in the snow, like snails on a sidewalk leaving behind their slime.

Slime like the parasites responsible for all of this. Kate imagined pouring salt on them, watching them wither into nothing. How many had already died because of them? How many more would die because of them?

Luke suddenly flooded her thoughts, and Kate tightened her grip on the backpack straps. Her son was down in Virginia at school, alone, and if this problem in New York had really become a nationwide epidemic, then she just couldn't leave him down there alone. She had to make sure he was safe. But Rodney's plan pulled her in the opposite direction.

Kate racked her brain for a solution, but aside from walking down there herself, she had nothing. And it would take a week to travel that far on foot in this weather. If she could just find a car, any car that would work, she could—

A memory prickled in the back of her head. Last spring, before she had requested to be relocated to New York, she had been running a flight from Miami to Newark. It was a one-off, but the trip consisted of a two-day stay in New Jersey before she could fly home to Atlanta. The hotel concierge noticed Kate's wings when she checked in and told her about an airshow happening in a small town to the west of the city.

With a free day to kill, Kate decided to check it out and was blown away by what she saw. Apparently, it was the biggest airshow in the northeast. Planes and jets from all over the world converged for the event, and Kate couldn't help but admire all of the aviation history that had come before her.

And while there were plenty of modern jets and military craft at the event, there were even more older planes. Old prop engines that had flown for sixty or seventy years. Planes that were stripped of modern aviation equipment that the EMP had rendered useless.

If Rodney was right about the EMP and the computer chips, then all she needed to do was find a plane with hydraulic controls. She could make the trip down to Virginia in a few hours, then fly up and meet Mark and Holly at Rodney's cabin with Luke in tow. It was a long shot, but it was something.

Mark slowed his pace and sidled up next to Kate. "I think her temperature is getting worse."

Kate touched Holly's forehead. It was hot as a stovetop. "Yeah."

"Her body's like a little furnace. She's actually making me sweat."

"Should we wake her up and give her some more medicine?"

"No, let her rest. I gave her a dose before we left the restaurant."

Kate nodded and then looked toward what remained of their group. Rodney was up ahead in the lead, guiding them to the docks.

"Listen, when we cross, I'm going to an airfield," Kate said.

Mark stopped. "What?"

Kate pulled him back into stride with her. "I think Rodney is right. I think that this... EMP has affected the entire country."

"You don't know that."

"Just listen." Kate placed her finger to her lips, and the pair tilted their ears toward the sky. "You hear that?"

"No," Mark answered.

"Exactly. No planes, no helicopters, nothing. It's been, what? Five or six hours since everything stopped working? If this was limited to New York, then there would be helicopters coming to the hospitals with supplies or to help evacuate critical patients. The Air Force would be sending jets over the city on patrol. But there's nothing."

"If you know that there aren't any planes working, then why the hell would you even try and go to the airfield?"

"If I can find a plane old enough, without any computer components, it might work."

Mark shook his head. "I don't like it, Kate. We need to stick together. Without any lines of communication, how are we supposed to keep track of one another?"

"I can have Rodney give me the coordinates of the cabin. Once I have Luke, I can meet up with you guys later."

Mark kept quiet. Whenever he shut down like that, she knew he was getting upset. The only way to get him out of that funk was to let him be, and so that's what she did.

And while her husband stewed, Kate reexamined her plan from every angle. She tried to recall the types of planes at the show and the owners who stored them in the hangars at the airfield. Fuel could be a problem, or at least retrieving it could be. Without power, the pumps were useless. She could siphon it so long as she could find some tubes to work with.

"Stop." Rodney spun around, arm extended like a crossing guard, and the group froze in their tracks. Then, after a minute, he gathered everyone close. "The docks are just down this road, but there is a big group of people there."

"How many?" Kate asked.

Rodney locked eyes with her. "More than we can take."

"So what do we do?" Mark asked, adjusting Holly on his shoulder. "The moment they see we have a working boat, they're going to be pissed."

"It looks like there's still a guard on duty, and they've kept the docks locked up." Rodney smiled in disbelief. "Who'd have thought of all the organizations, the New York Port Authority would have their shit together." Angered chants drifted from the mob at the docks. "We move through them quickly. Don't stop for anything."

Nervous nods answered in response, but Kate kept her eyes glued to the people searching for escape. They were no different than herself.

"If they charge, there is enough of them to bust down the gates," Rodney said. "If that happens, run. I'm the last slip on the dock. I'm going to move quickly, so you have to keep up." He paused. "We can't wait on anyone. Got it?"

More nervous nods, and then they walked to the city.

11

The chants grew louder on their approach to the docks, and Kate was suddenly reminded of the metro, the expressions of confusion, pain, and anger. She remembered the woman who'd fallen from the rail and smacked against the pavement—the sound had been so dull and ominous, and the unsettling silence that followed after her scream was cut short.

The crowd numbered around twenty. They huddled at the gated entrance and latched onto the chain-link fence, which swayed back and forth from the crowd's weight. The posts shook, but the fence held.

Everyone followed close behind as Rodney approached the dead center of the mob outside the gated entryway. Kate's heart rate quickened as they all shouldered their way through, and the deeper they penetrated the group, the more stares bored into the back of her head.

"Hey! What do you think you're doing?"

Because she was in the back, the shout drew closest to Kate, but she kept her eyes forward like Rodney had instructed. They were stopped now, and while the chanting had died down when they first arrived, the angered murmuring hadn't.

The guard at the post approached the gate, reaching for his

keys, and bodies were suddenly pressed into Kate's back, shoving her forward and smashing her into Mark.

"Hey, they're letting them in!"

"Give us a ride across!"

"Help us! Please!"

Kate's feet were driven forward against her own will, and she saw Holly awake on her father's shoulder. She was squeezing him tight, tears leaking from her eyes. Kate reached for her daughter's hand. "It's all right, Holly. We're okay."

"Let us in! Let us in!"

The mob pinned them against the gate, and Holly screamed.

"Stop it!" Kate rammed an elbow into a gut behind her, and for a moment, the pressure of the bodies slamming against her subsided. She spun around, shoving people back, but the mob didn't let up.

The gate swung open, and Rodney jumped onto the docks. Mark grabbed Kate and pulled her through the opening, and Kate watched as the mob flooded after her, filling the empty space where she had stood. The gate swung closed just as the bodies smashed against the mesh.

Fingers prodded through the holes, and the fence buckled from the mob's weight. Faces and bodies were mashed against the metal. Everyone's expressions faded from anger to desperation.

"Please!" Lips and mouths pleaded. "Help us."

Kate was pulled along the dock but kept her eyes on the faces she was leaving behind. Faces of those who wanted to survive. And then she heard the scream of an infant.

"Wait!" Kate yanked her arm free and stepped toward the fence.

"Kate, what are you doing?" Mark asked. "We have to go!"

"I heard something," Kate said, her eyes glued to the bodies on the fence. "I thought I heard—" And then she saw it. A woman was gently rocking a bundle in her arms. Her face was the only one not focused on their group. Like a mother, her attention was on the baby.

"Rodney!" Kate sprinted across the dock, the wooden boards groaning beneath her feet, then splintering as she skidded to a stop. She pressed her hands against Rodney's chest. "They have a baby."

"Kate, we don't have room." He tried to sidestep her, but she blocked him.

"We can't leave those people here," Kate said. "We have to help them."

"How?" Rodney asked. "How in the hell are we supposed to do that?" He pointed to the sailboat. "We can't fit more than ten at a time, and the moment we let those people through the gates, they'll sink us." Every word puffed another breath of icy air.

Kate looked up to the sky and then to Rodney. "The weather is holding. We have enough time to make two trips, and two should be enough to get everyone across."

Rodney finally turned back to the fence and the bodies pressed against it. Kate couldn't see his face, but when he turned back around to face her, the hardened expression softened into something more akin to despair. "Kate, we can't save everyone."

"I know," Kate said and then stepped closer. "But let's save the ones we can."

Rodney sighed with exhaustion and looked back to the people behind the fence. After a moment, he nodded. "All right, listen up!"

The plan was simple. The guard would let the people inside at a trickle, with the understanding that the kids go first. Each kid would have one parent escort, and after Rodney was on the other side of the river, he'd come back for everyone else.

"It's important everyone understand what that means," Rodney said. "It means that anyone who doesn't have a child stays on this side, and even if you do, the parents decide who goes with the kid." He turned to Kate and Mark. "You guys let me know who's staying."

Rodney disappeared to the front gate, and after he arrived, the angered murmurs slowly morphed into cries of thanks and relief.

"You should go with her," Mark said, leaning close, his voice a whisper. "Rodney will probably want your help on the boat anyway."

"No, Daddy!" Holly clutched her father tight. "I want you to come with me."

Kate stood there like an outsider to her own family. Her daughter latched onto her father's shoulder, and no amount of prodding or persuasion was able to pull her off.

"Holly, sweetheart, it's okay."

"Please, don't leave me, Daddy." The plea had turned into sobs, and Holly shook her head, rubbing her face deeper into the shoulder of her father's coat. "Please, don't let me go."

"It's all right," Kate said. She gently placed her hand on Holly's back. "Daddy's gonna stay with you." She tossed Mark a glare before he could protest. "It's fine. I'll be fine." Kate kissed Mark's cheek and then went to help Rodney at the gate.

"It's all right, Frank," Rodney said. "I'm taking them on my boat."

"But what if they start to jump on the other vessels?" Frank asked, his gaze switching between Rodney and the now-quiet mob at the front gate. "What happens—"

"We won't touch anything." The voice came from a man with his hands gripped through the chain mesh. "We just want to put our kids on the boat, get them out of here." Stubble covered his chin and cheeks and looked as rough as his voice sounded. "C'mon, pal. My boy, he's only six."

The guard looked away, fiddling with the keys in his hand, and then stepped between Kate and Rodney and unlocked the gate then returned to his post without a word.

"I'm at the end," Rodney said, gesturing the group to follow. "Kate, get me a head count."

Kate nodded, silently prodding the air in the direction of the heads that passed. Twenty-three for the group, nine for the kids. It would be a crowded two trips.

There were a handful of people without children, and Kate made sure to keep an eye on them. They were more fidgety than the rest, and she didn't want to have any unexpected accidents while everyone was getting on board.

The hull of Rodney's vessel squeaked against the dock as the river water lapped lazily against it. It was like the water itself was so cold that it too had given way to any quick movement. The boat was small, and Kate understood why Rodney had been hesitant to take so many.

Goodbyes were said, and children were peeled away from mothers and fathers, crying, all save for one. Kate's daughter was already nestled safely into the boat with Mark, her face tucked into his shoulder. Not once did she cry for her mother.

"Kate," Rodney said, stepping off and pulling her aside. "Listen, a lot could change between now and the time I come back." He handed her a pair of binoculars. "So you can keep an eye on us as we cross."

Kate took them and then looked past Rodney to Mark, who was helping Holly protect her face from the wind. "How long will it take?"

"With this wind?" Rodney asked, looking to the sky. "Twenty or thirty minutes. But, hey." He grabbed her arm and forced her attention back to him. "If the terrorists show up again and the dock is compromised, you need to take everyone farther north." He looked up toward the shoreline. "There's another dock about three blocks up. It's private but easy to get to. The name of the building that it sits behind is the Regency." He turned back toward her. "Take everyone there if things turn south here. If I come back and you're not here, I'll know where to go." He grabbed her other free hand and then covertly shoved a revolver into her palm. "In case things get bad."

Kate quickly hid the gun from sight, her body suddenly

humming with nerves. "And what if the private dock doesn't work out?"

A smile crept over Rodney's face. "I could just toss these people in the river, and we could go across now." He held up his hands defensively. "If you want to, of course."

Kate couldn't hide the snicker and punched him in the shoulder. He reminded her of the younger brother she'd never had. "Be safe. All right?"

"You too."

The ropes were untied, and Kate and a few of the other parents helped shove off. Mark raised his arm and waved, though Holly kept herself tucked into a ball in his lap. Kate blew a kiss that he caught, and smiled.

The others had gathered at the end of the dock as well, arms waving back and forth, a desperation clinging to the cold winter air. It was a desperation lined with the hope of return, the hope of another chance, the hope of one more embrace.

But as the sails opened and caught the breeze, taking the small vessel across the icy waters of the Hudson, Kate heard loud claps in the city behind her. They were distant but ominous.

"Was that thunder?" a man asked, turning toward the sound.

Kate stepped forward, separating herself from the pack. She shook her head. "It's gunfire." And while the noise sounded far off, as time passed and the boat grew smaller, the gunfire became louder. Kate removed the small revolver, hoping she wouldn't have to use it.

12

Twenty-five minutes had passed since the boat left, and Rodney had nearly reached the other side. Which meant she had about that much time until they came back. And while there was relief at the fact that her family was away from danger, Kate couldn't shake the fear of being alone on this side of the river.

Of course there were the people still here, and while they all shared the same desire for safety and to be with their families, she didn't know them.

It was almost funny. Kate had lived in New York for six months, and over the course of the past eight hours, she had spoken to more strangers than she had the entire time she'd been here. And for a pilot who flew strangers around the world, that was saying a lot.

"Hey, thanks."

Kate turned at the nudging of her arm. She turned to find the woman she had let borrow the binoculars. "You're welcome."

The woman smiled sadly and then hugged herself, trying to stay warm. She was an older woman, probably in her mid-fifties. She had faded red hair that flowed long down her back, wound tightly into springy curls. Wrinkles and freckles covered her face in patterns that had somehow made her more attractive.

"How old is your son?" Kate asked, trying not to wince at the sound of the growing gunfire.

The woman looked toward the sound of the gunshots, then answered with her gaze lingering in the same direction. "Nine." She looked back to Kate. "And your daughter?"

"She'll be eleven next month," Kate answered.

"Has she started the preteen phase yet?"

Kate rolled her eyes. "Last week she said she was going to the movies with friends, and the way she said it, you would have thought she was going to ask to use my car to take them."

Both women laughed, and it caught the attention of the others on the dock. Slowly, they gravitated toward the pair, and after a moment's pause and awkward silence, Kate introduced herself. Putting names to faces always helped bring down walls.

The fifteen people that remained on the dock varied in age and sex. A little more than half were men, most of them the fathers of the children who had gone across. Three were women. Kate did her best to remember their names, but after their interaction, she only remembered a handful of them. The woman with the red hair stood out the most. She reminded Kate of a girl she had known in college.

It was the freckles and the hair and the way that she smiled. Kate's friend had been sweet, smart, and reserved but also outlandishly crass upon occasion. Kate remembered one night during her sophomore year when the pair had streaked across their apartment complex with Halloween masks to hide their faces. They got quite a few honks and cheers out the window and more than one invitation for a sleepover. They circled back to their building and then dashed into the dorm. Of course that was before Luke was born. Before Dennis.

Kate had told Mark the story once, and she nearly spit out her wine when he asked if she wanted to do that with him. Which they did. On their honeymoon.

After college, Kate drifted apart from her red-haired, freckled friend. But today, somewhere beyond Manhattan, her friend was out there, wondering what the hell was going on. Maybe she was scared, maybe she was hurt, but Kate hoped that she wasn't. She hoped that she was making the best of the situation just like she had always done. But above all, Kate hoped that she was safe.

A gunshot thundered, this one too close for comfort. The group stepped backward, the wood dock groaning under the mass retreat. People turned back to the river, searching in desperation for the boat.

"How much longer is he going to take before he gets back?"

"Can't he go any faster?"

"They're getting closer."

Kate stepped in front of the group, holding up her hands. "He's moving as fast and as safely as possible. But as a precaution, we should stand by the gate. If the terrorists arrive before Rodney returns, we'll head to the second location."

Exhalations followed Kate's orders, and while everyone nodded in agreement, she tensed in preparation for the knife she was sure someone would stick in her back. And what was to stop them? They were strangers. Despite their good intentions, deep down, Kate started to feel the truth of what Rodney had warned.

Kate scanned the alleys between the buildings in front of the docks. The views only offered narrow glimpses into the streets. In a way, it was good, because the docks were kept hidden. It was why there were only a few dozen people at the gates instead of a few thousand.

Three more gunshots sounded, these slower than the automatic fire they'd heard before. Were there people fighting back? Kate latched onto the mesh of the chain-link fence.

People sprinted past the alleyways on the other side of the buildings, the gunfire reaching some crescendo, unintelligible screams echoing between blasts. Voices barked loudly in a language Kate didn't understand. She turned back toward the river. Rodney had just turned the boat around.

"We don't have enough time," Kate whispered to herself.

The group of people in her charge kept their faces glued toward the screams and gunfire. Kate's heart thumped quickly, and she grabbed their shoulders, pulling them toward her.

"Listen! We're going to move to the secondary location," Kate said.

"Are you crazy?" One of the men in the back shoved his way to the front. "Those people are out there, and they're going to kill us!"

"If we stay on the docks, we're sitting ducks," Kate said, her tone sharp.

"Maybe they won't see us?" a woman asked, a hint of skepticism to her voice. "Maybe they'll just pass right by."

"We can't risk that." Kate turned back toward the alleyway. People were heading north, which meant the gunmen were still to the south. "We need to go."

"And why the hell is it your decision?" The voice accompanied a harsh shove, and Kate bounced into the fence, the wire mesh buckling and cradling her as she looked at the big man staring her down. "Who put you in charge?"

"Hey, knock it off!" A woman and two other men stepped between the pair, but if the big man was nervous, he didn't show it.

"No," Kate said, pushing herself off the fence and adjusting her coat. "He's right. I'm not in charge. I don't have any real authority. But I can tell you that Rodney won't let any of you get on board if he doesn't see me." She eyed the big man. "So if you want across that river, then I'd suggest you shut your trap and start moving, because I'm leaving."

Kate reached for the gated door and swung it open, slipping down the fence as another round of gunfire spat into the evening air. It cracked loudly, echoing down the alleyways. Kate turned toward the sound just in time to watch the body collapse.

The distance and winter clothes made it hard to tell if it was a man or a woman. They wallowed on the ground, and their last gurgling breaths of life traveled down the alleyway.

Another person appeared, this one with a rifle tucked under their arm and a ski mask over their face. It aimed the weapon at the wounded person. Another gunshot. A yelp sounded behind Kate, and she turned to see one of the women covering her mouth, every group member looking on in horror.

The gunman shouted into the alley, and then three more armed terrorists were at his side.

"Run!" Kate sprinted just as the gunfire started. Her feet pounded the pavement, and adrenaline helped mask the fatigue and stiffness. She traversed the slick patches of pavement carefully, stealing glanced behind her to the group that followed. But with her eyes off the road, Kate landed on an ice patch and slipped.

A dull thud sounded as her ass greeted the pavement, and a sharp pain ran from her tailbone to the base of her neck. The cold numbed it quickly though, and the hot flash of pain dulled to a throbbing ache as she tried to stand. Then hands were suddenly on her shoulder and her arms, helping her off the ground.

"Are you all right?" The voice came from the red-haired woman.

"Yeah," Kate answered, not the least bit convincingly, as she frowned and grimaced from the pain in her back. She stole a glance behind her as the others caught up, and her eyes widened in terror as she saw the three gunmen exit the alleyway near the docks. "We need to move!"

Kate hobbled forward, her speed half of what it had been prior to the fall, and the herd of people shuffled forward. Gunfire chased them, and Kate refused to look back. Even when a cry bellowed to her right and she saw a body collapse in the periphery, Kate kept her eyes forward.

Wind numbed her face, and Kate tasted the snot dripping

from her nose. Everyone was screaming, crying, running. No one stopped. The primal instinct of survival guided them now.

Bullets zipped past, and a window shattered in an apartment complex to their right, the glass collapsing like a broken ice shelf that plummeted into the snow. And despite the cold, the pain, the heightened sense of danger, everything seemed to pass in slow motion. Kate looked to her left and saw strands of hair bouncing on a woman's face as she ran. She looked right and saw the muscles on a man's face twitch in fear at the sight behind him.

Finally, she looked back. The gunmen were still in pursuit. They were closer. And she saw the three casualties of their group from the gunfire.

Kate spun back around, looking for any place they could hide, anywhere they could run, and she thrust her arm out to a back door of a building that she prayed was open. "There!" She veered from the group, but not everyone followed.

The rest sprinted ahead, and when her hand curled around the handle of the door and she pulled it open, she caught only a glimpse of the fate of those that had gone straight, and it was of their bodies hitting the floor after a spray of gunfire.

Kate waited until everyone entered and caught one final glimpse of the gunmen before she slammed the door shut, still having the presence of mind to lock it, sealing them in darkness.

Bullets thumped against the door and exterior, and Kate hunched over, still pressing forward. "Go! Go! Go!" She shoved against the bodies in front of her, pushing everyone ahead blindly as more bullets ricocheted off of the door behind them.

The narrow hallway ended and opened into a lobby. Light drifted in through the front windows and revealed the huddled shapes of bodies on the floor. Frightened expressions covered everyone's faces, and before Kate could speak a word, another series of gunshots thundered from the back entrance, and the harsh crack of the door opening propelled her toward the front exit. "Get out! Everyone get out now!"

But the gunfire had already triggered the beginning of the stampede, and Kate was hurled in the middle of it. The herd carried her out of the doors like a wave, and suddenly the gunshots multiplied. They thundered like hail on a roof, and that same wave of bodies collapsed, and Kate was suddenly flattened to the sidewalk outside.

Kate thrust her hands out to try and catch herself, but the weight of the people behind her buckled her elbows, and she smacked the concrete hard. A bright white light flashed in her vision, and then suddenly things went dark as more bodies piled on top of her.

The screams suddenly faded, and the gunfire stopped. Kate lay still beneath the bodies, her visions limited to a small space between two bodies above her. But while she heard the thick, foreign accent of the gunmen as he drew closer, almost as if they were standing right next to her. Their tone was angered and hurried. And then, as she felt a pressure applied to her left ankle, she suddenly realized that they weren't next to her: they were on top of her.

The pressure from the boot heel drove a flurry of pain up the side of her leg, and she muffled a crying gasp. The heel ground into the tender joints of the ankle, but Kate neither screamed nor moved. Either meant death.

Finally, the pressure was relieved, and it took the same amount of concentration to keep herself from crying out in relief. Soundless puffs of breath passed through her nose, and then she dared herself to lift her eyes toward the small hole of light that broke between a shoulder and elbow that lay across from one another, forming a buttress of support that kept the bodies to her left slightly elevated.

An ear and then a shoulder passed overhead, and a sudden striking fear pulsed through her veins as the eye of the shooter appeared. She looked away quickly, still feeling the eye on her even after she did. There was more talk between them, and then another boot pressed into Kate's back through the body on top of her.

Kate bit her lip hard, drawing blood. She scrunched her eyes shut. A gunshot rang out, and a burst of warmth splattered her cheek as blood trickled down to her chin. She jumped from the sudden blast, but the body next to her jumped as well.

She froze, positive that she'd been discovered underneath the pile of bodies. She braced for the inevitable gunshot. Her thoughts ran to her children. Luke and Holly smiled at her. She thought of Mark, and she thought of her career, and then the flashes stopped as the terrorist's voices drifted away along with the gunshots.

Kate wasn't sure how long she lay there, but after a while, she wiggled underneath the bodies, shifting beneath the corpses. She grunted, pushing herself off the pavement, the dead rising with her. Her arms trembled from the weight of the bodies, but she finally burst from the mound. She gasped for breath as she quickly scurried back into the apartment building and into the safety of the lobby, which was empty save for the bodies of those that hadn't made it out in time.

A few bloodstains crept from beneath the corpses, but in the cold weather, the blood quickly congealed. Whatever warmth the building had once possessed before the power went out was gone. Death had taken its place and curled its icy fingers around everything.

Kate half collapsed, half lowered herself to the floor. She sat in the middle of the lobby, rocking back and forth. Her eyes darted between the bodies in the lobby and the bodies out front. The door was still open, propped by the foot of a man wearing black boots with bright neon laces. They caught the eye vividly and greedily.

As Kate rocked back and forth, shivering from both the cold and the brush with death, she couldn't take her eyes off those laces. And as she stared at them, she thought of all the people that had died, all the people that had followed her, and when she remembered the kids on the other side of the river, waiting for their parents, their mommies and daddies, she broke down.

The sobs rolled her shoulders, and she clutched her knees to her chest. The grief poured out of her, the tears stinging her cheeks as they froze from the cold.

They had followed her, and they had died. It was a realization that would haunt her for the rest of her life. But another thought broke through the cold of her mind, thawing her frozen body.

On the other side of that river was a child that still had a parent and a husband who still had a wife. And if she didn't get to that boat, she was sure that she'd never see them again.

"Get up," Kate said, her voice shaking as she forced the command from her lips. She pressed her gloved hand against the concrete and pushed, rising to a sitting position. Her boots scraped the lobby tile as she stood, her back hunched in pain.

When she finally straightened, she took shallow breaths, the cold like an anesthetic to help numb the pain. Slowly, she straightened again and this time avoided the sharp spasm in her back. Her ankle was tender as she broke into the rhythm of walking, and while her body clamored for her to stop, anger caused her to grit her teeth and press forward.

With her destination burned into her mind with a fresh determination, Kate limped forward, hobbling out the back, away from the bodies, away from the light, casting herself into the darkness of the hallway from which she had emerged.

The back door was cracked open from where the terrorists had entered, and the handle had disappeared, a ring of bullet holes around it. She pulled it open and squinted against the burst of light. She hobbled along, thinking of only getting to the docks.

Absentmindedly she reached for the revolver, forgetting she even had it. She gripped it firmly and glanced out to the river. She spied Rodney's boat making its way upstream. There was still time. The sight propelled her limp into a hobbled run, her movements more exaggerated by her arms as she used their momentum to swing herself forward.

But the wind had picked up, and when Kate looked out to the river, the boat had already sailed past. "No," she whispered. She attempted to hasten her pace but failed, her body too broken to follow her demands for speed.

Sweat trickled from her armpits, and her cheeks flushed from exertion. She couldn't miss that boat. She *wouldn't* miss that boat.

Up ahead, Kate saw the sign for the Regency through a pair of trees. Almost there.

Kate turned down the side of the building and immediately saw the docks. Hope swelled in her chest as she saw Rodney approach.

"Hey!" Kate shouted, but all that came out was crackled static. She cleared her throat and tried again. "Hey!"

Rodney waved.

Kate smiled and waved back excitedly. He had seen her. He would wait. She was going to make it. She was going to see her family again. And the more she centered her thoughts around that hope on her Frankenstein-like hobble toward her escape, the more real it felt. It solidified like concrete, and suddenly that was the only outcome. Everything else became fantasy.

Gunshots echoed to her left, and Kate stopped, her boots sliding against the slushy pavement. Flashes from the rifle muzzles were less than two blocks west of her. They chased a group of people sprinting in her direction. The impulse to flee, to live, triggered her face to look away and back toward Rodney and the boat.

But in that turn, her eyes caught a flash of something colorful. Afterward, Kate would reflect on the fact that if the sun hadn't appeared on the horizon, breaking through the clouds in that exact moment, she probably wouldn't have seen it. But it just so happened that she did, and that recognizable flash of red hair caught her eye.

Kate spun, this time her boots catching against solid ground, and saw a portion of the group that had run with her sprinting back.

They had a good lead on the gunmen, but they were closing fast. Kate stepped forward, gun raised. They were screaming, and Kate waved them forward. "Come on! Come on!" She finally intercepted them a quarter of the way down the alley. Bodies passed by her in a blur, and once they were clear, Kate squeezed the trigger.

The first shot missed wildly, and she had closed her eyes at the sound of the gunshot and the jerk of the pistol. But when she opened her eyes again, she saw the gunmen had stopped at the alleyway entrance, using the building walls for cover.

Kate fired again, her body adjusting to the recoil of the pistol, and though her eyelids fluttered, they didn't close. The bullet ricocheted off the right corner the alleyway, pushing one of the terrorists farther back. She fired again, taking a step closer, standing in the middle of the alley and void of cover. She squeezed and screamed, the reverberations from the gunshots issuing a throbbing ache in her forearm, and then suddenly everything stopped at the click of the hammer.

"Kate!"

She turned around, her arm still rigid and outstretched. She saw red hair and eyes wide with terror.

"RUN!"

Kate's joints stiffened, and even adrenaline couldn't ease the pain. Bullets pinged and bounced along the pavement and brick walls, the gunmen's retaliation more verbose and violent than anything Kate had thrust at them.

Bullets chased Kate all the way to the end of the alleyway, and the red-haired woman thrust out her hand, Kate reached for it, and one final yank pulled her from the clutches of danger.

Kate wrapped her arms tight around the woman, squeezing her firmly. "Thank God." She lifted her face from the woman's shoulder. There were five of them left. She smiled and nearly burst into tears.

More gunfire ended the reunion, and the red-haired woman pulled her toward the docks. "C'mon!"

Kate did her best to keep up, but fatigue had forced her to do little more than latch her hand around the red-haired woman's arm and hang on for dear life.

Out on the docks, the building provided cover from the gunshots. Kate tried to step over the high rails of the boat, but her body refused to cooperate. "I'm sorry." She stopped, trying to catch her breath. "I can't move."

"Help me." The red-haired woman motioned for a man, and he came and lifted Kate in his arms.

Kate smiled drunkenly, the solid ground suddenly shifting, and she swayed left and right, rocking with the boat. They set her down in a chair, and Kate's body sighed with relief. Her head lolled lazily on her shoulder, and she closed her eyes.

More shouts. More thunder. Suddenly everyone was in a hurry, and Rodney was screaming to shove off. But Kate didn't move. She finally felt warm, which was odd, because the river only made things colder. But here she was, closing her eyes, drifting off to sleep.

The boat rocked, and the wind rippled against the sails. Rodney was screaming for everyone to duck, but Kate just slouched lower in her chair. She was tired, but she was on the boat. And she was on her way to see her family.

13

A sharp pain woke Kate, her whole body screaming in protest. She blinked away the blurred vision and sat up, trying to get a grasp on her surroundings.

"Kate? Oh, thank god."

The words were followed by gentle hands, and Kate immediately leaned into their warmth. They were hands she knew, hands she remembered.

"How are you feeling?" Mark asked, crouched low by her side.

"Half dead," Kate answered, and then she suddenly sparked to life. "Holly? Where—"

"She's fine," Mark replied, gently pushing her back down on the cot. "The fever is still there, but it hasn't gone up. It seems like the medicine is helping."

Kate relaxed on her pillow, careful not to agitate her body any more than needed.

"There was a doctor over on this side, thank god," Mark said. "Aside from a few bumps and bruises and exhaustion, he said you're all right. He's been looking at everyone here."

Kate frowned, trying to figure out where "here" was, and then the events prior to her slumber flooded back. The boat, the docks, the gunfire, the shooters, the bodies, buried alive under all those corpses. Kate propped herself up, fighting past the pain that wanted to shove her back down. "How many made it back?"

Shadows engulfed Mark's face as he turned away. "We don't have to talk about that now."

But Kate couldn't stop thinking about it. She tried to recall the number of people that she had seen with the redheaded woman, but every time she tried, a terrible headache descended upon her and sent her back down to the pillow.

"They said they wouldn't have made it without you," Mark said. "The people that came back."

"And what about the kids with parents that didn't come back?" Kate lifted her head slightly and caught Mark's glare. "What about our group?"

"Glen and Laura made it," Mark answered.

The absence of the other names told her their fates. Kate nodded, staring blankly at a pile of blankets in the tent's corner.

"Holly was asking for you," Mark said. "Want me to get her?"

"Yes." Kate's answer was breathless, and her eyes immediately teared. Mark left and quickly returned with their daughter.

"Hey, Mom." Holly smiled.

"Hey, baby." Kate kissed the top of Holly's head and then squeezed her tight. There was a hunger in her arms, the same hunger that longed for her son, to hold him again like this and to make sure he was okay. "How are you feeling?"

"Still a little tired." Holly cast her face down but remained snuggled tightly against Kate. "My throat hurts."

"The medicine will help." Kate kissed her again and smiled. "I'm so happy to see you." She wrapped her daughter in a hug and shut her eyes, tears leaking from the corners. "So happy."

"You two should get some rest," Mark said. "Rodney wants to leave first thing in the morning. And he wanted to make sure everyone got a clean bill of health before we start the trip."

"Smart," Kate said, starting to drift off. Holly was putting off a lot of heat, and Kate yawned. "What time is it now?"

"Almost ten," Mark answered.

A sleeping bag lay to Kate's left, and Mark crawled inside it, the sound of his legs swooshing against the fabric as he positioned himself comfortably. Kate closed her eyes and kissed the back of Holly's head one more time.

During the night, the pain returned in flares and spasms, but they paled in comparison to the nightmares. The events of the day replayed in her head, blood and gore splashed liberally across every scene.

It started with the people on the metro train. When the power had gone out, their first reactions had been anger. It was nothing more than an accidental bump of a shoulder that ignited the whole car into a flurry of fists and boots and teeth.

After that it was the bridge, but instead of escaping safely to the other side, Kate plummeted into the icy waters, where she breathed lungful after lungful of icy river water. Other people fell with her, but while she could still breathe, they clawed for the surface, choking.

Halfway down into the water, Kate suddenly stopped, and there she was suspended, frozen, watching bodies rain all around her and delve deeper into the black abyss of the East River.

One quick yank and she was back at the docks, the gunmen spotting them from the alleyway. And while she hadn't gotten a very good look at them during the day, in her nightmare, they were wild, twisted things. Fangs jutted from mouths that dripped with saliva the color of blood.

Kate had tried to run from them, but her feet were cemented to the ground, and no matter how many times she tried to lift them, they wouldn't budge. The group of people that followed her suddenly stopped with her, looking for guidance.

"What do we do?"

"Where do we go?"

"Help us, Kate! Save us!"

But the moment Kate tried to open her mouth, she was

choked with silence. She clawed at her lips as the people around her looked on with desperation and confusion. She kept pointing for them to run, but they only repeated the same questions, and then Kate watched each of them die with a bullet to the head, their brains and bones spraying out across the dock.

Once they were all dead, the hungry wolves circled around Kate, drooling at the scent of more carnage. When they lunged, their jaws snapping, Kate was thrust to the final nightmare chamber, a place she hadn't been to in a very long time.

It was eighteen years ago. Kate lay in her bed in her studio apartment. Luke, barely six months old, lay sound asleep in the crib next to her bed. She was looking at him, watching the steady rise and fall of his chest. He had been a great baby. Never fussy, slept through the night, and Kate was young and naïve enough to believe that's how all babies were. It wasn't until she'd had Holly that she realized how lucky she was.

She had just turned twenty-one a few months ago, and the crummy apartment was the best she could afford after she was forced to leave the college dorms once Luke was born. How Luke slept through the neighbors' shouting match every night, Kate didn't know. But as she watched Luke and listened to Kent and Kara's (yes, those were their real names) arguments about who Kara was sleeping with when Kent wasn't around, she had no idea how she could love something so instantly with every fiber of her being.

But then a vicious knock sounded at Kate's door. It startled her and woke Luke. Three more hits against the door rattled the walls, and Luke belted out a shrieking scream.

"Shhh, it's okay, baby." Kate picked Luke out of the crib and rocked him on her way to the door. Her heart pounded just as loud as the door itself, and when she checked the peephole to see who was outside, she quickly stepped back. "Go away, Dennis! You're not supposed to be here!"

"Open this door, Kate!" The voice was angry and violent, and his words shook louder than the pounding of his fists. "Open it right fucking now!"

"No!" Kate screamed, but at the same time, her face twisted in preparation of tears. Luke continued to scream, and Kate hushed again.

The door buckled as Dennis rammed it repeatedly, and Kate retreated all the way to her bed. She held Luke tight, trying to soothe his tears while her own flowed freely from her eyes. "It's okay, Luke. Everything's going to be fine."

If she could have afforded a phone, she would have called the police, but she was barely making enough money at the diner to afford rent and power and diapers.

The door frame cracked, and one more blow knocked it inward. Kate screamed and trembled on the bed as Dennis stomped toward her. The muscles on his arms bulged from the sleeveless shirt that had a greasy brown stain on the chest. His face was covered in coarse black stubble, and his breath stank of whisky. He had a shotgun in one hand and a bag in the other.

"I told you to open the fucking door!"

Kate didn't respond, she simply kept her body between him and Luke.

Dennis dropped the bag, and she saw that the zipper was half open. A stack of cash poked out. He aimed the shotgun at Kate and then pumped it. "I want my kid, Kate."

"He's not yours."

"I fucked you, and then nine months later, that little cum stain popped out." He smiled. "He's mine all right. You haven't even been with anyone else."

It was a harsh truth and a mistake that Kate wished for the rest of her life that she could take back. "The courts said you can't be around me or him. Now go before I call the police."

"You don't have a phone," Dennis snarled. "I checked." He lunged an arm for Luke, and Kate fended him off. "Give him to me!"

"NO!" Kate ripped herself free and then sprinted for the

door. She was almost there when meaty fingers pulled her back. "Stop it! HELP! HELP ME!"

Dennis backhanded her and drew blood from her lip. The blow was more to keep her quiet than to hurt her, but she still wobbled on two legs after the crack. Then he wrapped his big hand around her throat and squeezed, moving her around the apartment like a ragdoll. "Give me my son!"

Kate used what concentration and strength remained to her to keep Luke in her arms, to protect him, to keep him from the madman that refused to leave her alone.

Dennis finally slugged a fist at Kate's cheek, and the blow knocked her to the ground. In the same motion, he ripped Luke from her arms, the boy's little cheeks red as he squealed at the top of his lungs. "There's my little insurance policy." He laughed and then reached for the bag with his money.

The ground rolled unevenly as Kate tried to stand. "Stop. You can't take him. You can't..." But the blow had knocked the fight from her, and what was meant to sound threatening came out only as a plea. "Let him go."

Dennis laughed, malice in his dark eyes as he forced Luke's little hand into a wave as her son screamed at the top of his lungs. "Say bye to Mommy."

"NO!" Kate forced herself up and tried to follow but crashed back onto the floor. Dennis disappeared with Luke into the darkness down the hallway, his voice echoing playfully amid Luke's screams. Kate veered into the hallway, and then as she screamed, she jolted awake.

Dawn had broken on the horizon, and Kate found herself covered in sweat. She looked down to Mark and Holly, who had climbed down to sleep with her father in the middle of the night, and she burst into tears.

She knew why that terrible memory had invaded her dreams tonight. It was because of the parole hearing, the one her lawyer had called her about before the EMP. Dennis Smith was Luke's father and a convicted murderer. It was that same night he came for Luke that he murdered a police officer who found him with the baby at a truck stop.

It took thirty-six hours for authorities to find Dennis and thirty-seven hours before Kate finally had Luke back in her arms. Dennis was sentenced to life but was eligible for parole after ten years. It was Kate's letter to the parole board that kept him in jail, a piece of information that she was sure Dennis knew.

And so every year around this time, Kate would go and speak to the parole board in upstate New York to make sure that the animal who had abducted her son to use as a hostage after his bank robbery remained behind bars.

Dennis was the culmination of a reckless moment in her youth, and while it had given her one of the best things in her life, Luke, it had also been the source of pain and loss.

After that incident, Kate made a promise to herself, a vow that she would never let her son be in harm's way again. No matter what, she would always find him. And as she stared at Mark and Holly as they slept, she knew that she wouldn't be joining them on their trip north to the cabin. She was going to the airfield. She was going to get her son.

* * *

WHILE MOST OF the camp slept in a mixture of sleeping bags and cots that had been pilfered from a camping store nearby, Rodney lay awake in his own bag. He had a spot near the river, where he watched the island of Manhattan sit glumly in the dark.

The water carried with it not just the chilling winds of cold but also random gunshots laced with screams. He didn't know what those people wanted, but he did know they would kill as many people as they could before any type of resistance formed to fight back. He figured that there would be pockets of terrorists scattered around the country, using the exact same guerilla tactics. But he doubted they'd find many in upstate

New York. And while they might not find any terrorists wielding AK-47s, there would be other people. People who wanted what Rodney had. And after a while, they'd do anything necessary to have it.

A ripping snore broke through one of the tents, and Rodney turned just as it ended. There was another, but then it stopped. He turned back to the self-destructing city, knowing that he wouldn't be able to take everyone he'd ferried across the river to his cabin. There were just too many.

He hoped that Kate wouldn't make a fuss about it when she woke, not that she was in any shape to do much fussing. She would slow them down, but with the old man in their group, he'd already factored in a slow pace. Another gunshot crossed the river. The distance turned it into nothing more than a faint pop of a firecracker, but it didn't lessen its lethalness.

Another body had fallen. More red slush was mixed up with the dirty grey of New York's finest pavement of Italian Ice. He rubbed his eyes and lay down, his eyes closed but his mind open and awake. He'd give them another hour. Then they'd have to start moving. It was going to be a long trip, and even when they got to the cabin, there wasn't a guarantee of survival. Winters had a way of weeding out the herd, and all the forecasts called for a bone-chilling season.

* * *

THE RESTLESS SLEEP had provided some relief from Kate's wounds, but not much. Despite Mark's protest, she hobbled around on her own, collecting their supplies and what they'd need. She still hadn't told him about her separate mission. He'd be upset, but she knew he'd let her go. It was her son.

"All right, folks, remember to top off your bottles and grab any of those protein bars at the main table," Rodney said, gesturing over to the "breakfast buffet" that had been set up for those that had stuck around. "We leave in five."

Rodney turned, and Kate hobbled to him. “Hey, you got a second?”

When he looked at her, Kate noticed that something in his face had changed. The lines that had set on his stoic expression had become defined overnight. He looked older. She expected they’d all be older when this was done.

Kate pulled him away from the others and kept her voice low. “Do you have the coordinates for your cabin?”

“Yeah,” Rodney answered. “Why?”

“I’m not going with you,” Kate said. “I’m going to get my son down in Virginia and then bring him back with me.”

Rodney ran his palm across his face and shook his head like a disappointed father. “Kate, that’s not a good idea. It’ll take too long on foot.”

“I’m not walking,” Kate said. “I’m flying.”

Rodney bellowed laughter, which he quickly reined in. “You plan on flapping your arms really hard? That’s quite the workout.”

“You said yourself that the EMP only affects computer chips, right?”

“Yeah,” Rodney answered.

“There’s an airfield a few miles southwest of here,” Kate said. “They do an airshow every spring, and a lot of old pilots show up there to do tricks and whatnot, show off their planes—shit.” A shot of pain radiated from her hip, and she bit her lip. She massaged the point of pain, and it seemed to help a little. When she lifted her face, Rodney greeted her with a “told you so” grin. “I’m fine.”

“Uh-huh,” Rodney said.

“Listen, a lot of those guys keep their old planes in storage at that airfield,” Kate said. “I might find one old enough to have hydraulic gears. If I do, I can fly it down to get my son and then fly back up to the coordinates of the cabin. Or at least get close.”

“It’s risky, Kate,” Rodney said. “And your family will want to go with you.”

"My family stays with you. That's nonnegotiable. It'll be safer away from populated areas." Without realizing it, she turned her gaze toward the city, which looked dead in the early morning light. Frozen like the icy waters of the river, immune to the warmth of the sun. "I'm going, Rodney. Now give me the damn coordinates."

Rodney hesitated a moment but eventually acceded to Kate's request. She folded the paper with the cabin's coordinates neatly into her pocket, making sure that it was secure behind the zipper, and muttered the numbers in her head to commit them to memory in case she lost the paper.

"Hey," Mark said, coming over as Rodney left. "What's going on?"

Spit disappeared from Kate's mouth, and she found herself just as tongue-tied as in her dream. But she wasn't going to let any more of her family be in harm's way, not when she had the ability to do something about it. "I'm going to get Luke."

"No." Mark shook his head, his flag firmly planted. "No way in hell you're going off somewhere alone in the condition you're in."

"It's not as bad as it looks," Kate said.

"Oh, no?" Mark barely shoved her shoulder, and the bad ankle folded and she started to fall, but Mark caught her. "You can barely walk, Kate." There was a bite to his tone, and the cold morning only made it worse.

"I'm not leaving him down there," Kate said, grumbling as Mark helped her up.

"Then we're coming with you," Mark said.

"No."

"Kate, you can't—"

"I'm not taking Holly back into that!" Kate thrust her arm out toward the city. "Not after what we saw, not after everything we went through to get out."

"But you're willing to put yourself back in it?"

"To get my son? Yes."

Mark spun in frustration. "For Christ's sakes, Kate, he's a man. He's been living on his own for the past year and a half. He can take care of himself, and when this blows over, we'll be able to call him when the power comes back on."

"You heard Rodney. That could take months!"

"It's suicide!"

"He's my son!" Her scream pierced the camp, and heads turned toward her, and she bowed her head, regaining her composure. When she faced Mark again, she couldn't hide the tears on her face anymore. "And I thought he was yours too."

"That's not fair, Kate." Mark stepped back. "You know I love him."

"Like he was your own?" Kate asked, and the moment the words left her lips and she saw the pain etched over his face, the anger deflated. "I'm sorry. I didn't—"

"It's fine." Mark waved a dismissive hand. "It's..." He walked toward her. "I love you. I love Luke. You are both important to me, just as important to me as Holly." He kissed her forehead. "You don't have to do this alone."

Kate hugged him, squeezing as hard as she could until her back hurt. "I know. But it'll be safer for Holly this way. Plus I can get there faster."

"Only if that plane idea of yours works." He sighed. "You want me to tell Holly?"

"No. I'll do it."

Kate found her daughter still sleeping in her father's sack, and she gently brushed Holly's hair back behind her ear and gave it a warm kiss. "Time to get up, baby."

Holly groaned and rolled away.

Kate reached for her daughter's shoulder and pulled her back. "Hey, listen, I need to tell you something."

Holly opened her eyes and rubbed them sleepily. "Can we go home yet?"

"No, not yet." Kate grabbed hold of Holly's leg, which she could still wrap her whole hand around. She remembered when she could still do that to Luke. "Daddy is going to take you someplace safe, but I'm going to get your brother and meet up with you guys later."

"Why can't Luke just meet us at the cabin?" Holly asked.

"Because he doesn't know where it is," Kate answered. "But Mommy is going to get him and bring him back, and we can all be together again. Just like it was at Christmas."

Holly smiled. "I liked Christmas."

"Me too."

The smile faded, and Holly picked at her blanket, her eyes cast down. "You promise you're coming back?"

Another round of tears appeared in her eyes, and Kate leaned forward and kissed Holly's cheek, inching her mouth close to Holly's ear. "I promise. And I love you so much. You know that, right? How much I love you?"

"I know," Holly said softly.

Kate pulled back but then bent down and kissed her again. She wiped her nose and then patted Holly's back. "I'll see you later, sweetheart."

And as she said her goodbyes, she tried to bury the lie that she'd told Mark. Even if there weren't planes, she wasn't coming back. Not without Luke. No matter what.

Kate forced her gaze to keep straight ahead, knowing that if she looked back, she might lose the grit to keep going. And while the first hundred yards were hard, it wasn't long before the cold and the pain of her body offered a distraction.

Winter bellowed its challenge with every frigid gust. It made the miles ahead stretch longer than their distance. Every step gained was one closer to her son—and farther away from her husband and daughter. Whatever direction she chose, it meant the loss of family. But she would come back to them. She would make her family whole.

14

YESTERDAY

The daily banter beyond the walls of the eight by four prison cell had already begun. It was all part of the morning routine between Renniger's insane guests and the correctional officers who "administered" their medicine.

Screams of resistance preceded the heavy thuds of contact between a baton and a body. It was a symphony that would last for the next few hours. And while the violence of the medical staff traversed the halls of one of New York's finest federal prisons, inmate 0946 in cell number 283 would be escorted past the crazies and into a small room where the next year of his life would be decided.

Dennis Smith lay on his side on his cot, dressed in his bright orange jumpsuit, his shoes on his feet. He always slept in his shoes. It was a habit he picked up when he was a kid. It was the fastest way to escape a beating from his father, who would come home in the middle of the night, drunk and looking for someone to wale on. It was either him or his mother, and Dennis wasn't taking a beating for that sour-faced bitch.

And it was a habit that had turned useful even into his adult years. It was rare he was caught with his pants down. Ever since that first car he boosted when he was sixteen, Dennis had lived a life of violence. It was a path that eventually led him here, tucked away in the far northern wilderness in the middle of BFE, New York, kept under lock and key.

Lock and key was just an expression, of course. Renniger was a state-of-the-art facility, run by sophisticated magnetized locks and security software. It was all digital and completely foolproof so long as the pistol-toting fat asses that ran this place were at the helm of the computers in the control room.

When the screams beyond his cell ended and the crazies had been sedated for yet another day, Dennis opened his eyes. They were a rich, dark brown, so dark that they almost blended into the black of his pupils. He frowned, the thin eyebrows accentuating his expression as he wiped his hand down his face and through the light-brown beard.

His joints groaned in pain as he stretched on the cot then grimaced. "Piece of shit." He propped himself up with his arms and examined the tiny living quarters where he had spent the last eighteen years of his life. He circled that thought for a moment. *Eighteen years.*

Time passed differently in prison. It was slower, painstakingly slower. The first few years were the worst. But eventually, time ceased to matter. Days bled into years, and years bled into decades, and the only thing that mattered was the survival of routine until one of two things happened: parole or death.

Dennis, like every other resident in Renniger, was a lifer. There wasn't a convict inside that didn't have multiple murder or rape charges. Dennis was tagged on six homicides, two of them cops. And if there was one thing the judicial system didn't like, it was cop killers. Prison guards weren't fond of them either.

For the first three years of Dennis's life sentence, the guards beat him within an inch of his life. Then, once he was healed, the beating was repeated, and so began his life cycle on the inside. But out of all the beatings and rapes and the struggle to maintain his sanity within his concrete coffin, it was today that he hated most. It had come every year for the past thirteen years. It was the day that hope was flaunted in front of him and then snatched away. It was parole-hearing day.

The springs of the cot groaned from Dennis's weight as he rolled over, resting his head on the flat pillow that was more cardboard than cushion, and faced the wall. He pressed down on the mattress to reveal a space on the wall near his pillow.

A name was etched into the concrete, one that had been retraced repeatedly over the past eighteen years. A flicker of rage brought the tip of his finger toward the carving. He traced the name slowly, mouthing it silently with his lips. *Kate.* Then, he punched it.

Bone and concrete offered little more than a dull thud, but the pain radiated from his knuckles all the way to his shoulder. His hand throbbed, and Dennis rolled to his back, shutting his eyes. If it weren't for that bitch, then he would have been out of here thirteen years ago. But she'd tricked him. She'd lied to him.

One of the stipulations of his conviction stated that he wasn't eligible for parole for five years after his sentencing, and it also prompted him to meet with a shrink once a month for "rehabilitation and observation." It took him a year to figure out that what the shrink wrote down on that fucking yellow notepad actually mattered.

That number-two-pencil-toting smug motherfucker had the ability to sway the parole board once he was eligible. So Dennis told the Poindexter what he wanted to hear. His father beat him, his mother wasn't around, blah, blah, blah.

But what he didn't tell them about was the bug stuck in his head. And how every now and then it burrowed through his brain, eroding his reason and control, driving him into violence and madness. It fed him, made him come alive. He loved it.

And after all of the sessions, all of the therapy, did he really change? No. It was all for show, and the long con was a struggle. He was more of a see it, want it, take it kind of person. But he pretended. Every day. For five years.

And when those five long, painfully slow years finally ended, the shrinks were in his pocket. He even had a written statement from the warden, commending him for his lack of "violent incidents." But there was one testimony that could put him over the edge. And it was from the very same woman whose name he had cursed since the day he was arrested.

Dennis wrote Kate once a month for two years prior to that first parole hearing. And just when he thought that she wasn't going to do anything, she finally replied. But what was more, the letter she wrote him back stated that she'd give him a favorable testimony.

When the day of that first parole hearing arrived, Dennis couldn't wipe the smile from his face. It would be a day he'd never forget. And like the name carved on the wall, he retraced it in his mind every single day.

"Mr. Smith, have a seat."

The voice of the chairman of the parole board echoed just as loudly in his thoughts as the rattles from the chains around his ankles and wrists. Back then, the parole hearings were performed in a room with a window, which granted a limited picture of the world beyond the walls and barbed-wire fence. It was sunny and beautiful outside.

"The board has reviewed your files as well as your written and audible testimony from both the trial and the team of psychologists that have been working with you here at the facility." The chairman lifted his eyes, his pupils magnified by thick lenses. "The board has already reached a decision regarding your case, but we wanted to offer you the opportunity to give a personal statement, in your own words, for the record."

Sweat broke under Dennis's shirt and beaded on his forehead. The chains rattled as he shifted in his chair. He cleared his throat, doing his best to keep the bug under control. "I committed a crime as a young man that is inexcusable. And I know the lives I changed, including my own, will never regain what they've lost." He dropped his hands, hunching slightly. "A man is dead because of me. He lost his life, and I lost my freedom." He took a dry swallow. "But I have a son who doesn't know me." He lifted his gaze, just like he'd practiced, and produced a single tear that ran down his cheek. "He'll be six next month. That's a long time for a boy to go without seeing his father." He wiped away the tear and cleared his throat, which had grown thick with phlegm. "I just want a second chance. I just want to prove to society and my family that I've changed. I think I deserve that chance. I hope you think so too." He sat down, the bug squirming and begging to be released, but he hung tight. He was close. He just needed to wait a little longer.

The committee leaned into each other's ears and whispered. And while they deliberated, Dennis searched the room for Kate.

At first he'd thought that he'd missed her when he entered. But now he was sure she wasn't here. He shifted in his chair uncomfortably at her absence. Had she come earlier and already given her testimony? Two knocks interrupted the parole board's deliberation, and Dennis turned to see Kate standing in the doorway. He smiled coyly. The dumb bitch decided to come.

"Sorry." Kate's voice was breathless and soft. She appeared in Dennis's peripheral vision, and she only brought her glance to his once. It was quick, dismissive.

"Mrs. Hillman," the chairman said. "We appreciate your attendance."

"I ran into some traffic on the way here," Kate said, keeping her eyes focused on the parole members. "Am I too late?"

"We've already received your written statement, but we haven't vocalized our decision," the chairman answered. "But seeing as you're here, would you like to speak on behalf of Mr. Smith?"

Kate opened her mouth, but after a long pause, she shook her head. "No."

Dennis's stomach soured, and the bug started to wiggle loose.

"Very well," the chairman said. "Let the record state that the parole for inmate 0946, Mr. Dennis Smith, is denied."

It took a few seconds for the chairman's words to register, and by the time they did, the correctional officers were already removing him from the room. "No, wait!" Dennis pivoted toward Kate, who kept her eyes on her shoes. "What did you tell them?" A sliver of malice snaked through the mask he'd practiced wearing. "What did you tell them, you bitch?"

Rough hands removed him from the room, and Dennis's bug broke free as he kicked and screamed and hollered all the way back to his cell. His elbow caught the cheek of one of the guards, and it cost him a week in isolation.

To this day, Dennis didn't know what Kate told the board. Those records were denied to him. But he was convinced that whatever she had told them was the reason for his continued incarceration. And so every year since that first parole meeting, for the past thirteen years, Kate arrived at his parole hearing, and he was denied release.

And so today would be another year of the same.

Dennis lay still on the cot and traced Kate's name. He imagined killing her. Then he imagined fucking her. He did both often. And then his manhood hardened, and he reached down to relieve himself. But before he could finish, the click of boots echoed outside his door, and a buzzer sounded, releasing the mechanical locks inside the six-inch steel door.

Dennis jumped from his bed, still erect, and placed his palms flat against the back of the wall, head down.

The hinges of the steel door groaned as it swung inward, and three pairs of boots echoed methodically inside until the guards were so close that Dennis felt their hot breath tickle his neck.

"Inmate 0946, turn around!" The orders were barked with a mechanical efficiency born from years of repetition.

Slowly, Dennis complied, the lack of vigor noted by the snarl on the sergeant's face, which quickly turned to a smirk at the sight of the erection. "Inmate 0946, did we catch you at a bad time?"

Dennis kept his lips tight. He wasn't in the mood for an ass kicking, not today, and especially not with a hard-on, though he suspected a beating would be the quickest way to get rid of it.

The sergeant stepped forward, still smirking. "Want us to bring you a friend in here to take care of that? Maybe one of the skinny Latin boys the fags like so much?" The other two officers snickered, the leather of their boots groaning as they swayed their weight from side to side.

"No, sir," Dennis answered. "But you're free to try." He looked the sergeant in the eye, smiling. "I wouldn't mind your wife in here, either."

The sergeant's smirk faded, and the two correctional officers behind him stepped forward as if they were going to beat the shit out of him, but the sergeant held up his hand, and they stopped. Instead, the sergeant removed his baton and then slapped it down hard on Dennis's erection.

The contact sent a shock of pain through him that was so immense that he simply collapsed to the floor, gasping for air and spasming. It wasn't until the tip of a guard's steel-toed boots connected with his stomach that he started to grunt in pain.

"Not his face!" the sergeant yelled. "I don't want the parole board feeling sorry for him."

After the kicking was finished, the sergeant spit on Dennis and then gestured for his men. "Chain him up."

Steel was clamped tight around Dennis's ankles and then his wrists, the chains stealing his mobility and slowly cutting the circulation to his hands and feet. It took less than a minute for them to throb and swell. Once the guards got him to his feet, his body screaming in pain, a hard jab to the back shoved him out of the cell.

The restraints and the beating made the long walk through the prison halls awkward and painful. He was sure that his dick was broken, and a few ribs weren't out of the question either. Before they entered the room with the parole board, the sergeant wiped the spit from Dennis's cheek and checked to make sure there weren't any physical signs of abuse. Once he was satisfied, Dennis was ushered in.

The parole board ended their idle chatter and focused their attention to Dennis's file. "All right." The parole chairman was young but just as dismissive as his predecessors. Dennis had been through a lot of parole chairmen during his tenure. "Mr. Smith, do you have anything to state for the record before this committee reads its decision?"

"No." The answer came out no louder than a whisper, and Dennis found that it hurt to speak.

"What was that, Mr. Smith?" the chairman asked.

Dennis gritted his teeth with seething anger. "I said, go fuck yourself."

"Very well." The chairman cleared his throat. "Mr. Smith, this committee does not grant you release in the form of parole. Your case for parole will be reexamined one year from now." The gavel banged, and just like that, the correctional officers collected him and dragged him from the room. The entire proceeding took less than two minutes.

Once he was back in the cell, the restraints were removed and Mr. Big Dick Sergeant smiled at Dennis, revealing a corn-yellow canine. "You're never getting out of here, asshole. Never."

"Never is a long time, Shit Breath."

The sergeant turned and took a step but then swung around, leading with his fist, which landed with a dull thud against Dennis's stomach.

Air exploded from Dennis's lungs as he dropped to his knees and tightly hugged his stomach. He leaned forward until his forehead touched the cool of the concrete floor, then he listened to the laughter and the click of boots until the steel door shut and the locks were reengaged.

Dennis rolled to his side, sipping gulps of air as the previous points of pain lit up his body like a Christmas tree. Once the pain subsided, he flicked a middle finger to the door then flashed another bird at the camera in the top left corner of the cell. The eye in the sky was everywhere. He couldn't take a shit without someone watching.

Slowly, Dennis pushed himself up, and as he sat on the edge of his cot, the halogen lights in his cell shut off, casting him in darkness.

Dennis sat still for a moment, unsure of what happened. It was barely past morning, and lights out didn't happen until eight o'clock. But this darkness was different from curfew. It was all-encompassing. All-shrouding.

The mattress squeaked as Dennis stood, and he limped toward the front of his cell and peered through the tiny rectangular window of his door. The darkness in the hall matched the same one in his cell. Had the power gone out?

A silhouette darted past the window, and Dennis jerked away in surprise. Suddenly, another shadow darted past, and another, and then a gunshot echoed down the hallway. He pressed his nose against the glass and realized they were inmates running in the halls, out of their cells.

Dennis pressed his hands against the door, feeling his way toward the cracks and the absence of a handle. He wedged his fingernails between door and the frame, his muscles tense, and then pulled.

He expected resistance, and the fantasy would end and he'd collapse back onto the cot and wait for the ache in his groin to disappear. But there was no resistance. The door opened. It was unlocked.

Even in the dark, the bright orange of the federal jumpsuits glowed, a stampede of inmates bolting toward the exit doors and out of the prison halls.

Another gunshot fired, and the stampede froze from the flash of a gun's muzzle, but after a quick scream and three more bullets, the shooter was suddenly silenced, swarmed by a mountain of shadows in the dark.

Dennis's legs unconsciously thrust him into the rat race. He sprinted through the darkness, the men in front of him guiding the way.

Shoulders and arms smacked into one another, and Dennis burst through the first set of double doors that led into the mess hall. The rush of men descended the staircase like water cascading down a mountain, and Dennis let himself be caught in the river's flow.

From the mess hall, they burst into the visitors' center, where the stream crashed into the dam of correctional officers that had barricaded the exit doors.

Daylight shone through the windows, and the officers had flipped the tables in the visiting room to be used as shields. They fired at random, shooting anyone that attempted the sprint from the mess hall toward the exit.

Dennis sidled up next to a group near the door. The herd of inmates behind was growing, along with the eagerness to escape.

An inmate broke from the pack, darting through the middle of the room, screaming. The officers opened fire, dropping him onto the growing pile of bodies.

"Fucking pricks!" an inmate close to Dennis screamed but then tucked himself back behind the safety of the walls. "God-damn motherfuckers!"

Another lone wolf broke from the pack. Three gunshots, and he hit the floor.

Dennis elbowed the men around him, pulling their attention away from the guards. Faces turned in the darkness, some of them viewable, most of them not. "You shit stains wanna get out of this place?"

"And miss mystery-meat Tuesday next week? You're out of your mind."

The words eased the tension, and a few chuckles escaped tight lips, Dennis's among them. "If we all rush the doors, we can overwhelm them."

"And who do you expect to go first?" a voice asked. "A dead man isn't a free man."

Dennis looked toward the pile of corpses. "We use the bodies as shields. Let the dead guys take the bullets."

A few heads nodded, and Dennis echoed his orders up to the front. Inmates reached for the closest legs and feet and pulled them back behind the walls, blood smearing the floor.

Dennis worked his way up to the front, a few of the guys in the back following him. He grabbed hold of one of the bodies with another inmate and looked to the eager faces around him. "On three!"

The group tensed, everyone inching forward, the bodies in the back acting like a pressure cooker ready to blow. "One!"

The officers on the other side braced for the rush. "Get ready to fire!"

"Two!" A pulse of energy jolted everyone forward a step, the number of inmates joining the rush growing with every breath.

"Three!"

The momentum from behind thrust Dennis forward, forcing his legs into a sprint, and he made good use of the dead man that he and another inmate carried.

"Open fire!"

Bullets vibrated against the body in Dennis's hands, and he peeked over the corpse's arm just in time to see the table come into view. A crash of orange jumpsuits broke the line of tables, and bodies rocketed forward like human missiles.

The collision caused a crescendo of screams and gunshots, and when Dennis dropped the corpse, he found himself staring down the barrel of a nine-millimeter. He smacked at the hand just before the officer pulled the trigger then tackled the guard to the floor, deafened by a high-pitched ringing.

The pair grappled, Dennis immediately reaching for the pistol. Two quick jabs to the officer's ribs loosened his grip, and Dennis yanked the gun free. He fired once, striking the officer's chest, but Kevlar kept the bullet from its lethal purpose. The air was knocked from the officer's lungs, and he lay stunned on the floor.

Dennis aimed for the head then fired again, sending the officer's brains out the back of his head and across the white tiled floor. He stood, pistol still gripped in his hand, and shouldered his way through the mass exodus of flailing arms and elbows.

The exertion and adrenaline had turned his legs to jelly, and each step over the bodies being trampled on the floor nearly sent him down to join the dead. But when Dennis crossed the threshold of the exit doors, the warmth of the sunlight was immediately knocked away by winter's icy grip.

Dennis froze, the cold overwhelming and shocking as he surveyed the snow-covered trees beyond the prison's fences. It wasn't until an inmate rammed into his back that Dennis trudged forward, his movements stiff and slow.

A few dozen men ran along the narrow corridor of chain-link fences, everyone less than fifty yards from freedom. The last barrier was the chained gate. The inmate next to Dennis turned and smiled at him, puffing wheezing breaths of icy air.

"You see that? We're gonna make it! We're gonna—"

A gunshot rang out, the man collapsed, and blood splattered against Dennis's cheek. He looked up and to the right, seeing two guards in the tower with sniper rifles. Men screamed as more gunshots thundered, producing the deadly hail of bullets. It was like shooting fish in a barrel.

Bodies in orange jumpsuits buckled against the chain mesh of the fence, and the first few inmates against the locked gate were shot in the back or the head.

More and more men tugged at the gate, flinging their bodies against it, as the guards picked them off one by one. When Dennis reached the back of the pack, he forced his way through the huddled masses, waving his pistol above his head. "Let me through! Let me through!" Bodies gave way, and once he was at the front, he aimed for the lock.

It took three bullets to shoot it off, and after that, the gates burst open, and a sea of orange flooded the snow-covered trees. Gunshots echoed through the forest, cracking the icy air. But after a few minutes of running, and as the sound of gunfire faded, Dennis glanced back at the prison.

There were still no sirens. No deployment of vehicles. And from what he could tell, they still hadn't plugged the dam as more and more orange flooded the forest.

Dennis didn't know why it happened or how it happened, but the deeper he cast himself into the forest, the more he didn't care. His mind was already circling the name he scribed on the walls of his prison cell.

15

PRESENT DAY

The highway had become a graveyard of abandoned vehicles. The snow that had fallen since the EMP detonated yesterday covered the hoods and roofs, creating tiny mounds of white for as far as the eye could see. And it wasn't just cars that stopped working.

Grey skies spit snow onto a world that had ceased to function. No power. No communication. No modern conveniences that so many relied on for food and water and shelter. The world had changed in the blink of an eye, and as it came to a standstill, the masses had worked themselves into panicked frenzies.

Cities were tearing themselves apart, either from the people fighting amongst themselves or from the terrorist group responsible for the EMP's detonation. The world had regressed to that primal function of survival; it had also become more dangerous.

Kate Hillman pulled her scarf tighter around her neck and face and flipped her jacket's collar up to help shield herself from the cold. She was covered from head to toe, only her eyes visible from beneath her winter clothes. But despite the layers she wore, the cold still seeped into her bones. It was unavoidable, and it was only going to get worse.

Snot crusted Kate's upper lip, frozen stiff, and her nose and cheeks were a bright cherry red beneath the cloth. She glanced behind her to the trail of footprints that stretched to the horizon. Somewhere to the north of Kate, her husband and daughter were traveling to the wilderness of upstate New York. She had fought so hard to find them in New York, but their reunion was cut short by her decision to head south.

Kate needed to get to Fairfax, Virginia. Her son, Luke, attended George Mason University, which sat on the outskirts of Washington, DC. And if the nation's capital was anything like New York City, then she needed to get him as far away from that place as she could.

Both her husband and Rodney had advised her against leaving, but she wouldn't abandon her son to a terrible fate. And she didn't plan on walking the whole way, either. She had a plan. It was a long shot, but it was still a plan. But first she had to get to the airfield.

The wind howled and kicked up snow that blasted Kate's face, stinging her eyes. Shivers rippled through her body as the cold continued to gnaw at her resolve. But the clock was running, and she didn't know how much time remained.

A trip that would have taken less than an hour had transformed into six, which was generous considering her slow pace. And right now, time wasn't something she could afford to lose. The only positive that she had been able to find in the situation was that the cold and movement had numbed the pain in her hip and ankle.

After everything that happened, she knew there had to be millions, maybe even hundreds of millions, of people just like her, trying to reunite with their loved ones. The internet and cell phones had made it so easy to connect to anyone, anywhere in the world. But the EMP stole that privilege in less than a second.

Kate squeezed her hands, pumping blood into them to keep them from getting stiff, but it did little help. She adjusted the pack on her shoulders, which grew heavier with every step. She had loaded herself down with as much gear as she could find at the camping store a mile back, and while Rodney had given her a list of supplies, she wasn't able to check off everything on the list. Not that she was complaining—the pack on her back already weighed close to sixty pounds.

After a few more miles were chewed up beneath her boots, the weather cleared up a bit. She looked up to find the sun trying to break through. She lowered the scarf, closing her eyes as she basked in the sun's warmth.

But more than the warmth, she was thankful for the light. It made the trip feel less dreary and lonesome. Since her departure from the little makeshift camp on the New Jersey side of the Hudson, she hadn't seen a single soul.

Another mile passed, Kate keeping track by the markers on the side of the highway, and shortly after, she spotted the exit for the airfield and smiled in relief. Excited, she reached for the map to check the remaining distance and then paused to drink some water. Despite the cold, the exertion of the walk had caused her to soak her undershirt with sweat.

The snow crunched beneath her feet, and her steps were slow and close together coming down the icy turnoff. Twice, she skidded half a foot before catching her balance, her muscles burning and her pulse racing. Any injury now could turn deadly. There was no 911 to call, no rescue team that could be summoned to find her frozen and broken body. She was on her own.

The curve of the off-ramp ended, and Kate veered along the shoulder of the road that would lead her through a small town and then to the New Jersey Scarborough Airfield, home of the annual Scarborough Air Stunt Spectacular.

Kate had gone to it once a few years back. She'd had a layover in New Jersey and a day to kill before her flight home. And despite the campy fare and homemade signs that acted as the event's advertisement, she had been glad she did.

They'd had planes of every size and shape from every era she could remember. She had walked through the airfield like a kid in a candy store, her jaw slack as she'd ran her fingertips down the welded metal of the fuselages of the planes that had flown for decades—DH-4 Biplanes, A-20 bombers, P-38's, and a slew of commercial planes.

The fact that people had done so much with instruments so basic in the early years of aviation was always an inspiration for her. History was riddled with talented pilots, some of whom had reached the status of legend, such as the likes of Earhart, Doolittle, and Wien. When she had been at the airfield and saw those planes that they'd piloted, it had been as if she was walking in those legends' footsteps. And now, like the greats that had come before her, Kate would need to rely on those early tried-and-true methods of aviation.

All of the electronics that she had grown accustomed to in her big 727s were gone. Along with the control towers, and runway crews, and mechanics to ensure that everything was running properly. It would be the plane, a compass, and a map. But that was really all a good pilot needed.

Still, she had never flown anything older than a nineties Gulf Stream. And the relics she would have to find without any onboard computers to run them were much older than that. But she'd have to figure it out. There wasn't any other option. Her son was two hundred miles south, and the time it would take to get to him on foot wasn't a luxury that she was afforded.

Kate carefully stepped through an icy patch, her arms thrust out as she kept her balance. She glanced up at the sky, hoping to still find the sliver of sun, but it had once again been swallowed up by the grey clouds that spit a light snowfall.

The road off the highway offered more of the same view. Broken down cars with their fenders and bumpers smashed into each other. It was hard to imagine so many graveyards like this across the country. Millions of vehicles left impotent from the EMP blast, and Kate wasn't sure if they were ever going to drive again.

"Hey!"

Kate skidded a few inches due to her abrupt stop. She turned, finding an outline of a man through the haze of snowfall. He had his hands in his pockets, a big black jacket zipped all the way to his chin, with a matching beanie covering the top of his head and ears.

As he grew closer, Kate stepped back. He removed his hands from his pockets and held them up passively.

"Whoa, hey, take it easy." Icy clouds puffed from his lips with each syllable. "I didn't mean to frighten you. I was under the overpass, and I saw you walk by. Haven't seen anyone around in a while." He glanced to his left and to his right quickly.

Kate's thoughts went to the gun tucked in her waistband at her back, and she suddenly felt foolish for not keeping it in a more convenient spot to reach. "I'm meeting up with a group." She blurted out the words, the cold and adrenaline forcing her voice to quiver.

The man smiled, taking quick steps closer to her. "Mind if I join you?"

As he neared, his features clarified. A short, unkempt beard was covered in snow, and his exposed hands were weathered and rough. The smile revealed yellow and crooked teeth.

"What do you say?" the man asked.

"No, I don't feel comfortable with that."

The man's eyes betrayed the forced smile as they darted quickly to Kate's left and then to her right. Before she had a chance to move, two pairs of hands grabbed her by the arms and threw her against the side of a car.

The force of the impact triggered a snowfall from the roof, and Kate hit the ground on her hip. She tried to stand, but before she could catch her breath, more hands lifted her off the pavement, pinning her against the car.

Kate shook and thrashed her body as hard as she could, but she couldn't overpower the two men. A cold sharpness pressed against her throat, and Kate stopped. She saw the handle of the blade in her peripheral vision, held by the man with yellow, crooked teeth.

"Out here all by yourself," he said, his breath as rotten as the rest of him. He smiled, looking her up and down as he pressed his body into her. "Such a pretty thing."

Kate thrust her knee up quickly and connected with his groin. The knife fell from his hand as he hobbled backward, cupping his balls.

"Goddamn! Fucking bitch!" A strand of spit dangled from his lips, and he smeared it across the sleeve of his jacket. His friends snickered as he leaned against another car, groaning.

"Don't have your cup?" the man on Kate's left asked.

"Fuck you, Mitch."

Kate focused her strength and gave another burst of thrashing.

"Hey, now, whoa, let's calm down, little lady." Both men moved closer, pinning her arms at her sides and pressing their bodies against her until she couldn't move. "All that aggression is only going to make it harder."

"And make us harder," the man on her right said, spurts of squealing laughter blasting into her ear.

"Yeah," Mitch replied, straightening himself out, a smile returning to his face. "Real hard."

The pressure from the car made the gun in Kate's waistband dig into her back. All she needed to do was get one hand free.

Mitch wrapped his hand around her throat and thrust her head back harshly, barking to the two guys on either side of her. "Find a car with a big backseat. I don't want to fuck her in the snow."

"Afraid it might get even smaller?" Kate asked, grunting through her teeth.

The two men snickered, but Mitch brought the tip of his blade to Kate's jugular. "Find one, now!" They disappeared, tugging at door handles that were locked.

Mitch applied pressure to the blade, Kate's skin so cold it was numb to the metal's touch, but she felt the warm trickle of blood roll down her throat.

"You know, you're the second woman we ran into today," Mitch said, smiling. "The first one wasn't as pretty as you." He leaned close to her ear, whispering like an angry lover. "I'm glad I get to go first."

Kate flinched from the tickle of his hot breath. All her thoughts ran to the pistol. A car door opened.

"Hey, Mitch! I think I've got one!"

Mitch laughed, turning his focus to the other rapists, which removed the edge of the blade from her neck, and Kate quickly jerked left, her back scraping against the car she was pinned against, her right hand reaching for the pistol behind her back.

Mitch's meaty hands grabbed her left arm, tugging hard at the sleeve. But she had the pistol in her hand now, and she aimed, her finger inching over the trigger. Mitch's eyes widened at the sight of the gun, and he immediately let her go, but it was too late.

Kate fired. The pistol jerked wildly in her hand, and the bullet missed, skimming to the left. Mitch ran, but Kate used her left hand to help steady the weapon. She lined up her second shot and fired again.

Sparks popped on the hood of a BMW as the bullet chased Mitch through the traffic lanes as he fled with his tail between his legs. Kate still lay on the snow, arms thrust out stiffly with her finger on the trigger as she scanned for the remaining two men. She spotted the tops of their heads passing behind a truck two lanes over. She fired, shattering the truck's window.

A slew of curses filtered through the air, and the pair followed their ringleader back toward the overpass. They were well out of range, and Kate's aim was too poor to hit them even if they were closer, but she squeezed the trigger again for good measure but only shattered another car window.

Kate panted heavily, the cold and the adrenaline fraying her nerves. She didn't move from the ground until she couldn't see the men in the distance anymore. Only then did she lower the weapon and then stand.

Exhausted, she leaned against the same car that they had pinned her against. With a shaky hand, she grazed the cut on her neck and found the blood already dried in the cold. She leaned her head back, lifting her gaze to the grey skies.

Memories from the city flashed in her mind. She had fled New York to escape the madness and the clamoring of people doing whatever they needed for survival. But in the chaos and the collapse of law and order, she had discovered something worse than people who wanted to survive. People who wanted to take.

Kate shut her eyes, letting her pulse slow, gathering her strength. After a minute passed, she pushed off the car. Her boots crunched through the snow, and she shuffled forward toward the airfield. She kept the gun in her hand, her eyes alert for any more people she might run into. And without realizing it, she placed her finger on the trigger.

16

The added layers of clothes didn't do much. The cold ate through everything. The grey skies were bursting at the seams, dying to release their flurries of snow. And even farther north was a storm that would make this weather seem like a walk in the park. But they still had time. So long as they kept pace.

Rodney Klatt glanced behind him at the four travelers that had hitched their wagon to his cart. Each of them had their heads down, feet shuffling through the snow. He reached into his pocket and removed a silver pocket watch that dangled from a thin chain. He cradled it carefully then checked the time. They'd only been walking for three hours. He snapped it shut and then gently ran his gloved thumb over the engraving on the top. *Be better.*

It had been almost four years since his dad passed. The watch in his pocket and the cabin up north were the only things that were left of him. And the moment the EMP went off, he was thankful for both.

Rodney clapped his hands, his attempt at motivation. "We've got less than two days to make it to the cabin." He glanced back toward the northwestern skies, where that blizzard was gaining steam.

Yesterday morning, before the EMP went off, Rodney had checked the three-day weather forecast, just as he did every morning. Meteorologists were tracking a massive storm coming down from Canada. Some had predicted ten to twelve feet of snow by Monday along with hail and sleet. It wasn't something Rodney wanted to be caught in, but with the miles yet to travel, they were already cutting it close.

The quick crunch of boots on snow was followed by a hand on Rodney's shoulder. He turned to find Mark, huffing from the short run. "Hey, we need to take a break."

Rodney looked past Mark to find Glen leaning up against a sedan, his head flung back with an expression of pain etched on his face. Glen was pushing seventy. A young woman, Laura, walked over to him, her short blond hair completely tucked beneath her purple knit beanie. She was small but pretty. And in the middle of the road, resting on a sled they picked off a van in the northbound lane, was Mark's sick daughter, Holly.

"We can't afford to stop before nightfall." Rodney sidestepped Mark as if that was the end of it, but the man followed, blocking him again.

"It's like fifteen degrees outside. I can't feel my toes, and Glen looks like he's about to have a heart attack."

"We can't stop every time someone gets tired. We're on a tight schedule. The storm's coming."

"Five minutes," Mark said. "That's all we need."

Rodney shook his head and grunted. "Fine. Five minutes."

"Thanks." Mark returned to Glen and Laura, giving them the good news, and then checked on his little girl, bringing a bottle of water to her lips. His daughter had been sick when they left New York. It was dangerous moving her like this, out in the cold. But survival had a tendency to outweigh common sense, and after what they'd seen in New York, Rodney knew why they wanted to come.

Cities had once been a beacon of civilization, but now that beacon had turned into a blazing fire that burned anything and everything within its domain. Anywhere with large and isolated portions of people had transformed into the most dangerous and violent areas in the country. So Rodney and his motley crew were heading north, into the wilderness, as far away from cities as they could get.

The cabin had enough supplies to last them for a long time, because Rodney had been preparing for a long time. But even after all of that preparation, watching the world unravel still didn't seem real.

Rodney leaned up against a sedan. He turned and glanced inside and then snickered. It was nice, one of the luxury cars. He bet that whoever owned that Beemer would trade every penny they had for a warm fire and some food in their belly. Money, retirement accounts, investments—none of that stuff held any value anymore.

He set his pack down and reached for the canteen bottle. He took a few swigs, the water so cold it burned his tongue and throat. He fought the urge to drain the rest of it, knowing it'd have to last. Clean water wouldn't be a problem once they made it to the cabin, but there wasn't any guarantee they'd find fresh, drinkable water on their journey. The farther north they trekked, the fewer towns and homes they'd come across to scavenge.

He was glad to see that everyone was taking his advice, staying hydrated. The cold was deceptive when it came to exertion, but just because the temperature dropped didn't mean you stopped sweating. He reached for the pocket watch and checked the time. "All right. Break's over!"

"Just a few more minutes," Mark said, still knelt down by Holly.

Rodney pocketed his father's watch and adjusted the pack on his back, making his way over to the group. He moved quickly, but his haste did little to stir the group. "We need to get moving."

Glen winced as he stood from leaning on the car, and Laura helped steady him. "How much farther is it?"

"Far," Rodney answered, slightly annoyed.

Mark fiddled with the straps on Holly's sled, whispering something to her that Rodney couldn't hear.

"Mark," Rodney said. "Let's go."

"Just a minute," Mark said, struggling with the sled's straps.

Rodney exhaled. "We don't have time for this. We need to—"

"Just hang on!"

Laura jumped, and Rodney took a step back in surprise from the outburst, but just as quickly as the anger appeared, it subsided.

Mark slouched. "I'm sorry, I didn't—"

"How long can a person without water?" Rodney asked, arching his eyebrows. "Or food? Anyone know?" He looked to each of them in turn. "What about freezing to death? Anyone know how long that'll take?"

Mark stood, wiping his palms on his legs. "All right, Rodney, you've made your—"

"The nights up here will dip below zero," Rodney said, looking at Mark. "At negative ten degrees, with only ten miles per hour of wind, exposed skin will be frostbitten in less than twenty minutes." He pointed to Holly. "You want her caught in that?" He gestured to the rest of the group. "We'll freeze to death if we don't get north before that storm. And it won't matter how many layers we put on. We'll be buried in snow. Visibility will be cut down to nothing more than a few inches in front of your face. You can't even see where you're stepping. A twisted an ankle, a broken leg, and your dead out here. Now, you might not like the pace I'm setting, but I think you'll like the alternative even less."

Heads lowered, all but Mark's. He nodded and reached for the rope attached to Holly's sled. "All right, Rodney. You're the boss." He tugged the sled behind him, and Laura and Glen slowly followed his lead, leaving Rodney alone and in the back of the pack.

Rodney shut his eyes, releasing the tension in his hands and body, exhaling. He didn't ask for this. All he was trying to do was the right thing. The road ahead would be tough, but they needed to be tougher. He knew they didn't like it. He knew they resented him. But he also knew that they'd be dead without him.

Rodney fished out the pocket watch, reading the engraved words one more time. *Be better.* He closed his fist around the silver case and started forward. He wanted to carry it for a little while, hold it. It made it feel as though his dad were with him when he did that. Tough love ran in his family. And that watch helped remind him of his own.

* * *

DESPITE THE FRIGID COLD, Holly's body had transformed into a tiny furnace. Every couple of minutes, she groaned, rolling from side to side on the sled.

"It's okay, baby," Mark said, the rope pulled taut over his shoulder. "Just hang on." But the medicine he'd given her didn't seem to be helping. If anything, he thought her condition had grown worse. His eyes flashed toward the back of Rodney's head. He was barely older than Luke, and while Mark didn't like being led by the nose by a twentysomething, he liked the thought of his daughter freezing to death even less.

The thought of Luke quickly shifted his mind toward Kate on her journey south to pick up her son. He shook his head. *Our son.* A pain of guilt flooded through him at having to say it to himself.

Luke was a good boy who had come out of a bad situation. And Kate was a good mother who'd done the same. It wasn't until after they'd married that Kate finally told him what happened. And it made him sick to his stomach.

But it explained a lot about the restlessness of the woman

Mark had fallen in love with. She always needed to be on the move, almost as if she was afraid to stay in one place. He suspected it was one of the reasons why she'd taken to the life of a pilot. Always moving, seeing new places—there was a romantic notion to it.

But the constant moving, the school changes for the kids, him being forced to find work every couple of years, starting over again and again and again—it was daunting. So when he finally convinced to settle in one spot, Mark was ecstatic. But none of that mattered anymore.

He wondered if she had made it to the airfield and wondered more if she'd found a plane that actually worked. He didn't like the idea of her flying through the air by herself in little more than a tin box, but when she set her mind to something, it was nearly impossible to convince her otherwise. But she was a damned good pilot. And that was what he held onto to make himself feel better.

Mark remembered the first time she took him flying. It was a little prop plane that she owned but sold a few years back. Aside from Luke, he was the first man that wasn't a copilot to go up with her.

It was a beautiful day outside, but despite the view, he couldn't take his eyes off her. She looked so at ease in the sky, and it was amazing to see her in her natural element. He nearly pissed himself when the engine failed, though. It wasn't until he was screaming for his mother and she was laughing her ass off that she revealed she had cut the fuel. It took a long time for him to live that down.

After they landed, Kate kept fiddling with her shirt the way she did when she was nervous. He immediately thought it was because of the few choice words he'd said in the air when he thought they were going to die, but when he started to apologize, Kate kissed him hard on the lips. When she pulled back, she was crying. Before he asked what was wrong, she blurted out that she loved him for the first time.

Mark had already told her those words three months before, and it was the longest three months of his life. He knew about her past and how difficult it was to trust again, so when she finally said those three words, he didn't take it lightly. He proposed six months later.

It took some coaxing before Kate agreed to having another child. The scars that Dennis left behind had healed, but weren't forgotten. He knew she'd never forget.

Holly coughed, her chest rattling with phlegm, then sniffled and pulled the blanket closer to her chin.

"Glen, will you get the medicine out of my pack?" Mark asked. He couldn't reach himself without stopping, and he wasn't in the mood for another lecture from their fearless leader.

"Is this it?" Glen asked, thrusting the bottle at Mark's face.

"Yeah," Mark answered. "Go ahead and give her one pill."

Mark didn't like the fact that the medicine wasn't helping. He didn't like the fact that his wife was heading hundreds of miles in the opposite direction. And he sure as shit didn't like the fact that he was being led by a guy who, up until yesterday, he barely knew.

"She's not getting better?" Glen asked, appearing at Mark's side and pretending not to wince with every step.

"I don't think so, but it's hard to tell," Mark answered.

"It's not too late to turn back," Glen said, a hint of hope in his voice. "We could be back at the camp before nightfall."

The "camp" Glen referred to was a makeshift shantytown with a few tents set up and run by a doctor. There was zero organization and enough food and water to last everyone a few more days. The doctor running it was betting on help showing up before that happened. But after what Mark had seen in the city, he knew help arriving was a long shot.

"If we change the plan now, then it messes with Kate's return." Which Mark hoped would be sooner rather than later.

"Rodney's been right about a lot of things so far. Not that he needs reminding of it."

Glen chuckled. "He's a young man but a good one." He rubbed his knobby, arthritic hands. "He could have left us to die, but he chose to take us with him. That's not a man I mind following."

Laura appeared on Mark's other side, her head down, and she wiped her nose, which had turned a bright cherry red. "He doesn't have to be so angry all the time, though, does he?"

"He's just inexperienced as a leader," Glen answered, keeping his voice low. Rodney had a good lead on them, but the quiet of the road made their voices feel louder. "He'll get better as he learns."

"Well, he could learn to say please every now and then." Laura kept her head down and gently prodded her lips. "It's so cold I can't feel anything."

"We just need to keep moving," Mark said, addressing them both. "The quicker we get to the cabin, the quicker we can put our feet up for a while and wait for all of this to blow over."

"You really think that?" Laura asked. "That this will blow over?"

"The country's been through tough times before," Glen answered, still limping along. "The Civil War, the Great Depression, both world wars. We've persevered through it all. We can get through this."

"But nothing's working!" Laura said, flipping off her hoodie and exposing the blond pixie haircut underneath. "No phones, no cars, no power. It's never been *this* bad."

"It has," Rodney said, still walking ahead of them, though the distance between them was shorter now. Without realizing it, Mark had caught up to him. "We didn't have power until the late nineteenth century. Technology still exists. It's just not what most people are used to." He turned around, stopping. "Over two thousand years ago, the Greeks had running water and sewage systems in their cities. They had specialized farming techniques and grew into one of the world's most powerful empires."

"So what?" Laura said. "We're supposed to be excited over the fact that we'll be dressing in togas in the summer?"

"I'm saying that people have ingenuity. Glen is right. People always find a way to survive. And plus, we have something the Greeks, the Romans, and the Aztecs didn't have."

"And what's that?" Laura asked.

"Knowledge. We have everything we need to start over, to rebuild. It's all just sitting around us in books, waiting to be relearned." Rodney looked at each of them in turn. "We're going to live. But if you don't believe that, then there isn't anything I can do for you."

Rodney turned and restarted his march north. The rest of them lingered for a moment, and it was Glen who spoke first.

"The boy's right," he said firmly, accentuating the affirmation with a hearty grunt. "It doesn't mean a damn what happens to us if we don't believe we can make it." He adjusted his pack and started forward. "We march on!"

Mark smiled at the sight of the old man and adjusted the rope on his shoulder. He looked back at Holly, who'd fallen asleep. He glanced over at Laura. "What do you say? You think we can make it?"

Laura shrugged then flipped up her hood. "I just want to get out of the cold." She stomped forward, her shoes crunching in the snow.

"Me too, kid," Mark said under his breath, following. "Me too."

17

The soles of her feet ached as Kate limped down the road. She still held the pistol, but like her feet, her fingers had gone numb around the weapon. Fatigue forced her head down, and it wasn't until she heard the murmur of voices on the horizon that she looked up.

The airfield was up ahead. Planes and jets dotted the sprawling fields, which had become whitewashed with snow. Thousands of people wandered aimlessly between the useless aircraft. And the closer Kate grew, the more those murmurs turned into dissent.

A plane wreck smoldered up on her left, and two more blanketed the field on her right. Nothing but shreds of metal were left, the aircraft, and presumably its passengers, smashed to smithereens. Car wrecks thickened the road the closer she moved toward the airfield's entrance, and so did the crowd.

With all the eyes watching, Kate tucked the pistol back inside her coat. She darted through the crowd, weaving her way deeper into the hangars on the field.

Whatever security the airfield possessed was no longer in place. Luggage and cars were parked right next to planes, and a line of jets was being pulled by ropes. Pilots and mechanics were hunched over open engine covers, tools on the ground, and the hands meant to use them were instead scratching heads.

Families huddled together in cars, children staring at the blank screens of phones. Empty oil drums had been placed along the airfield, billowing smoke from orange flames as people gathered around them for warmth.

A fight broke out past the fuel tanks, two men ramming fists into one another while their respective groups tried to pull them apart. Kate noted the red gas cans that each group held, and then scurried past before she was sucked into a brawl.

Tension and frustration had reached the boiling point. Fear was guiding people's decisions now. And Kate didn't want to be anywhere near here when those primal instincts surfaced. She'd seen enough of that in the city.

Kate slipped past unnoticed and headed for the south end of the field, away from the modern jets and planes that required circuit boards and digital navigation displays to pilot the skies. Judging by the way everyone was still standing around, it looked as though no one had thought of trying older planes as she had. Either that, or the old planes were already gone.

The silver hangar where she remembered that the old planes were stored was the last hangar on the left. The closer she drew to it, the faster she ran, and with only a few dozen yards left, she broke into a sprint, drawing attention be damned.

Shadows kept the inside of the hangar hidden, and it wasn't until Kate stepped inside and her vision adjusted to the darkness that her heart sank.

Empty. Not a single prop plane left. Canvas tarps littered the floor, and Kate lifted one up as if she could find one of the planes still hidden beneath. She dropped the tarp and then collapsed to the floor with it.

This was her chance, her one idea to get her son back. Walking wasn't an option, and neither was driving. She could find a bicycle maybe, but that would still take too long. Flying was her best chance, and now that had disappeared.

A heavy clang echoed outside the hangar walls, followed by an angry voice that muttered a flurry of curses. Kate arched an eyebrow and pushed herself off the cold concrete. She ventured out of the hangar and stepped around the side, following the random curses and clanks, which grew louder the closer she moved.

When Kate rounded the corner of the hangar's wall, a propeller came into view. The engine hatch was open, and Kate recognized the red-and-blue coloring of the rest of the plane. She'd seen it in the air show last spring.

It was a 1946 Commonwealth Skyranger 185. It was a single-pilot aircraft but could transport two people and had a range of around six hundred miles with a cruising speed of around one hundred miles per hour. Fairfax, Virginia, was around two hundred and twenty miles from the airfield. She could fly there and back before nightfall, with just enough fuel to make it to the cabin. Which was good, because it didn't look like the fuel pumps were working either.

Kate's eyes drifted to the gas cans near the tail of the plane then darted toward the cabin when she heard another sputtering curse as a pair of legs dangled out of the cockpit, kicking angrily.

"Damned machine!" The legs wiggled ferociously yet impotently, as they couldn't yet touch the ground. "Help!"

Kate darted over, grabbed hold of the pair of legs, and guided the man down, revealing an old man with snow-white hair sticking straight up, a pair of glasses sitting crookedly on his face. His cheeks were a cherry red, and a few stray whiskers protruded from his chin. He flattened his shirt, which had ridden up his stomach and chest, and then adjusted his glasses.

"Thank you," he said, still panting heavily. "I just don't seem to get in and out of there as easy as I used to." He glanced up at the plane and then gave it a few hearty pats. He was shorter than Kate, barely over five feet. "The old gal can be more stubborn than my late wife." He laughed at the joke, and Kate smiled. He extended his hand. "Roger Haywell."

"Kate Hillman." After they shook, she tried not to eyeball the craft too obviously. "Mr. Haywell, I'd like to buy your plane from you."

Roger laughed. "It's not for sale." He walked toward the tail and wiped his hands with an old rag.

Kate followed him. "Then I'd like to rent it from you for the next few hours."

Roger sighed, dropped the rag, and then placed his hands on his hips. "Young lady, you seem smarter than all of those other buffoons standing next to those jets, wondering why in the sam hell they're not working, so I'd like you to extend to me the same courtesy." He raised his thick white eyebrows when she didn't answer. "You and I both know that if I give you this plane, I'm not getting it back."

For a brief second, Kate thought of the pistol at her back in her waistband. All she had to do was shoot the man and then hop in the plane. She was close enough now to see that the gas cans were empty, which meant that the plane was fueled. And the old Skyranger was close enough to the field for her to wheel it over by herself. The more time she spent bickering with this old man was less time she had to get Luke.

And then she frowned, her cheeks reddening with shame. She stepped back from the old man, shaking her head. So she'd just take what she wanted because she could? If she did that, then she was no better than the men who attacked her on the road.

A sudden pain split through her head, and the past twenty-four hours caught up with her. She lowered her hand from her temple. "I need to get to Fairfax, Virginia."

"Virginia?" Roger asked, surprised. "Sweetheart, you don't want to go down there. It's a goddamn war zone."

"What?" Flashes of Luke lying in rubble, bloodied and dead, played in her mind. She gripped the old man by the shoulders, unaware of how hard she was squeezing him. "What's happened?"

Roger gently lifted his hands and removed Kate's arms from his shoulders. "There was a national guard unit that was stationed up here that marched through yesterday evening. Said they were ordered to go down and reinforce the capital. Whoever started all of this means to finish it."

The color drained from Kate's face, and she wobbled unsteadily on her feet, using the plane to keep herself from falling.

"Ma'am, are you all right?"

Kate swallowed, trying to steady her voice. "My son is down there." Tears were on the cusp of pouring down her cheeks, but she drew in a breath and fought them back. "Do you have children, Roger?"

"I do," he answered solemnly. "Three. They're all on the west coast." He chuckled and then looked off into the distance. "Got as far away from me as they possibly could, I suppose."

"Then help me," Kate said, pulling Roger's attention back to her.

Roger crossed his arms. "So you want to just take my plane and fly down into a war zone and try and find your son, who you have no way of contacting to see if he's even still there?" Roger gave a gut-busting burst of laughter and stepped back from Kate, shaking his head. "You know, I used to think my first ex-wife was the craziest woman to ever walk the earth, but she'll be glad to know I was wrong." He passed her and returned to the door to the cockpit. He paused and then tossed a glare back at Kate. "I assume you know how to fly."

"I've flown everything from seaplanes to 747s," Kate said, looking past Roger and to the Skyranger. "But none of them were this long in the tooth."

"Well, you're never too old to learn new things," Roger said, stepping inside the cabin. "I'll show you the controls."

Kate pulled on his shoulder. "You're letting me take it?"

"Listen, crazy woman, don't let me second-guess myself here, all right? And besides," he said, turning back toward the cabin door. "I wouldn't want you to shoot me with that .38 special in the back of your waistband."

Kate frowned and then reached back toward the weapon to make sure it was still there. "How'd you know I was carrying a gun?"

"I was a cop for thirty-five years," Roger said, focusing on the screwdriver in his hand, placing the control panel over the gauges. "And from the smell of things, it sounds like you've already had to use it today." He cast her a side-eye. "I suppose I should be thankful that action wasn't repeated on me."

"It was self-defense," Kate said. "I didn't want to add to the noise unless I had to."

Roger smiled. "I suppose I could be giving my plane away to someone less worthy." He finished screwing the cover back over the console. "She's pretty stubborn, so don't be afraid to knock her around a bit." Roger rattled the stick around like a concrete stirrer. "But she'll bite you back if you push it too hard. Just fiddle around with it for a bit while you're up there, and I'm sure you'll get the hang of it."

"Right," Kate said.

The rest of the controls were basic and self-explanatory as Roger went over them. Fuel, altimeter, airspeed indicator, turn and bank indicator, vertical speed indicator, artificial horizon, heading indicator. All completely analog, along with its engine.

"And you're sure it starts?" Kate asked. "I mean, have you tried it yet?"

"And grab the attention of those nut jobs down there? No." Roger opened his side door and nearly fell out before he managed to steady himself on the edge of the plane. Once he safely had both feet on the ground, Kate stepped out.

"So how do you know it'll work?" Kate asked.

"The same reason you were looking for one of these old planes, sweetheart." Roger tapped the engine casing. "Everything that has stopped working has a computer chip in it. My neighbor has an old 1959 Chevy, and while his wife's new Malibu wouldn't start, his fired up just fine. Whatever those people did was meant to wipe out our modern conveniences." He paused and then stared down the growing hordes of people arriving at the private airfield, hoping for a ride. "I heard people willing to pay all sorts of things for a ride out of here or to go and pick up family. Houses, investment fortunes, savings accounts—all of them were willing to empty everything for a chance to see someone that just yesterday they could have called on the phone."

Kate followed the old man's gaze and knew that the moment the engine started, they'd be swarmed. Having a plane that worked was akin to having a target strapped to her back, something she'd have to remember once she landed in Fairfax. "We'll need to push it over to the strip. And we'll need to do it quickly." She turned back to the old man. "It's already fueled, right?"

"Topped it off when I got here," Roger answered. "She should make it the full six hundred miles of range, but she's been prone to leakage lately, so I wouldn't push her past five hundred."

Kate bit her lip. That was pushing it. She ran the calculations through her head again. "It'll get me close enough." She climbed inside the cockpit and got a feel for the stick. "Walk me through the ignition sequence."

It only took her one try to get it down, and then she loaded her pack into the storage compartment and kicked off the blocks in front of the wheels. "You take the left wing, and I'll take the right."

They pushed the plane out to the field, and the moment they emerged from hiding, Kate looked toward the huddled masses and the graveyard of dead planes. They were far enough away to where she couldn't see the detail of their faces, but still she felt their stares.

Once on the stretch of field she'd use as a runway, Kate retreated toward the tail. "All right, let's straighten it out."

Snow broke free from the sky in lazy drifts, and once they had a clear path on the runway, Roger plugged in a starter for the engine. "Make sure you pump the primer three times. Any more, and she'll flood. Any less, and you'll have to use another starter."

Kate flashed a thumbs-up from the cockpit and pushed the rubber bulge three times. "Primer set!" She watched the old man reach for the prop to pull down, and just beyond him, a crowd had gathered along the field. They were pointing at her.

Roger pulled down on the prop hard, a series of firework-like pops belted from the engine, and the propeller spun wildly in front of her windshield, slightly distorting the field of view. She glanced over to Roger, who pointed up and to the left of the airfield and then wildly gestured for her to take off.

Hundreds more had gathered at the field's edge, and then a dozen men burst from the sideline, each of their hands holding something. It wasn't until she heard the first gunshot that she realized they were guns.

Roger banged on the door, making Kate jump, screaming at her to take off. She reached for the throttle and shoved it forward.

The plane's speed ticked up slowly, and the snow fell in heavier drifts. Kate bounced around the inside of the cockpit as the plane tumbled down the grassy runway. The gunmen drew closer, closing the gap, their weapons aimed, their screams muted by the engine.

The old Skyranger hopped, gaining some lift as the speed increased, but then thumped back onto grass and snow. A gust of wind vibrated the plane fiercely from the east and lifted the left side up. It flew up three feet before Kate corrected with the foot pedals and the stick, leaning her body into the turn that leveled the craft back to the ground.

Another gunshot fired, and Kate saw the gunmen were directly parallel with her now and close enough for her to see their expressions of panic. Their faces were filled with the same wild fear she had seen on the people in New York on the metro train, and then the bridge, and finally the docks where she barely escaped with her family and her life.

The Skyranger lifted again, this time with a steadier angle, and Kate jerked back hard on the stick. The engine whined in frustration from the steep climb, but between the gunmen and the end of the runway, Kate was out of time.

Another gunshot sounded, and a harsh thump immediately reverberated through the cabin, but it didn't matter. Kate glanced down at her altimeter, which climbed to twenty feet, then fifty feet, then ninety feet as she continued her angle toward the sky. She was off the ground. She was flying.

18

The cold was a relentless bitch. It curled its icy grip around everything it touched and numbed the mind and body. It clouded thoughts and judgment and made you slow and cumbersome, and Dennis wasn't sure how much more of it he could take.

Sleep had evaded him the night before, but by the time he awoke in the backseat of the Mercedes he found abandoned on the highway, the sun had been up for a long time. He groaned from the ache in his bones as he reached for the bottle of water he found in the backseat. It was half drunk, but it did the job of keeping him alive. He still hadn't found any food other than chips and crackers. He had walked all day yesterday, stealing what he could find to keep warm and alive.

The water had nearly frozen in the night, and Dennis felt the few chunks of ice that floated through the bottle's mouth and down his throat. He drained it and chucked it on the floorboard.

The windows of the sedan were frosted over, blocking his view to the outside. He wasn't sure how many other inmates were still here.

After the escape from the prison, anyone in an orange jump-suit huddled together, everyone weaving their way through the forest. But once they reached the road, people started to break apart. No one understood what had happened, and even if they did, they were too cold to care.

It was like the world had stopped. No matter where they turned, nothing worked. No phones. No cars. Nothing.

The freezing masses of inmates had a string of theories that worked their way through the ranks: aliens, invasion, some kind of super virus, the second coming, the final apocalypse. But while the bulk of the inmates chattered like schoolgirls, Dennis noticed a common thread—computers.

At first he thought it might have been just limited to the prison, but after seeing the cars and the phones and computers that he found left behind and broken. And the more he thought about it, the more sense it made. The prison was run on computers, and so were most cars nowadays. Hell, everything had some type of computer component to it, right?

Power plants, water treatment facilities, planes, every major consumer good or convenience were all attached to a grid that was run by software. But who had done it and why didn't matter. Hell, this was a godsend.

A fist knocked on the window, snapping Dennis out of his stupor. "Hey! You up?"

Dennis forced himself to an upright position, but the door opened before he could even reach it. A head poked inside, covered in a frost-thickened beard, dark circles beneath a pair of angry blue eyes. "What the fuck are you doing? Everyone's freezing their asses off out here. We going or what?"

Dennis kicked the door with his foot, flinging Jimmy back with it. "Yeah, we're fucking going." He grunted on his exit from the car and squinted back behind him to the sight of a few dozen men wrapped in whatever jackets they could find, but nearly everyone still in their orange jumpsuits underneath. Dennis included.

Jimmy stepped forward, those blue eyes as sharp as the bits of ice that formed in his beard. He was a wiry, energetic man, and the moment everyone started talking when they exited the forest, Jimmy was the first to point out that Dennis had a gun and that he had been the one to suggest using the dead bodies to rush the guards.

It was a thin thread to leadership, but the dumbasses behind him figured that it was enough to follow him. Over the course of yesterday and last night, almost half of the group they'd started with had disappeared. They slipped away in ones, twos, and threes, leaving without a word or cause.

One of the men behind him, a big man with a beard that stretched down to his chest, snuffed out the cigarette he was puffing and broke from the group of guys he was chatting up. He was really the only reason the majority of the people had stayed. John Mulls was Dennis's one friend in prison, and the pair had formed a strong relationship over the years. He was an older guy, and Dennis supposed that he looked at him like a son of sorts. But all Dennis cared about was the fact that after Mulls became his friend, the raping stopped. That was the only sign of friendship he needed.

"We rounded up as much food as we could get from the cars like you said." Mulls heaved a pillowcase onto the Mercedes's trunk. "Wasn't much. We need to find a place to recharge, or these guys aren't gonna hang around for much longer."

Dennis rummaged through the pillowcase with the hand that wasn't holding the gun. "I don't know why we need them at all."

"Hey!" Mulls stepped close, gritting his teeth. "We don't know what the hell is going on, and we've got a better chance of survival if we stick together." He frowned, looking Dennis up and down. "You'd have known that if you had any type of loyalty on the inside."

Dennis pulled out a Slim Jim and snapped into it greedily. "You were the only friend I needed, Mulls." He forced a smile then waved everyone forward. "C'mon, fellas! Breakfast is ready!"

The group limped forward like a zombie horde, rummaging through the sack of chips, crackers, dried meats, and nuts.

While the rest of the men ate, Mulls pulled Dennis to the side. "So where are we heading? We've got to be coming up to a town somewhere soon, right?"

Dennis practically swallowed the last few bites of his Slim Jim whole. He reached inside his jacket and pulled out a map. "I found this in the glove box. I had to check a dozen cars just to find one." With most cars coming with GPS, maps had gone the way of the dodo. He spread the old New York map across the Mercedes hood, shivering from the cold as he did. "Twelve miles south, we run into Duluth. It looks small, but we'll find something better than the backseat of a frozen car."

Mulls exhaled, an icy puff of air forming around his lips. "Christ, I miss the South. It never snowed in New Orleans."

Once breakfast was finished, Dennis led the slow stumble down the highway toward Duluth. Most of the men only nodded when he told them the plan, but a few still looked in high spirits. Dennis was sure the road ahead and the continued cold would take care of that, though.

And so they walked. What they were walking toward or why they were walking, Dennis still didn't know, but he had an itch to see people again, preferably a woman. But even aside from the itch of getting laid was the itch to see what the world had become, regardless of its momentary pause. He hadn't been outside that prison for eighteen years. Just from what he'd seen with some of the cars on the road, he could tell things had changed, and he wanted to see more.

And maybe old Mulls was right. The men at his back numbered close to forty, and a quarter of them were armed, stealing weapons off the dead guards on their way out. It was more than enough to handle any trouble up here.

Mile after mile passed, and the longer they trudged, the quieter the group became. A blast of icy wind froze Dennis in his tracks, and it wasn't until the gust ended that he started up again.

His feet had grown numb in the paper-thin material of his prison-issued shoes. Bits of ice formed over the thin orange pants, and everything below the waist was numb. Dennis grabbed his crotch, his fingers fumbling over his member, and prayed that frostbite take anything but that.

His lips quivered and turned blue. After a while, he wasn't cold anymore, and he knew that was a bad sign. Hypothermia was setting in, and if they didn't find a warm place soon, he might drop dead on the asphalt.

An elbow nudged Dennis, and he looked over to find Mulls pointing up ahead. "Hey, what's that?"

Dennis squinted, finding a green exit sign. The name of the town below it read Duluth, and next to it was another blue sign with the symbols for food, gas, and lodging.

A murmur rippled through the men, heads lifting at the sight of civilization. The cars thickened around the exit, and Dennis felt a jolt of adrenaline thrust him toward it, the same chemical imbalance propelling the inmates to follow him.

The embankment of the turn-off was clogged with cars, all of them abandoned. Ice and snow made the slope slick, and Dennis used the cars to help guide him safely toward the two-lane road that led off the highway.

He reached into his jacket, removing the map. He unfurled it quickly, like an eager child opening a present. "Shit! Which way is east?"

"That way," Mulls pointed, huffing and puffing as he joined Dennis on the road, more and more men following in their path.

"Less than a mile," Dennis said, smiling. "Hear that, boys? Party in Duluth tonight!"

The icy grip of winter was shattered as cheers erupted and fists thrust into the afternoon sky. The pack sensed prey, and they were ready to feast. And Dennis prayed that what they found in Duluth was worth their while, because he wasn't sure how much longer this pack was going to stick together.

* * *

GLASS SHATTERED THEN FELL to the carpet inside the house. Rodney had banged on the door for a solid minute, and when no one answered, he decided that no one was home. He knocked away the shards alongside the paneling and then thrust his hand through and grabbed hold of the lock. It clicked when he turned it, and he gently swung the door open.

Mark, Glen, and Laura stood behind Rodney, Mark carrying his daughter on his shoulder.

"Hello?" Rodney's voice echoed in the darkness, but like the knocks on the door, his question remained unanswered. "I think it's clear."

The others followed him inside, and Rodney did a quick sweep of the house while everyone piled into the living room. From what he gathered, it was a vacation home, seeing as how most of the cabinets were bare and there weren't many decorations on the wall.

After his quick sweep, Rodney returned to the living room and found everyone huddled by the fireplace. Mark was already stacking some logs in it, and both Glen and Laura stared at it longingly, as though they could wish a fire into existence. Mark wiped his nose and then extended his hand to Rodney.

"Matches?" Mark asked.

"And what makes you think I have matches?"

Mark dropped his head but kept his hand extended. "C'mon, man. Just give me the matches."

But instead, Rodney bypassed Mark, leaving him hanging, and knelt in front of the fire himself. "I don't want to have you waste the whole packet before we actually get a fire started." He picked up the logs, rearranging them into a cube-like structure.

He rose and then headed toward the door. "I'm gonna go find some tinder."

Despite Rodney's eyes adjusting to the darkness, he was still amazed at how black night had become now that the power was off. After he'd spent so much time in New York City, his eyes had become polluted from the constant stream of lights and activity.

He glanced down the darkened road that they'd used to turn off the highway. He'd picked the spot knowing that housing was sparse and what homes were out here had a lot of space between them. They'd made good time today, but he still would have preferred to be farther north.

For most people, it was a natural instinct to want to gather, cluster up in towns and groups. And while Rodney might have indulged that instinct a fair amount with the group he acquired getting out of the city, he wasn't willing to add any more travelers to his destination.

Most of the trees in the surrounding lots were dead, and he managed to find a few dry twigs that he snapped off to use for kindling and then scooped up some dead leaves, making sure to leave the damp ones in the snow. After he had what he thought was enough, he trudged back into the house.

Inside, his companions rubbed their hands together quickly in anticipation of the warmth to come. All of them were huddled close behind him, eager for the flames, but Rodney didn't rush it. Only when he had a good foundation and made sure the chimney vents were open did he strike a match.

The leaves went up quickly, and Rodney made sure to breathe air into the fire, stoking it until the kindling caught. From there, the logs grew warm, and then caught fire.

A sigh of relief echoed from nearly every mouth, and the five of them huddled next to the glow of the flames, as their ancestors had done for thousands of years before electricity.

With the exception of Mark's daughter, everyone was awake, though Glen looked to be fading quickly. Rodney reached into his pack and passed around some jerky. "Make it last. We still have at least another full day of hard walking ahead."

Hands reached for the food carefully.

"How much farther?" Laura asked, chewing little pieces of the jerky and staring into the fire.

"Forty miles, probably a little less. Longer if that storm catches us."

"You think we'll make it?" Glen asked, rubbing his eyes.

"If we hustle, yeah. But we can't have any slowdowns." Rodney locked eyes with Glen. "No matter how tired we get." He addressed the rest of the group. "We can rest when we get to the cabin. We all saw what happened in New York."

"We know, Rodney," Mark said, the fire flicking light on only the left side of his face. "No need for scare tactics."

"I'm not trying to scare anyone." Rodney got up. "But the truth sounds like that to some people." He looked at the rest of the group. "Get some rest. Morning will come early." He gestured to the couch in the room. "Holly can sleep there unless I find a mattress."

He left the group in the living room and found two twin beds in a bedroom in the rear of the house. He picked one of the mattresses off the frame and then dragged it from the room. He passed the kitchen and saw the glow of the fire spilling out of the living room when he stopped. They were whispering to one another.

Curiosity forced Rodney to put the mattress down slowly and then creep to the end of the hall. He leaned as close as he could, being mindful of his shadow. He closed his eyes and concentrated on their voices.

"Why can't we stay here?" Laura asked. "I mean, we hardly know him."

"And he hardly knows us," Mark answered. "Glen is right. He helped get us out of the city, and he's gotten us this far. He might be hard, but he's got a lot of pressure on him right now."

"What pressure?" Laura asked.

"Keeping us alive."

Rodney quietly retreated toward the mattress and sat down. He wiped the tears forming in his eyes before they could fall. Slow, deep breaths calmed him down, but he gave himself a minute to make sure his eyes didn't stay red.

Despite his preparation, he'd never truly been in this type of situation before. They were scared. He was scared. And what Mark had said was true. It wasn't as though he wanted to be the bad guy. But he didn't want anyone to die. Not on his watch.

Rodney gave himself another minute and then lifted the mattress and dragged it back into the living room. The whispers ended by the time he returned, and he plopped the mattress just behind Laura. "There's another one in the room back there. You and Glen can take them, and Holly can take the sofa. Me and Mark will take the floor." He looked over at Mark. "Didn't think you'd mind."

"At least it'll be warm." Mark pushed himself off the floor. "I'll give you a hand."

Rodney led him to the room, and as they positioned themselves on either end of the bed, Mark paused before they lifted it off the frame. "You're doing a good job. Despite my complaints."

Rodney felt the tears coming again and was thankful for the darkness. He knew Mark couldn't see his face, but just to be sure, he kept his head down. "I appreciate that."

"I'm serious."

Rodney looked up.

"You saved my family in that city. For that, I owe you everything."

"Well," Rodney said, starting to feel uncomfortable, "what was I supposed to do?" He cleared his throat and then gripped his end of the mattress. "We should get this moved."

They brought it into the living room, and it didn't take but thirty seconds for everyone to pass out. But while the others slept, Rodney lay restless. For most of his life, he'd stayed behind the walls he'd built for himself. He was safe behind those walls, protected. But now he had ventured from their safety, and he was with people he didn't know, in a world that wasn't recognizable. And no matter how much he wanted to, he couldn't go back behind those walls anymore. They were gone. And just before exhaustion finally took hold, Rodney whispered a little prayer to not screw it up.

19

The temperature inside the cockpit had dropped dramatically once night fell. The bitter cold ate through the layers and gnawed at Kate's bones. The altitude only made the cold worse. She had shivered for the past two hours. But recently that had stopped, and it wasn't because she was suddenly warmer.

Hypothermia wasn't a welcome passenger, not if she wanted to land this plane safely. She looked at the small wind-up watch she found beneath the dashboard after she was in the air to check her progress. Based off her speed, it was another twenty minutes before she was in Fairfax.

The trip had taken longer than expected because she adjusted her flight path to avoid the DC airspace. After what Roger had said about the capital being a war zone, she didn't want to risk making herself a target for either the terrorists or the United States military. But everything she'd experienced so far told her that she was alone in the sky.

There was no radio chatter, no other planes. And when she peered toward the ground, it was blanketed with darkness, which was going to provide trouble when it came time to land.

But the weather had held out, and despite the cold and loneliness, it was a beautiful night to fly.

Kate wiggled in her seat, trying to get the blood pumping again, and her thoughts drifted to Mark and Holly. She wondered how close they were to the cabin. She wondered if Holly was feeling better. She wondered if they were even still alive.

Stop it.

Of course they were still alive. Rodney knew what he was doing. They'd all still be fighting for their lives in the city if it weren't for him. The shivers returned after a few minutes of moving around, and she exhaled relief. She wasn't freezing to death. Not yet, at least.

It had been a while since she was up in the air like this, alone. At least six years. She'd forgotten how much she enjoyed it. There was something intimate about flying a two-seater by yourself.

She remembered her first solo flight at night. It was cross country. No flight instructor to help her prepare the aircraft, just her and the plane.

She had flown from Atlanta to Phoenix, and it was the first of many hours logged that she needed to acquire for her pilot's license. It was the worst mixture of excitement and nerves that she'd ever experienced. Earlier that day, she had dropped Luke off at the house of a friend whom she used frequently to watch him while she was attending school. He was two at the time and going through that "terrible" phase so popular among toddlers.

But that day when Kate dropped him off, he called for her just when she was at the door. Kate stopped, turned, and watched Luke sprint over on his chubby little legs, and he flung his arms around her knees.

"I love you, Mom." He raised his head and smiled. "Fly good."

Kate scooped him up off the floor and kissed him until he squealed. And that was all it took for the nerves to disappear.

Because as much as she enjoyed flying and for as long as she had wanted to be a pilot, there was a different purpose to her flight education once Luke was born. She was flying so she could make sure her kid had food and clothes and shelter.

The flight had gone off without a hitch, and she landed safely in Phoenix, finishing her required solo trip with ease. The next week, she took her pilot's exam and passed with flying colors. It was the beginning of something great for her and her son. And for the first time in a long time, she didn't have to look back on the past and dwell on it. The higher she flew, the farther she separated herself from her past mistakes. And even after all the years since, she was still flying for her son.

Kate descended to fifteen hundred feet so she had a better view of the ground. Her eyes had slowly adjusted to the dark, but it was still difficult to find a suitable landing site. After ten minutes, she saw a field break the monotony of trees. It was more box than rectangle, but it was still doable.

She practiced her approach twice, making sure that she had the timing down. With no lights, no tower, and in a plane that was older than her grandfather, she couldn't afford a mistake. And then, knowing it was as good as it could get, Kate began her final approach and descent.

The altimeter wound down, and Kate used it until the last four hundred feet, and then she eyeballed it, making sure she had clearance of the trees. The stick rumbled defiantly in her hands, but she kept the plane steady. The nose dipped twice, the engine waning and waxing due to the wobbly descent. She cleared the tree line on the field's edge and then dropped quickly, knowing her runway was short.

Kate pulled on the stick to level out, and the cockpit rumbled as the wheels made contact. She pulled back on the throttle quickly, hitting the brakes before she ran out of field, exhaling as she slowed to a stop.

Kate cut the engine, peeling her fingers off the stick. Stiff from the cold, she groaned as she exited the aircraft and landed awkwardly on her feet. Her back hurt, and a spasm from her hip made her wince on impact, but she was alive. She'd made it.

With the plane's engine cut, and the roar of the wind gone, the night was dead quiet. No cars, no people, no bugs, just silence. And in this kind of quiet, anyone within twenty miles would have heard her plane landing, and that was attention she could do without.

Kate searched the edge of the woods and found a small clearing in the trees. With some strained effort, she managed to push the Skyranger into it. Between the darkness, trees, and the branches she found, the plane was fairly well hidden.

One final sweep of the cockpit provided her with the map and her pack, and she checked the remaining bullets in her revolver. Only three shots left. She snapped the barrel shut and prayed that she wouldn't have to use any of them then limped into the forest.

The woods that surrounded the field were thick. Clusters of branches and bushes clawed at her arms and legs, doing their best to trap her in the wilderness. And despite her efforts to be quiet, each stomp of her boot and snap of a twig gave away her position for anyone within a mile's range.

The darkness and quiet of the woods put Kate on edge. Any gust of wind or rustle of leaves caused her to freeze in terror. She'd scan the forest with her eyes focused down the barrel of the gun and wait until she was sure she was alone, and then she would trudge forward.

Eventually, trees gave way to an embankment that led up to a road. Like the roads to the north, this one was littered with broken-down vehicles on both sides of the highway.

Kate walked a few hundred feet south in the direction of Fairfax and the campus and double-checked the road sign she found to make sure she was on the right path. Once she confirmed her heading, Kate broke into a jog. It took a few minutes to shake off the rust and push past the staleness of her muscles, but eventually she fell into a stride.

Every step toward the college brought with it anxiousness and excitement. She followed the exit sign off the highway that led her to Fairfax's main road, which led straight to George Mason's campus.

The graveyard of cars along the roads spilled onto the sidewalks, and it grew so thick that Kate was forced to walk, not that she was moving much quicker than that anymore.

Kate passed stores with broken windows, and her boots crunched on trash and snow. It was just as quiet in the town as it was in the forest. She kept a tight grip on her revolver, and her eyes alert in the darkness. Something felt off here.

A barrage of gunshots suddenly broke the night's silence, and Kate ducked behind the hood of a truck. The gunfire was distant, but it was quickly disrupted by a thunderous boom. Slowly, Kate lifted her head, the gunfire growing more sporadic, and another boom erupted on the horizon. It was coming from the direction of the capital.

With her focus on the sounds of war, Kate didn't hear the footsteps following her, and a massive weight tackled her to the pavement.

Kate whimpered just before her face planted into the pavement, thankful for the layer of snow that helped break her fall.

"Don't move, and keep your hands behind your back."

The voice was authoritative, male, and robotic.

Kate's arms were pinned, and a sharp pinch squeezed both wrists. She gasped and then tasted the blood dripping from her nose.

"Hostile secure, Sergeant Renly."

And then, just as quickly as she was slammed to the ground, pairs of hands lifted her off the pavement and held her upright.

Kate blinked, the pain from the fall lingering in the cold, but as her eyes adjusted, she saw four men surrounding her, all of them armed with rifles and decked out in camouflage. It wasn't until one of them started speaking to her that she realized they were soldiers. American soldiers.

"What's your name?" The man who spoke was tall and clean shaven and had a square jaw. The straps of his helmet that circled around his pointed chin moved the helmet as he spoke.

Kate stared at him in disbelief while the soldiers next to him kept their guns aimed at the surrounding area, keeping watch. A soldier who held her patted down her back side, inside her jacket, and then down her legs, taking the revolver off her.

The soldier handed the revolver to Sergeant Renly, who examined the weapon. "A .38, makes for a good concealed weapon." He handed the weapon off to another one of his men. "I'll ask you again. What's your name?"

"Kate. Kate Hillman."

"What are you doing out past curfew, Kate Hillman?" Renly asked.

"Curfew?" Kate asked. "I came down to get my son. He's enrolled at George Mason." Kate gestured down the road toward the campus's main entrance.

"Where are you from?" Renly asked.

"New York."

"New York?" Renly echoed the words like a surprised parrot. "How the hell did you get down here?"

"I flew."

Every head turned toward her, and one of the soldiers chuckled.

"Bullshit," he said. "What'd you do? Flap your ears like Dumbo?"

"I came down in a 1946 Commonwealth Skyranger," Kate answered. "Couldn't find an elephant."

"How the hell did you get a plane working?" Renly asked. "We don't have any coms or transportation."

"I didn't have to fix it. It was already working." Kate looked at them in turn and realized that they didn't know what happened.

"It was an EMP blast that took everything out. At least that's what I was told."

"You were told that?" Renly asked.

"She must be some kind of terrorist spy," a soldier said.

"Finest-looking spy I've seen," another soldier answered, smacking on some gum.

"Really, Parcy?" One of the other soldiers turned to him, raising his eyebrows.

"Shut it! All of you!" Renly barked, and the banter ended. "If she's a terrorist cell member, then I'm the goddamn queen of England. Take the cuffs off."

"Sarge, do you think—"

"I said take them off!"

The pressure around Kate's wrists ended, and she rubbed them in relief. "Thanks."

"Your face is all scratched to hell," Renly said. "We'll get you some medical attention back at the campus."

"I'm fine," Kate said. "What happened here?"

"Once the fighting started, our superior officer declared martial law," Renly answered. "We set a curfew for safety and gathered everyone in the town and shoved them down at the university. It was the easiest way to keep track of everyone."

"Yeah, and to make sure those rag heads don't get the drop on us," one of the soldiers said.

"Your son goes to George Mason?" Renly asked.

"Yeah," Kate answered.

"We'll escort you over," Renly said. "We have a team set up there as a FOB. Parcy, you're on point!"

"Yes, sir."

The unit moved forward, the sergeant and Kate in the middle of the pack as they traversed the sidewalk in the darkness. Boots scuffed snow and pavement, and the gear strapped to their bodies clanked in time with their steps.

"What happened in DC?" Kate asked.

"We're not sure. The last orders we received were to move to the university and secure the town. We were supposed to be a way station for troops coming to reinforce the capital. It's been over a day now, and we still haven't had anyone come through."

"Or heard shit from Command," Parcy said, barking from up front.

"How bad is it?" Kate asked.

"Bad," Renly answered. "Everything's fried. But we're working on getting an old Morris code transmitter we found in the college's engineering basement up and running." He regarded Kate again and then shook his head. "You really flew down here?"

"Yeah."

The sergeant laughed. "Goddamn."

The soldiers grew more relaxed the closer they moved to the campus, and once they passed a security checkpoint manned by a dozen soldiers, Kate started to relax. It was the first semblance of security that she'd felt since the EMP went off. It was hard to believe it'd only been a day since she left New York.

"Do you know what dorm your son was staying in?" the sergeant asked.

"The Commons," Kate answered.

"I'll have one of my guys take you over. You'll need the escort to get through the doors. If he's there, when you're done, one of my men will accompany you to the auditorium. I think we still have some bunks open there. Parcy!"

"I don't plan on staying, Sergeant. I'm taking my son and leaving."

"This campus is the safest place to be right now," Renly said. "And you should be thankful that we chose to take you in at all." And before she could make a rebuttal, the sergeant was gone.

As Kate was escorted through the campus, she noted how different everything looked. Darkness and silence had replaced the bustling grounds, soldiers marching instead of students learning.

Two guards were stationed at the door to Luke's dorm, and despite her military escort both soldiers raised their rifles.

"Got a mom who came to get her boy," Parcy said.

"I bet he's going to love that." The soldier smirked but stepped aside.

"I'll wait for you here," Parcy said. "Don't be long."

Kate was handed a flashlight to help guide her path inside. She found the stairwell and climbed to the third floor. Her nerves twisted her gut into knots on the way up, and by the time she exited the stairwell, she had to fight the urge to sprint toward Luke's room.

The old wooden floors in the hallway groaned with each step toward Luke's room. When she reached his door, Kate raised her fist and lightly knocked three times. She waited a moment, listening for any movement inside. When she heard nothing, Kate gripped the doorknob and turned it. It was unlocked.

The door cracked open, and Kate poked her head inside. "Luke?" she whispered, her eyes falling to his bed, where a massive lump lay under the covers with his back turned. But she recognized that mop of hair, and before she realized it, she was at his side. "Luke!" She shook his shoulder, and he groaned. He turned to face her, eyes blinking, and just when Kate's smile grew the widest, she finally noticed that he wasn't in bed alone.

"Holy shit, Mom!"

The girl next to him stirred and then jumped and screamed. Kate quickly retreated toward the door as the girl covered herself up. Luke's roommate jolted upright in his bed and then rolled off the mattress and hit the floor with a thud.

"I'm sorry," Kate said.

Doors opened in the hallway, and the sleepy students voiced their displeasure.

"Shut up in there!"

"We're trying to get some sleep!"

"Knock it off!"

Luke jumped out of bed, thankfully wearing gym shorts, and

then quickly shut the door. "Mom, what the hell are you doing here?"

"*Mom?*" The girl in the bed stared in horror, the sheet still clutched high on her chest, and then she let it drop, Kate thankfully noting that she was also clothed. "Oh my god." She slid out of bed and then quickly grabbed her shoes and a coat. "I have to go."

"Claire, no, wait." Luke tried to stop her, but the girl squeezed past Kate and disappeared down the hall. Luke slouched in defeat as he watched her leave then spun to face his mother. "Mom, *what* are you doing here? And how did you even *get* here?"

Kate knew he was mad and embarrassed, but seeing him standing there, alive, after everything she'd seen, after everything that she'd been through, she broke down in tears and threw her arms around him. "Thank God you're all right."

Luke's tone softened, and he returned the embrace. "Of course I'm all right." He broke off the embrace and walked the two of them to the edge of his bed, where he quickly moved a bra, and his cheeks reddened as he tossed it in the corner out of sight.

"Um..." Luke's roommate grabbed a shirt and got up from the floor. "I think I'll just wait outside." He left, his footsteps creaking down the hall.

Kate took Luke's hand. "Your father and I weren't sure how to get in contact with you after the power went out. We were so worried about you."

"I'm fine." Luke kept his voice calm. "Classes have been cancelled since... well, since whatever this is happened."

Kate hugged him again and kissed his cheek and then wiped her eyes, hoping he couldn't see her crying again in the dark. "And you're sure you're okay?" She gently prodded his face and shoulders.

Luke removed her hands, holding them in his own. "I'm fine, Mom." And then he frowned. "How did you get down here? The military hasn't been able to get anything working, let alone a car."

"I flew," Kate said.

"What?"

Kate stood and pulled Luke up off the bed with her. "We have to go. C'mon."

Luke removed his arm from her grip. "What? I can't leave."

"It's not safe here, Luke. We need to go, and we need to do it quickly."

"I'm not leaving Claire."

"Who's Claire?" And then Kate remembered the girl, and the bra, and Luke's cheeks reddened again. "Luke, now isn't the time to be romantic."

"We're surrounded by soldiers. This is the safest place I could be."

"If there are soldiers here, then that means there will be fighting here." Kate stiffened. "You're coming with me. And you're coming now."

"No." The defiance was short, stern, and immovable. "I'm not."

"We don't have time for this!" Kate's voice thundered in the room, but Luke just stood there, the threat from his mother neither intimidating nor effective.

Kate growled in frustration and then paced in a circle. She kept her eyes glued to the floor, fighting the urge to treat Luke like the child she believed he was acting like. "I know you think you really like this girl, and I know you think staying behind is the right thing, but it's not." She looked up to him. "Family is the most important thing right now, and your family needs you." She stepped toward him. "I need you."

Luke relaxed, his posture less standoffish, but he kept his distance. "I'm sorry, Mom. I am. But I can't leave."

The moment was surreal, worse than a nightmare. She had found Luke alive and well, but she recognized that stubborn tone in his voice. It sounded a lot like her own.

"We'll sleep on it," Kate said, and she suddenly felt exhausted. "They have a bed for me in the auditorium. There's a soldier waiting for me downstairs."

"I'll walk with you." Luke put on a shirt and shoes and then grabbed a coat.

Parcy followed behind them as Luke guided Kate toward the auditorium, and Luke put his arm around his mom as they walked. The quiet of the night was only interrupted by their footfalls crunching snow and the occasional gust of wind.

"I'm sorry about the girl," Luke said, almost blurting it out. "She's really nice, Mom. And I don't want you to think that just because—"

"It's fine, Luke," Kate said. "Really. I'm just glad that both of you were clothed."

Luke laughed. "That makes two of us."

Another silence fell between them, and it wasn't broken until they reached the gymnasium. Luke pocketed his hands and rocked back and forth on his feet nervously. "I love her. And I know all of the things that you'll tell me, that I've never really been in love, that we're both young, and that it won't work out." He broke eye contact and stared down at his feet. "And you might be right. But if this is a mistake, then you should let me make it. Just like you made yours."

Luke sheepishly lifted his gaze back toward Kate's, and while she wanted to confirm everything he said, she chose not to. Instead she pressed her hand against his cheek, feeling the rough stubble of hair growing. He wasn't a boy anymore. He had become a man when she wasn't paying attention. She dropped her hand and then kissed his cheek. "I'll see you in the morning."

"Night, Mom."

Kate lingered outside the gymnasium while she watched her son return to his dorm room. She wondered if the girl would come back or if he would go and find her, and then she quickly pushed that thought out of her head. She wasn't sure how she was going to convince Luke to come back with her, but she knew he couldn't stay here. Whatever enemy was attacking the capital didn't have plans to rest on their laurels. And if the soldiers she spoke to were correct, then the fighting could break out here at any moment. And she wanted her son to be as far away from that as possible.

20

Thirty-five convicts huddled in the trees behind Main Street in the town of Duluth. Fingers twitched anxiously, and knees bounced with nervous energy. Icy breaths escaped snarls surrounded by beards. The wolf pack was hungry and restless.

They had waited until night fall, scoping out the town to see if they were armed, and what supplies they had. But now everyone was asleep. Now was the time to strike.

"Christ, my balls are about to freeze off." Snow drifted off Jimmy's body as he rubbed his arms for warmth. "What the hell is taking them so long?"

Dennis examined the Glock in his hand then racked the slide back and stared at the bullet in the chamber. "I told them to be thorough."

"Well, I want my own bed," Jimmy said. "And a nice warm woman to go with it."

"Just remember not to hit her too hard before you drag her back to your cave," Mulls said. "Unless you want to be fucking a corpse."

"She'd only have to be warm for a minute." Jimmy wheezed laughter, his teeth chattering from the cold.

"We do this right," Dennis said, "and we can have whatever we want down there, and for as long as we want it."

Branches rustled to Dennis's right, followed by quick footfalls, and all three of them turned their weapons toward two men with scruffy beards and long, matted hair.

"Put those things down before you kill one of us." Martin waved his big hand and collapsed next to Dennis and tried to catch his breath as his brother, Billy, followed suit. Both brothers had been freelance killers before the FBI got ahold of them. Their skill sets also made them excellent trackers. They'd been part of Mulls's crew on the inside.

"Well?" Dennis asked.

"Eighty-plus people," Martin answered, clearing his throat, still huffing. The man's prime had ended more than a decade past. But his mind remained sharp. "Mostly vacationers up here for skiing. A few of the locals look like they had weapons, but no more than a dozen."

"Pigs?" Mulls asked.

"A sheriff and six deputies," Billy answered. The age gap between the brothers was enough that Billy could pass as Martin's son. "They've got two on watch, keeping their eyes on the only road into town, which is mostly asleep."

"We should hit them now," Mulls said. "We go in quick, round them up, and show 'em who's boss." He turned to Dennis. "They can't call anyone, can't drive anywhere, right?"

"Give me the rundown of the buildings," Dennis said.

Martin and Billy recited everything they'd seen, and Dennis was glad for the details. They'd counted the number of entrances and exits for every building in the town, which numbered at twelve. Once they finished, Dennis turned to Mulls.

"We take out the deputies first," he said. "And we do it quietly. We put three men to a building. All twelve groups need to have a gun and a point man. We funnel everyone out and take them—" He turned back to Martin. "You mentioned a town hall, where is it?"

"East end of the town."

"We corral them there," Dennis said. "We'll have to deal with a few hotheads, but once we take care of them, the rest of the sheep will fall into line. Won't take more than a few bullets to start flying before everyone shits their pants and just wants it to stop."

"And then we get to do whatever we want, right?" Jimmy's eyes grew wide, like a kid's on Christmas morning.

"You take what you want," Dennis answered. "Everybody gets a piece."

"I just want a piece of ass," Jimmy said then turned to Martin and Billy with longing in his eyes. "Women down there?"

"Yeah." A wide grin spread over Martin's face. "Plenty of them."

"Get everyone in position," Dennis said. "No one moves until the first gunshot."

Word spread, and all those twitching hands and bouncing knees exploded into action. The groups of three departed from the woods quietly and beelined toward their assigned buildings. It wasn't until everyone had left that Dennis, Mulls, and Jimmy snaked their way toward the sheriff's station.

The familiar surge of adrenaline that accompanied a heist returned, and Dennis had forgotten how much he'd missed it. Once a man had a taste of it, he never wanted anything else. There was rebellious freedom to it, violence that awakened the most primal human instincts. Every man in an orange jumpsuit knew that freedom. Crime was the worst kind of addiction, and every man was eager to have that needle prick their arms again.

Dennis and his group approached the back side of the sheriff's station. He peered down the alley and heard the voices of the two deputies on watch. He held out his palm, and Mulls handed him a knife. He curled his stiff and frozen fingers around it and crept down the alley, Mulls disappearing to the other side. Jimmy went in through the back door, taking care of the cops that slept.

With his feet frozen, it was nearly impossible for Dennis to keep his footfalls quiet, and each step was met with a cringe as he waited for his cover to be blown. But he grew nearer, and the banter between the cops at the front never broke.

Dennis glued himself to the building's wall, slithering toward the flickering glow of the candles the deputies had set out. He stopped just before the wall's end, knife poised to strike. He peered around the edge and saw the pair of deputies in the street, rifles hoisted over their shoulders, staring out into the darkness of the road.

Mulls appeared on the other side and locked eyes with Dennis. Both men nodded then crept from the shadows toward their victims.

Dennis had the knife raised high, his body stiff from cold and concentration, and when he was two steps from the deputy's throat, his shadow betrayed him, casting into the deputy's line of sight. The man spun, and Dennis led with the knife, metal digging into flesh just as the deputy squeezed the trigger, breaking the night's silence.

Blood splattered Dennis's face as the deputy clawed at Dennis's arm. He yanked the blade from the deputy's throat, blood dripping from the knife's tip. Crimson stained the snow, and he glanced over to find Mulls standing over the second deputy with his blood-soaked knife.

What took only seconds felt like an eternity. And Dennis barely had time to notice the shouts inside the sheriff's station before the entire town erupted with gunfire and screams. The inmates hooted and hollered, bloodlust taking control of their senses.

Frightened and confused townspeople were flung out into the cold, shivering in their pajamas, plucked from the warmth of their beds. One inmate held a young woman dressed in a lacy teddy, gripping her by the hair. Another prisoner came out holding her man at gunpoint.

"Oh, she's gonna warm me up real good!" He laughed, and the woman screamed.

"You don't fucking touch her!" But the man's threat fell empty as he was kicked to the ground, and the prisoner with the gun to his head pumped the shotgun.

The man froze at the sound and remained on his knees as he lifted his hands in the air. His woman looked back at him, crying, struggling against the inmate who would rape her. Dennis expected a lot of that for the next couple of nights. That and killing.

"Not here," Dennis said, icy clouds forming from his excited and labored breaths. "We wait until we've got everyone." He looked at the woman and then her husband. "Then the fun begins."

A gunshot thundered up ahead, and glass shattered, and Dennis caught the blur of an orange jumpsuit that was flung outside. The barrel of a rifle penetrated the open door, and then a bullet was fired into the prisoner's gut.

The door then slammed shut quickly, and Dennis joined the other inmates that swarmed the rebellious shooter, a smile on his face. They had a fighter on their hands.

Dennis, Jimmy, and Mulls paused at the door. Dennis peered through the broken window, the boards of the front porch groaning as he did. A gunshot thundered inside, and Dennis ducked out of the way of the bullet screaming into the street.

"Son of a bitch!" Mulls said, growling.

"He's heading out the back!" Jimmy said, staring down the side of the house.

Dennis led the pursuit, and the small backyard quickly gave way to a cluster of trees, spying to figures fleeing through the forest.

Deeper into the woods, the snow on the ground thickened, and both parties were forced to little more than a crawl. But Dennis raised his gun, bringing the man's back into his crosshairs. He forced his arm steady, and he squeezed the trigger.

The man flung his arms wildly as he plummeted face-first into the snow. The rifle flew from his hands, and the woman shrieked, dropping to her man's side, too hysterical to reach for the rifle in the snow.

"Drake, get up! *Get up!*" The woman flung her body over the dead man's, her face turned up toward Dennis, staring down the barrel of the pistol. "*What did you do?*"

"Sorry, sweetheart," Dennis said, catching his breath but smiling as Jimmy and Mulls caught up with him. He motioned to Mulls. "Take her back with the others."

The woman burst into sobbing wails and flopped back over the man. It took both Mulls and Jimmy to drag her back, the woman's cries echoing all the way back into town.

Dennis lingered behind for a moment, staring down at the dead man. He saw the glint of metal on the man's left ring finger. A wedding band, the gold shining brightly against the backdrop of the white snow that wasn't covered with the man's blood, melting it into a red slush.

It had been a long time since Dennis had seen blood spilled. It twinkled in his eyes like fire, and his grin stretched from ear to ear. He bent down and poked his finger in it, swirling the blood and ice in little circles.

The metallic scent of the blood filled his nostrils, and he inhaled it, lifting his head and closing his eyes. It was intoxicating. And it was a smell he missed.

Dennis reached for the dead man's left hand and then removed the wedding ring and pocketed the gold. "Thanks for the wife." He laughed and left the corpse to rot in the snow.

Back on Main Street, he saw the lines of people being shuttled into the auditorium.

Dennis approached Jimmy and Mulls, who still held the wife of the man he killed, and ran his bloodstained finger from her chin up along her jawline. "Get her a good seat up front." She turned away, making the smear worse, and that bug started to burrow.

A low murmuring anxiety had filled the massive town hall, which echoed from the high ceilings and tiled floors. Dennis remained in the back, looking at the huddled masses shivering and clutching their pajamas and robes.

The inmates circled around the group like a wolf pack, baring their teeth with their smiles and dripping saliva. There was a fair amount of women inside. Most of the inmates hadn't even smelled a woman in over a decade.

"Quiet!" Dennis said, his voice booming and triggering a faint shriek from the group, then everyone fell silent. He cut through the middle, forcing the huddled masses to part for him. Dennis liked that. Once he reached the front of the group, he spun around, smiling. "Good evening, Duluth! My name is Inmate 0946." He gestured to the rest of the prisoners. "And these are a few of my closest friends."

The inmates chuckled, a few of them pointing to different women in the group. No doubt choosing their favorites.

"My friends and I want a little taste of what you all have here." Dennis opened his arms, spreading them wide and welcoming. "We've been deprived of such luxuries for so long we thought we'd try and take a few from you here."

"You're criminals!" a man on his knees shouted. Red blotches covered his face, and his lips quivered uncontrollably like the rest of him. He glanced around accusingly. "You belong back behind bars!"

Two of the inmates made a move for the man, but Dennis held up his hands, and they stopped. He looked at the woman of the man he'd killed out in the snow. To her credit, she didn't look away when they made eye contact.

"Criminals?" Dennis spoke the question with his eyes still locked onto the woman then finally broke off and set his gaze upon that trembling man. "We're only criminals because society labeled us that way. But look at society now."

The people around the man who'd spoken up started to separate themselves from him. All but the woman next to him who clutched his arm nervously.

Dennis knelt when he reached the man, and he placed the end of his pistol against the man's left temple. "I could blow your brains out, and you know what would happen? You would die, and then I would let those two guys over there fuck your wife."

The woman whimpered, and the husband protectively tucked his wife behind him. "You can't do this. It's against—"

"The law?" Dennis asked. "What law?" He removed the pistol and then pointed it down toward the sheriff's office. "We killed the deputies and the sheriff. The law is dead." He leaned closer to the dead man's ear and dropped his voice to a whisper. "We're in charge now."

Dennis stood and then placed the end of his pistol's barrel against the man's forehead.

"Please," the woman said, poking out from behind her husband. "Please, don't do this. We'll cooperate. We'll do whatever you want."

"Did you hear that, fellas?" Dennis shouted. "She said they'll do whatever we want!"

Laughter and a few howls and cheers erupted from the inmates, more violence and anger than joy and excitement.

Dennis looked back at the woman, laughing as well. "You might regret saying that, lady." He squeezed the trigger, the ring of the gunshot cut short by the screams that filled the auditorium. Dennis returned to the front of the hall, stopping at the woman, and he gently ran his hands through her hair. It was soft. Softer than anything he'd felt in a long time. She jerked away after a few seconds, and then he grabbed a fistful of her hair and yanked her to her feet.

"This is our town now!" Dennis said. "We do what we want, to who we want, wherever we want. The more you fight it, the worse it'll be." He looked at the inmates, who were practically salivating. "Have fun, boys."

21

Morning came quickly, and it only brought trouble with it. Mark rolled to his side, his entire body as stiff as a board from his night on the floor, and found Holly on her stomach, drawing in gargled and raspy breaths.

"Holly?" Mark hurried to her side and gently rolled her to her back. Her face was slick with sweat, and the heat pouring off her was tremendous. "Christ, Holly, can you hear me?"

Only raspy breaths answered, and everyone else began to rise from their slumber. Rodney was up first, and he rolled over, concern on his face. "What happened?"

"I-I don't know!" Mark propped Holly up, but the raspy breaths continued.

"Did you give her medicine last night?" Rodney asked, his voice on the edge of calm.

"Of course I did!"

Glen and Laura roused, rubbing their eyes sleepily at the commotion.

"What's wrong?" Glen asked.

"Can't we just sleep a little longer?" Laura asked longingly.

"Holly's getting worse," Rodney answered, pausing briefly at the foot of their cushions where they slept, and then darted out the door.

"Oh my god," Laura said, flinging off the quilt that she'd used the night before, and she quickly knelt down by Mark's side. "What happened?"

"Her breathing is really bad," Mark said, rocking Holly in his arms as she wheezed for air.

"Did you give her the antibiotics?" Laura asked.

"Yeah. They're not working." Mark brushed back the wet and matted hair on Holly's forehead. In addition to the fever, the sweating, and the wheezing, Holly had grown incredibly pale. All the color from her face was drained, and his daughter looked more dead than alive.

And where was he supposed to take her? He couldn't call a doctor or drive to a hospital. He couldn't get online and search WebMD. He was alone with his daughter in a place he'd never been before, in the middle of winter, with no power and no transportation.

Glen and Laura kept quiet and close. Every once in a while, one of them would offer water or food from their pack.

Holly wouldn't take the food, but Mark forced water down her throat. She had to be dehydrated from sweating so much. He thought about taking her jacket off and stripping her down to her underwear but knew that she'd freeze the moment they stepped outside.

Mark had to concentrate to keep the tears from falling. Never in his life had he felt more helpless than he did at that moment. A father was supposed to protect his daughter, shield her from the horrors of the world, and he could do nothing.

The door burst open, and Rodney appeared, bringing with him the light of daybreak. He held a rope and pulled the sled behind him. "Help me get her outside."

"What?" Mark asked, pulling his daughter out of Rodney's reach. "We can't move her. She'll freeze out there!"

"Her lungs are filled with liquid. She's choking to death,"

Rodney answered, his breath labored as he hunched over with his hands on his knees. "There is hospital ten miles west of us. If we're lucky, then there still might be some staff that stayed behind after the EMP was triggered. I don't know if they'll be able to help, but I can promise you that if we stay here, she will die."

It wasn't the words that scared Mark. It was the confidence with which Rodney had spoken them. "All right." He carried Holly to the sled, setting her down gently, but Holly drew in another harsh rasp. She hacked and coughed, spitting green fluid over the front of her jacket.

Laura gasped, and Glen let out a throaty groan as if he were experiencing the same pain.

"It's all right, Holly," Mark said, shushing her whimpering cries. "Everything is going to be okay."

Holly's eyelids fluttered, and they cracked open. Her mouth turned down before she began to shed tears. "I want to go home."

Mark kissed her forehead while Rodney finished securing the sled's straps. "I know, baby. I know you do."

Laura rushed back inside and then returned with a pillow. "Here. For her head."

"Thanks." Mark jimmied the pillow into place, resting Holly's head down just as gently. And despite the fever and at Rodney's urging, they covered her with another blanket.

"Even with the fever, she could still freeze," Rodney said then turned to the others. "We'll need to move quickly, but it'll be hard since we're cutting through the woods to save time. The snow will be thick." He spoke to the group, but his eyes were on Glen.

"We won't slow you down," Glen said.

"We promise," Laura said, looking down at Holly.

"Let's go!"

Both Rodney and Mark pulled the sled, with Laura and Glen

bringing up the rear. Holly's limp body rocked back and forth over the snow and hills as they weaved through the forest.

Every few feet, Mark looked back, and Holly would cough, spewing more fluid onto her chest. He churned his legs faster through the snow. She was running out of time.

* * *

IT WAS WELL past dawn when Kate awoke in the auditorium. Almost everyone else was already awake, chatting amongst themselves, a few holding Styrofoam cups that piped steam. Kate stared at the sight, unsure if she was dreaming.

"Fresh off the fire." The voice accompanied a similar piping-hot cup thrust into the path of her gawking eyes. Kate followed the arm to a smiling face of a young man with shoulder-length hair and scruff over his face.

Kate wasn't sure how long she stared but knew that it was too long based off the man's nervous laughter.

"It's not poison." He leaned closer, dropping his voice to a whisper. "At least yours isn't." He gestured to a couple chatting nearby. "Never really liked those two." Kate's expression didn't break, and he cleared his throat uncomfortably. "I'm joking, of course."

"Right." Kate shook her head and then took the coffee. She pressed both palms against its warmth. It was the first warm thing she'd held since the EMP went off two days ago. She lingered on that last thought. Had it really been two days?

"I'm Rick." He extended his free hand, the smile returned to his face.

"Kate." She took it, and his grip was firm. She examined the cup. "I forgot you could heat things up without power."

Rick took a seat on her cot, though he kept his distance. "The military may be a drag when it comes to wanting to go where you want to go, but they did bring a lot of rations with them." He raised the cup then sipped and grimaced. "Not very good, though. But a lot of it."

Kate sipped, burning her tongue, but found that he was right. The black sludge was more of a distant cousin to coffee than the legitimate heir.

"Told you."

Kate set the coffee down and then stood. "I'm sorry, but I have to go and see my son."

"You have a kid here?"

"Yes," Kate answered, exhausted. "Now if you'll excuse me." She left him with his shitty coffee on the cot. She didn't glance behind her, afraid that he'd follow, but she eventually snuck a peek once she was outside. Thankfully, he wasn't there.

A group of armed soldiers walked past, and Kate flagged one of them down. "Excuse me, do you know where The Commons House is?"

"No, but all of the dormitories have been escorted to the cafeteria," he said then pointed behind her. "It's that big grey building. You'll see the line out front."

"Thank you—" But when she turned, the soldiers were already up ahead, chatting amongst themselves and adjusting the rifles on their shoulders.

When she'd arrived in the night, the darkness had concealed the number of soldiers, but in the light of day she saw the place was crawling with them.

Kate walked over to the cafeteria, racking her brain for a way to convince Luke to come back with her. She longed for the days when she could just pick him up and carry him. That would have made things much simpler.

She found the line for breakfast and bypassed it. Nerves and the desire to get out of here as soon as possible had replaced hunger. She prayed the plane was still in that field.

Inside, hundreds of people had already found their way to the tables, most of them shoveling the food around on their trays instead of eating it. And while it didn't look appetizing, the smell started to bring the hunger out.

"Mom!"

Kate's heart stopped, and she turned toward Luke's voice. He stood with his hand in the air, waving, and to her surprise, smiling. Once he knew that she'd seen him, he plopped back down into his seat, and Kate noticed the same girl from the night before sitting next to him, her head down, buried in a bowl of oatmeal.

"Scoot over, guys." Luke shooed some of his friends down the long bench seats but then stopped when he noticed Kate didn't have a tray in her hands. "You're not hungry?"

"No, I'm fine." Kate smiled politely at the others, not recognizing any of them.

"Everyone, this is my mom," Luke said. "Mom, this is Doug, Barry, Kit, Mace, and, um..." He cleared his throat and blushed. "This is Claire."

The young girl stood at the sound of her name, springing up like a fresh daisy that had longed for springtime. She thrust out her hand, her cheeks red. "It's very nice to meet you, Mrs. Hillman."

"It's very nice to meet you, Claire." Kate let go of the girl's hand and whispered into Luke's ear. "I need to talk to you for a minute."

Claire sat down, and Luke nodded.

Once they were a safe distance away from any ears, Kate spoke. "Luke, we have to leave." Her son stood there, towering six inches above her, the features of his face set like hard granite. She took his hand. "I know you don't want to leave, but—"

"I'm not leaving Claire behind, Mom." He didn't remove his hand from hers, and instead he squeezed them tighter. "I wasn't just blowing smoke at you last night. I love her. I'm staying."

Kate cupped Luke's face, desperation clinging to her like morning dew. "Son, I can't leave you here. You don't know what's going on out there. You don't— Even the military doesn't really know what's happening." She glanced around, making sure there weren't any soldiers nearby. "The power isn't coming back on, and we need to get out of any highly populated areas. If the fighting is as bad in the capital as I've heard, then it won't be long before the fighting comes here. And if we try to leave then, it'll be too late."

She waited for Luke to say something, anything, but he just stared at her, almost mockingly. But he had the good sense to stifle any smirks.

"Mom, we're surrounded by soldiers." He released her hands. "We have food, water, and shelter. This is the safest place we could possibly be."

Kate steeled herself, and her expression caused Luke's boyish features to return. A mother's scorn had that effect. "You think it's a good idea to keep you and your girlfriend in a circle of guns? What happens when those guns are used? What happens when the small semblance of order here falls?"

Luke laughed. "Mom, I don't—"

"No, you don't!" Kate raised her volume and pulled a few heads in their direction. "People have died, Luke. Killed by their neighbors, by strangers, by the terrorists responsible for all of this. The moment this place is under attack, law and order go out the window. Those men with the guns will fight for themselves, and you'll be stuck in the crosshairs." Her voice cracked. "I won't let you die here."

The tears flowed despite Kate's resistance, and Luke hugged her. It was a pitying embrace but one that she still welcomed.

"Mom, I'm not—"

Gunshots thundered. They were far enough away to be dulled by distance and the cafeteria's walls but close enough to end the senseless chatter as heads turned toward the commotion.

Soldiers shouted and sprinted past the windows. Kate stepped around her son, watching the soldiers rush toward the source of the gunfire. More of it thundered. It grew closer. She turned around and reached for Luke's hand.

"We have to go. Now." Her tone was hurried and frightened, but Luke just stared into the distance, past the windows and the soldiers, his eyes blank, his expression devoid of understanding.

An explosion erupted near one of the buildings. A plume of fire jettisoned into the morning sky, burning bright and hot. The cafeteria rumbled in coordination with the blast, and that stunned silence was quickly replaced by gasps of surprise, ducking heads, and panic.

Trays of food were flung in haste as people sprinted for the exits. Kate grabbed hold of Luke's hand, but he lunged back toward the table for Claire, who struggled to make her way through the crowd.

"Claire!" Luke clawed through the bodies, gunshots silencing the chorus of screams inside the mess hall.

Kate tried to stop him, but it was all she could do to simply hang on for the ride. Shoulders and arms bumped into her as Luke grabbed hold of Claire's hand and then pulled both of them toward the nearest door, which happened to be the one closest to the gunshots.

Outside, the cold air blasted Kate's face, and Luke turned north, away from the cluster of soldiers that had crouched behind the cover on the building closest to the explosion.

Kate caught only a glimpse of the fight as Luke yanked both her and Claire away from the danger.

She wasn't sure how long she sprinted, but Kate was the first to run out of gas. She gave Luke's arm a tug, and they jerked to a stop. She gasped for breath, her muscles turned to jelly.

"What do we do?" Claire asked.

A group of soldiers hurried past, and Luke grabbed hold of one of them, his hand clamped tight around his arm. "Where are they coming from?"

The soldier snarled and yanked his arm free then jogged to rejoin his men. "Fucking everywhere!"

Another explosion sounded, and both Kate and Claire stepped toward Luke. The blast was farther away than the first, toward the west side of the campus, but more ferocious gunfire followed it.

"Mom, how far is the plane?" Luke asked.

"A few miles." Kate looked around, trying to get her bearings. "We need to get back onto the main road that leads into the campus. I should be able to retrace my steps from there."

The trio sprinted off, Luke leading the way through the campus. They passed more soldiers, and every few seconds, they flinched from gunfire, but they never stopped running.

"There's the road." Luke pointed. "Now, where?"

Kate took the lead, though the pace she set was slower. They weaved between the vehicles on the highway, Kate glancing everywhere, her eyes peeled on the woods to her left and the open field to her right. With all of the abandoned vehicles, there were so many places for people to hide.

Every step forward, Kate couldn't help but think of what lay beyond. One of those terrorists with a gun, ready to plow the three of them down. Memories of New York flashed in her head. The bodies, the bullets, the blood and screams.

Kate stopped and steadied herself against the side of a truck. She gasped for breath, hyperventilating. She was suddenly beneath all of those bodies, the terrorists standing on top of her. The heat coming off them was like the heat from a dying fire.

"Mom, are you all right?" Luke asked, taking hold of her arm.

Kate shut her eyes and nodded, trying to reel herself back to the present. "I'm fine." She popped her eyes open and saw worried expressions on both Luke and Claire. "We need to keep moving."

After her little episode, Kate pulled them closer to the forest line, where they had a clearer path. Her eyes darted to the side more than they stayed in front of her as she searched for an enemy that wasn't there.

"How much farther?" Luke asked.

Kate squinted through the trees. She had no idea. "Should be just up ahead."

Leaves and snow crunched underfoot, and a breeze rustled dead branches and fallen leaves. Kate stopped, and Luke and Claire stopped with her.

"What?" Luke asked. "Mom, what—"

Kate waved at him angrily, hushing him. She perked her ear toward the direction of the voices carried through the trees, and Kate immediately pulled Luke down, with Claire following suit.

Her heart pounded wildly in her chest, her eyes scanning for the source of the noise, and then she spotted three men between the trees, each of them armed with rifles, dressed in long robes that concealed their faces, save for their eyes.

Kate turned to Luke and Claire, pressing her finger to her lips, and the terrorists grew louder, closer. When she turned back, she saw the trio had diverted their path toward them. Kate motioned Luke and Claire to follow, and they crawled through the snow.

Every creak of her joints, every crunch of her knees and hands into the snowfall brought with it a cringe. Kate kept a bead on the terrorists to her left. She stopped when they stopped. And so did Luke and Claire.

Once they were out of the terrorists' path, Kate stopped, hunched behind a dead tree, and waited for them to pass. It wasn't until they were out of sight and she could no longer hear their foreign tongue that she gave a long exhalation.

"Thank God," Kate said.

"Who are those people?" Luke asked, his eyes still trained on their footprints. "Are they the ones attacking us?"

"Yeah," Kate answered, turning back to where they disappeared.

"Who are they?" Claire asked.

"It doesn't matter." Kate stood and brushed the snow and leaves off of her. "We need to go." She stepped from the cover of the tree and froze when the barrel of a rifle bore down on her face.

"Tawaquf!" The words were shouted through the cloth covering the man's mouth. He shoved the end of his rifle into Kate's face. *"Ealaa Rakbataykl!"*

Kate kept her hands in the air and stepped back. Luke jumped to her side, throwing his body in front of hers, which she quickly peeled away. "No, don't!"

The soldier repeated his screams, shaking the rifle at them like a stick. After a minute, foreign voices returned the lone soldier's cries. Kate turned in horror to see the other fighters making their return. They were at least one hundred yards away, but they moved quickly.

The terrorist jammed the end of his rifle barrel into Kate's shoulder and shoved her backward, slamming her into Luke and Claire.

"Hey!" Luke reached for the rifle, and in the same instant, Kate heard a gunshot.

Claire screamed, and Kate watched the color drain from Luke's face as he collapsed into the snow. She dropped to his side, Claire falling with him. Kate's hands found the wound on the left side of his chest, and she applied pressure.

"Mom?" Luke's voice was little more than a whisper. He was suddenly pale and sweaty.

"It's all right, Luke." Kate steadied her voice, trying to remain focused, trying to hold it all together. "Shh, it's all right." Kate flicked her eyes up, and through the trees, she saw the terrorists sprinting toward her.

Kate's head tilted forward, the rifle barrel pressed hard into the back of her skull. Her eyes met the eyes of Claire, who was crying and on the edge of hysteria.

More blood oozed from Luke's bullet wound, warming Kate's hand and then spilling onto the snow. His eyes fluttered closed, and he stopped shaking.

Kate shut her eyes, adrenaline fueling the rage bubbling to

the precipice of action, and then exploded upward, turning and swinging both arms, knocking the rifle to the side. The gun fired, and the terrorist stumbled backward, eyes wide with surprise.

Kate snatched at the rifle, the steel cold against her grip. Another gunshot fired into the trees, vibrating her arms and hands, but she didn't let go.

The rifle's stock pressed into her throat, and Kate's airflow tightened. Her breaths transformed into raspy gasps, and the pressure increased.

Claire flung herself on the terrorist's back in an effort to help, and Kate wrestled the rifle from his grip. She flipped it around in her hands, her finger finding the trigger, and squeezed.

A red mark stained the terrorist's chest, spreading over the cloth as he was flung backward, crashing into the snow next to her son.

The terrorist's comrades screamed and sprinted faster through the woods at the sight of their fallen brother.

Kate took hold of Luke's left arm and tucked the rifle under her right shoulder. "Claire, grab his other hand!" The girl did as she was told, though she sobbed through the whole ordeal. "We need to pull him. C'mon!"

Luke's body jerked forward with a jolt, and a red smear trailed through the white snow, his back scraping against the rocks and roots beneath. He groaned. Kate stopped.

"We need to get him up." Kate dropped to Luke's side and looked up at Claire, who was glancing back toward the terrorists. "Claire, c'mon!"

Claire stepped away from Luke. "I'm sorry. I can't do this. I can't."

"Claire, don't!" Kate watched Claire disappear into the woods and then saw one of the terrorists break from his group to chase her down.

Kate squatted low and hooked her arms beneath Luke's pits.

Her boots scraped the frozen ground, and she dragged him four feet before she tripped over a rock and collapsed backward.

Claire screamed, and Kate shuddered when she heard the gunshot that silenced it. She found the two terrorists chasing her had cut the distance between them in half. Kate forced herself up and yanked Luke forward, a wild panic to her retreat. She wasn't going to let them die here, not after coming so far.

Kate pushed through a cluster of branches and high bushes, and then she saw it. Less than fifty feet away was the plane she stashed next to the clearing. She turned back toward the woods, the terrorists fifty yards away.

Kate propped Luke up against the plane and then opened the cabin door. She wrapped her arms around his stomach and then heaved him onto the seat. His legs dangled from the cabin door, and she awkwardly folded them inside.

Once Luke was inside the cockpit, Kate snatched one of the ignition starters, then pumped the primer three times, and pushed the aircraft from the tree line and onto the field.

A gunshot burst from the forest, and Kate jumped as she shoved the ignition starter into place. She reached high with both arms and pulled the propeller down with all her might. Her fatigued muscles strained from the effort, but they provided enough power to start the old Skyranger, and the terrorists' shouts were drowned out by the engine's throttling.

Kate jumped into the cockpit, frantically running through the prestart, her hands sticky with Luke's blood, and then released the brake and hit the throttle. The engine whined, but as loud as it was, she still heard the terrorist's gunfire.

The contact of the bullets vibrated through the cockpit, and Kate white-knuckled the throttle. As the speedometer ticked upward, the engine's roar drowned out the rest of the gunshots.

Kate pulled back on the stick. "C'mon, baby. C'mon!" The cockpit rattled, and the plane jumped with lift and then landed hard on its wheels. The end of the field was closing in, and Kate pushed the throttle down further, pulling back on the stick with all her might. "*Gaaahhh!*"

The Skyranger's nose lifted, and the wheels separated from the field. The top of the trees disappeared as Kate continued her strained pull on the stick, and the wheels scuffed the tip of a conifer just before clearing.

Kate's muscles relaxed, and she laughed in triumph. "*YES!*" She leveled the plane out a bit so the engine wouldn't stall and then turned to her son, who still lay unconscious in the seat. "Luke? Can you hear me?" She patted his cheeks, and when he groaned in response, she smiled. "Good boy." She pulled a first aid kid out of from behind her seat, her gloved fingers fumbling it open awkwardly, and then applied gauze over the wound. "Just hang on, Luke."

The plane tilted to the left, and Kate was forced to grab hold of the stick. She couldn't keep one hand on the stick and the other on her son. She found tape and strapped the gauze over the wound and prayed it would hold for the trip.

Luke groaned again, and Kate retook the stick. She looked back at Luke, sunlight reflecting on his bloody chest, and a tear broke free from her eye. She looked down at the fuel gauge, which hovered well below half a tank. She was short on time and fuel.

22

Mark and Rodney stomped through the forest, leaving a trail of churned up snow on their hastened trip toward the hospital. The cold burned Mark's lungs, and his muscles twitched and spasmed in protest, but he pushed through it. He glanced over at Rodney, who held the other rope attached to the sled that Holly rested on.

Ice formed in little bits along his eyebrows and the scruff of his face. His breathing was labored, but his pace was steady. He kept his eyes forward, the snow around his shins piling to the sides with every step.

Glen and Laura had fallen behind. It was mainly Glen, but Laura stayed with him to make sure he didn't collapse in the snow with a heart attack. Mark couldn't see them anymore through the trees.

"There it is," Rodney said with breathless relief.

Mark turned quickly and saw the large grey building. "Thank god." He turned back to Holly, whose wheezes and rasps had worsened.

The pair pulled Holly toward the ER doors, where two ambulances were parked with their back doors swung open.

Mark glanced around, surprised at how vacant the outside looked. Compared to what he'd seen in New York, this was a ghost town.

The inside of the ER was dark, but there was a woman stationed at the desk, bundled up in a jacket and rubbing her hands together, looking down at something on the desk.

"Hey!" Mark said, still dragging the rope and the sled inside with Rodney's help. "My daughter's sick!"

The woman didn't move. She just kept huddled at her desk, shivering, staring down.

"Hello!" Mark grew more agitated, and then he dropped the rope and went over to the desk. "Hey, I said—"

The woman looked up and hissed, flashing yellowed teeth.

"Christ!" Mark jumped backward, and the woman looked back down at whatever she'd been staring at before.

A woman wearing blue scrubs stepped through two swinging double doors, holding a candle.

"Can I help you?" The woman wore earmuffs and gloves but no jacket. And before Mark answered, she saw the woman at the station and beelined toward her. "Cara! How did you get out?" The woman hissed again, but the nurse ignored it and grabbed the woman by the arm. "Let's get you back to your room." She turned to Mark. "I'm sorry—"

"My daughter's needs help," Mark said. "She's—"

"Mark!"

The alarm in Rodney's voice caused both Mark and the nurse to spin around at the summons.

"She's not breathing!"

"Oh my god," the nurse said.

Mark sprinted over, sliding on his knees as Rodney untied the straps holding Holly down. "Holly!" Mark lifted his daughter in his arms, her lips blue as the nurse rushed to his side.

"Follow me. We'll get her to a room."

Mark sprinted after the nurse, bursting through the double

doors and into the darkened hallway. The candle in the nurse's hand provided the only light, and its glow didn't cast farther than the nurse herself. "Hang on, sweetheart."

"In here." The nurse opened the door and gestured to a table in the middle of the room. "Put her there."

The table was on wheels, and it jerked away from Mark as he set Holly down. The nurse was already at his side, putting over Holly's face a plastic mask that was attached to a small ball that the nurse squeezed to pump air into her lungs.

"What happened?" the nurse asked, pumping air and checking Holly's pulse.

Mark stammered, trying to put his thoughts together in an orderly fashion but failing. "She had a cold, and we've been giving her medicine, but it's not—"

"What do we have?" a doctor appeared, his white jacket trailing him and then wrapping around his legs when he came to a stop at Holly's side.

"She's not breathing," Mark answered. "She'd been wheezing a lot and coughing."

The doctor leaned down and pressed his ear to Holly's chest then straightened up. "Her lungs are full of liquid. She's choking herself to death. Stacy, take the mask off." The doctor whirled around, producing a massive needle and syringe. He positioned the needle at Holly's chest, and Mark reached out his hand to stop him from inserting the monstrous thing into his daughter's body.

"What the hell are you doing?" Mark asked.

"We need to get the liquid from her lungs," the doctor answered.

"She's still awake," Mark replied. "Shouldn't she get some anesthesia or—"

"We don't have anything for her." The doctor's voice was calmer than the expression on his face. "You either let me do this, or she dies on this table."

Mark examined Holly's pale complexion and her blue lips and then removed his arm.

"Get her shirt off, and sterilize the area," the doctor said.

The nurse complied, and the doctor inserted the needle through Holly's chest. It disappeared, deeper and deeper until Mark thought the damned thing was going to come out the other side.

The doctor slowly pulled back the pump, and greenish-yellow liquid filled the glass. Once it was full, he removed the tube. "Give her another pump with the mask."

The nurse complied, and Holly's chest expanded with the mask's compression. The doctor moved the nurse's hand away and leaned his ear down to Holly's nose. He lingered for a few seconds and then grabbed the mask himself, giving another pump. "C'mon, sweetheart." He removed the mask again and lowered his ear to her nose, listening for breath. He shook his head and repositioned the tube. "I'll have to get more of the liquid out."

"How much?" Mark asked.

"All of it." Holly's body spasmed. "Keep her still. If she thrashes too much, I might damage her lungs."

Mark dropped her daughter's hand and used his strength to keep her still as the bottle filled with more of the greenish liquid. Halfway through, Holly opened her eyes and started to cry. "Shh, it's okay, baby. Everything's fine."

"Keep her still!" the doctor shouted.

But when Mark tried to end his daughter's thrashing, she suddenly lay still. The doctor snatched Holly's wrist as quick as a snakebite. After a moment, he dropped her arm and removed the needle, tossing it with the bottle of liquid it collected on a table. He shooed the nurse and Mark away. He placed his hands over Holly's sternum and pressed down hard, a loud crunch echoing through the room like ice breaking.

"*What are you doing?*" Mark lunged, but Rodney held him back, pulling him from the room. He struggled against Rodney's hold, fighting to be at his daughter's side. "Holly!" He thrashed. "Let me go!"

"You need to let the doctor do his job, Mark." Rodney's voice trembled due to the concentrated effort to keep Mark in place. "You can't do anything in there for her."

"She's my daughter!"

"She knows that!" Rodney spit back. "But you can't save her, Mark." The fight started to slip out of Mark after that comment. Rodney's voice softened. "You did what you could do."

Slowly, Rodney let him go, and Mark slid to the floor, sobbing. He shook his head. And while Rodney attempted to offer words, they fell on deaf ears. It was a father's job to be prepared, to protect his family against the world. But the world dealt a hand that Mark couldn't beat. If Holly died, so did he.

* * *

DENNIS STOOD NAKED by the window, looking out onto the street from the second story of the house he'd commandeered as his. It cost well into the seven figures, maybe even eight considering the location in the mountains and all of the amenities.

Of course, most of those amenities no longer worked. He would have killed to get that Jacuzzi going. But it would sit outside beneath the awning, unused, at least until he could get the power going. He puffed a cigarette, taking a slow, deep drag.

He'd raided the local convenience store last night and picked up a few luxuries before the rest of the inmates got wise and started hoarding. He hadn't had a decent drink or a smoke since he'd been on the inside. And here he had both. He smiled. It was good to be king.

He'd been awake since before dawn but only recently moved himself from beneath the sheets. It was warm there and cold by the window. But he needed to wake up. He needed to think. The frigid air and the cigarette were better than a double espresso.

A scream echoed outside, loud enough to penetrate the walls

of the house next door and the walls of his place. He frowned, knowing the raping was going to have to be dealt with soon, but then chuckled. He was already thinking like a fucking politician.

He flicked the cigarette on the carpet and then stomped it out with his bare heel, smearing a black stain into the beige floor. He looked back at the bed. The woman was still asleep, with both hands cuffed to the headboard. The restraints were more for necessity than pleasure, at least for her.

The drugs he slipped her last night would wear off soon. It wasn't until after he had his way with her and she lay naked and passed out on the sheets that he thought maybe he'd given her too much. But she was still breathing, and he made sure that she slept on her stomach so she wouldn't vomit and then choke on her own puke.

He turned back to the window and looked down to the wedding ring that belonged to the woman's husband he'd killed. There was some blood on it, but instead of scrubbing it off, he let it be. He liked it bloody.

Dennis got dressed, and before he left, he paused at the door, leaning back inside the room. "Bye, baby. Time to make the donuts."

Downstairs, spread out over the kitchen table was a map. He'd found it when he raided the convenience store. It was of the surrounding area, and the longer Dennis stared at that map, the more that bug started to burrow. He snatched the map off the table and walked outside.

The temperature had dropped, made even worse by a stiff wind. Dennis glanced up at the clouds, which already looked dark. It looked like the makings of a bad blizzard.

"Hey, Dennis." Mulls took a swig from a nearly empty bottle of Jack Daniels, his voice gruff and scratchy like the stubble on his face. "Have a good night?" He chuckled and took another drink.

"Hell, we all had a good night!" Jimmy appeared, then punched Mulls playfully, his voice high pitched and quick like an excited teenager. But the playfulness made Mulls spill his drink, and the big man landed a hard hook into Jimmy's stomach that buckled him at the waist.

"You need to stop fucking around so much, Jimmy," Mulls said, wiping his mouth. "Shit's not funny."

But Jimmy straightened out quickly and bounced excitedly on his toes. "Aw, it's a little funny." He coughed, rubbed his stomach, and then gave another playful shadow box routine to a still unamused Mulls, who was too slow to stop him.

"Knock it off," Dennis said, and Jimmy dropped the act. "We've got work to do. Round all the guys up, and tell them to come to the hall."

"What do you want me to tell them?" John asked, cocking one eyebrow up.

"Tell them I said so." Dennis turned and left Jimmy and Mulls to their task. This was the first test. He hoped that after a night of fucking and drinking they'd be in a good mood. If even most of the guys showed up, then he was in good shape. If it was anything less than half, then he would hit the road and move on. The inmates he knew hoarded together like locusts. So long as the majority agreed, the rest went along for the ride. But he wasn't about to be the outsider looking in.

It took less than twenty minutes before the hall was filled with sleepy, drunk, and hungover prisoners from Renniger Penitentiary. And every single prick that had stayed in this town was up like morning wood. Reporting to him.

"I don't know about you fuckers," Dennis said, raising his voice to a loud boom. "But my dick is rubbed raw!"

Laughter echoed the response, and a few of the guys raised beers they'd brought with them in a salute.

Dennis paced the platform at the front hall. "We've been locked away for a long time, boys. We've sat behind bars while the rest of the world ate, drank, and fucked! Well, now it's our turn." Another round of cheers erupted, and Dennis felt the first swells of power flood through him. They were listening to him, they believed him, and now it was time to find out if they would follow him. "We have a good thing going here, fellas." He stopped walking, finding the center of the hall's platform. "But if we don't take measures, it won't last."

The cheer died down, some of the men grunting in confusion.

"If we don't stake our claim, then someone else will! The more time goes on, and people start figuring out whatever the hell happened, the more others will start to gather their strength. And when that happens, it'll be harder for us to get what we want." He hopped off the stage and into the group of inmates. "But if we strike now, while everyone is still disoriented, we can make sure we have enough to last us the rest of our lives." He found each of their eyes, and noticed the twinkle of lust as he ticked off everything that they could have. "Booze. Drugs. Food. Women. Houses. Gold. Whatever the fuck we want." He whirled toward Mulls. "You want a waterfront beach property? It's yours."

Laughter echoed in the hall, and Mulls clapped his hands together greedily. "Nothing like a little sand and surf!"

Dennis turned and pointed toward Jimmy. "You want a Lamborghini? It's sitting out on the highway."

Jimmy grabbed hold of an imaginary wheel, and turned it sharply left and right, spitting over his shirt because of the engine noises he made in coordination with his erratic driving.

The group of inmates turned to follow Dennis as he cut through the crowd, and he waited until there was a small uproar of cheers behind him before he turned with a smile on his face, unfurling the map that he'd been holding. "There are five other towns within ten square miles, just like this one. Outside of those towns is nothing but trees and mountains for forty miles. We control this hub, and we have ourselves a nice little setup." He rolled the map back up. "Now, some of these towns will have authorities in them. Others won't. But if we strike now... if we hit them when they're still fumbling around and trying to figure out what happened... then the easier it'll be to push them out."

"So what do we do?" The question was shouted by a man in the back.

"I want to send out scouting parties," Dennis answered. "I want to know everything that's around us, and then I want us to take it. And we need to figure out how to get some heat going in this place."

"I did some electrician trade schooling in the pen." A man stepped forward, shirtless despite the cold. Tattoos crawled over his stomach and chest and up both sides of his neck. "I might be able to take a look around, see what's going on."

"Good. I like that," Dennis said. "Anyone else with trade schooling?"

A few more hands shot up in the air, and Dennis couldn't help but smile at the irony. All of those rehabilitation programs that taxpayers had funded were finally coming full circle to further screw over those same taxpayers.

Dennis turned to Mulls. "Let's get a list going of everyone's skills. And make the rounds for everyone that's still alive. See what we can squeeze from them."

It took less than an hour to get everyone organized, and by the time it was over, Dennis received a roaring round of applause. The scouts were sent out in groups of two, and Dennis smiled as he watched them leave.

To celebrate, he walked down to the liquor store and grabbed a fresh bottle of Jack Daniels and a two-liter liter of Coke then returned to his house. He stopped in the driveway and looked up at the two-story cabin that reached toward the sky. In all his life, Dennis never lived in something so huge. He'd grown up in a trailer park in northern New Jersey.

It was a shit childhood, and it was a shit way to grow up. Dennis twisted the cap off the Jack Daniels bottle and took a swig then wiped his mouth as he stifled a cough with the back of his hand. The liquor instantly warmed his innards and spread to his hands and feet. He walked into the house, leaving the thoughts of the trailer park out on the driveway. He wasn't going back to that life. No way in hell. He was a king now. He was the one giving orders. And he wasn't going to let anyone take it away from him. No fucking way.

23

Kate balanced between keeping both hands on the stick and then reaching over to check Luke's pulse as he lay unconscious. She trembled each time she pressed her fingers onto the cold skin of his neck. The idea of her son dying right next to her on the plane was more than she wanted to think about. But each time she checked, she exhaled in relief at the bump of his pulse.

The blood looked as if it was clotting over the wound, but it had taken a while. Kate reached for the map, her gloved hands still covered in blood, which stuck to the paper. She peeled her fingers off and flattened out the map.

She was close to the cabin, only thirty or thirty-five miles away. Kate unfolded the scratch piece of paper that Rodney had written the coordinates on. She rechecked her calculations, adjusting for the head wind she'd run into and the time. It was all ballpark figures, but they lined up correctly with what she was seeing on the map.

The clouds had worsened, and snow was far off on the horizon. She knew it was that storm Rodney was worried about. She looked at Luke, praying that the cabin had good medical supplies. She hadn't the first clue what he needed, besides a doctor, and Kate was betting the chances of one being on hand close by were slim.

Her eyes drifted to the control panel, and the needle in the fuel gauge hovered on empty. A lot of chances were slim.

Kate had saved time by flying directly over DC on her way north. It was an area that she'd wanted to avoid going down, but she knew she didn't have the fuel to go around it on the way back. She kept as high as she could, but even so, she still heard the thundering booms from the fights below.

Curiosity got the better of her, and she tilted the plane to the side to get a better look at the capital. But most of what she saw from the air was nothing but blackened rubble.

There was movement below, huddles of men scattered about in small groups. The only recognizable building that was still standing that Kate could see was the White House. But it was thoroughly barricaded, with the bulk of the city's resources and forces stationed around it.

Kate had worried that the sight and sound of her plane would cause attention, but with everything going on down below, she was the least of everyone's worries. But even from her position high in the sky, Kate could still plainly see that the capital was plagued with the same problems that she had seen everywhere else. No lights. No power.

If the people who did this could cause so much trouble to her country, to a nation that was believed untouchable, then where would they stop? Kate shivered at the thought of this epidemic spread across the globe. It was a virus without a cure. Or at least that was what it felt like.

The present had suddenly become the most important aspect of everyone's lives. There was no time to dwell on the past, no hope to think of the future. Everything had shifted to right here and right now. She glanced over at Luke.

Kate knew that his future would never be the same. No more college, no more schooling. With them thrust back into the

Stone Age with zero law and order, his future was one of survival. It was a future that Kate's entire family shared.

Phlegm formed in the back of her throat in the preparation of tears, but Kate forced them back. She had to stay focused. "One problem at a time, Kate." She sniffled, wiping the cold snot from her upper lip.

Another fifteen minutes passed, and Kate knew she was close. She dropped her altitude and searched for a place to land, but she didn't have many options. What wasn't covered in snow was covered with trees.

She circled, scanning the terrain, her hopes wildly high that she would spot the cabin and there would be a clearing nearby. But the more she circled, the more those hopes sank.

Kate reached over and checked Luke's pulse again, feeling the faint thump of her heart when the engine sputtered.

The old Skyranger jerked forward, the engine bucking the plane a few times before it finally died. The loud hum of the motor was replaced by the howl of the wind, and the propeller spun a few more rotations before gliding to a stop.

Kate gripped both hands around the stick, doing her best to keep the craft level, though it cost her every bit of her strength to do it. She scanned the ground, searching for any place that she could land, but still saw nothing but trees and snow.

The altimeter spun downward, the elevation dropping dramatically, and with the low visibility and the rolling hills of the terrain, the situation was growing from bad to worse.

Kate tilted the stick hard to the right, slamming her foot on the steering pedals, but the old bird whined in defiance. Her eyes glanced between the fast-approaching ground, the instruments that spiraled backward, and Luke.

The altimeter dropped to fourteen thousand feet, then thirteen thousand, twelve thousand, ticking downward faster and faster. Kate continued her frantic search for any suitable landing spot but still saw nothing that gave them a chance at survival.

And then, just at the altimeter dropped below nine thousand, she saw it in the top right-hand corner of her windshield. There was a straight cut through the trees. It was a road.

Kate straightened the stick, the plane wobbling left and right, her entire body shaking due to the growing turbulence and rough controls. She reached across to Luke's seat and tightened the straps over his chest and waist, making sure he was secure. She wished she could have done something about his head and neck. The landing was going to be rough.

The tips of the trees and the ground grew closer. Kate leaned left, muscling the plane toward the highway. And when Kate finally had a good look at her approach, her stomach soured.

Abandoned cars, covered in snow, lined the highway, leaving zero gaps of flat land. She checked the altimeter—twenty-five hundred feet. She was out of options.

Kate tightened the straps on her belts and then let the flaps down on the plane as far as they would go to give her more control. She gripped the stick with both hands, the plane wobbling left and right despite her forced control.

"C'mon," Kate said, whispering to herself.

Sweat broke out on her forehead, and her body flushed with heat. She tensed once the altimeter dropped below five hundred feet, and she could make out the models of the cars on the road.

Kate kept the nose up and pulled the stick back hard. She took one quick glance over at the altimeter, the numbers rolling into the double digits. Kate stiffened her arms and then looked at her son just before impact.

The pair jerked wildly in the cockpit, and the moment the wheels hit the top of the first car, Kate lost control.

The stick flew out of her hand, and the plane spun ninety degrees to the left. Both Kate and Luke were suspended in the air for a moment as the plane's belly skipped between the roof of two cars, then it jolted down hard on the top of a van, and the thin metal sheeting ripped like a sheet of aluminum foil. Kate thrashed wildly in her chair, the cockpit a whirlwind of turbulence.

The pressure from the straps dug into Kate's coat, and Luke's left arm smacked her forehead as the right wing of the plane tilted and wedged itself between a front and back bumper before the pressure and speed of the craft snapped it off, and the plane finally jerked to a halt where the fuselage lay on its right side.

Kate's vision blurred, and she shut her eyes, waiting for her head and stomach to catch up with the rest of her body in the cockpit, then looked to her son.

Luke's head lolled to the right, the straps of the belt still snug over his shoulders and chest. Kate gingerly unbuckled herself and reached her fingers over to him.

"Luke?" Kate asked. "Luke, can you hear me?"

She didn't think he'd answer, but the questions came out regardless of the likelihood of his response. His skin was still cold to the touch, but when she pressed against the artery on his neck, her own heart stalled.

Nothing. No pulse. Kate frantically inched closer, crawling over to Luke, and quickly unstrapped the belts. "Luke!" Her voice grew more frantic when she saw the fresh blood oozing from the gunshot. It had torn open during the vicious landing.

Kate grabbed the old bloody gauze, brittle and sticky from the cold, and pressed it hard into the reopened wound. Blood oozed over her gloved fingers, and the tears froze to her cheeks as they fell from her eyes.

"Stay with me, Luke," Kate said, reaching for his neck again to check his pulse. "Please, hang on."

A thump pressed against her finger.

Kate's eyes widened with hope, and she steadied her hand where she felt another light bump. She sobbed and kissed Luke's forehead, his skin icy against her lips. He was alive, but she'd need to move quickly if she wanted him to stay that way.

Kate unbuckled Luke from his seatbelt, then reached for the door handle on his side, but with the way the plane landed, it jammed against the hood of a car, preventing escape. Kate turned, looking back toward her door, and climbed upward.

Kate protruded from the cabin of the busted Skyranger and was smacked with the frigid cold of the north. She heaved herself out of the cabin and nearly tumbled down the other side before catching herself on the plane.

Kate planted one foot on either side of the open door, and then squatted, reaching her arms into the cabin and grabbing hold of Luke's arm, then pulled.

The first tug barely budged Luke from his seat. Kate repositioned her grip then tried again, exploding upward with enough force to thrust Luke's torso from the plane before she lost her grip and tumbled backward into the snow.

Kate landed hard on her ass, but the snow was deep enough to cushion her landing. She wallowed to the left and right before she finally got her legs beneath her, and then she climbed back up to the plane's cabin door.

She removed the rest of Luke carefully from the cabin as he dangled over the side. Despite the thick cushion of snow, she lowered him down gently, making sure that she didn't break his neck.

Kate nearly had Luke all the way down when she heard a rustle in the woods behind her. She jerked sharply at the noise and then quickly leapt off the plane's side.

Voices drifted onto the road, followed by heavy panting.

"It was over here," a man said. "Damn thing fell right out of the sky."

"I thought everything was broken." A second man's voice drifted toward her, gruffer but just as breathless. "How the hell did someone get a plane working?"

Kate grabbed Luke beneath his arms and pulled him, staying as low as she could. She made it a few feet before she realized she was leaving a trail in the snow. They'd be able to follow it right to her. She scanned the area and spotted a van two cars down. She pulled Luke toward it and prayed that it was unlocked.

Kate tugged at the handle, and she breathed a sigh of relief when it opened. She lifted Luke inside, her legs shaking from the exertion, and he landed with a dull thud. Quietly, she shut the door then erased the tracks that led to it from the plane.

"There! See? I told you I saw a plane!"

The voice was closer now, and Kate's heart thumped wildly in her throat. She darted in the opposite direction of the van, her footsteps leading whoever those people were away from Luke. She kept low behind the cars but stopped when she heard the hurried crunch of boots in the snow.

"Shit! You see that?" The man's voice squeaked in excitement.

"Would you *shut up*?" The second man hushed him angrily. "You want to give our position away?"

Kate lifted her head to the rear driver side window of a sedan and peered through the frosted glass. The two men passed, and it was here that she saw the rifles in each of their hands.

"Get your gun up," the second man said. "We don't know if they're still alive."

"Well, they won't be for long." The first man giggled in the same high-pitched tone as before.

Kate quietly ducked beneath the window and waited for them to pass. She darted a few more car lengths away from them but then stopped at a truck near the edge of the road and waited. She wanted to make sure they took the bait and followed her tracks.

The distance caused their voices to muffle, but from her vantage point, she could see them circling the plane. The cramped space between the cars offered only glimpses, but Kate did see one of their heads fall to the ground, the man pointing to what had to be her footprints.

But then, just when the loudmouth took a step to follow, the man's friend pulled him back to the path that Kate had tried to cover up, and her heart sank like a stone into her stomach as they began to follow it.

Kate began to stand but then thought better of it. She stared at the car door in front of her and cocked her arm back, curling her fingers into a fist. She punched the door, and a dull thud rang out. She looked through the icy window and saw both men turn at the noise. She punched the door again, and this time both men started back toward her.

Kate kept low, shuffling backward, banging on doors every few cars that she passed, leading the gunmen away from her son. She kept it up until they broke out into a jog, and then Kate darted for the forest.

"Hey! I see 'em!"

Snow and branches smacked Kate's face and body. The snow deepened the farther she traversed into the forest, slowing her pace. She glanced behind her, watching the fragmented images of the men chasing her between the trees. Then she lowered her eyes to the trail she'd cut in the snow. A trail that they could follow right to her.

"Through here!" The voice huffed loudly, and Kate saw the man pointing down at her tracks.

She slowed her pace, trying to let her brain catch up with her body. She shut her eyes hard, breathing, panicking. She turned left, then right, looking for solid ground.

"C'mon!" the voice said excitedly. "She couldn't have gone far!"

"Slow down, you asshat! Hey, stop!"

And at that command, Kate darted behind a tree, peering around the side until she saw the second man walking to catch up. They were close, but with the thick tree cover and the cold, any distance was made three times as long.

"We're supposed to be scouting for that town, not running through the woods."

"That's what we're doing!" the high-pitched voice complained.

"You're just chasing ass." The man gripped his friend by the collar. "And I'm not gonna freeze my ass off out here just so you can go and chase through the woods some woman who doesn't want anything to do with your dick."

"But all we have to do is follow—"

A heavy thud preceded a groan, and Kate saw the high-pitched wailing man buckle at the hips, hunched over and clutching his stomach.

"Enough fucking around!" the big man roared, his cheeks reddening. "I don't want to be out in this frozen shitstorm longer than I have to! Dennis wants us back soon!"

Kate furrowed her brow at the name, and hollowness carved out her innards. She was lightheaded, and she pressed her back against the rough bark and slid down into the snow with a soft crunch. She shook her head.

"That's impossible." Kate whispered to herself, her eyes searching the blinding whiteness of the snow. Dennis was in prison. And that was where he was going to stay for the rest of his life. He couldn't have gotten out. Could he?

The parole hearing was scheduled for what, yesterday? Two days ago? Kate's eyes widened. It was the day of the EMP.

Institutions were failing, and basic services were cut off. She had flown over the capital herself and seen the fighting and destruction that ravaged the city. Plus, she was in the northern New York wilderness, close to Dennis's prison. It was possible he was out. But that didn't mean he was coming for her.

Kate relaxed. Of course he wasn't coming for her. He had no idea where she was. If anything, he'd go to New York and discover the chaos that she'd escaped from. She peered from behind the tree trunk, finding both men gone.

Clumps of snow fell from her legs and back as she carefully and slowly approached the road. She kept her eyes peeled. The men could have been talking as a trick. But the closer she moved to the forest's edge, the more confident she grew that they were really gone.

Kate hurried back to the van where she'd left Luke, praying that he was still alive. She ripped open the doors and struggled to pull his body closer to her. She checked his pulse. She sighed in relief at the light thump. But it was faint. Too faint. It was only a ghost of a heartbeat.

She hurried back to the wreckage and found the map but was unable to locate the coordinates that she'd written down. It didn't matter, though. She knew them by heart. She used the nearest mile marker on the highway to check her location on the map. She was close. Only ten or twelve miles.

Yeah, ten or twelve miles through snow and hills with a one hundred and sixty pound kid to carry. Kate leaned forward, her body and mind exhausted. She lifted her head and looked to the north. The storm clouds were growing closer. She wouldn't be able to move him fast enough by herself. She couldn't carry him farther than ten feet before collapsing.

Kate stuffed the map inside her jacket and searched the vehicles on the road, praying she'd find one sooner or later. She figured that most of the people were traveling up here on vacation, hitting the slopes, which meant—"Yes!"

Kate found a sled, a pair of skis, and poles in the back of a van. She grabbed the gear and dragged it back over to Luke. She strapped her son to the sled, found some rope and cord in the van where she'd stashed him, and then slipped into her skis.

She tied the rope around her waist. She had to be quick. She had to get to the cabin. She planted one of the poles firmly in the ground and then glided her left foot forward.

It was slow going at first, but once she had some momentum, she was cruising. She kept to the shoulder of the highway, which was mainly clear of any obstacles. She pushed through the burn of her muscles, and past the fatigue, and fell into a rhythm. She was almost there. She was so close to the finish line.

24

The sounds that echoed through the dark hospital hallways were dreadful, hopeless noises. If it wasn't someone crying, it was someone screaming. Pleas and prayers intermixed with the wailing cries of those who had survived longer than their loved ones, but after a while, they became nothing but background noise.

Mark kept his hands clasped together tightly. He had gotten up from his seat in the hallway and paced the floor repeatedly. But after a time, the strength had disappeared from his legs, and he collapsed into a chair.

Rodney had remained seated once Mark calmed down, but Mark noticed the light bounce of the young man's knee.

Footsteps inside Holly's room triggered both men to look toward the door, and Mark stood as the doctor finally emerged. It was a second, maybe less before the doctor spoke, but Mark watched the man's face carefully, studying the doctor's stoic expression. The moment dragged on for an eternity, and Mark's entire body ached with distress he'd never experienced.

"She's alive," The doctor said.

"Thank god," Rodney said, exhaling and then collapsing back in his seat.

But Mark just stood there, frozen. He wanted to speak but continued to watch the doctor's face. Despite the good news, he still looked worried. "What else?" He stepped closer, prompting the doctor to take a step back. "What's wrong?"

"Your daughter's infection is quite severe," the doctor answered. "I've got most of the fluid out of her lungs, but if they fill up like that again, and her condition doesn't improve, I'm not sure that her body will be able to go through that kind of procedure again."

Mark lost his balance, staggering sideways until he hit the wall. His gaze drifted away from the doctor's, and he struggled to focus on anything. The doctor continued to speak, but Mark didn't hear him. "What?"

"I said your daughter will need to stay here for a while."

Rodney appeared at Mark's side, shaking his head. "Doc, there's a storm coming, and if we don't get moving soon, we'll be snowed in."

"I'm sorry, but there really isn't anything else we can do except keep an eye on her and pray that the new strain of antibiotics we're giving her through the IV will knock out the infection. Some of her ribs were bruised during CPR, but I've wrapped them tight. If she needs any pain relief just flag down one of the nurses." He stepped away from the two men. "Now, if you'll excuse me, I need to make my rounds."

Mark and Rodney watched the doctor disappear into the darkness of the hallway, his shadow lingering behind him because of the flickering candles that provided light.

"Mark," Rodney said, his voice soft. "I know the doctor wants us to stay—"

"I'm not moving her," Mark said, his eyes still lingering on where the doctor had disappeared. "I'm not going to risk making her sick again."

"If we stay, we'll have bigger problems than your daughter's infection." Rodney stepped directly in front of Mark, blocking his view of the dark hallway. "This place is running on fumes.

They're running out of food, they're running out of medicine, and once that storm hits and snows everyone in, this place is going to explode in a powder keg."

"What am I supposed to do?" Mark spun around, asking the question more to himself than Rodney.

"We let her rest for another hour to see if the new medicine is working, and if it is, then we take enough to run it out of her system, and then we leave." Rodney held both of his hands up and together in front him as if he were praying. "It's our best chance."

"She almost died!" Mark lunged at him, thrusting his finger toward the room where Holly still lay, fighting for her life. "You don't have kids, so I don't expect you to understand, but that girl is everything to me." His words lingered in the air for a minute, and once the flash of anger subsided, he sat down. He rubbed his face, feeling the growing stubble along his cheeks and chin and neck. "I know that she would already be dead if it wasn't for you." He looked at Rodney. "You saved her life."

"I just got her here," Rodney said, taking a seat next to Mark. "The doctor saved her life."

"No," Mark replied. "It was you." He leaned back, exhaling. "You've saved our asses so many times since New York that I've lost count. And Glen and Laura are alive because of you too." He watched the back of Rodney's head as the boy leaned forward, resting his elbows on his knees. "I owe you my life ten times over."

Rodney shook his head. "You shouldn't say that."

"Why not?" Mark asked. "It's true."

Rodney turned to face him, and even in the dark, Mark saw the redness in his eyes. "I almost left you guys. Back in the city. I made it halfway down the stairwell before I turned around. I didn't want to take you, and the only reason I did was the hope that one of you would have a skill set that I didn't."

"Well, you struck out there." Mark smiled, and Rodney

laughed, wiping his nose. "Look, it doesn't matter what you *thought* about doing." He rested his hand on Rodney's shoulder. "It's what you *did*."

Rodney nodded. "Yeah. I guess you're right."

"I know I'm right." Mark patted the boy on the back and then stood, his knees and hips popping, making him a decade older. The hiking was catching up with him. So was the cold. He could see his breath even inside the hospital. He walked to the entrance of Holly's room and watched her from the hallway.

"When you have kids, you want to protect them from everything," Mark said. "It's a duty that you wear like a badge of honor. When you first hold them in your arms, you have such high hopes. You want to give them everything you didn't have, and you want them to surpass everything you've become." He focused on the light rise and fall of her chest then watched her little hand twitch as she slept. He looked up at one of the plastic casings that housed the halogen lights that no longer worked. "So what are they supposed to do now in a world like this?"

"Survive," Rodney said. "That's what they'll do." He stood. "That's what we'll all do."

"Yeah." Mark followed the needle of the IV that ran into Holly's arm up to the bag that slowly dripped the medicine into her body. "One hour. We can leave then."

Rodney's eyes widened. "You're sure?"

"You've been right about everything so far. Despite me not wanting you to be." He turned to Rodney with a sad smile. "You really think that right now our best chance is to head to the cabin?"

"Yes."

There was no hesitation in the young man's voice, and Mark rubbed his eyes. "Then we go."

"I'll tell Glen and Laura then track down that doctor to get some more medicine."

After Rodney left, Mark just stared at Holly from the doorway. He was hesitant to enter, afraid that his presence inside might somehow disturb her rest. Two voices caught Mark's attention, and he turned and found two nurses chatting with one another, both of them wearing expressions of worry.

"I told you I already checked."

"And you're sure?"

"Yes, less than two cases are left."

The shorter of the pair of nurses placed her hand on her forehead as they passed Mark, and he turned to follow their conversation.

"That's not enough water. That's nowhere near enough."

"I know. I don't know what we're going to do!"

The pair disappeared into the darkness, and sourness formed in the pit of his stomach. He thought of the powder keg that Rodney had mentioned, and he ticked another tally on the young man's side of the scoreboard.

Outside, the wind had started to howl, drowning out some of the crying from the other rooms. It was a wicked, harrowing sound. Almost worse than the woman screaming for the doctors to give her child back to her.

* * *

THE MAP WAS SPREAD over the kitchen table, the corners weighted down with half-filled liquor bottles. Dennis stood over the map, arms crossed, tapping a black marker against his shoulder. Everyone but Mulls and Jimmy had returned. They stood behind him, still knocking the ice and snow from their clothes and onto the authentic wood flooring of the house.

Numbers were written near each of the dots that represented the nearby towns: 39, 86, 309, and 55 respectively. He stared at those dots with hunger drilled into the pit of his stomach.

"You're sure there weren't any cops?" Dennis asked, his eyes still glued to the map.

"Nah, we didn't see anything."

"Nope."

"No stations at least, but we couldn't check the whole town without looking suspicious."

Dennis nodded to himself. He set the marker down and turned to the inmates. Looking at them standing there, waiting for him to speak, he suddenly felt the ludicrous idea that he was their warden. He repressed the smile, and they parted as he stepped between them.

A desk with rifles and handguns was behind them, and Dennis had his eyes on the shotgun. It was a twelve-gauge pump action with a pistol grip for better ease of use. He picked it up and opened the chamber. It was loaded. "And they're all still scrambling to try and figure out what's going on?"

"There were a few people in the town that we scouted that were trying to form a committee."

"Yeah, ours too."

"We didn't hear anything in ours."

"There were a couple people talking about how to get the power back on."

Dennis nodded, smiling to himself, and then slammed the chamber of the weapon closed. He turned, shotgun still in hand, and eyed the men that had returned to him. "We need to move quickly then. The more time we give them to prepare or get a grip on things, the harder it will be for us to take what we want." He stepped through the inmates again, heading back to the map, this time pulling the inmates with him toward the table. "The closest power station is fifty miles to the south. The odds of getting that back up and running, or even getting to it at all, are slim. Anyone dumb enough to make the trip will die before they get there." He picked up the marker, flicking off the cap with his thumb, and kept the shotgun gripped in his other hand. He marked three spots on the map. "Hardware store, sporting goods store, and grocery. That's where we'll find what we need." He turned to everyone. "Get a piece of paper and something to write with. Everyone's making a list."

The group looked at each other confusedly for a moment but slowly dispersed in search of the equipment while Dennis eyed the map. He'd used some of the local flyers down at the police station and town welcome center to learn the location of those stores. And it turned out that the sweet thing he kept upstairs was a local girl. All it took was the promise of being left alone for a night to get her to spill the beans. He still hadn't decided if he was going to keep good on that promise, though.

The inmates returned with their paper and writing utensils, which ranged from pens to crayons. Dennis leaned the shotgun against his shoulder and rested his ass against the table. "Generators, skis, gas cans, fuel, hunting knives, fishing gear, bows and arrows..." He rattled off dozens of other items, trying to be as specific as possible so that the simple-minded, narrow-viewed cretins could handle it. "As far as food goes, anything canned or packaged is what you want. The sporting goods store might have some survivalist meals. If it says MRE on it, then take it."

All heads were down as the inmates tried their best to keep up with his instructions. He couldn't imagine what the spelling on those lists looked like. Once he was finished, he repeated the list again, and just as much writing happened as the first round. But he hammered home a few of the more big-ticket items like diesel generators, fuel, and power cords. If he could just get a few houses running with heat, they'd be in a good spot.

"And the last item on the list, which I don't think needs to even be written down, are guns." Dennis tilted the shotgun off his shoulder, and it landed in his right palm with a smack. "Guns and ammo, as much as you can find. Eventually, other people are going to be doing what we're doing, and if they come knocking on our door, I want to make sure we have enough bullets to kill them ten times over."

Chuckles and nods greeted Dennis as the inmates looked up from their lists.

"We do have one roadblock now, and it could be a big one." Dennis smacked his finger on a small location off the highway.

"There's a state trooper station ten miles to the north of us. I doubt they'll be making their way to our sleepy little corner anytime soon, but I don't want to take any chances. Our next order of business after we get the supplies we're looking for and take those towns is to take out those pigs."

"*Yeah!*" Fists thrust into the air and then pounded cabinets and walls.

Dennis waited for the ruckus to die down before he spoke but didn't do anything to hurry them along. He wanted them to remain angry. He wanted them focused. So long as he kept feeding into that hate, they'd love him, and he needed that to stay in control.

"We kill all of them," Dennis said. "No surviv—"

The door burst open, and Mulls and Jimmy burst inside, bringing a gust of cold wind with them as they shook off the snow. They stomped out the frost and snow on their legs and brushed it from their arms.

"Christ's dick, it's cold outside," Jimmy said, squealing. "Looks like there's a bad storm coming down this way. Did you guys—"

"What'd you find?" Dennis asked, his voice cold like the weather the two men had brought back with them.

Mulls stepped in front of Jimmy before he could open his mouth. "The town wasn't more than a few buildings. Whoever had been there was gone. We did find something useful, though."

"What?" Dennis asked.

"A hospital," Jimmy answered, poking his head up from behind Mulls.

"It's a small one, but it's close by." Mulls walked to the map and pointed it out off the highway. "Right there."

Medicine was just as valuable as food now. And Dennis imagined it would be a good bartering tool in the days to come. He didn't want to pass the opportunity up.

Dennis clapped Mulls on the shoulder and nodded toward Jimmy. "Good work." He turned to the rest of the group. "I want everyone ready to roll out in the next twenty minutes. We can get to the hospital and back before dark. Gather up as many sacks and boxes as you can carry." He circled the spot on the map where Mulls had pointed. "We're going to do a little shopping."

25

The wind kicked up, and the sky darkened with a more sinister blanket of dark-grey clouds. Kate planted the ski pole in her left hand shakily in the ground. The cord tied around her waist that connected her to Luke's sled was taut. The momentum from the beginning of her trip had ended once she was forced to turn off the main highway and travel the back-roads to the cabin.

Kate hunched over, using the poles to keep herself from face-planting into the snow. She turned back to Luke and saw that her son was covered in a layer of fresh snow. He lay there lifeless, and she was unsure if he was still breathing.

The thought of dragging her son's lifeless carcass triggered an involuntary scream that quickly cut out and transformed into a sob. She collapsed to her knees, gulping deep breaths of icy air that burned her lungs.

Kate shut her eyes. He was alive. She knew he was. She just had to get him to the cabin before the storm worsened. She took a deep breath and then pushed herself up from the snow. Her legs trembled in the skis. She pulled herself forward then planted the pole in her left hand into the ground then repeated the action with the right one.

She had already followed the road off the highway as far as it would go, and now she trekked through the woods, in search of a cabin that was somewhere in the wilderness of upstate New York where she had never been.

More and more thoughts of Holly and Mark filled her head, and Kate focused on them to distract herself from the cold. The strands of hair that protruded from her beanie were frozen stiff. And while she couldn't see herself, she was convinced that she had turned a shade of blue.

Holly's laughter drifted through her mind, and she smiled as she watched Mark lift her off the ground. Her daughter was four, and they had taken a trip to the beach. Kate had a rare few days off, so they rented a beach house. It was the start of summer, so Luke wasn't in school, though he was nervous and anxious about going back. He was about to start high school.

It was three days of nothing but beautiful weather on the golden coast, and Kate remembered thinking that they could live there. She even so much as brought it up to Mark on the second day.

"Really?" he asked, his tone laced with a mixture of surprise, excitement, and skepticism. "You think you could get a permanent gig here with the airline?"

"It's possible," Kate answered, watching Holly bury Luke in the sand. She leaned into him, and even in the frigid winds of the north, she remembered the warmth of the sun on his skin. "I think it would be good for the kids. I know Luke's tired of having to switch schools every couple years, and it might actually give him a chance to make friends in high school."

"I think that would be great," Mark said. "You really want to give it a try?"

"Yeah," Kate answered, lifting her face toward his. "Let's do it."

But the memory faded, and suddenly, all those good feelings disappeared with it. When Kate went to make the request, she couldn't bring herself to do it.

Kate had moved around so much because she felt a lingering restlessness about what happened with Dennis. And back then she still hadn't rid herself of his memory. It wasn't until a few years ago that the nightmares finally stopped.

And now those men back on that road had mentioned a man named Dennis. They looked shady enough to be from prison. And she was in Dennis's territory. Could he be here? Could he find—

Kate stopped. She blinked a few times, staring straight ahead. She slid forward on one of the skis to get a better look. It was a wall. It was the side of a cabin.

Her legs and arms flailed wildly and in poor coordination as she struggled to pull Luke the last few yards. A smile creased her face, and she waved her arms as if her family were outside waiting for her. "Holly! Mark!" She dug into the snow with ferocity and enthusiasm that her body wasn't willing to match.

The snow thickened and deepened the closer she grew to the cabin, and twice, Luke's sled was stuck. Less than ten yards from the front door, Kate abandoned the skis and untied the cord around her waist. Her legs sank into the thick drifts of snow. She lifted her knees high, struggling in the drifts until her foot landed on the old wood of the front porch.

"Hello!" Kate lunged for the doorknob, and it offered the resistance of a locked door. She pounded her fists against the wood. "Mark! Rodney!" She rushed to the frosted windows, pressing her face against the cold glass.

Nothing but darkness and haze was visible from the outside, and Kate pushed off the wall in a fit of rage. She clawed at her head and then turned back to where she'd left Luke in the snow. She checked his vitals. He was still breathing. Still alive. She sprinted around to the back door and gave it a tug. Locked. She looked around, searching for anything. She found a nice-sized stick and thrust it at the window.

Glass shattered, and Kate waved the stick around, moving the shards away. She climbed inside, wiggling her way over the ledge of the broken window. She landed on hardwood and groaned as she sat up.

Silhouettes of furniture and cabinets lay spread out in an open floor plan, the only doors inside leading to bedrooms or closets. She rushed to the front door, unlocked it, and then dragged Luke inside.

A fireplace was on the south end of the house in what she considered the living room. There was a pile of wood and a few starter logs next to it. She piled them into the chimney, then her feet thumped against the floor as she scoured the kitchen in search of a lighter.

She found her prize in the fifth cabinet and then ripped up an old newspaper as she made her way back to the fireplace.

The lighter sparked a flame on the first flick of her thumb, and she held the piece of paper to it until it caught, then tossed it beneath the wood.

Smoke billowed up but then was pushed back in, and Kate realized the vents were closed. She held her breath and reached for the lever up inside the chimney and opened them, clearing the airways. She stepped back, coughing, as the first few flames caught the starter log. She heaved Luke close to the fire and sat there, rocking with him. "Okay, Luke. Time to get warm."

The pair sat in the living room, the fire growing along with the warmth, and Kate felt her body thaw. It felt so good it was almost painful. A few minutes later, the fire was raging. Kate reached for a pillow on the couch and gently laid it beneath Luke's head.

She pulled open kitchen cabinets, bypassing the canned foods, though her stomach growled at the sight of them. She reached for a closet door and finally found the stacks of bottled water she was looking for. They were cold.

Kate forced the water down Luke's throat, and much to her surprise, he drank it. His lips worked against the streaming current of water, though half the bottle ended up on the front of his shirt.

The wind howled outside, and a gust blew snow and frost through the back window, over the glass she'd broken to enter. With the storm coming, she'd need to cover it up, or the fire wouldn't do much good to keep them warm when they were sleeping in snow.

But even with that, there was a more pressing matter, and that was the bullet still currently lodged in her son's chest. The bloody bandages that she had used from the first aid kit on the Skyranger were now hard and crusted. They broke off in pieces as she peeled them back. She didn't know much about first aid, but she knew that the wound needed to be cleaned.

After another few minutes of searching, Kate found a bunch of gauze and bandages with other medical supplies, and she pushed past the bottles with names she didn't recognize until she found the hydrogen peroxide.

Armed with a mountain of gauze, the antiseptic, and a package of water bottles, Kate hesitated as she knelt by Luke's side. She feared what lay beneath those last strips of bandages. There was so much blood already, and while she had seen gunshot wounds on television and in movies, she had never seen a real one up close.

Finally, Kate gritted her teeth and pulled the old, dirty bandages back. She winced, squinting with only one eye at the wound, but once the bandage was off, she discovered that it was little more than old, crusted blood.

Kate poured water over it and scrubbed some of the frozen, stubborn slabs of blood. Luke moaned in pain in his unconscious stupor. She tried to move quickly, unsure of the exact procedure, and halfway through her cleaning, she realized that she should have sterilized her hands before touching him. She doused her fingers with the peroxide, hoping she wasn't too late, and went back to work.

Once she was finished, the flesh around the bullet wound on Luke's shoulder was light pink. She saw the entrance wound and the tiny bits of jagged, hanging flesh that surrounded the tiny crater. Kate lifted the lip of the bottle of peroxide near the wound and slowly tilted the bottle over.

Luke's body gave an involuntary spasm as she poured, but she kept going until she felt as if it was enough. He grew still when she stopped, and then Kate quickly wrapped the wound with the fresh bandages, making them snug but not overly tight. She remembered training from her early aircraft-safety days that told her to keep the blood flow pumping, so long as bleeding had stopped, which it had.

A thick sheen of sweat covered Kate's face as she finished, and she leaned back into the couch and sighed. Luke continued to lie still, and when she checked his pulse it was still weak.

Kate collected all of the old, dirty gauze and bandages and piled them in a trash bag that she set by the back door, where she was reminded of the broken window. She found some blue tarp in the same closet as the medical supplies and then found a hammer and nails.

The patch of blue tarp was stretched taut over the window. It was crude, but it kept the snow out—for now. Then she scraped up the glass shards and placed them in the sack with the medical waste.

After the cleanup, Kate's stomach growled. She searched the cabinets and plucked out two cans of tomato soup and poured them into pot that she sat next to the fire.

While it warmed, Kate fed Luke another bottle of water, of which he managed to drain three quarters. The fact that he was drinking and his skin was warming helped to ease her worries.

The shelter, warmth, water, and food were drastic improvements from an hour ago. She checked the soup and fished a spoonful out. It was lukewarm, but she nearly lifted the pot to her lips and drained it all.

Kate forced herself to eat slowly, savoring each bite. She ate half of it then tried feeding some to Luke. He ate a quarter, and then Kate polished off the rest. After that she rummaged for snacks and found some crackers that she munched on.

Luke's face glowed due to the flames, the fire offering a crackle and pop as if in challenge to the growing winds of the storm outside.

The longer she sat in that cabin by herself, the more she wondered what had happened to Mark and Holly. They had more than a day's head start on her. She tried to avoid traveling down all of the horrific scenarios that could have occurred, but there wasn't much else for her to do.

A thousand things could have happened. But she tried to rationalize. Holly's condition could have worsened, and maybe they stayed somewhere until she was better. After all, Mark probably wouldn't have wanted to move her if the flu worsened, though she knew that Rodney wouldn't have been happy about it.

But even if that was the case, or one of the other few positive scenarios, Rodney's whole concern was to have gotten to the cabin before that big storm blew through. What did he say? Trying to wade through the snow and find the cabin after twenty feet of powder dropped would be like trying to find a needle in a haystack.

Kate walked to the front window. She clasped her hands together tightly, staring out into the growing storm. The snowfall had thickened, and the wind had picked up. A branch snapped off a tree and crashed into the powder, kicking up more white into an already growing blizzard. It wouldn't be long until she couldn't see anything beyond the front porch.

But Kate stood there, waiting, hoping, wishing to see a few bodies pushing their way through the storm. She'd run out to greet them then help them to the fire. They'd joke about the cold, and then Rodney would be able to do something about Luke's wound. And everything would turn out just fine. She could live with that.

What she couldn't stand was being here alone with Luke, whom she no longer knew how to heal. What she couldn't stand was not knowing what was going to happen next. She was still flying blind.

26

Rodney paced nervously, checking the pocket watch every few seconds to see if the hour was up. It was only another five minutes, but Rodney was careful not push Mark too quickly. He could see it in the man's eyes that he was struggling with the decision to leave.

"How's she doing?" Rodney asked, still keeping his distance.

Mark hovered over her, his upper back hunched as he held her hand and gently stroked her hair. Her breathing was labored, but the wheezing hadn't returned, which was a good sign. "I don't know. It's hard to tell. She looks so tired."

The candle flames flickered and moved the shadows over Mark's face. They made him look older, hollowed. It was almost as if they were at a funeral home instead of a hospital. And with the number of sheet-covered bodies that Rodney had seen, it wasn't a far stretch.

Rodney checked the pocket watch again—two more minutes until the end of the hour. He stepped out of the room and into the hall. Even inside, the howl of the wind had picked up, and Rodney knew that it was the big storm from the northwest. They had to get going. Now.

"Mark, it's been an hour." Rodney stepped inside the room,

finding Mark in the exact same position. "We need to get going. Laura and Glen are waiting on us." He hoped that the fact that there were other lives at stake would provide the needed clout to go, but Mark didn't budge.

Rodney sidled up alongside Mark, looking down at Holly from his point of view. "She's stronger than you think. And I've been listening since our talk. She hasn't wheezed once." He pointed to the medicine. "It's working, and I have more packed with our gear. I've got the supplies needed at the cabin to set up an IV, but our window is closing fast. It's now or never, Mark."

Another howl of winter wind penetrated the walls, and Mark finally nodded. "All right."

Before Mark could change his mind, Rodney carefully removed the IV from Holly's arm and helped bundle the girl up as Mark scooped her up off the table.

"Glen and Laura are with the sled." Rodney led while Mark carried Holly, staying close behind. The trio weaved through the darkened halls, and a weight lifted from him.

They passed the open doors of the other rooms. Some of the rooms were dark and empty, others filled with the grief of sobbing survivors.

Rodney propped open the stairwell door, and they passed some doctors and nurses hurrying upstairs, carrying what looked like a packet of blood, which also covered their scrubs. Light penetrated the cracks of the first-floor door, and Rodney quickly reached for the bar and pushed it open.

The first floor was busier than the second, and Rodney and Mark had to dart between the scurrying bodies of staff and patients. Patches of conversations flooded Rodney's ears as he hurried toward the ER lobby.

"What do you mean you're out of water?"

"I need the doctor to check on my son."

"I don't know. He's not breathing anymore!"

Tones ranged from fear and confusion, to fury and anger. It was already happening. The boiling point had been reached.

Rodney shoulder-checked the double doors open and immediately spotted Laura, who shot up out of her seat and quickly patted Glen, who'd fallen asleep, on his shoulder. Rodney smiled, and she smiled, and with less than fifteen yards between Rodney and Laura, a shimmer of black caught Rodney's peripherals. He looked to his right just in time to see four men enter, all armed with shotguns, rifles, and pistols. And then they opened fire.

A brief roar of screams erupted before the cacophony of gunshots cut them short, and Rodney had just enough time to duck behind a row of chairs before the bullets started flying toward him.

He landed hard on the tile, the impact made worse by the cold, though he was so flooded with adrenaline that he barely felt it. He army-crawled farther behind the chairs and seats but then stopped himself, looking for Mark and Holly. He spotted Mark on the floor behind the next row of chairs, his body curled up around Holly, shielding her from gunfire.

"Mark!" His voice was barely audible over the gunfire and screams and... laughter? Was that what he was hearing? "Mark!"

Mark finally looked over, and Rodney pointed toward the wall, gesturing for him to follow and keep low. Rodney waited for Mark to nod in compliance, and then they started their trek toward the wall.

Rodney watched the shuffling and scattering of feet from beneath the chairs. When he and Mark reached the wall, they tucked themselves behind the chairs, curled up in balls, and Rodney held a finger to his lips for quiet.

"They runnin' for hell or high water! *Hah!*" The voice was high pitched, and despite the gunfire, there was still the shrill of laughter.

"Spread out! If you can't fuck it or it isn't a doctor, then shoot it." The second voice was low and angry. "You two stay and watch the exit!"

They grunted in annoyance but obeyed.

From his position against the wall, Rodney saw carnage in the lobby. Bodies littered the floor, and blood seeped onto the white tile. He tried to crane his neck to see the fates of Laura and Glen, but the wall that led up to the ER's exit doors blocked them from view.

More screams and random gunshots echoed in the hallways, and when a woman came sprinting through the double doors and into the lobby, shrieking, one of the men on guard shot her before she had a chance to stop and turn around.

"Now what the hell did you do that for?" one of the sentries asked.

"You heard Mulls. She was too ugly."

Rodney's heart hammered in his chest. He stared down the end of his aisle. He had a clear view of the woman who'd been shot. Her head had turned toward him as she fell. Her mouth twitched, the last bits of life draining from her as their eyes locked onto each other. She moved her arm along the tile and stretched her fingers toward him. And then she was still.

It took everything Rodney had not to scream or jump up and run at those bastards at full steam, screaming his fury until they shot him dead like that nurse. But he buried that urge, knowing that he'd have to be smart.

He waited until his heart rate calmed, and then caught Mark's attention. Luckily for both of them, Holly was so tired that she was practically sedated. Rodney gestured for Mark to follow him, and they crawled toward the wall next to the exit doors.

Once there, Rodney whispered into Mark's ear.

"I'm going to jump the guard nearest to us. I can kill him, but I don't know if I'll have time to get the friend. If I can't, you jump him when he comes over to get me. Then you take Holly and run as fast and as far as you can into the woods. Try and get to the cabin, but don't stop moving."

When Rodney pulled away, Mark was frantically shaking his head. But there wasn't any other play. They had to act, and they had to do it fast. There was no telling how many more of those people were around.

Rodney coiled his body in preparation. His muscles tensed, and he focused every bit of willpower on the sliver of an arm that he had in his view. A thousand different scenarios of what could happen ran through his mind. He lunged for the arm and wrestled the weapon away from the shooter, wrapping his hand around a cold, meaty arm.

At the same moment, someone shouted, and the man tried to yank free, but Rodney already had his other arm around the man's throat, spinning him around and using him as a human shield. From behind his human shield, he saw the barrel of a gun pointed at him. But that wasn't what caught his attention first.

Although Glen was lying on the ground, covered in blood, Rodney was still able to recognize his bald head immediately. But even more recognizable was the tuft of Laura's blond hair. Blood pooled from beneath her stomach, and while Glen's face was turned away from him, Laura's pretty blue eyes stared right through him.

Something shifted inside Rodney when he saw that. He stepped away from himself and inched closer to something primal, almost evil. He turned his gaze back to the man with the rifle. "Put it down. Or I kill him." The voice that escaped Rodney's lips wasn't one that he recognized. It was cold and feral.

The man in Rodney's choke hold squirmed, and he groaned something through his teeth that sounded like "Do it!"

Rodney added pressure to the blade, causing his hostage to stiffen. The partner grimaced, looked at the doors his friends had disappeared through, and then finally lowered the weapon.

"Toss it on the ground, and then kick it toward me."

"Shit." The inmate did as he was told, and the rifle skidded over the tile to Rodney's feet.

"Good."

Rodney ran the blade across his hostage's throat quickly, and a warm gush of blood rushed over his fingers. The man gargled and then collapsed to the ground, choking, both hands around his neck as he bled out.

"What the fuck!" The thug stared down at his friend in shock and then looked at Rodney, his face flashing anger. "You fucking prick—"

Rodney squeezed the trigger of the rifle he'd picked up off the floor, and the man buckled forward due to the bullet that entered his gut. He dropped to his knees and looked up at Rodney, blood dripping from his mouth. "What the—"

Rodney squeezed the trigger again, putting a bullet through his skull. Everything was quiet for a minute, nothing but the ringing of the gunshot in his ears.

"Rodney?" Mark stood behind him, clutching Holly close to his chest. "Rodney, are you all right?"

He heard the question, but he didn't respond. His eyes fell to Glen and Laura, and he walked to them, stepping through the blood and tracking footprints on the tile. He knelt by Laura's side. He felt himself take another step away from himself as he gently closed her eyes.

"Rodney, we have to go!"

"I know." Rodney kept his eyes on Laura's body. And then, after another pause, he stood, turning to Mark, who recoiled once Rodney faced him.

More shouts echoed from the behind the double doors that led deeper into the hospital. The hallway doors burst open, and three more men flooded into the ER lobby. For a brief moment, nothing happened. They simply stared at one another, and then when Rodney raised his rifle, the one in the middle screamed for his men to shoot, and the bullets started flying.

Rodney squeezed off two shots before he joined Mark's retreat into the cold. Wind and snow whipped their faces, the storm immediately slowing their escape.

Shouts and gunfire carried on the wind, and Rodney kept hold of Mark's arm as he held Holly close to his chest. Their shins kicked up piles of white, and they struggled against the sudden steep pitch of the terrain.

Snow concealed the rocks and boulders that tripped them and sent them tumbling into snowdrifts. With the howling wind, and subzero temperatures, Rodney knew they couldn't survive the storm. He forced Mark to stop. "We need to find shelter! We'll freeze before we get to the cabin!"

Mark nodded, his body shaking as he kept Holly's face buried against the front of his jacket. "So where do we go?" Their words were snatched quickly by the wind and muffled to obscurity.

Rodney gestured to the northeast, up a steep incline. "We'll follow the rocky terrain! A cave is our best bet!"

Mark shook his head. "I don't think I can make it that far!" He lifted Holly. "Not with her!"

"We have to try! C'mon!"

Rodney placed one sturdy foot on rock beneath the snow and pushed himself up, offering a hand to Mark, who took it to steady himself. It was painstakingly slow, but they pressed on.

Halfway up, Rodney turned to see if the hospital was still visible, but he couldn't even see the trees ten feet from his position. He patted Mark on the back as he climbed. "We're almost there!"

They spotted a cave between two big boulders, and Rodney steered Mark inside. Rodney produced a small hand-cranked light from the inside of his jacket and peered inside. It was deep. Deep enough to protect them from the storm. He motioned for Mark to come up. "C'mon!"

The three of them entered the cave, Rodney's light leading the way, and he checked the back for animals, following it as far as he could before the space grew too small. It was clear. He traveled back to Mark, who sat and leaned up against the wall.

"How are you doing?" Rodney knelt by him and took stock of what limited supplies remained on his person, but his fingers had frozen stiff, and it took nearly a minute of focus and practice to form a fist.

A few tools, a lighter, iodine tablets, a miniature first aid kit with bandages, needle, and string. A few small packs of dried fruits and nuts, along with some jerky. But no water. And no wood. Rodney, shivering himself, looked at Mark, who couldn't stop shaking either, rocking Holly in his arms. "We need a fire, or we won't last the storm."

He stood, hunched over because of the short ceiling, and Mark grabbed him before he was gone. "You'll freeze out there."

"I'll be back before that happens."

"What if one of those people finds you?"

It was a tone that Rodney hadn't heard in a long time. The concern, the fear, the touch of anger. It was the voice of a father.

"I'll be fine," Rodney said, having to peel Mark's hand off him. "Just try and keep her warm."

The wind and cold stopped him dead in his tracks the moment he left the protection of the cave. His body and even his mind screamed for him to go back inside. But he knew that if he didn't find wood, then all three of them wouldn't last the night.

Frozen stiff by the time he reached the bottom, Rodney found the nearest tree and reached up for the closest dead branches that he could feel. He tugged gently, seeing which would give way, and after three tries, one snapped off with ease. He made sure to keep his back toward the cliff, knowing how easy it would be to get lost in the sea of white.

Rodney bundled the sticks he found and then turned, the steep incline of rocks nowhere to be seen. He stumbled forward, hoping it was just the lack of visibility, but still there was nothing. His heart rate quickened, and his breathing grew so labored that he gasped for breath.

He pushed forward, holding on to the sticks that he'd gathered, looking for the rocks that led up to the cavern in a world that was nothing but a white backdrop. "Mark!" He felt the scream's vibrations along his throat, but he could barely hear himself above the whine of the wind.

But despite the fear, despite the confusion, Rodney stayed

true to the path, and he exhaled relief when he saw the familiar cropping of the rock formation above. He was careful with this footing on his ascent, balancing the wood and himself so he wouldn't fall. If he fell here, he wouldn't get back up.

Rodney dropped the sticks into the cave and shook off the snow. He found Mark and Holly in the same positions as when he left, and he started knocking the snow from the wood before it melted and wet the sticks.

He was forced to throw out a few that were too damp from the snow, but he had a decent pile ready, and enough to keep it burning, hopefully, through the night. He gripped the lighter and reached for one of the little strips of paper that he stored with it to act as tinder and set it ablaze.

Both Mark and Rodney stared at the flame as if it were a godsend. With shaking hands and holding his breath, Rodney brought the strip to the shavings. Smoke filtered up, and he carefully lifted the burning pile toward the larger branches. He continued to feed it shavings until flames flickered, and once the other sticks burned, the tension in his body relaxed.

"God, I don't think I've ever been so happy to see fire," Mark said, keeping Holly in his arms as she shivered. He stared at her. "We don't have the medicine."

"I know." Rodney stared into the flames and then looked toward the front of the cave and the blizzard outside. "We can't chance going back now." He turned to Mark. "Maybe in the morning."

"Yeah." But Mark looked at Holly. "Morning."

Both men understood what the night would tell them. Every howl of wind and flurry of snow that gusted into the cave's entrance reminded them of it. Morning would reveal them alive or dead.

But even if they survived until the morning, the likelihood of finding the cabin was limited. The roads would be snowed over and so deep that the cars would be buried, so long as the weatherman who'd predicted the storm was accurate.

The fire flickered, and Rodney and Mark inched closer to the flames.

"I'll take the first watch," Rodney said. "I'll wake you up in a few hours."

"Yeah," Mark said. "Rest would be good."

But despite their rotation, neither men would get any rest. They just took turns staring at the fire and into the storm, making sure that Holly was still breathing all right. After all of Rodney's preparation and all of his planning, it felt as if everything had come down to this one night.

Survive, Rodney thought. *Just survive.*

27

A blanket of fresh white snow covered the northernmost portion of New York State. The blizzard that blew through the day before and bellowed well into the next morning had finally passed. And aside from the ten feet of snow it dropped, nearly swallowing the cabin whole, it also brought the clearest blue skies that Kate had ever seen.

She planted the shovel firmly in the snow and wiped the sweat from her brow, glancing at the path she'd had to dig from the front porch. A narrow gulley was etched deep into the snow that sloped downward toward the door.

It had taken nearly an hour to get through all of it, but she was glad to have the activity. In the brief twenty-four hours that she'd been inside that cabin, she had already gone stir crazy.

Kate glanced at the horizon and the landscape, which looked just as pristine as the sky above. She bit her lip anxiously, hoping that at any moment she'd see Mark and Holly coming up over the snow. She lingered out there, feeling the burn of the sun despite the cold, watching and waiting.

"Mom?"

Kate turned back to the cabin and immediately descended the freshly shoveled snow path. Luke had awoken during the storm. He wasn't very coherent, but he was hungry, which she took as a good sign. Then he'd passed out again and slept, until now.

Luke lay on the couch, his head propped up on pillows, looking at her with a sleepy, pain-riddled stare. Kate knelt by his side, smiling, and removed the glove from her hand to touch his face. "Hey, how are you feeling?"

"Water?" Luke asked, pinching his eyebrows together, his voice scratchy and dry.

Kate reached for one of the half-drunk bottles on the floor and started to tip the bottle toward his mouth before he stopped her.

"No," Luke said. "I need to try." He shakily held the bottle, his grip barely strong enough to squeeze the plastic, but he drank it by himself. "Thanks."

Kate touched his forehead. He was sweating quite a bit, though she wasn't sure if it was because of the fire and blankets or something else. She reached for some of the wool quilts. "We'll take a few of these off, see if it helps cool you off." She made a mental note to check his bandage and clean it again now that he was awake.

Luke jolted upright quickly, his eyes frantic and wide. "Claire." He winced when he tried to turn, and the pain and fatigue dragged him back down. "Mom, where is she?"

For a second, Kate forgot that name. It had taken a backseat to the events since leaving the college. In all the time she had by herself, she hadn't spent a single second of it thinking of what to tell him, or how to tell him, what happened.

"Mom?" Luke's expression showed that he was on the verge of tears.

"She didn't come with us," Kate answered. "After you were shot, she helped me carry you to the plane, and there wasn't enough room for both of you." Kate tried to smile, but it felt false on her face. "She stayed behind to save you."

"What?" Luke's lip quivered. "You left her?" He shied away from her.

Kate reached for her hand, but he knocked it away. "The people who shot you were chasing us. We didn't have time to think it through. It was the best decision. She helped lead them away from you."

"How do you know that?" The words pricked like poisoned darts.

"There wasn't another choice—"

"There's always another choice!" Luke roared, his pallid cheeks flushing color. But the outburst sapped what little strength he had, and he collapsed back onto his pillow.

"Luke—" Kate buttoned her lips, unable to tell him the truth, because it would hurt him worse to know that Claire had discarded him the moment her own life was in danger. But in her lie, Kate could ease the burden of heartbreak.

Kate walked to one of the bedrooms, the mattress still covered in plastic. It crinkled as she collapsed onto it, curling up with the pillow, which was devoid of any cover. And so, even with her son awake, she was still alone.

She had to fight the repeated urges to march out there and tell him the truth, but she won out each time, knowing that he was hurting but that pain would heal. It would leave a scar, but it would heal, and life would go on.

But the more she thought about it, the less she believed that statement was true. Life hadn't gone on. It had stopped. The terrorists and their EMP had made sure of that. She balled her hands into fists and grimaced, feeling the hot tears roll down her cheeks.

What had they done it for? Some selfish idealism? Some sacrifice for their God so they'd get their virgins in heaven? Millions were suffering. Maybe even millions had died. Families had been torn apart, and Kate Hillman was one of the casualties.

Hadn't she been through enough? Hadn't she already paid for whatever sins she committed? The recklessness of her youth and the danger it had put her son in had haunted her for years. But now it had come full circle.

The tears eventually gave way to fatigue, and Kate's eyes fluttered closed. She drifted in that suspended animation between full sleep and being awake, but when she heard the voice, it was hard for her to determine if it was real.

Was it from a dream? Or could it be—

"Kate?"

She snapped her head up off the pillow, her mind foggy and her body heavy from the dazing nap. She wiggled herself off the mattress, the plastic crinkling madly from her wild, uncoordinated movements.

"Kate!"

The voice was closer now. It was heavy and out of breath, and Kate's knees buckled when her feet hit the floorboards. She sprinted from the bedroom, through the kitchen, and past Luke, who had propped his head up and tried looking out the door.

The snow brightened and whitewashed the landscape as Kate slipped up the slope she'd carved out earlier. She clawed with her hands, hunched over, and squinted as she broke the surface. "Mark!" Kate spun around, looking for him, but saw only the snow and the mountains. "Mark!"

"Oh my god, Kate!"

Kate spun around, following the voice. And when her head finally stopped spinning, she saw Mark and Rodney, pulling a sled behind them. Kate sprinted toward them, and Mark untied the cord around his belt, dropping it hastily into the snow.

They collided with a muffled smack due to their bulky coats and squeezed each other hungrily. Kate shut her eyes, clawing at his back as Mark lifted her up. "Thank God. Oh, thank God." She kissed his cheek, his cold skin stinging her lips. "Holly?"

"She got worse, but she's okay." He turned back to Rodney, who was still pulling the sled with their daughter. "That's what took us so long."

But as the sight of Rodney alone with her daughter started to sink in, Kate frowned, shaking her head. "Where are Glen and Laura?"

Mark lowered his head. "They didn't make it."

Kate pressed her hands to the sides of her head, taking a step back. "Christ."

But Mark reached for her and pulled her close, looking toward the house. "Is Luke inside?"

"He is, but..." Kate answered, reaching up to his face. "He needs a doctor."

It took a few minutes for each of them to get caught up, but on the way back to the cabin, and even when they were inside, Kate didn't leave Holly's side. Their daughter was still unconscious, and though Luke was still upset, he was glad to see Mark, and vice versa.

Aside from a quick hello, Rodney had said nothing upon his arrival. His silence wasn't noticeable at first, not when Kate was so consumed with her family, but once they were caught up, Kate knew something was wrong.

"Rodney?" Kate asked, slowly approaching him from behind as he stood at the living room window, which was caked with snow.

"We'll need to clear as much of the powder away from the front of the house as possible," Rodney answered, keeping his face toward the window. "It'll be a while before it melts, but I want to make sure we have at least two exits open in case we need to leave quickly."

"Rodney, are you all right?" Kate sidled up next to him, and he turned his face away, swiping at his eyes.

"Fine." Rodney cleared his throat, and then, after another pause, he finally turned to face Kate, the remnants of his tears almost invisible. "We'll take stock of our provisions, and then tomorrow, I'll go and see if we can find some materials back at the hospital to get the bullet out of Luke's shoulder. I have some medical books here on operating, and I might be able—"

Kate touched his shoulder, and Rodney seized up. "What

happened at the hospital wasn't your fault. You did what you could."

"We should have left sooner. If I had just—"

"You did exactly what you should have done." Kate stepped closer, and the stoic façade that was Rodney's expression cracked as he twisted the corner of his mouth. "Take it from someone whose job it was to be prepared for every outcome when they were a pilot. There wasn't any way of knowing that those people would show up. And if you didn't go there and you didn't wait for the medicine to work on Holly, then my daughter would be dead." She hugged him, and his arms hung limp at his sides. "You saved people. Even when you didn't have to. Laura knew that. Glen knew that. And they wouldn't blame you, either."

Rodney sniffled and whimpered at the sound of their names and then slowly lifted his arms and wrapped them around Kate, squeezing tightly. When he pulled away, he exhaled a shaky breath and then wiped his eyes. "We do need to get ready. Set up the rooms, check the provisions."

"I've gone through the closets already," Kate said. "Everything looks fully stocked."

"We still need to check the caches," Rodney said.

"What?" Kate asked.

"Around the cabin," Rodney answered. "I've got supplies buried all around the property. And we need to get our water system set up. C'mon, I'll show you where the lake is."

Kate followed Rodney to a bedroom, but Mark stopped her just before she entered.

"Hey, I need to talk to you." Mark eyed Rodney. "It'll just be a minute." Mark led them to another room, the same one where Kate had been sleeping. He took her hand as they sat on the plastic mattress covering, staring at her knees. "There's something I need to tell you. Something that I'm still not sure I really saw."

Kate frowned. "What?" Mark's apprehension was making her

nervous. Out of the two of them in their relationship, he was the one who was always forthright, the one willing to talk about anything. Seeing him with a tight lip wasn't a common occurrence.

"It was at the hospital, right before we left, right before Rodney killed—"

"What?" Kate gasped but kept her volume low. "Rodney killed somebody?"

Mark shook his head. "It's not what you think. It was after they'd killed Glen and Laura. And if he hadn't, then Holly and I would be dead."

"Christ, you didn't tell me that," Kate said, reclaiming her hands and twisting her fingers nervously.

"I didn't want to bring it up in front of Rodney, but listen." Mark inched closer. "The people who attacked the hospital, they weren't terrorists. I think they were inmates."

Color drained from Kate's face, and she thought of the pair of men that she'd seen on the road. Could it have been the same people?

"When we were making a run for it, I saw someone chasing us," Mark said, and he looked away, almost as if he was trying to convince himself that the memory wasn't true. "I only got a glimpse of him. And I wasn't completely sure until I heard the others say a name."

Kate stood, walking like a ghost to the wall in the room. Her mind was back on the highway, ducked behind those trees in the snow. She spoke his name before Mark had a chance. "Dennis."

It was quiet for a long time, and then Mark finally stood and walked to Kate, gently gripping her elbows.

Kate maintained a stoic expression; only the tears streaming down her face gave away the truth of her fear. She told Mark what she'd seen on the road, what happened with the inmates who chased her into the woods. She had tossed it aside as a trick of her mind, or that there were millions of others with the same name. But it was real.

"It doesn't mean anything," Mark said. "He doesn't know where we are. It may not have even been him. I could have just been seeing things. We were moving so quickly, and there was so much adrenaline that I—"

"It was him," Kate said, her voice an octave lower than it normally would have been. She raised her eyes to meet Mark's. "I know it's him."

"We'll be fine," Mark said. "We're in the middle of nowhere. He won't get us. He can't get us."

"That's what I told myself after Luke was born," Kate said, stepping away from Mark and moving toward the door, where she could see Luke watching over Holly in the living room. "But I was wrong."

* * *

DESPITE THE COLD, the stink of the bodies was overwhelming. And it wasn't just the dead. Plumbing had stopped working, and shit was starting to flood the halls. The storm had trapped them inside. It was like being locked up all over again. Except it was snow that kept them inside instead of iron bars.

"Dennis!" The scream bellowed down the dark hallways flickering with candlelight. "Dennis, where the fuck are you?"

Dennis rubbed his temples and slowly rose from the cot in the room he'd picked out on the first floor. It was the only one he could find that didn't have any dead people in it. He recognized the voice screaming his name, and he knew what the fat man wanted. It was the same thing everyone else wanted.

When Dennis stepped into the hallway, he spied the bulbous shadow that Carl's body cast due to the flickering candles. He was flanked by two other men, Tim and Vic, though they didn't share Carl's vigor and satisfaction in finding their leader.

"You said it was a better idea to stay!" Carl pointed his fat finger in Dennis's face, his breath reeking from a good five feet away, though that could have just been the shit. When it came to

Carl's breath, it was hard to tell the difference. "How much longer we have to be stuck in here?"

"You're free to leave whenever you want," Dennis answered. "I'm sure that fat ass of yours will keep you nice and warm." He smiled, and Tim and Vic snickered.

Carl's face flushed red. "You think you're fucking funny?" He removed the pistol from his waistband at the front and pointed it at Dennis's forehead, his finger on the trigger. "Well, I don't think it's fucking funny!" His voice thundered, and the two men beside him took a step backward.

Dennis stared down the pistol's barrel, and his smile slowly faded. "No. It's not." He raised his hand, which held no pistol, and snapped his fingers. In the quiet of the hall, the faint snap echoed loudly, and it took less than ten seconds for a dozen men to appear from the shadows of the hall behind Dennis.

All of the men that appeared were armed, and all of their guns were pointed at Carl. Dennis walked forward until his forehead rested against the end of Carl's pistol. The man frowned in confusion.

"What the fuck is your problem?" Carl asked, visibly shaking now. "Are you crazy?"

"I'm not the one with a dozen guns trained on me," Dennis answered. "You're the only crazy one I see around here." He quickly grabbed hold of Carl's thick wrists, and he felt the shock run through the fat man's body. "Go on, Carl. You're the big man on campus, right? The one with everything figured out? So get on with it."

Carl shifted his gaze between Dennis and the guns aimed at him. And when he tried to remove the pistol, Dennis tightened his grip so Carl couldn't move.

"What the hell?" Carl panicked, jerking wildly to try and free his arms. "Let go, man!" Carl dropped the pistol, and it clanged against the floor, but Dennis kept hold of Carl's hands. "I said let go!" He yanked his arms back hard, and that was when Dennis finally released his grip.

Carl tumbled backward, smacking against the floor with a thud, both Tim and Vic stepping away from him and merging with the crew behind Dennis.

Dennis towered over Carl who crawled backward, cowering.

"I-I'm sorry, Dennis. Hey, you know me, right? I've got a big fucking mouth and a hot temper, but I'm not a troublemaker. You know that, right?" Carl awkwardly wallowed from side to side, his weight making it difficult to stand, and when he finally did, he remained hunched in a cowering position. "Please. Dennis, it's just that we've been stuck in here for—"

"Less than a day," Dennis said then lowered his eyes to the pistol that Carl had dropped. He bent down and picked it up with casual effort that would have been appropriate for someone picking up a sock or some trash. He gave the pistol a shake up and down, feeling the weight of it.

"Dennis, look I—*Gah!*" Carl shot his hands up in the air and looked away as Dennis pointed the gun at him. "P-Please. Don't do this."

Even with the limited light from the candles, Dennis could still see the sweat dripping from Carl's face. He liked that look. It was the look of a broken dog, a beast that recognized its inferiority. But like all bad dogs, it was time to put this one down.

The pistol jerked Dennis's hand back as he fired, and the bullet went straight through Carl's skull. The man dropped dead, collapsing into a worthless meat sack in less than the blink of an eye. Dennis tossed the pistol onto the man's stomach, which jiggled when it landed, and the visual made him laugh. "Fat shit."

When he turned, he saw that Tim and Vic were the only ones not laughing. They kept their heads down, and when the rest of Dennis's men parted to let him through, Vic whimpered.

"You went along with him?" Dennis asked.

"No." Tim looked Dennis in the eye, the effort causing his neck to strain. "We didn't know he was going to do that."

"We just wanted to get out of here. There isn't any food or

water left." Vic kept his head down, his shoulders shaking like leaves in the wind.

Dennis grabbed each of their shoulders. "We all want to get out of here." He craned his neck back at Carl. He laughed then clapped Vic and Tim on the back and walked past them. He snapped his fingers, and the hallway lit up with gunfire.

It took less than an hour to shovel their way out of the ER lobby, but when Dennis felt the sun on his face, he took a deep breath of cold mountain air. "Now this is more like it." He looked back at the men penetrating the surface of the hole they had dug, and the imagery of convicts tunneling from prison forced Dennis to laugh again.

"Mulls!" Dennis hollered for the man the moment he was out, catching him in the middle of stretching his back.

The big man sauntered over, gasping for breath. "Yeah?"

"Those people we saw escape yesterday. You think Martin and Billy can track them?"

Mulls gazed out into the sweeping landscape of white. "I doubt they made it far in the storm. They probably found a place someplace close and waited until it passed. If we can find where they laid up, then they might be able to."

Dennis grunted. Those bastards had killed two of his men. And while he didn't share any fondness for the rapists and murders he'd assembled, he was trying to build a reputation in this new world. And if there was one thing that would break him faster than anything with the group of men he surrounded himself with, it was looking weak.

"Do it," Dennis said. "But if it takes you longer than two hours, come back to town." He turned to see the medical supplies being lifted from the snow. "I'd come with you myself, but I want to make sure none of these former junkies lift any of the good stuff. Which reminds me..." He turned back to Mulls. "If you do find the tracks, come and get me before you hunt those little pricks down. I'd like to be there and shoot them myself."

"All right," Mulls said, and without another word, the old inmate snatched up two men and waddled into the woods in search of the murderers.

Dennis watched them disappear into the vastness of the white forest and thought of the face of one of the men who'd run from them yesterday. It was only for a second, and he could be remembering it wrong, but the man looked as if he was surprised to see him.

And it wasn't a surprise of fear—it was more the way someone would look when they recognized a person they hadn't seen in a long time. But what had been driving Dennis mad was the fact that he didn't know who that man was. Hopefully, Martin and Billy would find their little hideout, and Dennis would be able to scratch that itch.

But until then, he had business to attend to. There were another forty men waiting for his orders back at the town, and five more settlements to take over. But if he wanted to expand he needed to recruit. "Jimmy!"

The skinny, wiry stalk of muscle bounced close. "Yeah, boss?"

"I want you to take a trip back upstate," Dennis answered. "Look for any more inmates that are wandering around, and tell them what we have, what we're doing."

Jimmy smiled. "Yeah, sure boss."

"Pack up when we get back to town." Dennis patted Jimmy on the back and then stepped out into the snow. It was a brave new world. And soon it would be all his.

28

Morning had arrived three hours earlier, and the sun shone brightly on the picturesque ski village below. Pitched snow-covered roofs of cabins and small inns dotted the main street with a few shops sprinkled between.

The highway that fed into the small town was clogged with broken-down vehicles buried beneath the blizzard that had blown through the day before. Only roofs and antennas protruded through the snow. The cars were abandoned without a second thought as people fled, seeking the safety and refuge of shelter.

Dennis Smith stood on a ridge that over looked the town. Frost and blood covered his face, mixing to produce a shimmering red beneath the sun. On either side of him stretched fifteen men, all of them armed, all of them sporting the same frosty red glower.

Tongues ran over cracked lips, appetites eager for the taste of chaos and death. Adrenaline pulsed wildly through their veins. They turned toward Dennis. They waited for him. The man who had brought them here, the man who had quenched their thirst for blood and women and booze. There was more of it down there, just waiting for someone strong enough to take it.

A cold, stiff wind blew from behind them, casting their scent toward the unsuspecting victims below. They were nothing more than sheep ready for slaughter. The wolves had arrived. The wolves were hungry. The breeze died. Dennis nodded.

The escaped inmates swarmed the town like locusts. Houses were searched, one by one, people cowering and hiding beneath beds and in closets. No one was spared, and no one was left behind. Rebellion was dealt with swiftly, the remnants of defiance staining the white snow with crimson.

Wives and children cried as they passed their slain husbands and fathers, shoved along by men who laughed and howled and reveled in their pain. Dennis smiled from his perch on the ridge.

Mulls, Dennis's right-hand man, ascended the ridge when it was finished. His gut hung over the belt at his waist, and he puffed labored breaths as he crested the top, icy clouds spitting from his mouth like dragon's breath. "We've rounded all of them up." He gestured to the bodies and bloodstained patches below. "They don't have a town hall like the others, but one of the inns has a big lobby. That's where we put them."

Dennis kept his gaze fixed on the town below. He waited for the inevitable. Movement flickered in his left peripheral. Five people sprinted from the back of a house, weaving through the thick snow beneath the cover of trees. "Not all of them." He turned his dark eyes on Mulls, and with a flick of his head, he gestured toward the fleeing townspeople. "Bring them back."

"Shit." Mulls hurried back down the ridge, triggering small avalanches on his descent.

Dennis knelt in the snow and reached inside his jacket. He removed the folded map that detailed their small section of upstate New York, and smoothed out the creases over the snow.

The map revealed six small towns within twenty square miles. Two of them had *X*s crossed over them. Dennis reached into his pocket and removed a black marker, plucked the cap off, added a third *X* to the map, and smiled.

A square box stood out among the circles, and Dennis stared

at it for a half second longer than the other marks on the map. It was a highway patrol station, and it represented the one obstacle and hazard that could upend all of Dennis's work. He needed to wipe those pigs off the map before they decided to organize. But he wanted to make sure he had a good foothold in the area before that happened. Their time would come. And he would kill them all.

With the same care with which someone would handle an infant, Dennis refolded the map, paying attention to the original creases, and returned the compacted little square inside his jacket along with the pen. He stood, wiping the snow from his knees, and then descended the hill.

Broken glass and blood littered the snow along Main Street. Dennis passed the open front doors of businesses, houses, and hotels. He maintained a leisurely pace, hands folded behind his back. He'd enjoyed taking his time outdoors since his escape from prison. For eighteen years, he was held to a regimented schedule. He had his own schedule now. He was in charge. He was the warden.

Dennis veered toward the middle of the street, and his boots sank into the red slush that circled the dead. Limbs and heads extended from the mound of corpses, and he stopped to examine the bulbous nose of a man near the bottom. Dennis stared into the pair of lifeless eyes and slowly touched the tip of the deceased's enormous beak. He smiled, chuckling to himself, and then proceeded toward the inn.

Inside the lobby Dennis saw the group of men, women, and children that shivered on their knees, heads down. Quiet sobs and whispers of reassurance between loved ones drifted from the huddled prisoners.

"Good morning." Dennis smiled widely, his tone cordial. He tracked bloody boot prints inside as he circled the cowering cluster. "I know you're scared. I know you're confused." Faces remained tilted down as he slowly circled, his steps rhythmic and hypnotic. "You don't know why the power is off. You don't know why your phones aren't working, and you don't know why there has been no one to come and help you."

Dennis stopped, the sound of his steps replaced by those quiet sobs and nervous breaths. He spread his arms wide and smiled, exposing his yellowed teeth. "You're safe now." He spoke with a warm, soothing tone, his eyes scanning the group in search of the ones he'd seen at the hospital who'd killed two of his men. Billy and Martin's attempt to track them after the storm had passed had failed. And the fact that there were people out there who could escape him drove that little bug inside of his head mad. "The worst is over, so long as everyone here does exactly as they're told." His gaze focused on a middle-aged woman who clutched two young children to her sides. She kept her head down, shivering, but the little boy to her left looked up at Dennis, his expression more curious than afraid. "You just have to follow the rules." Dennis dropped to one knee and ruffled the little boy's hair. "You're good at following rules, aren't you?"

The woman shuddered and pulled her boy closer. Dennis grabbed her chin and tilted her face toward his. Tears streaked down her cheeks, her face haggard and fatigued. He dropped his tone an octave, his expression stoic save for a few spasms of anger that erupted in little twitches around his eyes and mouth. "The rules are simple. Do what we say, when we say it." His eyes drifted toward the little boy. "And no one gets hurt."

Jake Stows jogged in through the front door, covered in snow up to his waist. He panted and leaned against the wall to keep himself upright, his tongue lolling like a tired dog. "I couldn't—" Spit rained from his mouth as he coughed. He wiped his mouth, straightening himself out. "The ones that ran off, I couldn't get them. The snow in the forest is too high."

Dennis turned to Mulls on his right. "That's the man you sent?"

Mulls nodded.

Dennis pinched the bridge of his nose, nodding, that bug

burrowing through his mind. It tunneled quickly, scrambling reason and control, and Dennis felt his grip on restraint slip. "They escaped?"

"They ran like fucking rabbits," Jake answered, triggering a laugh from a few of the men.

Dennis joined in the laughter then slowly stepped around the huddled mass of the shivering cattle and grabbed hold of Jake's shoulder. "Like rabbits, huh?" He kept hold of Jake and turned to the group, his laughter growing more hysterical, that bug in his head burrowing faster and faster. Tears squeezed from the corners of his eyes, and he let go of Jake's shoulder to wipe them away. "Like rabbits!" Another burst of high-pitched squeals escaped his lips, and the laughter of the men faded until it was only Dennis.

Jake shifted uneasily, and Dennis's delirium ended.

"Oh, that's funny." Dennis smiled and gave three quick pats on his shoulder. "That's too bad."

One swift motion of the hand, and Dennis aimed his pistol at Jake's forehead then squeezed.

Gasps and screams erupted with the gunshot, and Jake's head jolted backward, blood and bone spraying in a trail due to the bullet's exit from the back of the skull, and Jake collapsed to the floor.

Smoke drifted from the end of the pistol's barrel, and Dennis lowered it to his side. He turned an angry glare to the rest of his men. "We are fucking wolves!" He stomped his foot, his knuckles flashing white against the pistol's black grip.

Dennis paced the room, turning his gaze to each and every one of his men until their eyes dropped to the tips of their boots. "If you cannot hunt, then you cannot kill, and if you cannot kill, then you will be killed!" Spittle dripped from Dennis's mouth and landed on the brown, matted beard that covered his chin and cheeks. He looked back down to the woman with the two children, and the little boy who was staring up at him, wide-eyed, his cheeks white as snow. "Remember that, boy."

Dennis ran his hand through his hair, the bug in his head finally resting. He closed his eyes and took a deep breath then exhaled slowly. "Okay." He opened his eyes, his stature more relaxed. He examined the cowering prisoners and then gestured to his men. "Make it quick."

The inmates broke into a frenzy as Dennis stepped over Jake's body on his exit. Screams and pleas of mercy erupted behind him as the men fought over the prettiest women in the group. Outside, the frigid mountain air cooled the rage. He closed his eyes and lifted his head toward the sky, basking in the howls from his pack and the screams from their victims. He reached for his map. Only three towns left.

29

The fresh powder from the blizzard had covered the landscape with a sheet of white that sparkled beneath the sunlight, which made the forest look alive.

Kate held the shovel but remained motionless as she stared at the mountains on the horizon that climbed high until it looked as though they touched the sky itself. It was one of the most beautiful sights she'd ever seen. But the view had come at a cost.

She lowered her gaze and saw the two rifles leaning up against a tree trunk, snapping her back to reality. The past three days had been an education for Kate and her family in the harsh realities of their new lives. They had no power, no phones, no transportation. The EMP stole every modern convenience, leaving millions ill prepared to survive the aftermath.

"Hey!" Rodney shoveled a scoop of snow and added it to the growing pile beside the hole. "C'mon, this is the last one. And we still need to do our water run." The snow crunched as he scooped another shovelful and tossed it aside.

Kate wiped the sweat from her brow and then started digging. "Why the hell did you bury all of this stuff?"

"If something is easy to find, then it's easy to steal."

Kate conceded the point. Rodney had been one of the few

who were ready. Up until the EMP, she didn't even know that Rodney Klatt existed. But over the past few days, he had become the little brother she'd never had. And while he was barely older than her nineteen-year-old son, he carried himself like a man in his forties.

Twenty minutes later, Kate's shovel vibrated from a heavy clunk in the ground. "Finally." Both dropped their shovels and cleared off the frozen soil. When the box was finally unearthed, they stood on either side, each gripping a handle.

"On three," Rodney said. "One, two, three!"

Kate's muscles drew taut, and her back strained as she lifted the heavy stash. The metal box scraped the side of the hole, and it hit the ground with a thud as Kate and Rodney dropped it. She rotated her shoulder, wincing. "Did you bury rocks?"

The inside was lined with plastic, and when Rodney peeled away the layers of clear sheets, she saw three letters stamped in large bold letters on matching bags: MRE.

Kate plucked one from the box and read the back. "Steak and garlic mashed potatoes." She arched her eyebrows, flashing the pack to Rodney. "Just add water." She tossed it back with the others as Rodney pulled a piece of paper and a pen from the container's side.

"Let's get an inventory, and then we'll bring it back to the cabin."

With this being the fourth box of supplies they'd dug up, Kate and Rodney fell into their practiced rhythm easily.

Once finished, Kate and Rodney slung their rifles over their shoulders then picked up the box. None of them went outside without a gun, per Rodney's request. But Kate didn't object. She understood the need for weapons now. They had supplies that people would kill to take. And she didn't plan on leaving her family with nothing.

The pair kicked their way through the tall drifts of snow, Kate dragging the shovel behind her, the pointed tip cutting a fine line through the soft powder. She lifted her knees high, the pair of snowshoes feeling more like a hindrance than a help.

"How long will the snow be this deep?" Kate asked.

"Until spring," Rodney answered. "The roads are near impassible now unless you've got the right gear." He gestured to their feet. "I know they're a pain, but it'd be a lot worse without them. Trust me."

Kate lifted her foot, and snow smacked her face. "I can't imagine."

The view of the back of the cabin brought with it the harsh whack of wood that echoed from the front and formed a methodical rhythm as Kate rounded the corner and saw Mark near the front porch, his back to the high walls of snow that boxed him into a rectangle-shaped crater.

Mark stood just over six feet, and the white walls behind him stretched four feet taller. The blizzard had buried the cabin, and they reclaimed it from the snowy earth one shovelful at a time.

Mark rested the head of the axe on the chopping block, his chest heaving up and down beneath his bulky coat. "I've already got two piles done. You said we want at least three per day, right?"

"Yeah," Rodney answered. "Three per day for the next four months."

Kate bumped Mark's arm on the way past. "Just don't chop your hand off."

Mark removed his left arm from behind his back. He'd worked his coat sleeve over his hand to make it look like it was amputated. "Too late."

Kate snorted and dropped the container of goods they'd carried from their cache. She kicked the snow from the large contraptions around her feet then peeled them off, chucking them in the corner with Rodney's.

"We'll need to match up what we found with my master list," Rodney said. "It's in the kitchen pantry. C'mon." He removed his gloves as he stepped inside, but before Kate followed, she turned back to Mark.

"Luke come out?" she asked.

"No," Mark answered, the playfulness gone as he pulled back his sleeve and picked up the axe. "I'll go and check on him in a minute. You finish up with Rodney. I know you still have the water run." He heaved the axe high again and split a log in two.

"Thanks," Kate said then mouthed, "I love you," and Mark did the same.

Rodney was already at the pantry, a binder in his hands that was three inches thick. "All we have left to do is make sure the numbers from the caches match up with the ones here."

Kate uncrumpled the list she'd balled into her pocket. The redundancies that Rodney had in place reminded her of the preflight checklists for the airlines—something she wasn't sure if she'd ever get the chance to do again.

"Mom?"

Kate turned, finding Holly in the entrance of the galley-style kitchen. "Hey, sweetheart. What's wrong?"

"Can I go outside?"

It was a request that had been repeated numerous times over the past few days, and Kate was reluctant to grant it. She knew that they were in the middle of nowhere, and she had rationalized their situation repeatedly. Still, she couldn't shake the danger of this new world.

There were no more police, no more ambulances, no justice system. The country's technological clock and been wound back one hundred years. Holly had nearly died from infection a few days ago, and the bruising around her ribs hadn't fully healed. But she knew that she couldn't keep her daughter locked inside the cabin as if it were an ivory tower.

"It's pretty cold out there," Kate answered, wrinkling her nose. "You might freeze."

"I can put on an extra coat," Holly said, stepping forward as she clasped her hands together, her movements still slow and restricted from the bandages around her ribs. "Please, Mom? Please, please, pleeeeease?"

With Holly batting those long eyelashes and puffing her lip, Kate caved. "All right, but put your gloves on, okay?"

"Yes!" Holly hugged Kate's legs. "Thanks, Mom!"

Kate smiled and smoothed the unruly hairs that broke free from Holly's ponytail. "You're welcome." She watched Holly grab her coat and sprint out the door. She stepped forward, extending her hand as if she could reach her daughter from twenty feet away. "And stay where your father can see you!"

Giggles answered back, and Holly squealed as she burst outside.

Kate smiled. It was good to be on speaking terms with her daughter again. In fact, it was the only good thing that she had been able to salvage from the situation. Her life as a pilot had given her wonderful opportunities, but it had also kept her away from home. Gone days at a time, she had missed a lot of Holly growing up, and that had strained their relationship. But it was slowly starting to turn around. But she had traded one child's indifference for another.

"All right," Rodney said. "We're all set here. Let's go to the lake."

Rodney stepped out first, and Kate lingered behind, staring at the closed door to Luke's room. It had stayed like that upon arrival. Her son had refused to come out, refused to talk to anyone, and wouldn't even look Kate in the eyes.

Luke's bitterness was Kate's own doing. She had fed him a lie to spare him pain, and from that lie was borne an inevitable anger. But she knew the truth would hurt him worse. All that mattered now was that he was alive. And even though her family was finally all together, it still didn't feel whole.

Outside, Kate found Mark and Holly engaged in a snowball fight. She smiled, donning her snowshoes, as small clusters of white exploded on their jackets. Holly ducked behind the piles of wood for cover then resurfaced, flinging a snowball that missed her father and smacked Rodney in the face.

Holly covered her mouth, freezing in place like a child who knew she'd done something wrong. But when Kate burst into laughter, Holly squealed with excitement.

Rodney spit out bits of snow and wiped his face, trying to hide his smile. "How about a little warning next time?"

"Sorry," Holly answered, giggling.

"I'll get her back for you, Rodney," Mark said, packing another snowball that sent Holly running.

Kate helped Rodney carry the pump and turned back as Mark chased after their daughter. "Don't go easy on him, Holl!"

"I won't!" Holly answered, laughing as Mark chased her around the side of the cabin.

The lake's close proximity to the cabin made water retrieval slightly easier, but it was far from convenient. Most of it was frozen, and every day, they were forced to chop away at the six inches of ice before they struck water.

The embankment to the lake's edge was steep, and Kate's knees groaned about the harsh decline, but she didn't stop until she felt the hard surface of ice. They set the pump down, and Rodney lifted the sledgehammer high then slammed it down hard.

Ice splintered, spreading spiderweb cracks from the point of contact. Rodney whacked again, the cracks multiplying, sending bits of ice shavings against the front of his pants. Six heavy hits later, and water bubbled up. Breathless, Rodney squeezed his hands, the cold wearing on his joints.

Kate slid the tube into the hole and then siphoned water until the twelve-gallon tank was full. It was enough for them to drink, cook, and bathe for one day. Though "bathe" was a loose term. With the freezing temperatures, they had done little more than just splash water under their arms and over their faces.

"All right," Rodney said, pulling the pump's tube from the lake. "We should be good."

"Weather's been holding up pretty well," Kate said, dismantling the pump to make it easier to carry.

Rodney glanced up toward the sky and nodded. "That blizzard probably took a lot of the bad weather with it." He wiped the snot dripping from his nose, and Kate mimed the motion.

"I think we should take advantage of it," Kate said. "Before things turn bad again."

Rodney paused. With one arm propped against a bent knee, he turned toward her. "Kate, I told you that we need to keep our heads down." He stood and grabbed the pump from her hands.

"But we don't know what's out there," Kate said. "What if we need help? What if we need—"

"Why would we need help?" Rodney spread his arms wide and turned in a circle. "We have everything we need right here. Food, water, shelter."

Kate glanced around at the frozen tundra, the dead and barren trees covered in snow. "Yeah, it's a real paradise."

"It's better if we stay put," Rodney said, grabbing the left handle of their water tank, as if that meant the discussion was over. But Kate pressed on.

"Luke has a bullet lodged in his chest," Kate said. "He needs a doctor."

"Mark and I told you what happened to the hospital," Rodney said. "I'll have to fish the bullet out myself."

Kate knocked the pump's tubing from Rodney's hand and stepped closer. "And you think you can get close without striking an artery near his heart? Well, I don't. You're skilled, Rodney, but you're not a surgeon."

"Kate, we don't—"

"And what if those people you saw at the hospital come back?" Kate felt herself tremble beneath the bulky winter clothes. "What if they find us? From the numbers you saw, they could—"

Footfalls echoed to the east, and Rodney and Kate both

reached for their rifles. Rodney aimed with his finger on the trigger before Kate could even get into position.

Rodney placed a finger to his lips and then slowly crested the slope, his feet soundless with each step, while their intruders stumbled loudly.

Kate followed, staying to Rodney's right. The sights of her rifle wavered, her muscles twitching with a mixture of adrenaline and fear. She couldn't rid herself of the thoughts of finding Dennis at the top of that slope, those dark eyes smiling at her.

After another minute, breathless voices were paired with the crunch of feet in snow. And while Kate couldn't hear what they were saying, she recognized the tone. It was a tone of panic.

"Don't move!" Rodney barked the order at the top of the embankment, rifle aimed, his composure still and calm. "Hands up where I can see them. Nice and slow."

Kate crested the top next. She saw their hands first and then their reddened cheeks and shivering bodies. But what caught her eyes the most was the shimmer of blood.

There were five of them, all underdressed for the freezing temperatures. It hadn't gotten above twelve degrees all morning, but they were in nothing more than flannel pajamas, with boots on their feet. They wore no gloves, no hats, and from what Kate saw, they carried no weapons.

An older man stood in the center. He was flanked by two older women on his left and a middle-aged woman around Kate's age on his right, who cradled a boy in her arms. The mother stepped forward, sobbing.

"Please," she said, her voice hysterical. "My son." She glanced at the boy in her arms. "He's hurt." She stepped forward quickly.

"Stay where you are," Rodney said, his tone stern, but remaining calm.

"Please," the old man said, his glasses halfway down his nose, and shivering. "I'm a physician." He gestured to the mother and son. "He was shot as we were trying to escape. If you have shelter, I can—"

"He's dying!" The woman shrieked, unable to control her heaving sobs, adjusting the boy in her arms, separating herself from the others until she stood halfway between her group and Rodney with his rifle. "Help us!"

Kate lowered her rifle. "Rodney. They're not here to hurt us. Look at what they're wearing, for Christ's sake."

The seven of them stood like frozen statues, and the mother in no man's land dropped to her knees. Tears had frozen to her cheeks, shimmering like the blood that covered her body. Her son's blood. Kate reached for Rodney's arm and for a moment felt his muscles stiffen beneath her grip.

But the moment passed, and Rodney finally lowered the rifle, and the torn and tattered survivors lowered their arms.

"Follow me," Rodney said.

30

Holly had collapsed into the snow, her arms and legs thrust out in straight, rigid lines for her third attempt at a snow angel. Mark watched from the chopping block, smiling as he split another log.

"Okay! I'm done!"

Mark wedged the axe's head into the stump and walked over, yanking Holly from the snow. He spun her around so she could see. "Looks like third time is the charm."

"I messed up on the wings a little bit," Holly said, frowning, and then turned to her dad, a tiny smirk creeping through the frown. "I think I need to try it again."

"Well, I think you need to go inside and warm up." Mark directed her toward the cabin door, and she gave a little *humph* as he patted her bottom and ushered her forward. "We'll see how your brother is doing. I need to check his bandages anyway."

Holly reluctantly sat by the fire, defiantly crossing her arms as Mark made his way toward the kitchen. "Are you hungry?"

"No." Holly kept her face toward the fire, away from her father.

Mark reached for a can of chicken soup, which was her favorite food. When she was little, she'd pretended to be sick on several occasions just to have it. And it wasn't until Mark and Kate explained to her that she didn't have to be sick to eat chicken soup that she finally ended the charade.

"No?" Mark asked, his voice curiously high. "Not even for a little, oh, I don't know." He quickly slammed the can onto the counter in a dramatic fashion, and the commotion made Holly turn around. "Chicken soup?"

Holly smiled, the anger melting away. "Okay."

"Come here and get it ready. I need to check on your brother." Mark kissed the top of Holly's head and moved past her toward the bedrooms.

The cabin was a good size, having four bedrooms. Three were clustered on one side, the kitchen and living room in the middle, and on the other end was the master bedroom where Rodney slept. The three bedrooms behind the kitchen were smaller, more closet than bedroom, and the beds were uncomfortable, but the fireplace kept everything warm.

Mark gently tapped on Luke's door, his mouth a breath away from the old wood. "Luke?" He grabbed the cold bronze of the doorknob and slowly pushed it open. The hinges groaned, and the sliver of space between the door and the frame widened as Mark squeezed his way into the gap. "Luke?"

His son was asleep on the bed, with the sheets up to his chin. His head lolled lazily to the left, revealing the growing scruff on his cheeks. Mark involuntarily reached for his own cheek, finding the start of a beard. It was dark brown and thicker than Luke's, coarse from age and the cold. He could break off a hair like an icicle if he wanted to.

Mark pressed his hand against the boy's forehead. Luke's head was like a stovetop, and Mark immediately ripped the covers off him and tried to stir him awake. "Luke? Can you hear me?"

Luke groaned. "I don't want to go. You can't leave her. I won't — Can't go. Don't go. Claire." The words faded like a whisper, and Luke's eyelids fluttered.

Mark hurried into the kitchen and opened the pantry, where his fingers tore open the nearest plastic case of water. He ripped the bottle out and grabbed Holly's arm. "Go outside and scream for your mom to come back."

"What's wrong?" Holly asked, her voice trembling with fear.

And before Mark could explain, he saw figures dart past the widows, Kate leading a crying woman in boots and pajamas that carried a bloodied boy inside, followed by three others dressed in similar garb. Rodney followed suit, shutting the door.

Kate cleared off the round kitchen table, and the woman gently laid the injured boy down, and Mark noted how still the boy looked.

Rodney hurried past Mark in the galley, forcing him flush against the counter and cabinets, and then he snatched a bag from the pantry and brought it to the table, where an old man hovered over the boy.

"I'll need to sterilize the wound," the old man said, rolling up his sleeves, exposing frost, dirt, and blood. Rodney handed him a bottle of peroxide, and he doused his arms with it, the excess spilling onto the table and floor.

"Scissors." The old man held out his hand, and Rodney handed him the silver-plated tool. He cut the boy's shirt from the collar straight down the middle and flung the tattered remnants aside.

What small patches of the boy's stomach and chest weren't covered in blood were pale shapes of white flesh. A gruesome wound rested to the left-hand side of the boy's navel, oozing fresh blood. The old man snatched a handful of gauze and pressed it hard against the exposed wound.

"I need a hand, quickly." The doctor's orders were frantic but mechanically efficient. Rodney offered his hand for assistance but was knocked away. "No, I need you to keep handing me the tools. You." He pointed at Kate, who stepped up. The old man grabbed her hand and placed it over the wound. "Press hard."

"O-Okay, I got it," Kate said.

Mark watched as the old man frantically gathered the tools from Rodney's bag, smearing blood over the clean silver of the instruments. And though his arms and hands trembled from the cold, they moved with skill.

The woman who carried the boy inside kept hold of his hand, pressing it tight against her lips, and then whispered prayers and pleaded to God the way only a mother could.

"Move the gauze." The old man waved Kate out of the way and then plunged small metal tweezers into the boy's gut, which triggered the first signs of life.

"*Ahhhh!*" The boy bucked wildly on the table, and the tweezers were thrown to the floor at Mark's feet.

"Hold him down! Keep him still!" the old man said.

Kate, Rodney, and the mother placed their hands on the boy's shoulders, arms, and legs. The screams curdled the blood in Mark's veins, and he couldn't take his eyes off the boy's kicking legs, the blood, the—

"Mark!" Kate said, whipping her head back at him, then gestured to the floor. "The tweezers!"

Mark stared at the bloodied piece of silver circled by scattered blood droplets at his toes. He picked it up and then put it in the doctor's extended hand.

"Give me the peroxide." The old man poured more of the liquid over the tweezers, and Mark lingered close by and watched him plunge the tweezers back into the wound, which produced another eardrum-shattering scream. But after a few seconds, the scream died as the boy passed out, his head lolling limply to the side.

"Chris!" The boy's mother reached for his face, pulling it toward her.

"Got it." The old man removed the tweezers and dropped the nine-millimeter bullet on the table, where it rolled off and clanked against the floor. He then stuck his fingers in the hole, examining the rest of the wound. "I can't tell if any organs were struck." He removed his finger and pressed around the abdomen. "Needle and thread. I need to sew this up quickly."

Rodney handed the old man the requested supplies, but the mother stepped in the old man's way, her eyes frantic and wide. She was a frightened animal, a creature unsure of any future. She reminded Mark of Kate when she first arrived at their apartment in New York after the EMP.

"Is he going to live?" the mother asked.

The words hung in the air, and when the doctor remained silent, she gasped, stepping backward until she hit the wall and collapsed.

The old man ran the needle and thread through the boy's skin, pulling the wound closed, until there was nothing there but blood and lines of thread. "We need to get him to a bed, and we need fluids in him."

"I have an IV bag," Rodney said, getting his arms beneath the boy. "Kate, you know where they are." He lifted the boy off the table and carried him to Holly's room, the mother trailing behind.

Mark stood motionless in the kitchen amid the flurry of action. He stared at the fresh blood on the table and the floor. Crimson droplets hit the floor in slow, methodical drops at the table's edge. He saw the bullet near one of the table's legs, and he picked it up. He rolled the metal between his fingers. It was still warm from the boy's gut.

Kate stepped out of the room and staggered a little bit, unsure of her footing. She clamped her hand around Mark's arm and snapped his attention away from the bullet. "Are you all right?"

Mark peered into her concerned eyes and then looked back at the bullet. "Luke is sick. I think he has an infection."

"What? He was fine last night." Kate walked toward Luke's room and disappeared inside. Mark was still staring down at the bullet when she rushed past Mark and retrieved the old man, dragging him to Luke's room. There was silence for a minute, and then Kate was screaming.

"Help him!"

His wife's hysteria triggered Mark back into action, and he joined Rodney in the room. Kate stood at the head of Luke's bed, the veins in her neck throbbing and her jaw square. The old man was at the foot of the bed, his back toward the door. Kate was fuming.

"We helped you!" Kate shoved the old man hard in the chest, and he stumbled backward to the floor. She hovered over him, fist raised, and it took both Mark and Rodney to keep her still.

"Whoa, hey, what is going on?" Mark asked.

Kate's eyes bored into the old man, and while her snarl remained, the tension in her body released. "He won't help Luke."

Rodney and Mark both turned to the old man. Mark stepped first, picking the old man up to his feet and then slamming him against the wall.

"Help. Him." Mark spoke through gritted teeth, the old man's shivering throat in his hand.

"My niece," he said, limply groping at Mark's arm. "She's back at the town. With those people who attacked us." He leaned into Mark's hand. "Help me get her back."

"If you don't help him, I will throw you out into the cold," Rodney said.

"And then he'll die!" the old man fired back. "The wound's infected. And the only way to treat him now is with antibiotics and removing the infected tissue. You might have the supplies to perform the task, but that bullet is close to the arteries that run into his heart. You try and pull it out yourself, and he could bleed to death."

Mark gave a slow turn of his head toward Rodney. The stare that passed between them told Mark that the old man was right. With gritted teeth, he let the old man go.

Four red finger marks lingered on the old man's skin, and he gently rubbed them as he stepped from the room and rejoined his group.

"Where's the town?" Mark asked.

* * *

THE DOCTOR, whose name was Harold, sat at the kitchen table, where he removed the bullet from the boy just moments before. The older woman he brought was his wife, Marie, and the younger girl was his daughter, Lisa. The mother with the wounded son, Chris, was Gwen.

"Who are they?" Rodney asked.

"We don't know." Harold clasped his hands tightly between his knees and rocked back and forth in the chair.

"They were armed?" Kate asked.

The doctor nodded, and then his wife touched his shoulder.

"They shot anyone that tried to fight back," she said, tears glistening in her eyes.

"I watched them kill my brother from our living room window," Harold said. "After I saw that, I took my family and ran out the back." He gestured back to the room where they put Chris and Gwen. "I found them on the way, and we all ran. They followed, but they gave up quickly. The snow was thick. There were a lot of trees—"

"Did you see your niece?" Rodney asked. "Did you see that she was alive?"

"I-I don't know," Harold answered.

"I'm not going over there to bring back a dead body." Rodney pushed himself from the wall of the living room. "And I'm not letting any of my people die, so you can—"

"We're wasting time!" Kate stepped between Rodney and the doctor, looking at Rodney. "Can you help Luke? Can you get the bullet out without killing him?"

Rodney ground his teeth, the muscles along his jaw twitching. He shook his head.

Kate walked toward him, her eyes pleading. "Then I need his help." She stopped just short of reaching for his hand. "Luke will die if we don't go." She turned to the doctor. "But if she is dead, our deal still stands. You will operate on Luke."

"If I see the body," the doctor said. "Yes."

Kate turned back to Rodney, those eyes still pleading. If there was one thing Rodney couldn't stand, it was blackmail. But the choices were shit either way. If the bullet had just gone into Luke's arm, the shoulder—hell the stomach—he could have risked fishing it out himself. But he knew the old doctor was right, and he hated it.

Kate leaned closer, her voice a whisper. "The same people that attacked their town could be the same ones that hit the hospital. We need to find out what we're dealing with."

Without a word, Rodney disappeared into his room. A desk sat in the far corner, and he opened the top drawer. He removed a rolled-up piece of paper and then returned to the kitchen and slapped the paper on the table.

"Open it," Rodney said, looking at the old man.

Harold hesitated but then reached for the paper and slowly unrolled the parchment. As he did, he unveiled a map of upstate New York.

"Show me where the town is," Rodney said.

Kate sidled up next to him, gently holding his arm. "Thank you."

Rodney nodded and then looked at Mark while the old doctor examined the map. "Do you know how to shoot?"

"It's been a while," Mark answered.

"I'll give you some pointers."

31

The town was easier to find than Kate thought, but it was closer to the cabin than she would have liked. And from the expression on Rodney's face, he thought so too, and she wondered if that was the motivation for him to come. Despite the noble quest to help her son, Kate knew Rodney was pragmatic. He wouldn't have gotten them this far if he weren't. But in the end, it didn't matter. They were here, and they needed to find the girl.

The doctor didn't have a picture, but luckily his niece had very striking purple dye in her hair. So long as Dennis's men hadn't scalped her, finding her wouldn't be a problem.

"We'll stay toward the town's north side," Rodney said, pointing through the trees and toward a ridge. "With the town in a valley, we'll have the high ground."

Kate peeked around Mark at Lisa, the doctor's daughter, who had come with them. Rodney wanted someone who had some knowledge of the town, and Kate wanted an insurance policy for her son. She didn't think the doctor would go back on his word, but he'd be less tempted so long as Kate kept the girl close.

"There were a lot of them." Lisa spoke warily, staring at the town as if a monster slept below. "More than we have."

"That's why we're going to scout it first," Rodney said. "Keep your eyes peeled."

The foursome crawled along the top of the ridge, Rodney using the binoculars every twenty yards to check for the inmates below. They worked their way down the ridgeline until they reached the end, and their view was blocked by forest.

Rodney waved them close, and they formed a small, broken circle. "All right, unless all of the inmates have moved inside the buildings, it doesn't look like they have the same numbers anymore. I saw two guards at the town's entrance and two stationed outside a single building." He turned to Lisa. "I'm assuming that's the inn?"

"Yeah," Lisa answered, glancing back into the town. "That's where we saw them putting everyone."

Rodney removed his binoculars and handed them to Kate, and just when he was about to descend the ridge, she snatched his arm.

"What are you doing?" Kate asked, her voice a harsh whisper.

"We need to confirm the people are still inside," Rodney answered. "It'll be easier for me to go down alone."

"What if someone sees you? What if you get hurt? What if you—"

"I'll be fine." Rodney removed her hand from his arm. "Keep an eye on me with the binoculars. If things go bad, head back to the cabin."

"If we can't get the girl back, then Luke dies," Mark said. "No cowboy stuff. Just go down there, peek through the windows, and then come right back."

Rodney nodded and then slipped down the mountain, gliding through the snow on his backside until it leveled out to where he could walk.

The binoculars made Kate feel as if she'd been thrust into the valley, and she tightened her grip as Rodney crept toward the window on the back side of a building.

For a moment, Kate considered the possibility of failure. Her thoughts crossed the line of morality, into the dark company of the very inmates they were fighting. She peeled her eyes away from the binoculars and found Lisa. If they failed, and the doctor still wouldn't help her, then she would force him to—by any means necessary.

"Kate." Mark touched her shoulder, pointing toward Rodney on his return.

Rodney kept low on the climb up, crawling on all fours, and Mark offered his hand to help him over the ridge. "I didn't see her inside." He turned toward the town, still catching his breath. "But I could hear them talking. One of the guards has taken a few of the women to the building next door. She might be there."

"How many guards?" Mark asked.

"I saw four inside plus the two I saw stationed at the town's road entrance," Rodney answered. "And two more in the building next door."

"Shit," Mark said breathlessly. He shifted toward Kate. "It won't take anything but a scream to break our cover."

Kate nodded. It was riskier than she would have preferred, but they were out of choices. She turned toward Lisa, who trembled under Kate's hand. "How good of a shot are you?"

"I-I don't know," Lisa said, staring at the rifle in her hands as if it were a foreign object. "I had a boyfriend that took me hunting a few times. He showed me a few things."

Without asking, Kate took the weapon away from her and checked their position through the scope. Both buildings had back doors, but from their vantage point, even with the trees, it was a clear shot. She handed the weapon back to Lisa. "If you hear screams or gunshots, we're coming out of those doors. You shoot anything that's not us, understand?"

Lisa nodded and tried to position herself comfortably as Kate turned to Mark.

"Stay with her." Kate's eyes told the rest of her thoughts, and just before she descended the ridge, Mark pulled her close and kissed her. She tensed but then fell into him.

Mark slowly pulled back, tugging her lips slightly with him before they parted. He opened his eyes first. "Come back."

Rodney took the lead, Kate struggling to keep her balance on the steep descent. At the bottom, they ducked below the windows on the cabin's back side, creeping their way toward the door. Muffled laughter echoed through the log walls, followed by intermittent screams.

Kate held back the impulse to burst inside and open fire. This needed to be done quietly and quickly.

Rodney laid his rifle in the snow and removed a hunting blade from his belt. He carefully pressed his ear to the door, his free hand reaching for the knob.

Kate positioned herself near the window, and she raised her eyes to the windowsill. The room appeared in fragments. A chair, a desk, a fur rug, and then a bed. A man was on it, naked from the waist down. A girl lay beneath him, her hands bound and tied. Kate's knuckles whitened against the rifle.

Rodney opened the door, exposing them to more laughter and the grunts from the bedroom. The doorway opened into a hallway with the bedroom on the right, its door closed.

Kate eyed the door as Rodney crept down the hallway toward the voices up front. Kate started to follow, but then gestured for her to stay put.

As Rodney crept farther down the hall, the grunts in the bedroom grew louder. And before Kate knew it, her fingers were already on the brass knob, turning it slowly. She couldn't leave that woman to her fate. Not when she could do something about it.

The door cracked open, and another helpless whimper drifted past. The inmate's back was turned to Kate as she stepped inside. The man's thrusts were quick and violent. The woman beneath him kept her face turned away, her eyes shut. Her lower lip was smeared with blood.

Kate glanced down the hall, finding Rodney nearing the

other guard. She needed to be quick. She raised the butt of her rifle, and three quick steps brought her toward the bed.

The boards groaned from Kate's movement, and the big man turned around. "What the hell, I'm not even done ye—"

The rifle struck the brute's forehead, eliciting a crack that drew blood and collapsed the piece of scum on top of the woman. Quickly, Kate knocked the man off the bed, and he hit the floor with a heavy thump.

Kate set the rifle down and then reached for the woman's restraints. When Kate's fingers grazed the woman's wrist, she bucked wildly in fear.

"It's all right, shh," Kate said, keeping her voice down as she quickly untied the ropes. "I'm here to help. We're going to—"

A woman's scream wailed like a siren from the front of the cabin, but it was overpowered by two gunshots, followed by hurried footsteps. Kate reached for the rifle, aiming it at the door, poised to fire.

Rodney appeared, a girl with a mop of purple in her hair draped under his arm. "We need to move!"

Kate turned back to the woman she'd freed, finding her standing and naked from the waist down, quickly trying to dress. Rodney shifted anxiously as Kate tried to help the woman with her shoes. Men shouted next door.

"Hurry!" Rodney said.

The woman finished, and Kate grabbed her arm, yanking her out of the room. Rodney was out the door first, the purple-haired girl limping next to him. Kate followed, pulling the second woman behind her. She landed in the snow, Rodney already making his ascent up the ridge, when the back door to the inn opened.

Kate raised her rifle, ready to fire, when bullets bombarded the back side of the house, forcing the door closed. She glanced up toward the ridge, Mark and Lisa invisible save for the sound of their gunshots.

The foursome churned up the ridge, their retreat frantic

amid the gunfire blasting both in front of them and behind. Kate's muscles burned on the ascent as she pulled the woman, who could barely keep herself upright.

Mark, Lisa, and the security of the ridgeline came into view, and just before they crested the top, the woman yanked her hand from Kate's grip.

"Stop!" the woman screamed, waving her arms at Mark and Lisa, who lifted their gaze from their scopes. She hyperventilated, gasping deep breaths of air and pointing back toward the cabin. "My son!" She turned her face away then clawed her nails through her knotted and tangled hair.

"Kate, c'mon!" Rodney said, now with the doctor's niece draped over his shoulder.

Hands were suddenly on Kate, and she turned to find the woman, her eyes wild with fear, her lower lip swollen and crusted with blood. Bruises lined her neck and cheek. "My son. They'll kill him. They told me they would." She sank her nails deeper into the sleeve of Kate's jacket until she felt the pinpoint pressure beneath each finger. "Help me."

Below, inmates flooded out of the cabin and onto the town's main street. They circled around a different building, and Kate looked at Rodney and Mark.

"Please!" the woman cried.

Kate stomped toward Lisa, snatching the rifle from her hands, and thrust it into the woman's chest. "You know how to use one?"

The woman stared at it a second too long, but just when Kate was about to lower the weapon and forgo the rescue, she snatched it from her hands. She spun the rifle around, staring down the sight, handling the weapon deftly. She opened the chamber then ejected the magazine, examining the bullets.

Kate turned toward Mark. "Help Rodney get Lisa and the niece to the cabin."

"Kate, this is—"

She kissed him hard, longer than she should have, and this

time when she peeled her face away, his eyes were still closed. "Have the doctor start working on Luke. I won't be far behind. I promise."

Rodney handed the purple-haired girl over to Mark before he could protest, and then Kate, Rodney, and the woman descended the ridge, back into the storm.

Kate fought the urge to look back up the ridge. If she gave in to it, she knew she'd leave. This was a risk that took her away from her family, but she understood a mother's drive to save her child. That was what cemented her decision to stay. Rodney had helped her, and now she could help another.

"Stay on me!" Rodney said as the snow leveled out at the ridge's bottom.

Kate kept the butt of her rifle locked into the crook of her arm, and her vision narrowed to the pinpoint accuracy of the weapon's sight. She placed her gloved finger over the trigger, careful not to squeeze as she brought up the rear of their pack as they entered an alleyway toward Main Street.

Rodney held up a fist, and their movement ended at the alley's exit. Kate covered their rear, and angry shouts and footsteps circled.

"All right," Rodney said, still peering through the scope. "We're four buildings down from the inn. That's where your son is?"

"Yeah," the woman answered.

"I'm gonna head for that building across the street. There's a good sniper window on the second floor." Rodney turned to the woman. "I'll make sure no one sneaks up behind you."

The woman nodded.

"Kate, are you good to go with her?" Rodney asked.

"Yeah."

"Don't move until I'm in position." Rodney sprinted across the street, his feet crunching quickly over the snow, and Kate took his place at the alley's exit.

The woman adjusted her aim, providing Rodney cover. Kate

joined the cause, but just before Rodney entered the building, a bullet splintered the wood over the woman's head.

Instinct pushed both women from the alley, Kate turning and firing blindly at the pair of thugs at the alley's opposite end. They sprinted for the inn on Main Street, Kate stealing glances down the alleys they passed as the men followed on the building's back side.

Breathless, Kate and the woman crouched on either side of the inn's front door. Angry shouts rattled inside, followed by the quivering whimpers of those that were trapped.

"Shut up!" a man ordered, hushing the growing dissent of the hostages. "I'll put a bullet in every single one of you. Now shut—"

In one swift motion, the woman stood, kicked open the door, and stepped into the room, firing before Kate had a chance to stand. A scream erupted in time with the gunshot, and Kate followed, rifle up, but her sights only bore down on a huddled group of women and children.

"Danny!" The woman lowered her rifle and rushed to a small boy wedged between two older women. He lifted his head at his name and then flung his arms around his mother's neck, and both burst into tears.

For a moment, everything was still, and Kate watched the reunion of the family. But the relief ended with the shattering of glass and the thunder of gunshots behind her.

Kate hit the floor, ducking along with everyone else, the world fading to black with a soundtrack of gunshots, groans, and screams. She waited for the surge of men or hands on her to whisk her away to a dark room to be raped, but as she lingered on the floor, the commotion ended.

Kate lifted her head, turning her neck sharply to see that the windows behind her were devoid of the hulking figures she expected, and saw only shards of broken glass.

Kate scrambled forward on hands and knees. "We need to move! Everyone, get out!" She leaned into the group, her haste triggering action as she spun around, rifle up, waiting for anyone else to come through. But none came.

A hand clapped Kate's shoulder, and she turned to find the woman. "Let's go."

The group stopped at the back door, and Kate hurried past them. A gunshot pulled everyone back to the floor, but Kate opened the door. Snow and trees came into view, and then the quick dart of a body.

Kate kicked the door the rest of the way open and brought the thug in her crosshairs. She fired, the first bullet missing wide, and then steadied her aim. The second sent a geyser of blood out of the man's back and a spray of crimson across the white snow.

Kate held her position, waiting for another inmate to appear, but none came. The coast was clear. She turned back toward the group, finally getting a sense of their size. Twenty faces looked to her for guidance, a mix of men, women, and children.

"Everyone run up the ridge and wait there."

"What if they start shooting us?" a woman asked, terror laced in her voice.

"The trees will provide good cover," Kate answered. "Now go!" She barked the order, and the group trickled out into the snow, most of them ill prepared for the cold, but freezing was better than dying.

Kate swiveled to her left and right, rifle aimed, making sure the coast remained clear as the last few refugees scurried up the hill. Sporadic gunfire echoed from the building's front side, and when the woman Kate had saved brought up the rear, she lowered her weapon.

"Thank you," she said, the rifle still clutched in her chest, her eyes watering.

Kate nodded, and the woman joined the retreat with her son. Once she couldn't see them anymore, Kate turned back into the building, finger over the trigger, her eyes scanning the front of the building for anymore hostiles.

A puddle of blood formed around one of the dead men, and Kate skirted the gore and found two more bodies on the street, littering the snow, their limbs sprawled out at awkward angles, the rifles they'd carried still clutched in their dead hands.

Kate found the second floor of the building where Rodney had left the window open. The front door opened on the first floor, causing her to cast her eyes downward, and Rodney jogged into the street, away from her and toward the east end.

"Two got away from me," Rodney said, jogging away. "I'm going to finish this."

"Rodney, wait!"

Kate sprinted after him, following him into the building where the road dead-ended. Some souvenirs and trinkets lay piled on tables and shelves, but most of the store's merchandise was broken and scattered on the floor. Kate crunched glass beneath her boots, and Rodney fired from somewhere out the back.

Rodney was already aimed, firing at two figures darting up the mountain, feet churning up snow in a hasty retreat. Kate sidled up beside him and took a breath, taking her time to line up her shot. The crosshairs fell against the man's back. She followed his path for a minute, then squeezed the trigger.

The man ducked, and the bullet disappeared into the snow, and before Kate could readjust, the man vanished behind a cluster of trees.

Rodney followed the second man, his finger gently placed on the trigger. "I've got him." He kept his right eye glued to the scope, his body still as the frozen tundra outside. He exhaled a slow breath and then squeezed the trigger.

A splash of red burst from the convict's back, and he sprawled forward into the snow. The ring of the gunshot clung to the air as the man lay still, his body firmly planted in the soft, frozen powder.

Rodney raised his rifle to search for the inmate that Kate had missed, but quickly lowered it. "He's gone." He spun around, angry. "Shit."

"We should go," Kate said.

Rodney nodded. "Yeah, we need to get out of here before he tells the rest of his buddies what happened."

32

Frozen, stiff, and exhausted, Dennis shuffled into town. The entire trip back, there were only two thoughts that circled his mind. Bed, and laying that woman still chained up in his room.

A mechanical hum echoed from the large diesel generators that Dennis had sent his people to find, and he was glad to find them already hooked up to his house and the sleeping quarters of his men. Billy and Martin appeared from the big hunk of machinery, passing a whiskey bottle between them. They were brothers, and the best trackers that Dennis had ever seen. And while they fell short of finding the bastards who'd killed their men at the hospital, the supplies they sniffed out were even better. Though he knew most of the work was done by the younger sibling, Billy.

Dennis clapped excitedly. "About damn time. I hope you hooked that thing up to the Jacuzzi around back." He snatched the bottle away, took a few swills of liquor, then handed it to Mulls. "How many houses are hooked up?"

"Three," Martin said. "And we're getting ready to haul another one in before nightfall. We have enough fuel to last us a few months, so long as we don't go overboard with running it day and night."

"Hell no. Those fuckers are never going off!" Dennis spun around, arms spread wide, a yellow smile on his face. "We're the pioneers of the new world, boys! There's an ocean of fuel out there just ready to be taken!" He clapped his hands vigorously. "Let's get to it!"

The men behind Mulls remained quiet, as he dangled the bottle of booze from his fingertips. "Jimmy still hasn't come back. It's been almost two days now."

Dennis spun around, his good mood disappeared. "What do you want me to do? If the dumbass got lost, then there is nothing we can do about it." He headed for his house, that little bug in his head starting to stir, but Mulls followed, and so did the others, causing him to stop. He felt an uneasy shift in the pecking order, and he didn't like it. "Something you want to share with me, Mulls?"

"We've been collecting supplies nonstop for the past three days," Mulls answered. "We've got food, we've got water, we've got enough guns for an army." He separated himself from the group. "Everybody wants to enjoy what we've got for a little while."

Dennis looked past Mulls, toward the convicts, who lowered their heads, staring at their boots. He stepped past Mulls, confronting the men who'd been whining behind his back. "Is that true? Everyone just wants to have a little fun?" The men retreated, taking steps back every time Dennis stepped forward. "Well, I don't want you all to be left out! How about this—everyone can take turns screwing the woman I've got at my place." He leaned forward, bouncing his eyebrows, and raised his left hand, which exposed the golden band. "I'll even let you wear the wedding ring, huh?"

"Dennis, we've done everything you've asked," Mulls answered. "We just want a break."

Dennis spun around, then swiveled his attention between

Mulls and the inmates who followed him. "Is that all?" He feigned an expression of empathy. "Well, if that's all anybody wants—Oh." He pressed a finger to his lips. "Oh, but there is something else, isn't there?" He nodded to himself, the group parting for him to pass. "What was it again? It was on the tip of my tongue—Ah!" He smiled, lifting his finger up. "The cops." He eyed each of the convicts in turn. "You remember? The little highway patrol center that holds the one group of people that can stop us? But hey, if you guys want to take it easy for a while, lay back and relax, I'm sure that station can wait."

"Dennis, that's not what we're—"

"No!" Dennis barked, and the men cowered as he snarled his lips and exposed his teeth. "You want this place to last two months or the rest of our lives?" He hammered his fist angrily. "We take out that station, and we don't have anyone to oppose us until the spring. Do you know what happens if those pigs find us? We go back in a cell." He shook his head, wiping the spit that dribbled from his lower lip. "I'm not going back in a cell. Are you?" He shoved the nearest man hard then turned to another. "Are you?"

There was a series of headshakes, and a few muffled *nos* escaped tight lips.

"*Are you?*" Dennis roared.

"No!"

He smiled at the echoed war cry and nodded, turning back toward Mulls slowly, deliberately. And to the big bear's credit, he never looked away. "We take out the station, and then we can start to relax."

"With what men?" Mulls asked, matching Dennis's anger. "We're spread too thin. Jimmy was supposed to fix that problem, but he's god knows where now."

"We send out more scouts," Dennis said.

"And lose even more men?" Mulls shook his head and lowered his voice. "Let's go back to the other towns, drag the people we want back here, and then torch the places. We need to centralize."

Dennis leaned close enough for a kiss, and he got a nasty whiff of Mulls's rotten stench. "No." The defiance rolled off his tongue slowly. "I'm not giving up what we've taken."

"All right, Dennis." Mulls nodded, unsmiling. "All right." He shook his head and then chuckled. "Christ, you think you would—"

But Mulls stopped, looking past Dennis down Main Street. Dennis frowned and then turned, his expression morphing into a smile.

Covered in snow and ice and looking half dead, Jimmy strutted into town at the helm of a large cluster of snow-covered orange jumpsuits.

"Son of a bitch." Dennis laughed, performing a slow clap as he walked to meet Jimmy and wrapped him in a bear hug. "You squirrely son of a bitch! Look at you!" He clapped Jimmy on the shoulders, and bits of ice broke away from his clothes. "We thought the storm got you."

Jimmy chattered his teeth together, and a goofy grin crinkled the left side of his face. "I-I-I t-t-thought-t-t w-e-e, co-co—" He shut his eyes, trying to concentrate. "Could make it through." He huffed in fatigue and wobbled on both legs.

"Let's get you warmed up." Dennis stepped around Jimmy and opened his arms in welcome to the fresh meat for his grinder. "We've got heat, women, and booze, gentlemen. Just head on down to the Convict Motel." Dennis laughed, and the frozen masses shuffled past.

Once they were gone and inside, only Mulls and Dennis remained on the street. The pair of men stared each other down, but it was Mulls who shook his head and backed down first. And when the big man had walked away, Dennis slowly recounted the number of men that Jimmy had just added to his arsenal. Fifty. Fifty to his already robust forty.

Once fed, bathed, and satisfied with a woman, they'd do

whatever he told them to do. Because just as Mulls understood, Dennis was the hand that fed them. Those pigs wouldn't know what hit them.

"Dennis!"

He stopped and turned to find another breathless man wandering into his town. It took a minute for him to recognize him, but the tuft of red hair gave Ken away. That little fire crotch was supposed to be in the valley town.

Ken skidded on his heels to a stop, hunched over with his hands on his knees, gasping for breath. He finally straightened himself out, wiping away a stringy collection of spit and snot. "The town's gone."

The muscles along Dennis's face tightened in anger, his tone flat but stern. "What?"

Ken rubbed his palms on his thighs again. "Christ, I barely made it out of there alive."

Dennis twitched, and the bug burrowed. The madness crept over him, and he turned away from Ken, stumbling aimlessly around Main Street. Rage gained momentum as the realization sunk in.

His town was gone? One of *his* towns?

Dennis froze, but that bug inside his head tunneled through his reason and control. "How many?"

"What?" Ken asked.

Dennis turned, his eyes focused on that red-haired bastard in the middle of his street. "How. Many. Were there?"

Ken took one step backward. "I-I don't know. I didn't really get a good look, but if I had to guess, um..." He swallowed and trembled. "A few?"

Surprise flashed over Dennis's face, but only a moment before anger retook control. "A few?" Snow crunched beneath Dennis's boot as he stepped forward slowly. "We had eight men stationed in the valley." Quick as a snakebite, Dennis lunged and curled both hands around Ken's throat, pulling him intimately close. "A few fucking people took back a town that had eight armed inmates?"

Ken struggled for breath. "We didn't see them coming."

The bug in Dennis's mind burrowed faster and faster, eating up his brain as his hand tightened around Ken's throat. The man whacked at Dennis's arm, fighting for his life, and then just as quickly as Dennis grabbed him, he let go.

Ken collapsed to his knees, hands on his throat, coughing and gasping for air.

Dennis turned away from Ken, hiding the pistol that he removed from his holster. "Three people killed eight of my men."

"They only killed seven," Ken said.

Dennis spun around and fired, spraying Ken's brain over the snow. He holstered the pistol. "No. Eight." The bug in his brain calmed, and he watched blood crawl from Ken's body like crimson fingers along the ground.

Dennis wasn't sure how long he stood there, but when he turned around, Mulls was behind him. "They lost the town. He ran." He strutted over to Mulls, whose eyes were still locked on Ken's body. It wasn't until Dennis clapped him on the back that Mulls finally looked away. "Cowards die, Mulls." He laughed and then headed back inside. "Get the boys ready. We've got work to do!"

33

Kate sat outside Luke's room, the door closed as the doctor made good on his promise to remove the bullet from his chest. The inside of the cabin was dead quiet save for the occasional whisper. Kate had wanted to be inside during the surgery, but the doctor didn't want any distractions. The procedure was hard enough without all the necessary equipment, and he didn't need her breathing down his neck. It took every ounce of Kate's willpower not to choke him.

She and Mark had resigned themselves to the kitchen, each of them tapping a foot or hand nervously. Luke's condition had worsened by the time they'd returned, and even if the doctor was able to get the bullet out, there was no guarantee that the infection wouldn't have spread or that the antibiotics that Rodney had would kill it.

Kate turned left, eyeing the twenty-plus people in the living room, sipping water and nibbling on crackers and soup. She didn't know what they were going to do with them. There wasn't enough room in the cabin for an entire town to survive.

Rodney stepped from his room on the opposite side, weaving around the huddled bodies on the floor, and joined her and

Mark in the kitchen. He crossed his arms and gestured toward the door. "Anything?"

"Not yet," Kate answered, her voice hoarse from staying quiet.

Rodney checked the pocket watch he carried. "It's been almost an hour."

"I know." Kate eyed the wooden slats on the door. She had stared at that door for so long that she had every groove of the wood memorized.

"Listen, we need to talk," Rodney said, looking at both Kate and Mark. "Outside."

"Yeah." Kate was the last to leave the kitchen, and though she didn't want anything to steal her attention away from Luke's surgery, a part of her thought the distraction might help speed things along.

The contrast from the warmth of the cabin and the cold outside shocked Kate's senses when she stepped outside. She flipped her collar up to guard herself against the stiff wind and joined Mark and Rodney in the snow.

"I think we all know we don't have the room for these people," Rodney said. "As much as I'd like for them to stay, logistically, it's just not possible."

"Can't we take them back to the town?" Mark asked. "I mean, all of the bad guys are dead, right?"

"One got away," Kate answered, her eyes lost in the sheer whiteness that blanketed the forest.

"I think having them return to the town is the best option," Rodney answered. "I just don't know how we're going to convince them. They don't have food, or water, and they know we have both here. There's nothing stopping them from overpowering us."

"How many people did you say attacked the hospital?" Kate asked, looking to Rodney.

"It was hard to tell, but it looked like at least a dozen."

"Then let's assume they have three times that," Kate replied, pointing toward the cabin. "We get these people on our side, and we've got a chance at fighting back."

"We don't need to fight back, Kate," Rodney said. "Those people aren't our problem."

"You saw what those animals were doing," Kate said, her tone laced with accusation. "God knows who else they're doing it to."

"You want to throw us in the middle of some kind of war?" Rodney asked. "People will die, Kate. Hiding might not be the most noble thing to do, but it's the smartest. We've risked too much already."

"It'll only be a matter of time before they find this place."

The three of them turned back toward the cabin door. Stacy, the woman whom Kate freed from rape, clutched a blanket around her shoulders.

Shivering, she stepped forward, nearing the circle but not joining. "They talked about spreading through this part of the state like some type of conquerors. They're a disease. And if they find this place they'll kill it."

"And what would you have us do?" Rodney asked.

"Fight them."

Rodney laughed, shaking his head. "And who will do the fighting? The people in that town didn't bother fighting back, and the ones that did are dead." He looked to Kate and Mark. "You think taking in those people will give us an army? It doesn't."

Stacy stepped closer. "Those men talked a lot. I don't know how much of it was truth, but I can tell you what I know. We can use it to bring them down."

"All right," Mark said, raising his hands to calm the growing eagerness. "Let's just take this one step at a time." He gestured Stacy into the circle. "What do you know?"

Stacy's blanket was lifted by a strong gust of wind, and she pulled it tighter around her body. "They're taking over towns. There are six of them up here that are strung pretty close together. I don't know if they have all of them under their thumb, but from the number of men I saw sweep through our town, I'd bet they do." She winced and touched the lump on her lip.

"How many were there?" Rodney asked.

"A few dozen," Stacy answered. "But from the sound of it, they had more that stayed behind at the other towns like ours."

"Did they say what they're doing?" Mark asked.

"They're doing whatever they want," Stacy answered. "They think there isn't anyone around to stop them." She turned to Rodney. "I guess they were right."

Rodney crossed his arms. "Listen, lady, I understand your worry. I really do, but we don't have the resources to fight them."

"Sure we do," Kate said. "We have guns, and ammunition, and—"

"Nobody that knows how to use them," Rodney said.

"We could teach them," Kate said, looking at Rodney. "You taught us."

Rodney sighed and rubbed his forehead. "We don't know what we're up against. We don't know how many men they really have, and we don't know what kind of weaponry they're packing." He eyed Kate and then Stacy. "I'm sorry, but the best I can do is take you back to the town with some supplies."

"I can help you train," Stacy said, trying her best not to sound desperate. "I was in the military. I wasn't in combat, but I helped with logistical preparation with the army. We can set up a system. I can help get us organized."

Rodney laughed and flapped his arms at his sides. "This is crazy. I'm not looking to start a war."

"One's already been started," Stacy said. "Look, if you think that those people won't eventually stumble onto this place, then you're a fool. You need the numbers to fight back." She straightened, fighting the cold. "One of the guards mentioned a highway patrol station off the highway. They're worried that they'll be found out, put back in jail."

"There aren't any more jails," Rodney said. "And if there were cops in that station, they're long gone by now."

"How do you know that?" Kate asked.

"Look around, Kate!" Rodney gestured to the empty forest. "People ran. People fled. We fled. We came here to survive, and that's not going to happen if we decide to go looking for a fight!" He spun around and violently kicked the snow, sending up a drift that caught in the wind. He kept his back to them for a long time, hands on his hips, his head lowered.

Kate walked to him slowly but didn't step around to face him. "Rodney." When he didn't answer, she took another half step, her voice dropping to a whisper. "Rodney."

He turned his head slowly. "You're willing to expose us? Expose your family?"

"I'm doing this to keep them safe," Kate answered. "To keep us all safe."

Rodney slumped his shoulders then turned, his face still turned down to his boots. "All right, Kate." He looked at Stacy. "Can you show me where the highway patrol station is?"

Stacy nodded. "Yeah. I caught a glimpse of one of their maps."

Rodney shook his head as he stepped past them and headed toward the door. Stacy looked back at Kate and mouthed "Thank you" as she followed Rodney inside, leaving Kate and Mark in the snow alone.

"He's not wrong," Mark said.

"I know," Kate replied, watching the front door close behind Stacy. "But neither am I."

Mark took her hand, and the pair walked back inside, returning to their sentry post in the kitchen, and time returned to its slow, crawling pace. She closed her eyes, still clutching Mark's hand, and for the first time since Luke was born, she whispered a prayer in her head.

Don't take him from me. Don't let me have brought him this far for nothing. He's a good boy. Her lip quivered. *He's my son.*

Mark noticed the tears and pulled Kate close. They held onto each other for a long time, and Kate sniffled, trying not to lose control. She just had to believe it would turn out okay. For once, she had to push aside the odds and the logic and the calculations. She needed faith.

The door opened, and the doctor stepped out. Blood covered both hands and stretched up to his elbows, with matching stains on the front of his shirt. He wiped the crimson away in dark smears on a towel, and the sight of so much blood made Kate fear the worst.

"I was able to get the bullet out," the doctor said. "And I was able to remove a lot of the infected tissue. But he lost a lot of blood." He turned back inside the room. "He's resting now, but it'll take some time before we know for sure if he'll pull through."

"But he's okay?" Kate asked, holding back tears.

"Yes," the doctor said. "For now."

"Can we see him?" Mark asked.

"Yes, but try not to wake him."

The doctor stepped aside, and Kate walked in first, fighting to keep her steps quiet and calm as she approached Luke's bedside. A fresh white bandage was stretched over his chest and shoulder. Blood covered most of the sheets. His cheeks were pale, and when Kate grabbed his hand, Luke's fingers were ice cold.

Mark stood behind her, both hands on her shoulders. "He's going to be okay. He just needs some rest, and he'll be fine in the morning."

Kate nodded, her lips pursed as more tears fell. She kissed Luke's hand, and then she started to cry. "I don't want to lose him. I can't lose him."

"You won't," Mark said, whispering into her ear.

The couple held each other tight and close, watching over their son. They remained still and quiet for a long time, both hoping for the best.

* * *

RODNEY MADE Stacy go over the locations a few times, and the exact conversation she'd heard from the men who'd attacked the town. He wanted to see if he could find inconsistencies with her story. He couldn't, which made the situation even more dangerous.

If the woman's estimates were correct, then there were close to forty men spread over the remaining five towns. Forty armed and dangerous convicts against two dozen scared men, women, and children. He didn't like those odds at all.

Their only hope rested in the highway patrol station. He wasn't sure how many officers would still be there, especially with so much time passed since the EMP struck, but if anything, they might be able to find additional ammunition and guns.

Rodney looked at his closet, hoping he wouldn't have to use what was behind those doors. It was a last resort. He examined the map for a final time and then walked back toward the living room.

Most of the refugees camped in his living room were asleep, exhausted by the walk from town. The food they'd eaten was probably the first real stuff they'd tasted in a couple days. And with full bellies and heavy eyes, they passed out right where they sat. All but two.

A mother and daughter sat in the corner. The daughter sobbed quietly, her only signs of distress the gentle shake of her shoulders. Her mother stroked the girl's hair, her eyes closed, the motion repetitive, the sight reminding Rodney of a swing that had been pushed and never lost momentum.

"You're the man who saved us?"

Rodney jumped a little at the question, not realizing he'd been staring at her the whole time. He cleared his throat, keeping his voice down. "I was one of the people that came into the town, yes."

The mother smiled. "My name is Yvonne." She looked down

to her daughter. "This is the first time she's slept since those men came into town." The smile faded, and the wrinkles along her eyes and mouth smoothed out. "They tried to take her from me. Made all of these threats. My husband, he—"

The tear fell first, and the wrinkles returned as she scrunched her face and lifted her hand from her daughter's light brown hair. It hovered there for a moment, and then she covered her mouth, stifling some sobs.

Rodney watched from afar, at least three other sleeping bodies between the two of them, making any attempt at physical contact impossible. "I'm sorry for your loss."

Yvonne wiped her eyes. "Thank you." She restarted the stroking of the daughter's hair, and kept her voice low. "It was very nice of you, taking us all in like you did."

Rodney nodded, keeping the knowledge that he'd only gone to retrieve the doctor's daughter. He never had any intention of bringing all of these people back. But then again, he never had the intention of letting Kate and her family tag along.

"Did you," she paused, raising her eyebrows, "lose anyone?"

"No." Rodney fidgeted with his hands. "I was alone before the EMP." When the mother frowned at that last word, Rodney leaned forward. "It's what caused all of this to happen. Killed every piece of technology controlled with a computer chip." He snapped his fingers. "Faster than the blink of an eye."

Yvonne shook her head in disbelief. Her eyes remained red, the tiny veins highlighted by the glow of the fire. "It's hard to believe that people can become so violent in times like these."

"Fear is a powerful emotion," Rodney answered. "It can push you to do things you could never imagine."

Yvonne brushed her daughter's hair back behind her ear, and then let her palm rest on the little girl's shoulder, her voice dropping an octave but remaining quiet. "What those men did, what they are, it's more than just fear that drives them." She locked eyes with Rodney, her gaze like a magnet pulling him closer. "I'd never seen anything like it. Not even in films. It was animalistic. It was… evil. And it's spreading."

Rodney finally looked away, his eyes falling to anything save for the woman's ghostlike glare. "We're heading to the police station. I'm sure we'll be able to find you all some help there."

"The police?" Yvonne's voice fluttered into a laughing whimper. "They can't stop what I saw. They can't stop what those people are."

Unable to settle his eyes on anything else, Rodney finally looked back to the woman, who he found still staring at him. He shifted uneasily. "You speak like there isn't any hope."

At that, Yvonne finally broke away from her locked stare, and lowered her eyes to her daughter. "I'd love nothing more than to believe that everything will turn out all right. That my daughter will grow up in a world where she doesn't have to fear for her life." She traced her daughter's jaw with the lightest touch, and then finally lifted her eyes. "Do you know what the last thing I said to my husband was before those animals killed him?" Her lips quivered. "We were fighting about money, and I told him that if he was a real man then he would be able to provide a better life for his family." The tears fell freely now. "You tell me what kind of hopeful world lets those words be the last spoken between a man and a woman who've been married for fifteen years." She cast her head down, her hand trembling as she restarted the motion of her stroking her daughter's hair.

Rodney waited for a moment, unsure if she would speak, and unsure of what he should say. But thankfully the mother kept her head down, and allowed Rodney a moment of reflection. With so much talk of family and death, Rodney couldn't help but think of his own family. Especially his dad.

He couldn't keep track of the number of times he wanted to call his dad up just to hear his voice and that boisterous laugh. To this day, he still hadn't ever heard a laugh so full of life. And he'd kill for one of his mother's pies. Any pie. So long as she was the one who made it.

Just one more dinner, one more trip up here to the cabin during the spring or summer to go fishing. One more hello, good night, or I love you. But his *one mores* weren't in the cards. Cancer and heart failure made sure of that.

Rodney looked at the huddled masses asleep on the floor and wondered how many of them had lost loved ones. How many of them wanted "one more"? He knew that mother wanted one more goodbye, a chance to do it the right way.

Their family and friends were left for dead back at the town, their hasty retreat leaving no time for proper goodbyes or funerals. Burials were hard, but despite the pain, they brought acceptance, a sense of peace.

The couch groaned in relief when Rodney stood, and his footsteps were hurried toward Luke's room. He found Mark and Kate inside, both kneeling by Luke's bed, and he gently knocked on the doorframe. They turned, smiling with sad eyes.

"Hey," Rodney said. "How's he doing?"

"The doctor said time will tell." Kate had her arms crossed over her chest, her hands rubbing her shoulders.

"Listen, I'm not going with you to the highway patrol station," Rodney said.

"What?" Kate and Mark both stood, walking to him at the door. "Rodney, you said—"

"You guys should still go, but I need to go back to the town," Rodney said. "I'll take the people who lost their loved ones. I want us to bury them." He glanced back at the group. "I want them to have a chance to say goodbye."

"Rodney," Kate said, shaking her head. "I don't think that's a good—"

"I lost both my parents within the same year," Rodney said. "Cancer took my dad, and then a broken heart took my mom. I was able to say goodbye to both before they were gone." He gestured to the people inside. "They didn't. But I can right that wrong."

"I'll go with you," Mark said then looked at Kate. "You can lead the group to the station. They'll follow you."

"He's right," Rodney replied. "They will."

Rodney watched Kate process his request, and when she finally worked through it, she simply nodded.

34

It didn't take much coaxing for Rodney to convince the townspeople to head back and bury their dead. He waited until Kate and Stacy and the eight others made their trek toward the highway patrol station before he led the charge back to town with Mark, Harold, a young woman named Dalia, and Yvonne in tow. They were the only ones with family that had died. Everyone else had either perished with their loved ones or were vacationers with no family.

But Rodney figured the others that died had family somewhere, and even though they'd never see each other again, he still felt an obligation to bury them properly. That was what he hoped someone would do for him.

The return to the valley town was quick, despite the heavier snowfall. One hand gripped a shovel, and the other held the rifle strapped to his shoulder should he need to put anyone else beneath the ground.

They found the town deserted when they arrived, but Rodney still performed a thorough sweep before he let anyone enter. Once they did, the doctor, Harold, and the mother, Yvonne, and the young woman, Dalia, found their family members piled in the snow behind one of the cabins.

The cold had already turned their skin blue, and frostbite was showing on their fingertips. One by one, they pulled the bodies from the pile and laid them in a row. Final goodbyes were whispered, and then Rodney planted his shovel into the icy earth.

Winter made the digging difficult, but they didn't need to be deep graves. The bodies would freeze and then decay in the spring, but by then, with any luck, the world would be back standing on at least one leg.

Rodney smirked. Kate's optimism was starting to wear off on him. No, it wasn't her optimism—it was something else. He'd been touched with a purpose that went beyond him. For as long as he could remember prepping, Rodney was always concerned with making sure that he was ready, but not once had he ever considered making sure everyone else was ready. Because if everyone was ready, they wouldn't have been in this position in the first place.

Each grave was marked with a small cross that the doctor constructed from dead tree branches. He planted them firmly at the head of each mound when it was finished, and then they moved on to the next.

It took almost two hours, and by the time they finished, the snowfall had worsened, bringing with it colder temperatures.

Mark appeared through the white haze, lifting his arm to shield his eyes from the snowfall. "We should get heading back."

Rodney nodded and then looked at the last grave they'd finished. It belonged to Yvonne's husband, and she knelt at the foot of the grave while the doctor finished up the cross at the grave's head. She had her hands clasped together tightly, her body curled forward in the position of prayer. How someone could still have faith after something like this, Rodney had no idea.

"Rodney," Mark said, prodding his arm.

"Right." Rodney stepped toward the woman, having to lift his feet higher in the snow now that it was starting to pile up again.

He placed a gloved hand on her shoulder so lightly that she didn't even realize he was there until he spoke. "We need to leave."

Yvonne jumped, slightly startled, and then nodded, pursing her lips as she wiped her eyes. The doctor walked around to join them, and then he stopped in his tracks. He held up his hand and began to retreat toward the main road between the building alleyways.

"I'll be right back! My daughter wanted something from our cabin. It'll just take a minute." The old doctor broke into a half-hearted jog that stole his breath.

It wasn't until Harold was out of view, and Rodney turned away, that he heard the gunshot. He spun around, dropping his shovel in favor of his rifle, and sprinted down the alley toward the gunfire just in time to find the doctor on his knees, his arms limp at his side, and then face planted onto the icy pavement.

Rodney tried to bring the rifle up to his shoulder to aim, but a hand stopped him. He turned to find Mark holding him still, and another gunshot thundered through the hazy white of the snowfall. And then, toward the town's entrance, a light glow of orange burned through the snow like a rising sun.

"Burn it! Shoot it! Kill anything that's still alive in this place!"

The order boomed from the haze of falling snow, and Mark pulled Rodney backward. "C'mon!" he whispered harshly, heading toward the safety of the ridge.

Rodney stole one last glance on his ascent, just before the snow and trees blocked the town from view. He saw a man with a torch, standing over the slain doctor's body. He aimed a pistol at the doctor's head and then fired again, the doctor's lifeless body twitching on the pavement.

Rage flooded Rodney's veins, and he stopped his climb while Mark, Dalia, and Yvonne continued their ascent. Rodney reached for the rifle, letting go of the steep ledge, and slid down with an avalanche of snow.

"Rodney, no!" Mark yelled, but his voice was snuffed out by

the growing wind. Rodney's boots planted against the snow and ice, and he cranked the lever of his rifle to load a bullet. He wanted to see these people. He wanted to meet the man in charge of those that would kill and rape so willingly. He wanted to see the face of the men he planned to kill.

Rodney leaned against the back side of one of the cabins near the town's east end. Flames grew hotter and wilder on the west end, the convicts marching their way down, torching the buildings one by one.

Heat from the flames burned a hole through the cold, and ash drifted down with the snow, staining the pure white with grey. He hurried down the nearest alley and stopped at the edge. He craned his head around the corner, and what he saw burning in the light of the flames made him gasp.

It wasn't a group of thugs, or a gang laced together with matching tattoos marching into town. The numbers that they'd estimated weren't even close. What Rodney got a look at was a group of eighty-plus armed men. It was an army.

He quickly scanned the line of men, all of them marching without any type of structural ranking. He crouched to one knee and aimed. He could pick off four of them before they even knew what hit them.

The first man came into Rodney's crosshairs. He steadied then squeezed the trigger. The man dropped, and Rodney moved to his right, finding a confused and frightened man aimlessly gripping a shotgun. Rodney fired again.

The second convict joined his comrade on the ground. The ranks panicked now, most of them firing blindly to the east. A few bullets nicked the front of the porch that Rodney was tucked behind, but none of them got close enough for him to even feel the breeze.

Rodney lined up another shot and fired again, this time pushing the front lines back as a third convict dropped to the ground. A brass casing ejected from the rifle's side as another quickly took its place. He gritted his teeth and lined up another shot, but the crosshairs at the end of the scope wavered. He was shaking now. Trembling from anger, and from fear, and from the cold at his back.

One of the inmates screamed, charging forward, firing at anything that looked funny, and a few stray bullets pushed Rodney from the alley. He cut behind the back of the building and leaned against the wall, the rifle barrel tilted toward the sky. He shut his eyes, which stung with sweat. He knew he couldn't take them all on by himself. It was a suicide mission.

In one swift movement, Rodney darted from the cabin, sprinting as fast as his legs would carry him toward the ridge. His muscles burned as he ascended the slope, and once he was at the top, he turned to find the valley below in flames.

The fire burned bright and hot, and Rodney saw the clusters of inmates forced back toward the west end near the highway. Rodney wasn't sure how long he watched the buildings smolder into nothing but ash, but by the time he turned around, his eyes burned along with the town.

Rodney broke into a sprint and eventually found Mark and Dalia up ahead. Mark kept asking him questions. What did he see? What did he do? But Rodney kept silent. They needed to put distance between them and the army. And they needed to get to Kate before she left the highway patrol station. If it was even still there.

* * *

DENNIS LEANED BACK on the hood of an old F-150 and closed his eyes, but the light of the fire was even visible through his eyelids. He smiled, listening to a few of the men hoot and holler as they watched the place burn.

But then Dennis heard the gunshots. When he watched four of his men go down, he leapt off the truck with the agility of a cat, landing gracefully on his feet. He watched from the road as his men were pushed back. He squinted up ahead to find the shooter, but the flames were too bright, and the fire cast too many shadows.

"You don't back down!" Dennis spit the order from behind safety, and when they didn't heed his words, they heeded his bullets. Dennis fired four shots next to the feet of the men in the rear, and pushed them forward. "Find them, you cowards!"

One of his men broke free at the front, charging wildly, but by then the flames had caught the rest of the houses, and it forced everyone back. The fire raged so hot that Dennis had forgotten about the cold. He found Mulls and ordered Martin and Billy to him immediately.

When the pair arrived, he grabbed Billy by his collar. "I want you to search the area. You find any tracks, and you stick to them until you find whoever made them. And do not come back to me without a body or another place to burn, you got it?"

They nodded, and Dennis flung the younger sibling back, sending them off into the storm. Dennis lifted his face toward the sky, squinting due to the snowfall. He wondered if it would be another bad one like they had before, but he didn't think so. Those types of storms they'd experienced tended to be one in a season.

The prospect of the townspeople escaping was more troublesome. He thought of the people who'd killed his men at the hospital. The fact that there were people out there that slipped away made that bug in his head skitter. But they wouldn't be able to evade his best trackers again. Those brothers were more bloodhound than human.

"Boss," Mulls said, coming up behind him. "Let's get out of here. There's nothing to salvage, and we don't know when this storm is going to end."

"No," Dennis said.

"Dennis, we have to—"

"We hit the trooper station, now!" He hammered his fist in the air and leaned toward Mulls in the process. "Get the guys, and tell them to get back on the highway."

Mulls gestured toward the sky, the wind picking up and blasting a sheet of snow against his body. "The storm is only going to get worse! We won't even be able to see what we're shooting at, and we haven't sent scouts to the station to see what we're up against!"

The bug gnawed at the bits of wiring in his brain, tearing violence and rage loose. The rest of the signals suddenly fried, and he whirled around, fist aimed for Mulls's face, and the harsh contact caused the bone to emit a loud crack in the cold that bit and stung both men.

Mulls cupped the cheek that Dennis had hit. "Son of a bitch!" The big bear charged Dennis, tackling him hard to the pavement. His sheer weight and size gave him the upper hand as they sprawled over the snow, fists clenched and arms ramming them into whatever flesh they could find.

Dennis lifted his knee and connected with Mulls's groin. Mulls yelped in pain, seizing up long enough for Dennis to fling him off.

Mulls rolled to his back on the pavement, scrunching his face in pain, as Dennis jumped on him to seize the opportunity.

Every punch into Mulls's face bloodied Dennis's knuckles. The cartilage in his nose crunched and dissolved with each blow. The tension in Mulls's body released, and his arms and limbs lay limp at his sides. Dennis's arm grew heavy, and he strained, but he kept beating the man's face. The bug burrowed deeper and deeper into his mind.

"My way!" Dennis screamed into Mulls's lifeless face. "My way! My way! My way! My way!" Each phrase was met with another blow until Mulls's face was no longer recognizable.

Gasping for air, and exhausted, Dennis rolled off Mulls and sprawled out on the snowy pavement next to him. Blood covered his right arm, his face, and his chest. He coughed and then glanced over at Mulls's lifeless body.

The bug stopped digging, and Dennis rolled to his side, pushing himself up off the ground. He wobbled back on his feet, and when he looked down at Mulls, he knew the big bear was dead. He turned around, finding Jimmy standing behind him, rifle in hand.

Jimmy's gaze fell from Dennis to Mulls then back to Dennis. The thickened snowfall made it difficult to make out the features on Jimmy's face, but it was easy to see the shotgun aimed at him.

"What did you do?" Jimmy said, his arms trembling, his voice stuck in that high octave. Three quick steps put him an arm's length away from Dennis, and the anger on his face was clear as day now. "*What did you do?*"

Dennis glanced down at Mulls's body and then back to the end of Jimmy's shotgun. "You going to shoot me, Jimmy?" He made it one step before the familiar *tha-chunk* of a pump-action twelve gauge stopped him cold.

Jimmy lowered his eyes to Mulls once again, and the anger faded to sadness, but it was gone by the time they returned to Dennis. "Christ. You killed him!"

"And what did Mulls ever do for you?" Dennis asked, his eyes searching for any more of his men that could be lurking, growing bolder when he realized they were still alone. "It was my idea to take the towns. It was my idea to gather supplies." He shuffled very careful steps toward Jimmy with each sentence, unnoticeable in their small increments. "You know what Mulls wanted? He wanted us to lie low, forget about it." Dennis pointed toward the smoldering town. "This is what happens when you lie low!"

"Maybe." Jimmy shook his head, raising the shotgun to his shoulder and taking aim. "But you didn't do shit for me on the inside. It was all Mulls. And he did the same for you! Go to hell—"

With his arm now within the reach of the shotgun's barrel, Dennis lunged his hand out, ducking his head out of the way as Jimmy squeezed the trigger. The blast deafened Dennis to the world, and he felt a light pinch in his shoulder, but with Jimmy surprised by the blow, he easily snatched the gun away.

A quick adjust of his grip, and Dennis squeezed the trigger, shooting from the waist. The slug tore through Jimmy's stomach, and blood and intestines slid down the ridges of his ribs as he tumbled backward and lay still, falling snow slowly covering the exposed wound.

With the shotgun in his hand, standing between two dead men, he heard the shouts of the others heading his way. He quickly aimed the gun at Mulls's stomach and fired, blasting a slug through the dead man's big stomach, and a few seconds later, Dennis was surrounded.

The convicts appeared like ghosts through the sheets of snow, and every one of their faces fell to Mulls first, then to Jimmy, and finally to Dennis. As the circle of spectators grew, so did the number of angry expressions. Before any of them could shoot, Dennis lowered the shotgun and pointed at Jimmy.

"The skinny bastard tried to kill Mulls!" Dennis heaved exhausted breaths, shaking his head. "I tried to stop him."

"Bullshit!" A voice echoed from the circle, and a few murmurs of agreement followed. "Jimmy wouldn't do that!"

"No?" Dennis asked, laughing. "You don't think those two didn't have history? You don't think Jimmy got tired of following orders?" He searched for the source of the voice in the crowd but had no luck in finding it. "I told Mulls we should go to the highway patrol station now, and when he told Jimmy that, the bastard shot him then started whaling on him." He pointed toward the bullet wound that he fired just moments before everyone had arrived, to help corroborate his story. "And you know why Mulls wanted us to attack the pigpen? Because of that!" he shouted, thrusting his hand toward the town they'd just turned to ash. "I told everyone here that people would eventually push back! And what happens if the people that were here find that highway patrol station before we take it out? Huh?" He walked to one of the men on the circle's edge. "You want to give up your warm bed?" He turned to the man next to him. "You want to go back to wanking it with your hand instead of having a woman?" Slowly, the heads started to shake in response, and a few *nos* filtered through the air, and Dennis retreated into the circle, and the majority of the inmates' mood shifted. "If we don't act now, then we can lose everything! And I'm telling you right now, boys, that I'm not going back in a cell. I'll be six feet under before that happens."

The agreement rippled through the crowd, and it wasn't long before even those that had been friends with and loyal to Mulls nodded. It never ceased to amaze Dennis how far fear would push people. The fear of loss, of death, of pain. Humans had fought against that fear since the beginning of time. And in that battle, there was violence that had ravaged civilization and killed millions. And now Dennis would use that violence to kill every living thing that stood against him. His wolves were hungry now, and he had no intention of keeping them that way.

* * *

BY THE TIME they returned to the cabin, Rodney, Mark, Yvonne, and Dalia were cloaked in snow and ice. They burst through the front door like a group of snow monsters in search of fire to free them from their curse. Questions were thrust at them, but Rodney could only think of the relief that the flames brought to his body. As he thawed, his mind returned to the present.

"What happened?" Marie, the doctor's wife, asked, and then, as if she had forgotten to count the number of bodies that returned, she gasped, covering her mouth.

Marie collapsed into a chair, sobbing. Rodney walked over, placing his still snow-covered gloved hand on her shoulder.

"I'm sorry." His voice cracked, his body still raw and stiff from the cold. He turned to an elderly woman. "They haven't come back yet?"

The grey-haired woman shook her head.

Holly scooted past Rodney and Mark scooped her up. “How far is the station from here?”

“Forty minutes,” Rodney answered. “In good weather.” The snow had thickened outside, but it still hadn’t reached blizzard levels yet. It was uncomfortable outside but still traversable.

“You think they’d stay at the station to wait for this to blow over?” Mark asked.

“Maybe.” But as Rodney spoke, he was already on his way toward his room. Snow tracked him all the way to his bed, and when he opened the closet door to the tall, black safe that rested inside, his fingers were so cold that he still couldn’t feel the dial as he spun it. The lock opened, and Rodney swung the door open.

Inside were the components to put together a fifty-caliber machine gun, and he grabbed the pieces, his hands moving over the metal deftly. It was heavy put together, close to ninety pounds, and the tripod mount added another forty. He’d need a sled to carry it.

When he brought the gun out and rested it against the wall by the front door, its sight was greeted by a series of gasps that ended with Mark’s “What the hell is that?”

“An M2 fifty-cal machine gun,” Rodney answered, heading to his room to grab the tripod mount. “The inmates that attacked that town were close to one hundred.” He went back into his room, grabbing the crates of ammunition. The box hit the ground with a heavy thud, and Rodney grabbed the sled from the closet, along with rope. When he came back out, there were still confused faces glaring at the weapon.

Mark grabbed Rodney’s arm, stopping him in the middle of tying his knot through the sled’s loops. “What is it that you’re planning here?”

“The plan? The plan is to kill as many of those bastards as I can.”

“Jesus Christ,” Mark said, running his hands through his hair, flinging the melted bits of snow from his head.

"We need to get to the trooper station, get those cops out of there." Rodney returned to the work on his knot. "If they're still alive."

Mark bent down to help Rodney with the ropes, but Rodney stopped him.

"No," Rodney said. "You're staying here."

"You can't pull this thing by yourself."

"I've done it before." Which was true. But he'd only done it once, a year ago, and it wasn't storming outside. Rodney set the last piece of the weaponry on the sled. "You need to stay here with your kids." Rodney stared at the weapon. Even with the glow of the firelight, the gleaming metal looked cold. He grabbed the ropes and headed for the door.

Mark gripped Rodney's arm. He worked his mouth, at first unable to find the words, and then he sighed and wrapped Rodney in a hug. "Be careful out there, huh?"

Rodney nodded, and then Mark stepped aside, opening the path to the cold wilderness.

The slack of the rope disappeared, and it grew taut as Rodney dug his snow boots into the ground, lugging the hulking machine into the storm. He kept a steady pace, the sled easier to pull than he thought even with the snowfall. He could get there in time so long as he kept this pace. He just hoped there would still be people alive when he arrived.

35

The snowfall had just begun when Kate and her group arrived at the highway patrol station. And despite the road signs, they'd nearly missed it. All but the roof was buried in snow, save for a single trench that led down to the front doors, which meant that there was still a good chance the troopers inside were alive; if they hadn't already fled.

"Get your weapons handy," Kate said, getting close to the door. "I don't know what we'll find inside, so keep your eyes peeled."

Nervous nods answered, and Kate prayed silently to herself that she wouldn't get anyone killed. Slowly, carefully, she reached for the door handle, and with a light tug, it cracked open.

It was dark inside. The snow that covered the windows also blocked out the light. Behind her, the snowfall worsened, and Kate entered the station, the end of her rifle barrel guiding her way. "Hello?" Her voice echoed over empty office chairs, spreading through the darkness like sonar, searching for a response in the cold.

Chair legs scraped against tile to her left, and in the same sweeping motion, every gun moved toward the commotion.

"Who's there?" Kate asked, her eyes still not entirely adjusted to the dark. She stepped forward. "*Who's there?*"

"Put the guns down." The voice accompanied two figures that took shape in the dark, and then one of them stepped forward, pistol in hand, and wearing a highway patrolman uniform. The officer spoke like a man who'd given orders his entire life, and the greying stubble along his face suggested he'd been doing it for a long time.

No one in Kate's group lowered their weapons. She kept the bead on the officer, her eyes scanning the rest of the office, and slowly she made out two more shapes off to her right. More officers, with guns trained on them. She flicked her eyes back toward the officer who spoke. "We didn't come here for trouble."

"Then put the guns down."

Slowly, Kate submitted, and so did her group. She raised her brow in response to the officer's pistol, and then they lowered their weapons, though he didn't holster it. Instead it remained at his side as he stepped forward.

"Are any of you hurt?"

Whatever doubts that Kate felt toward the officers ended with those words. "No. How about yours?"

He holstered his weapon. "Hungry, but okay."

"Good." Kate stepped close enough to read the name on his uniform. Captain Harley. "Captain, we need to talk."

"Well," Captain Harley said. "Might as well talk about it with the doors closed. It's cold enough in here already." He gestured to his men, and they shut the doors.

Kate followed the officers toward the back rooms and offices of the station. When they were all together, they totaled only five. It didn't take long for Kate to tell them what she knew. And she was surprised at how much the officers didn't know.

After the power had gone out, most of the troopers were sent out to assist stranded motorists. But after the first day, most of his men started disappearing without word. Captain Harley suspected most fled toward home, to be with their families, but he knew some of them probably froze to death in the blizzard that passed through.

The officers that remained included Captain Harley, Lieutenant Benson, Officer Terry, Officer Luis, and Officer Thomas.

"And you think the inmates are going to come here?" Lieutenant Benson asked.

"They had your station marked on a map of theirs we found," Stacy said.

"And they already have six towns under their control." Captain Harley looked at no one as he crossed his arms, nodding to himself. When he did meet a pair of eyes, it was Kate's. "How many men do they have?"

"More than us," Kate answered. "We weren't sure we'd get to you before they ambushed. I'm glad we did."

"Us too." Captain Harley pushed himself off the desk. He wasn't a big man, but he held a presence, and it was on display as the rest of his men rose with him. "What do you need from us?"

"Gather as much food, weapons, and ammunition as you can carry. We'll help, but we need to move quickly. I don't know how much time we have."

Captain Harley nodded. "You heard the lady! Let's move!"

The officers scattered to the various dark corners of the station, Kate sending her people to help, until only she and Captain Harley remained.

Two piles quickly formed near the station's exit, one of food, and the other of weapons. The weapons pile was nearly twice the size of the food pile.

Lieutenant Benson added two more rifles to the cache and then wiped his hands. "Do you want me to grab it, Captain?"

"No. It hasn't gotten us anything so far, and we won't have the connections to—"

"Grab what?" Kate asked.

Captain Harley exhaled, tilting his head to the side as if he were annoyed to answer. "When communications went down after this"—he frowned, looking at Kate for confirmation—"EMP? We didn't think we could reach anyone. But after the blizzard, we started scouring every nook and cranny of this place to look for food or water. We didn't find much, but we did find an old Morse code machine. It was used here back in the sixties as a means to contact emergency services if someone was sick on the mountain."

"Morse code?" Kate asked, a well of hope rising within her despite the captain's expression. "Were you able to—"

"Yes," Harley answered. "But we haven't heard from them since we set it up."

"Who answered?" Kate asked.

"It was a National Guard unit stationed to the south," Benson answered. "I told them where we were and that we needed assistance, but we never heard back."

"National Guard?" The words left Kate's lips like a balloon of hope, drifting toward the sky. "Have you tried since then?"

"Every day," Benson answered. "It's been radio silence."

Three quick steps brought Kate within inches of the lieutenant. "We need to try again. We need to send another message."

"Kate, we've tried—"

"We can't beat these guys on our own," Kate said. "But with the National Guard at our backs, we might have a chance." She flapped her arms at her sides. "What could it hurt?"

Benson glanced toward Captain Harley, and Kate knew that everything hinged on the thoughts behind that stoic expression. And then Kate's chest swelled with hope when Harley nodded. "Don't be long."

The machine itself was small and surprisingly simple. It was hooked to a string of copper wires that ran up toward the radio tower on the roof, and the sight of the well-worn technology made her smile as she thought of the man who'd given her the old Skyranger Commonwealth that brought her up here. She had a small bit of knowledge of Morse code from her early days as a pilot, but she was on the tail end of the generation that was required to have some proficiency in it.

"Send exactly what I say," Kate said and then cleared her throat as Lieutenant Benson poised his finger over the brass tab. "Mayday, mayday, mayday. Threat to life imminent." She then provided the longitude and latitude coordinates for Rodney's cabin, which she still had memorized. "Mayday, mayday, mayday."

The machine produced the series of dits and dahs that were transmitted via radio waves. When it was finished, Kate stood there, praying for a return response through the headphones that Lieutenant Benson wore, but they heard nothing.

"Let's send it again," Kate said.

And they did. Three more times. And it would have been more, but Captain Harley found them, and despite her persistence, the captain's authority won out. Kate lingered behind, looking at the machine, the one piece of equipment that could connect them to the outside world. She wanted to bring it but knew it was useless without the radio tower, and they didn't have the time or resources to make that happen.

Supplies and people waited at the station's exit when Kate walked up. She retrieved her gun and flicked the safety off, looking at the still-falling snow outside. The door swung open, and Lieutenant Benson was the first man to step out, and the first one to die.

The gunfire erupted like a thunderstorm, dozens of bullets turning the doors into Swiss cheese. Everyone ducked for cover, leaping behind desks and walls or whatever sturdy material that was close.

Captain Harley was the first to return fire, and Kate fumbled for the rifle she dropped on her hasty retreat. She joined the captain, planting her elbows on the desk as she fired in the direction of the doors, which were closed. But it wasn't until the captain placed his hand on her shoulder that she stopped.

"Hold your fire!" Harley bellowed.

A high-pitched whine of the wind replaced gunfire, and Kate's eyes fell to the lieutenant's body, his legs and arms twisted to the point of breaking. The pool of blood that spread from his right side resembled black tar instead of the flood of life that went through his veins.

"Thomas, Luis, on me," Harley said, and with their pistols still trained on the door, they moved efficiently through the darkness until they were side by side with the captain. "There's only one way inside this place, and it's through those doors. We can dig out way out the back while keeping them distracted out front."

"My people should go," Kate said. "Most of them are worse shots than all of you. They'd be better off digging."

"All right," Captain Harley said. "Anyone that's never handled a weapon before leaves."

A few more bullets hit the door, the enemy outside prodding them. But Kate knew that the convicts' army would charge. Especially if Dennis was leading them. He had no qualms about killing, least of all if they were cops. But Dennis and his people didn't know how many officers were inside. It was something they could use toward their advantage.

"No one goes toward the door," Kate said, looking at Harley when Thomas and Luis returned from showing Kate's people where to start digging. "So long as they think we've got thirty officers down here, they won't charge."

Harley nodded. "Terry, did you pack the riot gear?"

"No, I-I didn't think we'd—"

"Go and grab it," Harley said. "We'll shoot enough tear gas outside to blind them. If anything, it'll buy us some time."

Terry sprinted off, leaving Kate, Stacy, Captain Harley, Luis, and Thomas to hold the entrance. Despite the cold, sweat poured off Kate in buckets.

Their weapon barrels remained trained on the doors, the wind whistling through the bullet holes. It was the only sound inside, and as Kate's vision began to grow fuzzy from staring, the doors burst open.

Two men sprinted inside, the flashes from their gun muzzles striking the darkness like lightning. But the spurt of violence was short lived as over a dozen bullets dropped both men to the ground, dead before the double doors swung closed behind them.

Bullet casings clinked on the tile, the heated metal cooling the moment it was ejected from its chamber. Kate trembled, her adrenaline forcing the muscles along her arms to shake. The dead convicts collapsed near Lieutenant Benson, their hands almost touching.

Terry returned with the riot gear, dumping a bag of tear gas, flash grenades, and the appropriate launchers needed to send the convicts outside running away in tears.

"On me," Captain Harley said, the tear gas launcher in hand, the rest of his men in tow.

Kate hung back, rifle still aimed at the doors, as the troopers filed next to the exit, two on each side. She only saw their silhouettes, and then the quick nod from Harley as they shouldered open the doors, sending four cans of tear gas streaming into the air.

Shouts echoed inside before the doors swung shut, and Harley and his boys retreated toward Kate, Harley nudging her elbow. "Let's hope that keeps them busy for a little while. Why don't you go and check on your people?"

Kate nodded and then grabbed a candle to help light her path. The flame wiggled in time with her shaking, the light exposing her fear. But that was what light was for, wasn't it? To cast out the darkness, to fight against the fear? She forced her hand steady, and by the time she reached her people, it had stopped.

The progress was slow, the snow was thick and compacted. Kate stayed for a while to help but kept one ear toward the front.

She kept waiting for a series of screams or cries of terror, ending in a flurry of gunshots.

But with each pile of snow and ice they added to the floor while making their escape tunnel, Kate heard nothing. Maybe they could get out alive. Maybe this would work. She glanced at the small candle to her left, the flame wiggling in defiance of the darkness, holding on to hope.

* * *

THE SNOWFALL OFFERED POOR VISIBILITY, especially from the back of the group. After what happened with Mulls and Jimmy in town, he didn't want any of these guys with a gun in their hands standing behind him. Who knew what kind of stray bullet would find its way into the base of his skull.

And when the tear gas was thrown from the only entrance and exit of the building, Dennis was glad to have been in the rear.

Thick streams of gas left the cylinder canisters, blending with the white of the snowfall. Smoke crawled over the snow, spreading outward, forcing the inmates to retreat. Dennis stepped back, shielding his face with the front of his shirt, which he pulled up from beneath his coat. Three more canisters were flung from the station's entrance, and the poisonous fog continued to blanket the ground, lingering in the air.

"Watch the doors!" Dennis barked. "They could be coming out in masks! Be ready! Be ready!" But while a few of the inmates trained their weapons back on the station, most were too busy fending off the effects of the gas.

A burning sensation filled Dennis's eyes and throat, his nasal cavity growing thick with phlegm. He hacked with the rest of his men, who continued to backpedal from the gas. But the longer they stood out there in the cold, the more Dennis realized that the officers weren't coming out. Which meant one of two things:

either they had enough supplies inside to wait them out, or they didn't have the numbers.

Dennis shielded his nose and mouth from the gas that still lingered, and while he tried to avoid it, he didn't always succeed. His eyes teared and burned, blurring his vision, but he kept his concentration on the station's entrance.

After a while the gas dissipated, and the retreated masses slowly crept back to their original front line. Dennis remained in the back, wiping the freezing snot from his face, flinging it on the snow. The smoke had cleared, but his vision remained blurred from the watery effects of the gas.

The slope they'd dug to the front doors was steep, and Dennis only saw the very top of the doors. He clenched his fists. He was so close. All of the days and nights where he was locked away in that cell flooded back to him. The endless hours that stretched for eternity. In prison, there was no horizon, no dawn of a new day. It was only the repetition of the same day, over and over and over again. All of the same atrocities and horrors, the monotony, the hopelessness of being locked in a cell where you would rot into nothing for the rest of your life.

The bug stirred in his mind, then burrowed, tunneling its way deeper into Dennis's brain, igniting all of the ways he'd like to kill the officers inside. There would be no quarter given to those that dropped their weapons, only torture. It would be slow, methodical. Maybe he would leave them to freeze out in the cold, cutting them open to let the animals in the woods feast while they were still alive. And once every pig inside had been slaughtered, then there was no one left to oppose him.

Dennis smiled, enjoying that idea as the bug burrowed deeper, deeper… deeper. He marched back to his men, most of whom were sitting on cars or rocks. "Everyone up! We need to move! We need to move now!" When his words didn't stir them, he fired three shots into the air. "I said up, goddammit!"

Asses lifted from the snow, the thunder of gunshots enough to stir the people from their hazy stupor.

"I want thirty men by the entrance! And I want to circle around the back!" Dennis cut the group in half right where they stood. "Shoot anything that moves, and if they surrender themselves, I want them brought to me." He passed over the squinted faces, making sure everyone understood. "Those aren't men in that station! They're pigs! They're the cowards who hide behind badges. But those badges mean nothing now!" He pointed to the group, the inmates swelling with anger at his words. "This is our world! This is our time! And no one will take that from us!"

Cheers erupted into the evening sky, and Dennis raised his arms high as his people rattled their fists and weapons. Chants of violence and anger washed over the group, and Dennis smiled as everyone departed toward their assignments. This was a fight that they would win, and Dennis didn't care how many of his people would die.

* * *

KATE DROPPED THE SHOVEL, her hands frozen and aching, the joints screaming now. She worked her way from the front of the pack, needing a break.

The front of the station had remained quiet for the past twenty minutes, and while Kate tried to keep her attention on the progress of the tunnel, she found herself looking down the hall, waiting for the inevitable symphony of gunfire.

"I'm going to check the front," Kate said. "See how we're doing."

A few grunts of affirmation answered back, and Kate continued to pump her hands into fists, trying to get the blood flowing again.

Stacy, Harley, and his men still had their guns trained on the bullet-ridden door. The captain noticed her first. "How are we looking?"

"It's slow," Kate answered.

"How close?"

Kate shook her head in uncertainty, and Harley nodded in response. She cleared her throat. "Have they sent anyone else down?"

"No," Harley answered. "The gas seems to be doing the trick, but it'll be running its course soon." He turned back to Kate. "Better keep digging."

Urgency was laced in the request, and Kate nodded in response, her hands throbbing again at just the idea having to curl around the handle of a shovel again.

"Kate!" The voice was breathless, and a silhouette took shape in the darkness. "We're through! We've reached the top!"

Before Kate turned around, Harley and his men reached for their gear, retreating from their position. When they turned the corner of the hallway toward the back, everyone froze at the sound of an uproar that broke through the howl of wind and snow.

"What was that?" Luis asked, his worried expression made more ominous by the flickering candlelight in his hand.

"We need to move," Harley said. "Now!"

The captain led the sprinted retreat down the hall, and when they reached the back doors, Kate shoved her people forward and up. Feet and hands slipped on the ice, and the howl of wild men and gunfire forced Kate to turn her gaze backward.

From the narrow view inside the tunnel, Kate saw Harley and his men, in the hall, firing at the enemy. The small space amplified the gunshots, making them thunder with a fiercer bang.

The bodies behind Kate propelled her forward. Two people were ahead of her. The first broke the surface and turned around, extending a hand to help the woman in front of Kate. They clasped hands, and another gunshot thundered, striking the man in his shoulder and severing his grip on the woman's hand. She slid backward, slamming into Kate, who dug the tips of her boots into the compacted snow.

Time slowed. Any way Kate turned meant certain death. She

suddenly felt hands on her and then looked at Stacy. She was screaming something at her, a terrified expression on her face.

Kate couldn't make out the words, but they weren't needed as Harley funneled his men up the icy embankment. They pushed Kate toward the surface. Seconds later, snow whipped the top of Kate's head as she squinted into the storm.

Amongst the white were figures hunched over in the snow. The weather had made them faceless, but Kate knew they were Dennis's men. And when she reached for her pistol, she prayed that Mark made it back safely, and her mind flashed images of her children. Holly and Luke laughed, and as she straightened her arm to fire, Kate wished that she had been given another chance with Luke. She wished that they had been on better terms the last time they spoke. And she hoped that her son wasn't tormented by the fact he never got to say goodbye. Because she knew she was.

"Kate, get down!"

The voice thundered from behind her, and Kate didn't have time to get a good look at Rodney before hell rained over her head.

Kate clamped her hands over her ears, but her palms did little to muffle the gunfire above. Each gunshot vibrated her body, and when she lifted her face, she saw bullets flash in brilliant streaks of light, her cheeks warmed by the heat generated by the constant barrage of gunfire.

Minutes passed, and still the thunderous roar of whatever weapon Rodney had brought with him continued its assault on the convicts, and it wasn't until she looked down into the hallway that she realized that Harley and his men had ceased firing as well.

And then it was suddenly over, the gunfire ended, only their continuous vibrations rattling through Kate's body as she lifted her head toward the sky. She watched the snow fall, deaf to the world.

A rush of cold drifted toward her, and then Rodney was near, his lips moving quickly, extending his hand into the tunnel. But she just stared at him as if he were some type of mirage. A shove from behind propelled her body forward, and without thinking, she raised her hand to meet Rodney's as his firm grip wrapped around her wrist.

Rodney pulled her from the tunnel, and Kate stumbled blindly through the snow. She turned toward the direction where the prisoners had attacked, but the faceless silhouettes had been transformed into bloody piles in the snow.

Kate's jaw dropped at the number of corpses. It looked as if it stretched farther than she could see through the snowfall. Blotches of crimson and black contrasted with the white. And when she turned back around, everyone had already been pulled from the station, and Rodney was gripping her by the shoulders with both hands. Again his lips moved quickly, but she stared past him toward the hulking gun that was planted on a sled, smoke still rising from the weapon's thick barrel.

"Kate!" This time Rodney's voice broke through as he shook her harshly. "Kate, we have to go, now!" He pulled her with him on his retreat, but even as her feet moved, her eyes remained glued to the dead, and then as they passed the weapon that Rodney left behind, her eyes fell to it, and the mountain of bullet casings that rested beside it.

36

The snowfall didn't make the tracks any easier to follow, but Billy had once tracked a deer for six miles through a worse storm than this, and that was in the Rockies. Now, those were real mountains, not the hills he and his brother found himself in now. He missed the mountains of his youth. But if he had to choose between being back in a cell or stuck in these hills, he'd gladly choose the latter.

Martin brought up the rear, huffing and grumbling louder than he should have. He leaned against a tree trunk, his shoulder eliciting a loud thump against the bark, triggering snowfall from the dead branches. "Find it?" He hacked and then spit a wad of phlegm in the snow.

"No," Billy answered, his eyes scanning the endless sea of white, the rolling mounds of snow blurring together for the past dozen miles they'd already chewed up.

"Let's head back," Martin said. "The trail's cold."

Billy placed his gloved hand in the snow. He was tired. He was hungry. But unlike his brother, he wanted to get on Dennis's good side. Despite his older brother's apathy, he understood what Dennis was doing, and he wanted to ensure himself a seat at the table.

"We're close," Billy said, continuing his trek through the snow.

Martin groaned and shoved himself off the tree, continuing his labored breathing.

The group had done a good job of covering their tracks. Whoever was leading them made a smart move in having them walk in a single-file line, but the real problem was the fresh snowfall. It was like searching for a piece of paper in a sea of white. The trail was nothing more than a subtle break in the pattern of the snow.

Billy stopped, his eyes catching a hint of that path up to his left. "C'mon." He waved his brother forward and hastened his pace. He was close. He could feel it in bones like a radar signal.

Tracking had come second nature to him ever since he was a boy, when his mother used to send him out to fetch his father from the bar. Martin was good, but to Billy, tracking was like breathing. There wasn't anything he couldn't find.

Growing up dirt poor as a kid, Billy turned tracking into a game for himself. He'd time himself, blindfold himself, anything to make it more of a challenge. But he'd always find his target. It was a skill that his brother noticed quickly, and by the time he was sixteen, Billy was already running in a gang with Martin, hunting down men for anyone who'd pay.

In a way, he was a bounty hunter, though most of the time, the people that paid him wanted them not only found but also dead. Billy had never liked killing. That was Martin's forte.

But if they could pull this off, they would have a seat at the table, just like they did when they performed all of those jobs for those mobsters in New York.

Billy remembered all of the perks that came with working for men in a position of power. The girls, the food, the liquor, the parties, the cars, and all of the shiny stuff he'd seen in magazines and on television as a dirt-poor kid in the mountains were suddenly his. And after six years of being locked up, he was ready to do whatever he could to get those things back.

He followed the broken trail, losing it once more before finding it again, and as his eyes scanned the endless forest, he stopped cold. Just ahead, between two groups of trees, he saw an unnatural mound of snow. It was pitched downward, lying flat, like snow that had fallen on a roof.

"What the hell are you stopping for—"

Billy held up his hand, and his brother froze. Then after a second's pause, Martin crept as quietly as a mouse—each footfall in the snow was soundless. Billy pointed, and Martin followed his brother's hand toward the slanted roof.

"Son of a bitch," Martin said, whispering to himself in disbelief. "And here I was thinking you'd gotten rusty." He clapped his brother on the shoulder. "All right, let's go back and—"

"No," Billy said, removing the pistol from his holster. He'd only fired it a couple of times. But ever since his hookup with Dennis, he'd gotten better at killing. Though he still didn't like it, he didn't mind it as much anymore. "The place doesn't look big. Can't be more than a dozen people inside." He scanned the area. "And they don't have any guards set. We can take them by surprise."

Martin spun his brother around, shaking his head. "No. You remember what Dennis said. He wants us to come and get him."

"By the time we find him, things could have changed. It's better if we take care of this now. It'll be less he has to deal with when he gets back from the trooper station."

"What the hell's gotten into you?" Martin asked. "Why do you care so much about what that asshole wants? You think he cares about you?"

"No," Billy answered, though his tone was more defensive than he meant it to be. "I just don't want us to get left behind." He knew there was safety in numbers. And right now, Dennis had the most. If that changed, then maybe so would Billy's opinion, but he'd go down that road when he crossed it.

Martin laughed. "God, you always were worried about shit

like that, weren't you?" He grunted and then removed his pistol. "You sure you can handle this? We'll be outnumbered."

Billy turned back to the cabin, tightening his grip on the pistol. "Not for long."

* * *

LUKE AWOKE, sweaty and sore and alone in his bed. He blinked away the sleep in his eyes and saw the bandage across his chest. He lifted a hand and gently grazed the fabric. An aching pain throbbed his entire chest, his surroundings foreign.

He moved his tongue around his lips, which were rough and chapped. He tilted his head to the left on his pillow, finding a glass of water on the nightstand. He reached a shaking hand and curled his fingers around the cool glass. His grip was weak, and he could barely lift his head to drink, but when he tasted the water, he drank thirstily.

Luke emptied the cup and then weakly set the glass back on the nightstand, nearly dropping it as it hit the wood with a heavy thunk.

Lines of water ran down the corners of his mouth, and he shut his eyes. Slowly, his memory of events returned. Images from their escape from Fairfax, and then arriving here at the cabin flashed in his mind. And then his anger flared at the remembrance of his conversation with his mother.

The door opened, the knock that accompanied it more ceremonial than practical. "Luke?"

He smiled. "Hey, Holly."

The door remained cracked, and Holly was only a tiny sliver in the narrow space. "Can I come in with you, or are you still sick?"

"You can come in, but don't—"

Holly burst inside and then catapulted herself onto the bed, landing on Luke's stomach and sending a bright flash of pain throughout the wound on his chest. He yelped, and Holly's playful giggle turned to a gasp, and she slinked away, afraid she was in trouble.

"Jump on the bed," Luke said through gritted teeth.

Holly lowered her head sheepishly. "I'm sorry."

Luke closed his eyes, taking deep breaths until the pain eased. "It's all right." He opened his eyes and found her still sulking, and the rest of the anger melted away. "I'm fine. Really." He forced a cheesy grin. "See?"

Holly approached, taking a seat on the edge of the bed. She picked up his hand, and started playing with his fingers. "Are you still mad at Mom?"

Luke frowned. "Who told you I was mad at Mom?"

She flashed him a teenager-like stare, and for a moment she looked older. He didn't like that.

"There's very thin walls in here," Holly answered, then she paused. "So are you? Still mad?"

Luke sighed. "I don't know, Holls. I guess a little."

"You shouldn't be mad," Holly said.

"Says the girl who's been mad at her for the past year," Luke replied accusingly. "What's changed your tune?"

"I don't know." The words matched a genuinely unsure tone as Holly tried to bend Luke's pinky finger to an unnatural angle. "I like having her around."

Luke had forgotten how much she missed as a kid. Their mom was gone a lot more than when he was little. Better jobs at bigger airlines meant longer hours and more time away from home. "You missed her, huh?"

"Yeah," Holly answered. "I guess I did." She plucked at his leg hair, and she giggled when he winced.

Luke tried to smack her hand away but couldn't reach due to his limited mobility. "Stop, you freak." But that only made her try it again and increased the level of giggles, and even Luke started to laugh. "Ugh! You're lucky I was shot!"

Luke took her hand, engulfing it quickly with one snatch, his grip gentle but firm. "Hey. I want you to do something for me, okay?"

"What?" Holly widened her eyes, making them grow big and round like full moons. They always looked so green whenever she was worried. It was as though the emotion brightened them.

"You know it's not safe, right? That there are people out there who want to hurt us?"

"I know," she answered. "I'm not a kid."

"Good, because if something ever happens and we are in trouble, I want you to hide somewhere good and don't make a sound, no matter what."

"But—"

Luke tightened his grip. "No buts, Holly." And before she opened her mouth to answer, he pulled her close, dropping his voice to a whisper. "And this isn't a promise you can break." He held up his left hand, extending his pinky.

Holly regarded the pinky, those eyes still wide and bright green. She nodded and then wrapped her pinky around his. "I promise."

Luke exhaled, knowing she meant it. She might act like a teenager, but a younger sibling never forgets the promises from childhood. For them, that was the pinky promise. Whenever either of them did that, they knew the other meant business.

Luke kissed her forehead and then rested his head back on the pillow, yawning. Fatigue had gripped him again, and the room started to fade to black. "I love you… Holls…"

Holly reached up on her tippy toes and kissed Luke's cheek. "I love you too," she whispered in his ear and then left.

* * *

OUTSIDE, the snow had picked up, and it made it hard for Mark to see very deep into the woods. But he still kept his eyes glued to the horizon, waiting for Kate to return. Over the course of his relationship with his wife, he had become very good at waiting. He could argue that he was the most patient man in the world. But this kind of waiting was different than before. It was dangerous.

Mark squinted, thinking he saw something in the snow, but once his eyes set on it, it didn't move. Nothing but sheets of white waved against a sky fading into night. Uneasy, he walked to the kitchen and grabbed Luke's medication, passing the townspeople who had taken up whatever space they could find on the floor.

Most of them were asleep. Mark imagined that they hadn't had a good rest in a while—either that, or the adrenaline from the sprint here had finally worn off. But for the number of people crammed inside the cabin, it was quiet.

Mark tapped on Luke's door. When there wasn't an answer, he cracked it open. "Luke?"

The boy was asleep on the bed, his head turned away from the door, and the covers pulled all the way up to the white bandages that covered his shoulder and chest, which rose and fell steadily with each breath.

Mark watched him for a moment and then stepped as quietly as the old wooden floorboards allowed him.

Luke may have not been his biological son, but that didn't mean he loved the boy any less. Luke was eight when he first started dating his mom. And for a child that had experienced so much pain and trauma, he was wonderfully kind. There wasn't a trace of the evil that controlled his father.

But it was a thought that lingered in the back of Mark's mind, the question of "what if?" What if the smiling boy had that evil inside of him? Because despite the teachings of his mother and the guidance Mark had tried to give the boy, there was no guarantee that he would be good.

Luke knew the truth about his real father. He knew what happened to him as a baby, and the crimes his father committed. But now, all those worries that Mark had experienced about the boy's future when he was younger resurfaced. Dennis wasn't locked away anymore. He was out there, somewhere in the cold, killing people who did nothing to deserve to die.

And what would happen if Dennis found him here? What would the father do to the son he kidnapped all those years ago and used as a hostage to escape the authorities? History enjoyed repeating itself. And Mark feared that another repetition was close at hand.

"Luke?" Mark asked, gently shaking Luke's arm. "Luke, you need to get up."

The boy groaned, his eyes fluttering open.

"Hey, it's time for your medicine." Mark extended his hand, his open palm holding two pills.

Luke reached for them lazily and then downed them with a swig of water. When he was finished, he leaned his head back onto the pillow, closing his eyes again. But sensing Mark was still in the room, he opened them.

"What's wrong?" Luke's voice croaked as he frowned with concern.

Mark battled with telling him the truth, about everything. About what happened with Claire back in Fairfax, about the fact that his real father was out there in the storm, trying to kill anyone that opposed him. And the more he thought about it, the more he realized what he needed to say.

"Your mother lied to you," Mark said. "About what happened in Fairfax. About Claire."

Luke tensed. "What?"

"After you were shot, your mother and Claire carried you through the forest," Mark answered, gathering his nerve for the truth. "But they had trouble moving you. There was a lot of gunfire, and you need to understand that everyone was scared, including your mother—"

"What. Happened." The words came out more as growls than actual speech, and Luke's eyes glinted with fear and anger and confusion. And for a moment, Mark wondered if he'd made a mistake, if he'd gone too far.

"Claire left you," Mark said, his tone blunt. "She left you to save herself, and it was your mother who dragged you to the plane and got you to safety."

The words swirled through the air, and it looked as though Luke were examining them before he finally let himself hear them.

"Your mother wanted to spare you from that truth," Mark said, watching Luke's face contort to further confusion. "But I'm not going to sit here and watch you make her feel bad for trying to spare your feelings. You're old enough for the hard truths of life."

And so Mark waited, the silence passing between them building anxiousness.

"Why?" Again Luke's words came out cracked and broken. "Why are you telling me this?"

"Because I want you to make your own decisions and form your own thoughts, and you can't do that without the truth."

Luke nodded, his eyes drifting to the foot of the bed.

"And there's something else," Mark said, the spit disappearing from his mouth. "Something you need to know about the people that are out there."

Mark reached for Luke's hand when a gunshot thundered, followed quickly by shattering glass. Screams came next, and by the time Mark was at the door, there was already a bloodied body on the floor and two men with guns in the living room.

Mark stepped out of the room, closing the door behind him. The pair of intruders were dressed like the men at the town.

"Well, look what we've got here." The older of the pair spoke first, the end of his pistol switching between the huddled group by the fire and Mark. "A party? And we weren't invited?" He shook his head, clucking his tongue.

The second one, younger and thinner, stepped toward the

group, his weapon trained on them as well. Holly was in that group.

Mark's gun rested beneath the counter, blocked from view of the inmates by a short wall. It was just out of arm's reach. He stepped toward it, and the fat man brought Mark into his crosshairs.

"Go on," he said. "Join the others." Then he looked past Mark to the closed door. "What you hiding in there?"

Mark shuffled closer to the gun, his eyes falling to the bloodied body on the floor, then looked back up to the big man. He slowly raised his hands, stopping them at waist level, just high enough for the gun.

"Don't move," the big man said.

But Mark's hand was only inches away. He could almost feel the cold of the metal, the hardened steel. He didn't dare look for Holly in the group. She was tucked away safe in the back somewhere.

"I said don't move!" The big man stomped forward, finger on the trigger.

It happened quickly. Mark reached for the pistol and curled his fingers around the handle, placing his index finger on the trigger. The recoil from the gunshot caused him to miss, then a bullet entered his chest and slammed him back into the wall.

Cold washed over him, blood leaking through his clothes and staining the front of him red. A few screams filtered up through the air, but the only one he recognized was "Daddy!" His legs gave out, and he slid to the floor. The big man who'd shot him stomped over and knocked the pistol out of his hands before he had a chance to use it again.

"Shut up! All of you!" the big guy shouted, keeping his gun aimed at Mark's head, and then pushed open Luke's door. "Got another one in here, Billy."

Mark wanted to speak, he wanted to reach out and call for Holly, but darkness was falling over him now. Death pulled the veil over his eyes, and all sensation disappeared from his body.

The last few noises he heard were the screams of women and Luke's defiant grunting as the big man pulled him from bed and dragged him out with the others. He wanted to tell Luke that he loved him. He wanted to say the same thing to Holly. But all faded to black.

37

Kate wasn't sure how long they kept up their sprint before exhaustion finally gripped its relentless and inevitable fingers around their bodies. She only knew of what happened when they stopped.

"I can't." A puff of icy air flew from Stacy's mouth. "I need a break." Her legs stumbled along with her words, and finally she collapsed to her knees.

"We can rest at the cabin," Rodney said, though his tone sounded as if he was as weary as the woman. "We're close. It's not that much farther."

Captain Hurley squinted through a blast of snow, his officers clustering around him, most of them ill prepared for the sudden escape, finding themselves half frozen. "We can push it. C'mon."

Whimpering, Stacy complied and started walking. Kate waited for the officers to catch up to her, letting Harley pass, and then found Luis, who'd showed her the Morse code machine. "What are the chances that the message went through?"

Luis huffed, shuffling through the snow, his head down and his shoulders hunched forward. "One hundred percent." He groaned, fatigue catching up with him as well. "But the chances that the National Guard troop actually listened to it?" He shrugged, shaking his head.

"And you're sure it was the National Guard that you were hearing?" Kate asked. "It wasn't something else? Something you weren't—"

"I know what I heard," Luis answered.

Kate dropped the subject. She was pushing her hopes onto a situation she wasn't even sure would come to fruition. But that gun Rodney had brought with him to save them killed a lot of Dennis's men, and they now had more trained shooters on their side. Even if the message didn't go through, their circumstances were improving despite the cold, and despite the odds.

A light flickered up ahead, breaking the monotony of the darkness and the shape of the cabin came into view. Kate hastened her pace, stumbling past the other tired bodies and taking the lead. But as she drew closer Kate realized that something was wrong.

The front door was open, and despite the distance, Kate saw someone sprawled out across the floor.

"No," Kate whispered and then sprinted from the group.

"Kate, wait!" Rodney shouted after her, no doubt having the same tingling suspicions as she, but she had too much of a head start on him.

Hot tears streaked down Kate's cheeks, running back into her ears and hair because of the wind, only to freeze in place due to the cold.

Kate leapt over the body and the pool of blood on the floor, launching herself into the living room.

"Holly! Luke! Mark!"

Four more bodies lay on the living room floor, the glow of the fire illuminating blank and lifeless stares of the dead. Relief flooded her veins when she didn't see Holly or Luke among them, and then when she stepped around the kitchen counter toward Luke's door, she froze.

When she first opened her mouth to scream, there was nothing. She shuddered, gasping cold air, and then it came slowly, her cry bellowing up and out of her like some ancient, primal thing born from nothing but pain.

She dropped to her knees, screaming until her throat went raw, and Rodney was standing next to her, staring at Mark's dead body. She tried to crawl to him, but Rodney held her back. She viciously smacked his hands away. "Let me go! *Let me go*!"

Rodney released her, and sobbing, Kate crawled to her husband. Her fingers hovered above his body, as if she were almost afraid to touch him. Her mouth quivered as tears dripped onto the wound that killed Mark.

Kate ripped off her gloves and tossed them aside in anger then cupped Mark's face, the scruff of his beard coarse and cold against her palms. She ran her hands through his hair, whimpering. Behind her, she heard the gasps and cries of the others who had lost loved ones, the others who had dead waiting for them to collect.

Luke's door was open, and Kate lifted her red and tear-soaked eyes to the empty bed. The sheets had been torn off messily, and a cup lay on the floor, its liquid staining the wood a darker shade of brown.

Slowly, grief gave way to rage. Luke's body wasn't here. Neither was Holly's. Which meant they were taken. And Kate knew who had done it.

Anger pushed Kate to her feet, propelling her past Rodney and the others toward the front door. She was going to kill him. She was going to kill all of them.

The cold touched her face, and then Rodney grabbed hold of her, yanking her back inside.

"No, Kate."

"Let me go!"

Rodney pulled her close, keeping her from escape. "You can't do this by yourself."

"I'm not losing my children to him!" Kate huffed and lunged

at Rodney like a wounded animal. "You don't know him. You don't know what he'll do." She turned away, stomping out into the snow.

"Who?" Rodney asked, screaming and following her into the woods, catching up to her and stopping her once again. "Kate, you'll die."

Kate stopped and collapsed into the snow on her knees. Rodney was right. She couldn't march into town alone, armed with nothing but a pistol. That would only get her killed, and that wouldn't help her children.

"We can get them back," Rodney said. "But the only way we get them back is if we're smart about it. And the only way we're smart about it is if we take our time."

"I don't have time," Kate said.

Rodney smirked. "We didn't have time in New York. We didn't have time on the road here. And I didn't have time to make it to the patrol station." He gripped her shoulders. "But we did it." He inched close, only a breath separating the two of them. "I swear on my life that I won't let them get away with it, and I swear I will do everything I can to get your kids back to you safely. Let me help you."

Kate wrapped her arms around Rodney, squeezing him tight, and she cried. The same guttural screams that she let go in the cabin escaped into the night air, which echoed her grief, and Rodney held her until it had run its course.

Kate peeled herself off of him and then looked Rodney in the eyes, wiping the tears from her own. She took a breath, clearing her throat and doing her best to compose herself. "There's something you don't know. Something that's important for you to understand before we go any further."

Rodney pressed his eyebrows together questioningly. "What is it?"

"That man, the one who is in charge of the inmates, he's Luke's father."

Rodney laughed, as most people do who are given such news, but when Kate's expression didn't break, when she said nothing else, the smile and laughter disappeared. He stepped away, running his hands through his hair, shaking his head in disbelief. "How is—" He turned around in a circle. "How?"

"That doesn't matter now," Kate answered. "All that matters now is getting them back. I don't know what he'll do if he finds out who he has. He's never met Luke, and Luke's never met him. But I know that if he does find out who he is, he'll do whatever he thinks will hurt me the most. And that will involve my children."

* * *

THE MARCH back to town was quick and then painfully slow. Dennis wasn't sure how many men he'd lost, but from the looks of the survivors, he would have thought they'd all died. Every once in a while, he would scream, that bug of his burrowing around in his head, and he'd fire his pistol into the woods, striking nothing but snow, rocks, and trees.

A man clutching his stomach, struck by shrapnel from the big gun's bullets, collapsed to his knees and face-planted into the snow. There he lay still, none of the inmates around even glancing down as they passed. It was just another dead man. All of them had seen plenty of dead men in their lifetime.

Firelight from the windows of Duluth fanned the flames of hope, and everyone sighed with relief. The fires of the town brought warmth from the bitter cold, the layers of ice on everyone's body starting to thaw.

The moment Dennis's men were back in their home base, anyone who wasn't seriously wounded grabbed liquor and food. But mostly liquor. One of them passed by Dennis, and he snatched the bottle from the man's hands and then smashed it on the ground.

"What the hell are you doing?" Dennis roared, turning every

head in camp. "You think that you're taking a break? *No!*" He pointed to the building that acted as their armory. "We're going to find those pigs and kill them!"

"You saw what they had," a voice cried out from the crowd. "It was a fucking machine gun. Heavy artillery. They mowed us down like cattle. That's not a fight—that's a massacre. I'm not going back out there."

Nods of agreement rippled like a wave through the crowd, and Dennis watched his authority slip away. He wanted to shoot all of them. And the bug that burrowed deep into his mind, urging him to grab a cluster of grenades that they'd found and start flinging them around, was suddenly silenced by a single word.

"Boss," Billy said, catching his breath, tapping Dennis on the shoulder. "We found them." He was grinning, smiling from ear to ear, his fucked-up teeth and rancid breath up close and personal.

"What?" Dennis asked, but then he saw the string of bodies that Billy's brother, Martin, pushed forward aggressively. They all had their faces down, all of them shivering, dressed in the same clothes that they were wearing tucked away in their warm houses.

"These are the ones who attacked the town," Billy said proudly. "And I know where their cabin is if you want to take a look."

Dennis clapped Billy on the back, his sour mood salvaged by this wonderful new gift. "Good work, Billy." He gestured to his house. "My woman is inside. Help yourself to some fun. Hell, take your brother with you." He laughed, rubbing his hands together greedily as Billy and Martin hopped off to Dennis's cabin. He didn't care. He was going to kill the bitch anyway to make him feel better. But this—this was a gift he didn't see coming.

"So," Dennis said, walking down the line of lowered heads. "You are the little bandits that got away." He smiled, noting there weren't as many as he hoped. "And which one of you was the one in charge?" He lifted the chin of an old woman who was crying, trembling wildly from his touch. "No, not you, I suppose." He flicked her nose and moved on to the next person, a middle-aged woman, whom he undressed with his eyes. "Was it you?" He leaned close, tilting his ear toward her. "Speak up."

"She's not here," the woman said, her voice shaking like her body. "The woman who helped us. She's not here."

"She's not?" Dennis asked, his voice innocent, almost sweet. And then, like flicking a switch, he grabbed the woman by the throat, his hand clamping down hard, and roared. "*Then where is she?*"

The woman could only choke, and she clawed at his arm. She looked at him the way everyone did when you killed someone with your bare hands. She was afraid, and her fear only made him feel stronger.

"She's dead." The voice came from farther down the line. It belonged to young man, shirtless and with a bandage over most of his chest. His skin was a shiny red and white. He fidgeted in the cold. Another few hours exposed in the weather dressed like he was, and he'd pass out then freeze to death in the snow. "A bullet caught her on the way back from the town. We buried her in the snow."

"Buried?" Dennis asked, then released the woman who collapsed to her knees, gasping for air. He walked to the young man. "Why? Plan on visiting her grave, boy?" Dennis noted the young girl at his side, clutching on his leg, acting like a crutch to keep him upright. He dropped to his knee and forced her gaze toward him. "Is that true? Did she die?"

The girl's face scrunched up in preparation in tears. "I-I don't know."

Dennis laughed and released the girl's face, which she buried in the boy's leg. He glanced up at the boy's face, and gauging from his expression, the little girl meant something to him.

"So," Dennis said, standing, the boy nearly meeting his eye

line. "This woman died and left you all to fend for yourselves." He stepped close. "And you're sure she's really dead?" His voice was threatening, though his tone was barely above a whisper.

The boy didn't move, didn't even blink. It was one of the best poker faces that Dennis had ever seen.

"C'mon," Dennis said. "Let's go to my place and chat." He grabbed the boy by the back of his neck with his right hand, and used his left to swallow up the little girl's hand, forcing both toward his house.

In the kitchen, they could still hear the moans from Billy's good time upstairs, and Dennis spit a sharp and fast laugh as he shoved the kid into a chair, the legs screeching against the wood as it slid back. But he kept hold of the little girl's hand, keeping her close, which triggered an angered snarl from his new captive.

Dennis nodded to the bandage on the boy's chest. "What happened there? Girlfriend beat you up?" Dennis laughed, but the boy didn't react. "Oh, sorry. Boyfriend?"

The boy grimaced, and Dennis released a sympathetic moan. "Aww, don't be like that. Hey, I'm not offended if you like to take it up the ass. Believe me, after a few years in prison, there were a lot of guys that didn't mind it either."

The little girl whimpered, and Dennis looked down to see the tears streaming off her face. When he looked back at the boy, his eyes were focused on her.

"So how do you two know each other?" Dennis asked, the innocence in his tone contrasting against the malevolent stare in his eyes. He kept both hands on the girl. "You two..." He bounced his eyebrows suggestively, and when the boy clenched his fists in anger, Dennis released another hearty laugh. "No? Well, then you probably don't mind if I take a stab then, do you?"

"Ahh!"

The boy launched himself off the chair and at Dennis, his movements lethargically slow, and swung his fists like a windmill. But the boy was so weak it only took Dennis one arm to keep him at bay.

"Whoa! Easy there, cowboy!" Dennis thrust the boy back into his seat and brandished a knife that he placed against the girl's throat. "Let's not do anything rash."

The boy tensed, but he stayed in his chair.

"We're going to play a game," Dennis said. "I'm going to ask you a question, and then you're going to give me an answer. If I think you're lying to me, then I cut her."

The girl shivered, the boy's eyes locked onto the knife at the girl's throat.

"Now," Dennis said. "Is the woman still alive?"

The boy's Adam's apple bobbed as he swallowed before he answered, "Yes."

"Where is she now?"

"She went to a highway patrol station,"

"How many more of you are there?"

"Ten left the cabin to go to the station," the boy answered. "I don't know how many came back."

The girl was crying hysterically now.

Slowly, Dennis glanced down at the girl, and when he raised his eyes back toward the boy, he smiled. "Is this your sister?"

The words hung in the air between them, and the boy moved his lips to speak, but the silence spoke volumes.

Dennis applied enough pressure against the girl's throat to draw blood. "Is. This. Your. Sis—"

"Yes." The answer left his lips quickly, and for the first time since their interaction, the anger gave way to grief and fear, and the boy's eyes watered. "Please, let her go. If you want to hurt someone, then hurt me."

Dennis smiled then looked down at the little girl, pulling her hair back and exposing the soft pale flesh of her throat. "You know, I've never killed a kid before. Came close once, though."

More blood trickled down the girl's throat and into her shirt, staining the collar red. She sobbed violently now. "Luke, please, help me."

That bug in Dennis's head turned its gaze on the boy. The name sparked memories like hot flashes of flint and steel, stoking a blaze that meant to burn and ravage.

Dennis narrowed his eyes, his vision tunneling on the boy. He slowly lowered the blade from the girl's throat. It was too surreal, and he started to question whether or not he'd misheard what the girl had said. But the longer he stared at the boy, the more that fire grew, revealing the truth right in front of his eyes.

"I knew a boy," Dennis said. "A long time ago. He had your name. But he was just a baby then." He released the girl, and she hurried to Luke and flung her arms around him. But all Dennis focused on was the boy. The eyes he stared at were just like his own, so dark that they were practically black.

Dennis grabbed the boy by the throat and slowly lifted him from the chair, the vibrations from the boy's body thrumming against his hand. "I have one more question before our game is done." He adjusted his grip to the back of the boy's neck then raised the blade to the throat. "That woman. The one who went to the patrol station, the one who killed a lot of my men today." He paused. "Is she your mother?"

The boy trembled. "Yes."

The bug ignited into a fury Dennis had never known, that stretched beyond madness as his eyes widened and his voice dropped to a whisper. "What's her name?"

"Kate."

The name released the boy from Dennis's hold, and he stepped back, his breathing labored and painful. And at the slow realization of what he had, Dennis trembled with exaltation. The laughter rolled out from him triumphantly, causing both Luke and his sister to retreat against the wall, holding onto one another.

Dennis opened the cabinet where he stored the whiskey and dropped the knife, opening the bottle and taking a long swig.

The burn of the liquor helped steady him, and he walked over to Luke, a grin still plastered on his face and the hairs on his chin shiny with drips of whiskey. He extended the bottle to Luke, who stared at it with uncertainty. “Go on. Take it.” His smile widened. “I’ve always wanted to have a drink with my son.”

38

The bodies had been moved outside. No one could think or plan with them lying on the floor, their eyes still open, the flames from the fire offering the illusion of life behind their expressionless stares.

There was nothing to be done about the bloodstains. And while the map was sprawled out on the kitchen table, with Rodney, Kate, and the remaining group hovering over it, their eyes continued to fall to the stains where their loved ones once rested.

"Kate?" Rodney asked, his tone suggesting that it wasn't the first time he'd called her name.

"Hmm?" Kate peeled her gaze from the kitchen and the bloodstain where Mark had been. Every face was on her, expressions ranging from empathy to violence.

"What do you think?" Rodney asked, gesturing down at the map.

Kate pressed her palms against the table's edge, her weight causing it to groan. And while her eyes examined their attack on the town, her mind was still very much focused on Mark's dead body.

Captain Harley spoke up at Kate's silence. "Any way we slice it, we're outnumbered. The only good thing about our plan is the element of surprise. We've already experienced the bulk of their forces, and for all they know, we still have more bullets for the fifty cal." Harley rapped his knuckles against the table and crossed his arms. "If we go in quiet, do some recon, we have a chance at getting everyone back alive."

Kate's eyes returned to the bloodstain where Mark's body had been. Her thoughts drifted to Luke and Holly, both of them abducted by murderers and rapists. She knew that Luke would try to keep his sister safe, but he was so weak from the surgery. She wasn't sure if they'd last till dawn.

"There's only one way we get them back alive," Kate said, ending the bickering at the table, as she turned her gaze back to Rodney and Captain Harley. "I give myself over to them."

Confusion and a hint of skepticism circled the expressions around the table, but it was Captain Harley that spoke first. "You walk into that camp, and you're dead."

"They won't kill me," Kate answered.

"And how do you know that?" Officer Thomas asked.

"Because the man in charge will want to meet me," Kate answered. "I imagine he's been thinking about our meeting for nineteen years." Her eyes found the bloodstain again, but they didn't linger on it for long. "The man in charge of their group is my son's biological father. He was serving a life sentence at Renniger State Prison." She nodded. "At the very least, he'll want to speak to me before he kills me. And I know he'll have my children there, which means I'll be able to get in close." She looked at Rodney. "But once I'm inside, I'll need a distraction to get out."

Heads turned with Kate, glaring at Rodney, who was already shaking his head. "You walk in there, and you're not walking out."

"I'll go with her," Stacy said.

"No," Kate replied.

"You're not the only one with a child that was taken."

Kate wasn't going to argue. And the truth was that if Dennis had discovered who he had, she knew the bastard would want to keep them from the rest of the group. Kate stared at the little town of Duluth, marked on the map, that was Dennis's base of operations. She looked at Rodney again. "What kind of distraction can you work up?"

Rodney left the table, and while he was gone, a few of Harley's deputies whispered in the captain's ears, all the while his eyes not leaving Kate's face.

Rodney returned with a bag and a box that he laid carefully in the center of the table. "C-4 and detonators. I won't be able to trigger them remotely, but I've got enough wire to keep us safely away from the explosions. We'll place them behind the buildings, funnel everyone into Main Street, and then shoot as many of them as we can before they realize what's going on." He looked at Kate and Stacy. "And hopefully give you enough time to get our people out of there."

"What we're dealing with here is a hostage situation," Harley said then gestured to the explosives. "And what you're suggesting here dramatically lowers the survival percentage for those hostages—physical confrontation always does." He looked at every face of the people who had loved ones who were taken, staring at Kate last. "It's important for all of you to understand those consequences."

"Do you really think you can get them out?" Lisa, the doctor's daughter, asked. "Do you really think that guy will let you get that close?"

"Yes," Kate answered, and then turned to Stacy. "But I don't know what he'll do with you."

"It's all right," Stacy replied. "I can handle myself."

Heads nodded, and Rodney picked the bag and the box up off the table. "All right. I'll start wiring these. Everyone else, get plenty of ammo and magazines loaded. The more the merrier. I have a feeling these guys won't have a weapons shortage."

"All right then," Captain Harley said, a thick reluctance in his voice. "It'll be best if we can get them right before dawn, which gives us about seven hours to set everything up. Let's move."

The room broke apart, everyone leaving the table save for Rodney and Kate. Rodney had his eyes on Kate, and Kate had her eyes on the bloodstain again.

"Kate, listen," Rodney said. "Even with the distraction, there isn't a guarantee that it'll do what you want it to. And Captain Harley is right. The use of physical force will drop survival chances dramatically." He placed his hand on her shoulder. "Kate—"

She left, heading out the door before he could finish.

The cold stunned her senses, and she gasped as if she were emerging from a frozen lake. The clouds above had cleared, and the moon and stars blanketed the black of the night sky. Her legs immediately started walking toward the bodies that they'd stacked on the left side of the cabin.

Tears fell before Kate even turned the corner. The bodies were lined in a row, covered with plastic tarps. Mark's body was covered at the very end. She just stood there for a while, staring at him, her body frozen by apprehension and cold. She hadn't helped pull the bodies from inside. It was Captain Harley and his men who'd done all of the work.

It still didn't feel real. Kate kept expecting to wake up from the nightmare, and that she'd be in bed with her husband back in New York. Holly would be getting ready for school, and Luke would be down at George Mason.

But this wasn't a dream. Her dead husband was beneath that tarp, and her children were now under the murderous watch of a madman who happened to be Luke's father.

The past had come back to haunt not just *her* future, but also the future of her children. Her mistakes were now her children's burden, and she was the only one that could lift it.

Kate understood what would happen the moment she surrendered herself to the convicts in that town. But if she could get her children out, if she could save what was left of her family, then maybe she could save what was left of her.

She wasn't going to let the past define her future, or the future of her family. She wouldn't allow herself to fail her family now, and no matter what Dennis said, no matter what he had in store for her, she would endure it. She had already made it this far. She could survive a little longer.

Kate grabbed the shovel leaning up against the cabin's wall. She would let the others prepare their weapons and their bombs. She needed to put her husband to rest before she left. If she could do that, then she could go without reservations, without fear.

If Mark were here, she knew what he would tell her, how he would react. But he would do the same thing. He loved their children. He died trying to protect them. And she would give her life if it meant saving them from further harm.

39

Outside Duluth, Rodney and the group had determined that most of the inmates were confined to Main Street. They'd set up guards on the east and west ends, the bulk being stationed on the west end by the highway's entry point.

Rodney crept along the back side of Main Street, planting charges, his head on a swivel. But it was so dark that even if the goons were looking right at him, he didn't think they'd see him in the black. He was just another lump of shadows in the forest.

Officer Thomas accompanied Rodney. He had some explosives training at the academy and in his brief stint in the military.

The cold and the darkness made the work difficult, not to mention the sheer exhaustion plaguing Rodney. But his adrenaline kept him alert, and for the moment, it was enough to keep him going.

They positioned the charges close enough to the buildings to cause a rumble but far enough away to not kill anyone. He wanted to make sure the blasts maintained their purpose as a distraction. And with the amount of C-4 they had in their bags, it would be quite the fireworks show.

Rodney and Thomas finished and slunk back into the darkness. Unlike the previous town they helped liberate, this one was not located in a valley that provided a useful high ground for an attack. But they did manage to find a hilltop with a limited view of the main drag. At the very least, they'd be able to see the building where Kate was taken. If they didn't kill her on sight.

When Rodney and Thomas returned, Captain Harley and the rest were nothing but frozen shadows nestled in the snow.

With Kate near the west entrance, waiting until it was her time to turn herself in, there were thirteen of them to assault a group that probably numbered somewhere in the forties. Their only hope was that they could pick them off from the hill, getting as many as possible until they had to change position.

"What's the time?" Captain Harley asked.

Rodney checked the pocket watch, his eyes taking a minute to adjust to reading in the darkness. "Just under fifteen minutes." He snapped it shut and then placed it back in his pocket as he made sure to place the detonator in a secure position.

The wires extended from the silver metal box like veins eager to pump life into the frozen hearts buried in the snow.

"You think she'll actually do it?" Thomas asked. "I mean, just walk in there like that and give herself up?"

"Without hesitation." And while he had accepted her decision, Rodney didn't like it any more than he had to. But it wasn't his place to deny her request, nor anyone else's. It was her life. It was her children. It was her choice.

But whether he would ever see Kate Hillman again was another matter. He was suddenly regretful for not saying goodbye. In the heat of things, they had gone their separate ways without even a good luck. But he suspected that she had other things on her mind, and the last thing he wanted to do was distract her from her concentration on getting her children out alive.

The time passed slowly in the cold snow. And the added anxiety about the fight to come only made it worse. No one spoke, the silence pulled over them like the blanket of snow. But

Rodney could sense the humming of thoughts behind the mixture of expressions.

Each of them with their own worries, their own concerns, their own fears about what would happen when Kate walked into town and set things into motion. They all had something to lose, some more than others. But they were together. And they would fight together. A cluster of strangers who shared nothing in common but survival and the fight against evil.

If Rodney could pull one good thing from the events triggered by the EMP, it was that the haze of apathy was lifted. All of the little petty things that people clung to in their day-to-day life were gone. There were no more traffic jams filled with motorists brimming with road rage. Gone were the lines at coffee shops filled with people who were on their phones, huffing and puffing about their boss or office gossip, all the while ignoring one another and building a fake life on social media. The like buttons were gone, the emojis no longer mattered, and the plug had been pulled. And it had led to this.

A group of people fighting for life, uniting against a threat that was born from evil and greed. Of all the ways for his life to end, Rodney suspected it could be worse. He was no longer that guy hiding out in a city of millions, waiting for the world to end. And it had taken the memory of his late father and the righteous cause of a mother and her family, to show him the path of purpose, to see that without real human connections, a life wasn't truly lived.

Rodney checked his watch again—less than three minutes remained. He looked at the faces glued to the riflescopes.

"Do you have family, Captain Harley?" Rodney asked.

The question turned the captain's gaze, and everyone else's, toward him. He nodded curtly. "Two boys out in California. One of them has a wife with my first grandchild on the way."

A few smiles cracked along the worried expressions. Gena, one of the middle-aged women who had a sister that was taken, was one of them. "I have an aunt that lives in San Diego."

"That's where my oldest is," Captain Harley replied.

A whisper of conversation helped cast out the dark and their fears.

"Remember them," Rodney said. "Remember what we're doing here, because I can promise you that this isn't the only evil happening in the world. And remember that we're not the only ones fighting it."

The swell of confidence lifted the group, everyone sitting up straighter, hands and bodies steadier as they took up their aim on the town.

Rodney fished out his pocket watch again, and ran his thumb over the engraving, remembering the words his father told him just before the cancer wasted him away to nothing. A father's final challenge to a son who hoped he could answer.

"People want to do the right thing, Rodney. It's just that most of the time they're scared to. It's that fear that's the hardest thing to get over. It'll rot you from the inside out until there's nothing left. Be the person who helps rid people of that fear. Be the person who shows them the way. You'll get hurt, and you'll get knocked down and burned, but those wounds will heal, and those failures will fade. But what sticks with you, what others will see in you, is that courage in the face of fear. Be better, Rodney. Always be better."

The minute hand finally ticked toward the final sixty seconds until Kate walked into town, and Rodney peered through the scope of his rifle to watch Main Street. Rodney had never been sure about the afterlife, but in that moment, as the final seconds of their preparation came to end, Rodney hoped there was, and he hoped that his dad was up there watching.

* * *

NEITHER STACY or Kate spoke to one another. Both mothers were lost in their own minds. Kate figured Stacy had her own fears to deal with. Kate knew she had her hands full with her own.

Standing motionless in the cold had only made the waiting worse. But for some reason, Kate couldn't force herself to move. It was almost as if any movement before the time on her watch expired meant failure. And she couldn't fail, not this mission.

A million thoughts raced through Kate's mind as she waited for the hour to end. And of all those thoughts, of all the memories that could have resurfaced, one replayed like a broken record.

The memory was older than her past with Dennis, or Mark, or even her children. It was of her sixteenth birthday, which was also the day that she had chosen to become a pilot.

Before the incident with Dennis, and before she had gotten pregnant and her parents disowned her, Kate was the apple of her family's eye. She had excelled in high school and already had a slew of promising prospects for college and scholarships. She was at the top of her class, and her parents had promised to reward all of her hard work with a very special birthday gift.

When she woke up that morning, praying that her wish for a car would come true, Kate rushed to the living room and saw her present sitting in the driveway. They had even put a bow on it.

She drove to school that day and bragged to her friends who were still bumming rides from their parents. By the time she'd gotten out of class that day, the high from her present still hadn't worn off, and when she received a text from her father to come home quickly, another surge of excitement filled her on the drive home.

The next "surprise" turned out to be a three-hour road trip to the coast and a dinner at her favorite seafood restaurant, The Crab Shack. They had a great view of the sunset at the table, but her father quickly paid the check and then rushed her outside and back in the car, their mother staying behind, laughing at Kate's confused face.

Another twenty-minute drive north led them to an airfield, and Kate shook her head in confusion. "Am I getting my own private plane too?"

"You wish," her dad answered. "Now come on, we might miss it."

"Miss what?" But her father was already running out to a man standing next to a small twin-prop Gulfstream that he had rented for the next hour.

Kate rode co-pilot, and from the moment she reclined in the seat of the cockpit and donned the headset, she was hooked. She'd never been in a plane before, and her father had arranged for them to fly along the coast so she could watch the sunset from the sky. And it was the most beautiful thing she had ever seen.

"Remember this, sweetheart," her dad said. "When things get tough at school and you feel like quitting, remember that you can fly above it all. And that when you get to the top, there won't be anyone that can stop you. You can do whatever you want, Kate. Anything in the world."

And while the lesson was meant to teach her to aspire to greatness, the only thing Kate wanted to do when they landed was go back up again. Everything else faded from her mind—college, the car, her friends. The only thing that mattered was flying. She wanted to learn everything she could about planes, and from that point on, she knew nothing would stop her from becoming a pilot, and it was an endeavor that her parents supported wholeheartedly.

And then, three years later, Kate remembered telling that same father, who told her that she could do anything, that she was pregnant. And she also remembered that same father telling her if she didn't get an abortion to kill that thing "he" put inside her, then she shouldn't bother coming home again. So she didn't. Not even to their funerals.

But while the adoration of her family disappeared, the passion for flying only intensified. Every penny that she saved went toward flight lessons, and her college aspirations transformed from Stanford to Embry-Riddle. Every night, she dreamed of being up in the sky again, and every waking hour was spent trying to make those dreams a reality.

The passion didn't leave much time for anything else, and slowly, one by one, her friends stopped calling, and Kate stopped caring. She didn't date, didn't go out, and didn't socialize. And then after Luke was born, she grew even more into herself and providing a good life for her son.

But over the course of the years, Kate became so focused on and busy with providing a better life for her family that she began to leave her family behind. She had lost touch with her daughter and put a strain on everyone by moving them from city to city until Mark had to issue her an ultimatum of either settling down or having the family split up for good.

Kate thought those memories of her parent's scorn resurfaced because it was such a stark contrast to how she had approached her parenting. After giving birth to Luke and Holly, she couldn't imagine disowning them, no matter what path they chose to walk. A parent doesn't give up. No matter the odd or circumstances.

Kate checked the time, and the minute hand ticked past the hour mark. She turned to Stacy. "It's time."

Stacy nodded, and started to walk. Kate stared down at her feet, unsure if her body would even move after staying motionless in the cold for so long. But her right foot moved, and then her left, and then she was halfway down to the road that would lead her into town.

She kept a slow pace, taking her time but moving forward. She fought the urge to look to the north where Rodney and the rest were watching, because she knew that if she let herself turn once, she'd lose her focus.

As she approached the guarded front entrance, Kate made sure that the pair could see her coming from a long way off.

"Hey!" The first man who spotted her immediately lifted his

rifle, aiming at her chest in the darkness. "What are you doing out there?"

Kate slowed, raising both hands in the air, and the second sentry raised his rifle as well. Smiles spread on their faces when they realized they were both women.

"Sweethearts, are you two alright?" The guard on the left was big and muscular, his beard thick and wild around his face and stretched down to his chest. A few silver teeth glinted in the darkness, and even with a bulky coat clasped tight around his neck, the top of a few tattoos still crawled out from beneath.

"Yeah, baby." The guard on the right lowered his rifle. He was short, shorter than Kate, and bald, without a beard, and missing a few teeth. "You looking to get warm?" He grabbed himself and laughed.

Kate retained her stoic expression, while Stacy remained quiet, both fighting the urge to shake from the cold.

"My name is Kate Hillman," she said. "I am here to speak with Dennis Smith. He knows who I am." She stared at each of the guards in turn. "And he will want to meet me as I am right now. I suggest you take me to him immediately."

"And what about her?" The shorter bald one gestured to Stacy.

"I'm here for my son."

The playfulness of both the big man and the shorter one ended, and the short man raised his rifle at her once again as the pair exchanged a glance.

"Ladies," the bearded inmate said, his voice with a glint of warning, "you are the dumbest pair of bitches I have ever met."

The shorter one circled behind Kate and then prodded her forward with the tip of his rifle. "Move!"

The little man trailed Kate all the way down Main Street, while the big man walked behind Stacy. Kate's eyes searched for the source of a monotonous hum, and she found it in what looked like a large generator, feeding power into three separate buildings.

The big guard knocked on one of the door's attached to the building powered by the generator and then stepped back. Kate's stomach twisted and flipped, her nerves threatening to shatter what remained of her resolve as she waited for Dennis to come out.

The sound of footsteps triggered her heart into a hastened rhythm. She tightened her hands into fists, squeezing until it hurt, and when the door opened and she saw Dennis's expression morph from anger to surprise, her heart stopped dead.

The big man turned, pointing toward Kate, his tone nervous. "She came into town, said she knew you and that you'd want to see her."

Dennis walked past the guard without a word, his eyes focused only on Kate, and he moved within a breath's distance. He then grabbed her roughly by the arms, forcing her body flush against his, and kissed her.

Kate tried to turn away, but he kept his mouth pressed against hers until her lip bled. He pulled away and then slapped her across the face so hard it sent her to her knees.

The contact between bare hand and cheek made her face throb, and it was made worse by the cold and Dennis's hysterical laughter.

"You don't know how long I've waited to do that!" Dennis circled her, rubbing his hands together with enough vigor to start a fire. "Kate, Kate, Kate, Kate, Kate!" He tilted his head from side to side every time he spoke her name, and then he stopped his pacing when he faced her again. "Of all the little towns in all the little corners of the world, here you are."

Kate lifted her face to meet his gaze, and she stood. A red handprint had formed on her cheek. "Where are they?"

The smile dissolved. Dennis again closed the gap between them to a breath's distance. He shook his head and slowly lifted his hand, curling his fingers around her throat. The touch was soft at first and then slowly tightened as Dennis bared his teeth. "I know a lot about you, Kate. I know that it was you who fucked me over with the parole committee. I know it was you that called the cops on me and got me put in jail in the first place." The grip around Kate's throat closed her airway, and he dropped his voice to a whisper. "And I know that I have your children tied up inside my house."

Kate clawed at Dennis's arm, her muscles giving way and her vision fading as she choked. Black spots covered Dennis's snarling face, and just before everything faded to black, Dennis let go.

Kate clawed her fingers into the snow, her face red and purple, and drew in deep, raspy breaths. She swayed from side to side, coughing. And just when she felt the effects of the asphyxiation fading, a bright flash of pain erupted in her left side as Dennis kicked her.

The force rolled her to her back, and Kate shrieked as her hands immediately rushed to guard the wounded ribs. She lay still, her back cold against the snow, Dennis towering over her.

"Do you know what I went through in prison?" Dennis's cheeks grew red with rage. "Do you know what it was like?" He spit in her face and then kicked her again, harder, this time cracking ribs.

"*Ahh!*" Kate cried out, whatever resolve she had carried with her crumbling beneath her feet as she rolled to protect her injured side, only exacerbating the pain radiating from her ribs and spreading to the rest of her body.

"And do you know the one thing that kept me going?" Dennis squatted low, shoving his face near Kate's. "The one thing that I held onto that got me through the rapes and the insanity that being stuck in an eight- by four-foot cell does to you?" He grabbed her face, forcing her gaze onto his. "This moment. Right here. The hope that I would one day get to hurt you so bad that you wouldn't be whole again. So bad that you couldn't bear the thought of trying to live one more day. Because that's what it was like on the inside for me." He smiled, but the expression looked forced amidst the anger. "So thank you." He slammed her head back hard into the snow and stood. "Drag her inside, and take her friend and put her with the others. And get some men to search the area. I doubt they came here alone."

* * *

RODNEY'S STOMACH TIGHTENED, and it took every ounce of control in him to not flick the switches on the detonator box as he watched Kate take a beating. They all felt the urge to pull the trigger, but they had known that it could be like this, and they had to wait.

They still didn't know where the kids were being held, and when the beating was over and Kate was finally taken into Dennis's house, Rodney started the clock again. Five minutes. That was all the time she said she'd need.

"We've got something," Captain Harley said, peering through the scope of his rifle and catching the attention of group. "We've got six armed men heading into the woods."

"Shit." Rodney adjusted his rifle's scope from Dennis's house to the men heading into the woods. No doubt the bastards thought Kate had people waiting for her. He removed his eye from the rifle. "All right, everyone, listen up." Heads turned, including the captain's, and he didn't look too accustomed to receiving orders. "We split up. Make it harder for them find us. But we stay in pairs." He looked at Captain Harley. "Captain, you assign one of your men to each pair of civilians, and you can stay with me." He turned back to the group. "Find a good position where you can still see the street, and be mindful to stay back far enough from the explosives. The distance we are at right now is good."

Heads nodded quickly, and Rodney kept his voice down as he tapped on the detonator box. "Our signal is still with the explosives." He checked his watch. "We've got less than four minutes."

Harley assigned everyone quickly, and they disappeared into

the darkness, hunched low in the night. Rodney returned his eye to the scope, searching for the inmates under the cover of darkness, praying that he wouldn't have to blow the charges early.

* * *

EVERY BREATH HURT. It was as though glass had been ground up in Kate's body, and any movement sent the shards into muscles and bones and organs. She collapsed into the kitchen chair that Dennis shoved her into and tried to find a position where the pain wasn't so intense. She didn't find one.

The pain was so blinding that Kate wasn't sure how long Luke and Holly were standing in front of her before she saw them. Gags were shoved in their mouths, and their arms were tied behind their backs, with Dennis lording over them, large and in charge, the man who called the shots. The judge, the jury, and the executioner.

"Oh," Dennis said, smiling as he watched the realization spread over Kate's face. "Looks like someone is finally back with us." He looked down at both Luke and Holly. "Wave hello to your mother, kids! Oh, wait." He spun them around so Kate could see the rope tied around their wrists. "They can't. Ha ha!" He spun them back around and then shoved them into two chairs across from Kate, with him standing behind but still between them.

"Are you guys okay?" Kate asked, her voice shaking, her mind trying to process only three things: her pain, her children's safety, and any weapons that were nearby.

Luke nodded, and Holly cried. Kate tried to stand, but the moment she pushed herself from the chair, another bout of pain planted her ass back in the seat.

"So what do we talk about first?" Dennis asked. "I've already had a good conversation with my son about his heritage." He stared at Luke. "Medical history, girls, my time in prison." He flicked his eyes back toward Kate. "Mark."

Kate grimaced and tried another lunge, but an even bigger

flash of pain pushed her back down into her seat, and Dennis let out a slow, methodical laugh, shaking his head.

"I can't imagine what it was like going back to that cabin and finding your children gone and your husband dead. But then again, I can't imagine what it would have been like to be married to you." He wiped his nose, sniffling. "So how do you want to do this, Kate? Do I pick one to kill? Should I have you pick one to kill?"

Kate watched Dennis's eyes. They had always been the tell in his poker face. And at that moment, they looked as they had on the night over nineteen years ago. He was going to take one of them from her. And she would have to pick.

"Well, Kate?" Dennis asked, those eyes boring into her soul, his hands massaging Luke and Holly's shoulders. "What do you say?"

Time. That was all Kate needed. Just enough time for the distraction. She closed her eyes, drawing in quick gasps of breath as she remained hunched in her chair. She opened them again, a bit of clarity returning, and she spied a cluster of steak knives on the counter. Six or seven big steps—that was all she'd need to grab one. How much time was left till the detonators went off? She couldn't remember. The pain had blinded her to it.

"Tick tock, Kate," Dennis said. "C'mon! Don't keep me in suspense!"

Kate straightened, adjusting her posture in the chair, gritting her teeth, and groaning in pain as a thick sheen of sweat appeared on her forehead. She was weak, and she knew Dennis saw it. But she just needed to pull his attention away from her kids.

"So that's what you want to do?" Kate asked, trying to play off a sense of apathy. "Play a game? I think you spent too much time playing with yourself on the inside." She laughed, and Dennis's expression slowly faded to match his murderous eyes. "You know, that letter that I submitted to the parole board, I think I rewrote it a dozen times before it was just right. Before I knew that it would keep you in that jail cell for the rest of your life."

Dennis released his hold on the kids and stepped toward her, but she didn't let up.

"My lawyer told me that I didn't have to come to the meeting, but I said that I wanted to be there. I wanted to make sure I saw the look on your face." Kate forced a smile, and that was the straw that broke the camel's back.

Dennis screamed, lunging for Kate in the chair, leading with his fist. The first blow broke her nose, spraying blood down the front of her shirt, and knocked her from the chair. She rolled on the ground, her mind conscious enough for her to see Luke lunge at Dennis only to be backhanded to the ground.

Another scream filled the room, and before Kate could determine whether it was hers or Holly's, Dennis lifted her off the floor, triggering more stabbing pain in her sides as he slammed her against the wall hard enough to knock the pictures of the family that had lived there previously to the floor.

"You've always been a hard one to nail down, Kate," Dennis said, tightening his hand around her throat like a vise. She clawed at his arm and swiped impotently at his face. "You were always smart, but you never knew when to quit." With one heavy flick of his arm, he flung her halfway across the kitchen, her shoulder landing hard on tile, eliciting another debilitating crack from her ribs.

The pain was so immense that when Kate opened her mouth to scream, nothing came out, and the screams that she heard now were coming from Holly, her daughter's face red and tearstained as her voice cracked with grief.

"Mommy!"

Kate could do nothing but stare at her daughter, as Dennis was on her once again, ramming his fist into her cheek, numbing her head and leaving her ears ringing. The next hit, she couldn't feel, and it took her a moment to realize that she was standing upright, Dennis holding her up against the counter as her body sagged.

"I thought about raping you before I killed you, but now that I've gotten a real good look at your face, I think I'll pass," Dennis said, his dark eyes wild with anger and violence. "But I bet there are a few guys out there that wouldn't mind it. Women have been in short supply, especially with our influx of men." He smiled, the specks of Kate's blood that had sprayed over his face filling the wrinkles around his eyes.

Kate moved her lips to speak, but the pain and exhaustion had numbed her tongue. She could see Luke trying to get up from the floor and could hear Holly screaming bloody murder. All sense of time disappeared, and Kate tried to remember what she was waiting for, but any attempt at remembrance disappeared with another punch to the gut.

Dennis released her, and Kate crumbled into a lifeless pile of meat on the tile. She blinked, which was the only movement allowed to her that didn't elicit a screaming symphony of pain. Her position on the floor granted her a view of her son. He was screaming something at her, but Kate could only watch the movement of his lips. She thought of how good a man he had become. She thought of how good of a man that he would be.

Would be.

Kate circled that thought, a meaning in it that the pain in her body wouldn't allow her to grasp, but when she felt the vibrations from Rodney's detonations, she remembered.

Dennis turned toward the blasts, and Kate lifted her head, the effort requiring what remained of her strength. The knife rested above her, but it was too high, too far for her to reach. But Dennis had his back turned, and she knew it wouldn't stay that way forever. She had to act, and she had to do it now.

With what remained of her strength, Kate pushed herself to her knees, buckling over at the waist and her clutching her chest as her ribs shrieked in pain and defiance. Kate extended her arm, her hand shaking as her fingertips grazed the knife's handle.

A scream escaped her lips as she raised it high, and Dennis turned, his eyes widening as she brought the blade down. He jerked away at the last second, only the knife's tip catching the meat of his chest, spraying a line of blood to the floor.

"*Gahhh!*" Dennis stumbled backward into the table as Kate collapsed to her knees, the strength from her body gone as she looked at her children.

"Run," Kate said, the word coming out cracked and inaudible. She tried again, screaming from the depths of her soul. "*Run!*"

Holly was out of her chair first, then Luke pushed her out the kitchen door. Dennis watched them leave and then turned his murderous glare to Kate. "You bitch!" But something at the door caught his eye, and at the last second, he sprinted out of the kitchen and deeper into the house as a gunshot thundered at the kitchen's exit.

Rodney burst inside, rifle up, scanning the kitchen until his eyes fell on Kate, and he flung the rifle's strap over his shoulder. Kate collapsed into his arms, forcing him to hold up her weight as she struggled for breath.

"Holly," Kate said, clutching Rodney's shoulder. "Luke—"

"They're outside," Rodney said. "C'mon, we have to get out of here, quick."

Rodney dragged Kate through the door, and she was surprised to feel nothing from the cold as the bottoms of her feet skidded across the snow.

Bodies littered Main Street, some of the buildings catching fire from the blasts that were set off, and up ahead, Kate saw Luke and Holly with Captain Harley near the highway exit. She then saw Stacy leading a group of people from one of the buildings.

Random gunshots erupted in the night, and despite the violence around her, Kate swelled with hope. She was almost out. Her body was broken, but she was almost free.

"Just hang on, Kate," Rodney said, his voice strained as he practically carried her away. "We're almost there. Just hang—"

The gunshot and the sudden taste of snow in her mouth were simultaneous. Kate barely felt the scrape of the concrete as she and Rodney face-planted to the ground.

Kate lifted her head and found a red blotch rising on the back of Rodney's shoulder. She reached for his arm, her face swollen and numb. "Rodney!"

More gunshots thundered, and screams followed the violent mechanical thunder as Kate watched a group of gunmen surround Captain Harley and her children.

"I want them alive!"

Kate turned back toward the house, finding Dennis with his arm extended with a pistol in his hand. The blood from the knife wound was still dripping, but the cold slowed the crawl of blood down his stomach.

More of Dennis's men emerged from the houses and the woods, some of them leading her people by gunpoint. She felt hands on her, and Kate was lifted off the pavement, her body devoid of all feeling as Dennis pressed the end of his pistol against her cheek.

"Eighteen years," he said, his voice haggard, and on the verge of tears. "Eighteen years in a concrete cell, eighteen years lost because of you and my bastard son."

Luke was thrust to his knees next to Kate, and Dennis removed the pistol from her cheek and pressed it against Luke's temple.

"Mom?" Luke asked, crying.

But she couldn't answer. She could barely keep herself conscious.

"I want you to know that I take no pleasure in killing our son," Dennis said, his voice steadying but that mad look returning to those dark eyes. "But I do take pleasure in watching his death cause you pain."

Kate drew in a ragged breath and focused on those dark eyes that a foolish nineteen-year-old girl once found attractive but now made her sick. "He was never your son. You were never a part of him, no matter what you say."

Dennis cocked the hammer on his pistol. "Fuck you, Kate."

Gunfire rained over the town, the explosions erupting from behind her, and Kate only caught a glimpse of Dennis's face as he removed the pistol from Luke's head and fired above their heads, retreating down the street.

And as Kate fell forward, she saw the bullets that cut through Dennis's chest and stomach, brilliant plumes of red spreading across his shirt as his body jerked wildly with each gunshot until he lay on the pavement, covered in blood. Dead.

A few more gunshots echoed, and then Kate felt hands up and down her body.

"Medic! We need a medic!"

"Ma'am, can you hear me? Ma'am? We're with the United States National Guard. Are you the one who sent the Morse code message? Ma'am?"

Kate wanted to answer, but everything had suddenly turned cold, and the white of the snow faded to grey. She couldn't feel her breathing anymore, and as she closed her eyes, she knew that she could find peace with the knowledge that her children were alive.

CHAPTER 40 (SIX MONTHS LATER)

Weeds and grass crept over the highway, trapping the broken cars and clogged road. The snows of winter had long since melted, and the heat of summer had descended upon northern New York State.

But while the days had grown long and hot, not a single man, woman, or child complained. The icy grip of winter had left a mark, and it would take a long time before that cold finally thawed.

Rodney adjusted the strap of his rifle as he weaved through the line of cars, Luke behind him, dragging a deer with him.

"You don't want to help me with this?" Luke asked, panting.

"You said you wanted to go hunting," Rodney answered, turning back with a smile over his thick beard, which was shiny with sweat. "Number-one rule of hunting is that the guy that does the killing doesn't have to do the carrying."

Luke rotated his shoulder as he gave the heavy buck another tug by the rope and tarp that he was dragging across the grass. "Last time, you said it was the hunter who does the killing that does the carrying."

Rodney laughed. "Well, that's the good thing about being the teacher. I get to make the rules." They walked another mile before Rodney finally broke down and helped Luke pull it. They walked all the way toward Duluth's exit then rolled the buck down the ramp to the highway into town.

It was almost evening by the time they returned, and the street was busy with chatter. Tables were already being set out for dinner, a mishmash of dining ware that stretched from one end of Main Street to the other.

Smiles and friendly faces greeted Rodney and Luke's entrance, and when they flipped open the tarp to reveal the fresh game, applause erupted.

"Looks a little smaller than the one I brought home yesterday," Harley said, leaning up against the doorway, finally looking comfortable in clothing that wasn't a uniform.

"It's a bit shorter," Rodney said. "But it's most definitely thicker."

Harley laughed and then helped Dana Miles set the table outside their little general store. Rodney had discovered that he liked hearing the old state trooper's laugh, and he tried to elicit a chuckle as often as he could.

"You remember how to gut it?" Rodney asked as they approached Luke's place.

"Yeah, I remember," Luke answered, blushing as Sarah walked out of their first-floor apartment and planted a kiss on his cheek.

Rodney watched the pair embrace and smiled as he returned to his little one-room studio on the back side of Main Street.

He'd stopped staying at the cabin after the last group of survivors that came through three months ago. With the numbers that were coming in from the highway, they had a nice linked group of community members now. Good people. Rodney forgot how much he missed good people.

Rodney leaned his rifle in the corner between the front door and the side wall, and before he could wipe the blood off his hands, the watch horn blared.

As quick as a snakebite, Rodney snatched the rifle from the

corner and hurried outside. A stream of people followed him toward the town's entrance, all of them armed. They'd prepared for something like this. Another confrontation was inevitable. But they were ready to face it. Together.

Rodney met Harley with his newly deputized officers at the town's entrance, moving the cars across the road to form a blockade. Dean Smultz sprinted down the road from his watch post, the sky turning a golden hue behind him as the sun set.

"What is it?" Rodney asked, elbows planted on the hood of a rusted Buick.

"Trucks," Dean answered, sliding over the Buick's trunk and repositioning his rifle. "They're armed to the teeth."

The town behind Rodney was quickly boarded up, everyone knowing their role. They had evacuation routes planned to the neighboring communities, and there was already a runner in the woods, sprinting to let everyone else in the other towns know that something was coming.

An engine rumbled, the noise foreign after so many months without traffic, and when the first truck made its way down the embankment, followed by a dozen more, Rodney tensed.

"If they charge, fall back!" Rodney said, his eyes still locked on the front grill of the first truck. "But do not fire until fired upon!" This was their group's first real test of strength, and Rodney knew there was a flurry of nerves attached to those trigger fingers.

Through the scope, Rodney noted the soldier uniforms. They hadn't had any contact with the United States military since the National Guard intervened, but he wasn't sure how these fighters planned to greet them.

The lead truck slowed a few dozen yards before the barricade, and doors opened and two soldiers stepped out, brandishing their weapons behind the cover of their armor-plated cavalry.

"Drop your weapons!" But when the order wasn't obeyed, the soldier scooted forward. "I said drop your—"

"Lieutenant!" The breathless voice was attached to a very small man dressed in a suit and tie, his glasses falling down the bridge of his nose, waving his arms. "Stop!" He slowed down at the convoy's front, stepping between the two groups, arms extended to both parties. "We don't need any bloodshed." He looked at Rodney then at the lieutenant. "How about a show of good faith, huh?"

A few seconds passed, and the lieutenant lowered his rifle.

"Stand down." The lieutenant's order echoed down the line, and once all of the weapons were lowered, the small man in the business suit looked toward Rodney and the line of guns still trained on the military.

"Please," the suited man said, his hands folded together. "I'm sure you have all been through quite a lot, but we're not here to take anything or hurt anyone. We're here to help."

Rodney wasn't sure of the man's agenda, but the fact that they weren't pointing their guns at them provided enough good will for him to reciprocate, and Rodney lowered his weapon, ordering the rest of his group to do the same. "Let's get these cars pushed back."

The old rust buckets were wheeled off, and Rodney was the first to cross the line to shake the little guy's hand. He was even smaller up close.

"Bob Gally," he said, wiping the sweat from his forehead. "The gentlemen you see behind me are with the army's Eighty-Seventh Infantry. We were stationed in DC when the EMP went off. I, um... oh." He patted his jacket, searching his pockets for something, which he found and handed over to Rodney for inspection. It was a badge. "I'm with the Department of Reconstruction."

Harley joined Rodney on his left as he handed the badge back to Bob Gally. "Never heard of it."

"No, you wouldn't have," Bob said, laughing, which he quickly stopped once neither Rodney nor Harley joined in. He cleared his throat. "It's a new department the president and his staff put together once we secured the capital. We're in the process of reestablishing communications across the country, and our group is part of the northeastern efforts." He looked back at Rodney's group, offering a friendly wave, which wasn't returned. "Are you the person in charge here?"

Rodney sized up the little man. If this was a charade, then it was one of the most elaborate charades that he'd ever seen. He looked at Harley, who gave him a slight nod, and Rodney exhaled. "Follow me." He started to walk. "But your military stays outside the town."

Bob Gally obliged and quickly fell into step behind Rodney, his short legs churning twice as fast.

Every eye turned toward Rodney, who led the representative of the Department of Reconstruction toward the town hall, where the bulk of their people were trained to go to during their practice drills.

Rodney didn't like the idea of having her stay when something like this happened. His original plan was to send her to the next community with their runner. But she wouldn't budge. He didn't know how it was possible, but she'd grown even more stubborn.

Golden sunlight flooded through the door as Rodney stepped inside. Faces turned. Some of the people were armed, but they lowered their weapons when they saw it was him. He saw her at the other end of the hall, helping Holly with a pair of elderly women that couldn't move on their own anymore.

"Kate," Rodney said, his voice echoing in the open space.

When she turned, those golden rays lit up her scarred face and slightly crooked nose that came from a bad set by the medical team who'd revived her. The medic who worked on her told him that she had been dead for nearly thirty seconds. After she woke up, Rodney told her what happened and asked her what she saw during those thirty seconds that she was dead.

"This is Bob Gally," Rodney said. "He's with the United States government."

Kate shook Bob's extended hand but didn't reciprocate the smile. "I didn't realize we still had one of those."

"We do, or at least we will," Bob said, that nervous laughter slipping through again. "So I'm told that you're the person in charge here?"

"That's what they tell me," Kate said, looking at Rodney.

Bob examined the hall and clapped his hands together. "You've got quite the setup. Very organized, which makes the transition back onto the grid easier."

Bob talked about sending Kate to DC to join the other "elected" leaders from similar communities that had assembled all around the country after the wake of the EMP. He spoke of the small pockets of resistance that still remained in the larger cities where the terrorists' strongholds were starting to dwindle away. But the only thing that Rodney focused on, the only thing that was repeated in his mind, was what she told him when she woke up.

"It was dark for a long time," Kate said, her voice so weak but her eyes alive as she lay on the cot set up in the tent. "But then everything was white, like snow, and it melted away. Grass and flowers, and life sprang up around me. It was warm, and I closed my eyes, thinking this was where I was meant to be." A tear fell out of the corner of her eye. "But I was alone."

Rodney squeezed Kate's hand and wiped the tear from her cheek, repeating the same words that she'd spoken to him when they left their apartment building in New York. "A world where you're by yourself isn't much of a world to live in, is it?"

And over the course of that harsh winter, Kate and Rodney kept as many people alive as they could. And then when the snows thawed, more people found their way to their towns. They built a community together. And now that community was on a journey to rejoin the rest of the world.

Bob Gally clapped his hands again, snapping Rodney from the memory. "Shall we get started?"

And to that Kate smiled. "We already have."

Made in United States
Troutdale, OR
11/22/2024